PRAISE FOR

SHERRYL
WOODS

"Strong supporting characters, a vivid sense
of place, and a strong appreciation for the
past add to the appeal of Woods'
contemporary romance."
—*Booklist* on *The Backup Plan*

"Clever characters and snappy, realistic dialogue
add zest...making this a delightful read."
—*Publishers Weekly* on *About that Man*

A "gripping, emotionally wrenching
but satisfying tale."
—*Booklist* on *Flamingo Diner*

"Sherryl Woods gives her characters depth,
intensity and the right amount of humor."
—*Romantic Times*

"Energetic pacing, snappy dialogue and
an appealing romantic hero."
—*Publishers Weekly* on *After Tex*

Dear Reader,

Usually when I write connected books, I plan in great detail well in advance, but when I came to the end of *The Backup Plan,* I suddenly realized that Maggie needed to have her own story. Here was a bright, spirited, successful woman who'd had the world's worst luck with men, a mother who considered her a failure at love, and a safe, predictable ex-fiancé who'd called off their wedding at the last minute. Maggie's self-esteem was pretty much trashed.

And so she ran...straight to a beach house to try to get a grip on her life. When three people show up to save her from herself—including her ex-fiancé—Maggie's pretty sure that her future is about as bleak as it can get.

Her best friend, though, has a plan...and a man for Maggie.

Josh Parker has issues of his own, including a mother whose maternal instincts leave a whole lot to be desired. What fun to have this strong, sexy man try to battle his feelings for Maggie and wrestle with all those old issues when his exuberant, offbeat mother zips in from Las Vegas after yet another disastrous marriage!

Once I had the right guy for Maggie, the rest of the story came together the second I saw the Reba McEntire commercial for Habitat for Humanity. Every single time I see it, I get choked up and think about all the families this wonderful organization has helped to move into their first real homes. It's a church that's building a home this time, but the philosophy of giving people a fresh chance is the same.

I hope you'll enjoy Maggie and Josh's story and that you'll have fun catching up with Dinah and Cord and meeting Amanda and Caleb. You guessed it! Those two will have their own remarkable story in *Waking Up in Charleston,* coming out in May 2006.

All best,
Sherryl

SHERRYL WOODS

Flirting
WITH
DISASTER

MIRA®

ISBN 0-7783-2238-6

FLIRTING WITH DISASTER

www.MIRABooks.com

Printed in U.S.A.

1

At six, running away from home had been a scary proposition. It should have been easier and less traumatic at thirty-two.

It wasn't, Maggie concluded with regret after three weeks in hiding. Oh, the logistics were easier, but the emotional wear and tear were about the same.

Way back then, lugging a Barbie suitcase packed with Oreos and her favorite stuffed toys, Maggie had set out to show her parents that she didn't need them anymore. But by the time she'd wandered a few blocks away from their Charleston home onto unfamiliar streets, and by the time darkness had closed in with its eerie shadows, she'd begun to wonder if she hadn't made a terrible mistake.

Still, she'd been far too stubborn to consider backing down. She'd climbed onto a wicker rocking chair deep in the shadows of a deserted front porch and, tightly clutching her tattered Winnie the Pooh, gone to sleep. Her frantic parents had found her there the next morning, thanks to a call from the owner of the house, who'd been alerted to her presence by his son. Leave it to terrible Tommy Henderson to rat her out. No wonder no one in first grade liked the little tattletale.

It seemed more than a bit ironic that twenty-six years later, Maggie was running away from home again and that she was still trying to prove things to her parents. The only difference this time was that Tommy Henderson was nowhere around. Last she'd heard, he was working somewhere overseas as a CIA operative for the United States government. At least he'd put his capacity for sneakiness to good use.

Sitting in a rocker on the front porch of a tiny rented beach house on Sullivan's Island, Maggie sipped her third glass of sweetened iced tea and watched the fireflies flicker in their endless game of tag in the evening sky. The air was still and thick with humidity, the night quiet and lonely. Even though she was all grown up, in many ways she was just as scared now as she had been at six, and just as stubbornly determined to stay away till she made sense of things.

She couldn't recall exactly what had sent her fleeing into the night back then, but now it was all about a man, of course. What else could possibly drive a reasonably sane and mature woman to run away from her home and business and fill her with enough self-doubt to keep her on a shrink's couch for years? She didn't miss the irony that it was, in fact, a shrink who'd turned her world upside down.

Safe, solid, dependable Warren Blake, Ph.D., had been the kind of respectable, charming man her family had always wanted for her. Her father had approved of him. Predictably, her mother had adored him. Warren didn't make waves. He didn't have any pierced or tattooed body parts. He could carry on an intelligent conversation. And he was Southern. What more could they have asked, after the parade of unlikely candidates Maggie had flaunted in front of them for years?

Basking in all that parental approval for the first time in her life, Maggie had convinced herself she loved Warren and wanted to marry him. The wedding date had been set.

And then, with the invitations already in the mail, Warren had called the whole thing off, saying he had come to his senses and realized their marriage would be a mistake. He'd done it so gently, at first Maggie hadn't even understood what he was trying to say. But when the full import had finally sunk in, she'd been furious, then devastated. Here she'd finally done the right thing, made the right choice, and what had she gotten in return? Total humiliation.

She'd packed her bags—Louis Vuitton this time—and run away from home again. In terms of distance, it really wasn't that much farther than she'd run all those years ago, but Sullivan's Island was light-years away from Charleston in terms of demands on her shattered psyche. She could sit on this porch, swatting lazily at mosquitoes, and never once have to make a decision that she'd come to regret the way she regretted her decision to get engaged to Warren.

She could eat tomato sandwiches on white bread slathered with Miracle Whip for breakfast and an entire pint of peach ice cream for lunch. She could play the radio at top volume and dance around the living room at any hour of the day or night, if she could summon the energy for it. She could go for a swim without waiting a whole hour after eating, and she could track sand through the house, if she felt like it.

In fact, she'd been doing all that for a while now and,

she was forced to admit, it was getting on her nerves. She was a social creature. She liked people. She missed her art gallery in Charleston. She was almost ready to start seeing her friends again, at least in small doses.

But she'd made up her mind that she wasn't going home until she'd come to grips with why the devil she'd been so determined to marry Warren in the first place. There had to be a reason she'd talked herself into being in love with a man who was the complete opposite of every other male she'd ever dated in her life. When she was willing to give Warren credit for anything, she conceded that he'd only saved them both a lot of misery. So why had the broken engagement sent her packing?

It wasn't the humiliation. Not entirely, anyway. Maggie had never given two figs what anyone thought of her, unlike her mother, who obsessed about everyone's opinion and had been horrified by her daughter's broken engagement.

It certainly wasn't a broken heart. Her ego might have been a little bruised, but her heart had been just fine. In fact, in a very short time she'd found herself breathing a sigh of relief. Not that she intended to admit that to Warren. Let the man squirm.

So, if it wasn't her heart or her pride that had been wounded, what was it? Maybe nothing more than watching a last desperate dream crash at her feet, leaving her with no more dreams, no more options.

On that disturbing note, Maggie dragged herself out of the rocker and went inside to retrieve another pint of ice cream—chocolate-chocolate chip this time—from the freezer. At this rate she'd be the size of a blimp by the time she decided to go back to Charleston. She shrugged off the possibility and dipped her spoon into the decadent treat. If she never intended to date again, what difference did it make if she was the size of a truck? Or a blimp?

She flipped on the radio and found an oldies station. She preferred country, but wallowing in love-gone-wrong songs at this particular moment in her life struck her as overkill.

She was dancing her way back toward the porch when she spotted three people on the other side of the screen door. Unfortunately, even in the dark, she knew exactly who they were—her best friend, Dinah Davis Beaufort, Dinah's new husband, Cordell, and the traitorous Warren.

If she'd had the energy, she would have bolted for the back door. As it was, she resigned herself to greeting them like the proper Southern belle she'd been raised to be. She could hear her mother's words echoing in her head. Company, even unwanted company, was always to be welcomed politely.

But even as she forced a smile and opened the door, she also vowed that the next time she ran away from home, she was going to choose someplace on the other side of the world where absolutely no one could find her.

As interventions went, this one pretty much sucked. Not that Maggie knew a whole lot about interventions, never having been addicted to much of anything—with the possible exception of truly lousy choices in men. She was fairly certain, though, that having only three people sitting before her with anxious expressions—one of them the very man responsible for her current state of mind—was not the way this sort of thing ought to work.

Then, again, Warren should know. He'd probably done hundreds of them for his alcohol- or drug-addicted clients. Hell, maybe he'd even done a few for women he'd dumped, like Maggie. Maybe that was how he'd built up his practice, the louse.

"Magnolia Forsythe, are you listening to a word we're saying?" Dinah Davis Beaufort demanded impatiently, a worried frown etched on her otherwise perfect face.

Dinah and Maggie had been friends forever. It was one reason, possibly the only reason, Maggie didn't summon the energy to slap Dinah for using her much-hated given name. Magnolia, for goodness' sakes! What had her parents been thinking?

Maggie regarded her best friend—her *former* best friend, she decided in that instant—with a scowl. "No." She didn't want to hear anything these three had to say. Every one of them had played a role in sending her into this depression. She doubted they had any advice that would drag her out of it.

"I told you she was going to hate this," Cordell Beaufort said.

Of everyone there, Cord looked the most relaxed, the most normal, Maggie concluded. In fact, he had the audacity to give her a wink. Because Maggie's futile attempt to seduce him before Dinah's return to town last year from a foreign assignment was another reason she was in this dark state of mind, she ignored the wink and concentrated on identifying all the escape routes from this room. Not that a woman should have to flee her own damn living room to get any peace. She ought to be able to kick the well-meaning intruders out, but—her mother's stern admonitions be damned—she'd tried that not five minutes after their arrival and not a one of them had budged. Perhaps she ought to consider telling them whatever they wanted to hear so they'd go away.

"I don't care if she does hate it," Dinah said, her expression grim. "We have to convince her to stop moping around in this house. Look at her. She hasn't even combed her hair or put on makeup." She surveyed Maggie with a practiced eye. "And what is that she's wearing? It looks as if she chopped off her jeans with gardening shears."

"I'm at the beach, for heaven's sake! And stop talking about me as if I've left the room," Maggie snapped.

Dinah ignored Maggie and went right on addressing Cord. "It's not healthy. She needs to come home. She needs to get out and do something. This project of ours is perfect."

"In your opinion," Cord chided. "Maggie might not agree."

Dinah frowned. "Well, if she doesn't want to help us with that, then she at least ought to remember that she has a business to run, a life to live."

Maggie felt the last thread holding her temper in check snap. "What life is that?" Maggie inquired. "The one I had before Warren here decided I wasn't his type and dumped me two weeks before our wedding? Or the humiliating one I have now, facing all my friends and trying to explain how I got it so wrong? Or perhaps you're referring to my pitiful and unsuccessful attempt to seduce Cord before you waltzed back into town from overseas and claimed him for yourself?"

Of all of them, only Warren had the grace to look chagrined. "Maggie, you know it would never have worked with us," he explained with great patience, just as he had on the night he'd first broken the news that the wedding was off. "I'm just the one who had the courage to say it."

"Well, you picked a damn fine time to figure it out," she said, despite the fact that she'd long since conceded to herself that he'd done exactly the right thing. "What kind of psychologist are you that you couldn't recognize something like our complete incompatibility a year before the wedding or even six months before the wedding?"

Warren regarded her with an unblinking gaze. "We were only engaged for a few weeks, Maggie," he reminded her in that same annoyingly patient tone. "You were the one who was in a rush to get married. Neither one of us had much time to think."

"I was in love with you!" she practically shouted, irritated by his determination to be logical when she was an emotional wreck. "Why would I want to waste time on a long engagement?"

Warren's tolerant expression never wavered. It was one of the things she'd grown to hate about him. He wouldn't fight with her. He was always so damn reasonable. It might be a terrific trait in a shrink, but in a boyfriend it had been infuriating, especially for a woman who enjoyed a good argument.

"Maggie, as much as I would love to think that you fell head over heels in love with me so quickly we both know the rush was all about keeping up with Dinah and Cord. The minute they got married, you started to panic. You hated being left behind and I was handy."

"You're wrong," she protested stubbornly, not liking the picture he was painting.

"Am I?" he asked mildly. "We'd already stopped seeing each other after just a few mostly disastrous dates, but right in the middle of Cord and Dinah's wedding reception, you decided we should give it another chance."

"Because my family adored you, because everyone said you were perfect for me. I was being open-minded," she countered. "Isn't that what the sensible women you so admire do?"

Cord tried unsuccessfully to swallow a chuckle. Warren and Dinah scowled at him.

"I have to say, I think Warren is right," Dinah chimed in. "I think you latched on to Warren as if he were the last life raft in the ocean."

"Oh, what do you know?" Maggie retorted. "You and Cord are so into each other you barely know anyone else is around."

"We're here, aren't we?" Dinah asked, completely unfazed by Maggie's nasty tone. "We can't be that self-absorbed."

"How did you find me, by the way? I thought I'd covered my tracks pretty well." The truth was, she hadn't tried all that hard. In fact, in her state of self-pity, she hadn't been able to imagine anyone caring enough to come after her.

"I'm a journalist," Dinah reminded her. "I know how to make phone calls. Besides, I know you. I knew you'd never go too far from home. Charleston is in your blood."

"More's the pity," Maggie grumbled. She really did need to broaden her horizons. Maybe that was what was wrong with her life. She'd never had any desire to be anyplace except South Carolina's Low Country. Maybe if she'd traveled the world the way Dinah had during her career as a foreign correspondent for a TV network, Maggie would have discovered some other place where she could be perfectly happy. At least it would have gotten her out from under her mother's judgmental gaze.

"Do you really want to talk about the pros and cons of living in Charleston?" Dinah inquired tartly.

"Not particularly," Maggie said.

"Then let's focus on getting your life back on track. Moping around out here all by yourself is not you, Maggie."

"I'm not moping," Maggie retorted. "I'm on vacation."

"Oh, please. You were halfway through that pint of ice cream when we walked in," Dinah responded. "That's moping. Believe me, I know all the signs. It's obvious you're in trouble and we want to help."

"I really don't need the three of you sitting here with these gloomy expressions on your faces trying to plan out my life. Hell, Dinah, you're the one who talked Warren into going out with me in the first place. Considering how things turned out, I should hate you for that."

In fact, she *was* pretty darn irritated about it. If it hadn't been for Dinah's meddling, Maggie would never in a million years have fallen, however halfheartedly, for a man like Warren Blake. Rock-steady and dependable might suit a lot of women, but such traits had always bored Maggie to tears. She preferred dark, dangerous and sexy. Men like Cord Beaufort, as a matter of fact.

If she were being totally honest, she'd have to admit she'd known all along that with Warren, she was settling for someone safe. He might not rock her world, but

he'd never hurt her, either. As it turned out, she'd been
wrong. He *had* hurt her, though mostly it was her ego
that was bruised. If a man like Warren couldn't truly
love her, who would?

That was what she'd been pondering in her Sullivan's
Island hideaway for a few weeks now. If she wasn't interesting enough, sexy enough or lovable enough for
Warren, then she might as well resign herself to spin-
sterhood. He was her last chance. Her sure thing. Sort
of the way Bobby Beaufort, Cord's sweet, but dull-as-
dishwater brother, had been Dinah's backup plan till her
hormones and good sense had interceded.

Even as Maggie was struck by that notion, she realized she should have seen the handwriting on the wall.
Wasn't she the one who'd told Dinah that safe was never
going to be enough? If it wasn't good enough for Dinah,
why had she, Maggie, ever thought it would work for
her? They'd always been like two peas in a pod when it
came to choosing between conventional and unconventional.

"Mind if I say something?" Cord asked, his gaze
filled with surprising compassion. He spoke in that
slow, lazy drawl that had once sent shivers down Maggie's spine till she'd realized he'd never want anyone but
Dinah. She'd learned to ignore the attraction and look
in other directions. Warren, unfortunately, had been in
the vicinity.

Maggie shrugged. "Suit yourself."

"Here's the way I see it," he began. "Nothing's stop-
ping you from sitting in this cozy little beach house all
the live-long day, if that's what you want to do. I'm sure
your art and antiques gallery can pretty much run itself,
thanks to those competent employees you've hired. And

if it doesn't, so what? You've got a nice little trust fund from your daddy. You don't need to do a thing."

Maggie bristled. She'd never liked thinking of herself as a spoiled little rich girl who didn't need to work for a living. She'd poured heart and soul into Images, a high-end shop that catered to Charleston's wealthier citizens and the tourists who visited the city's historic district. She'd never treated it like a hobby, and had taken pride in its success. She also felt a certain amount of perverse satisfaction just knowing that it drove her mother crazy to think of her daughter being in "trade," as she put it. Juliette Forsythe should have lived in some earlier century.

As for her employees, Maggie didn't know where Cord had gotten the idea they were competent. She'd be lucky if they didn't run the place into bankruptcy. Although, until right this second with Cord taunting her, she hadn't much cared.

But if Cord was aware of her growing indignation, he gave no indication. "Maggie's a smart woman," he continued mildly, aiming his words at Dinah and Warren and leaving Maggie to draw her own conclusions. "This has obviously been a trying time for her. I think we should let her decide for herself how she wants to spend her days. She can go back to work running her business, if that's what matters to her. She can come on out and help us with our project and make a real difference in someone's life. Or she can sit right here and feel sorry for herself. It's her choice. I think once we clear out and give her some breathing room, she'll make the right decision."

Maggie saw the trap at once. If she did what she wanted to do and hung around here wallowing in self-pity and Häagen-Daz ice cream, they'd worry, but they'd let her do it and they wouldn't think any the less of her, because they loved her. But in her heart, she'd see herself for the ridiculously self-indulgent idiot she was being.

She'd lost a man. So what? Warren wasn't the first and undoubtedly he wouldn't be the last, despite her current vow to avoid all males from here to eternity. Leave it to a man as sneaky and surprisingly insightful as Cordell to appeal to her floundering self-respect.

"Okay, okay, I get it. Tell me again about this stupid project," she said grudgingly.

Cord, bless his devious little heart, bit back a grin. "We're going to be building a house for someone who needs one. The church's congregation got the idea, a benefactor donated the land, and the preacher asked me to put together a volunteer construction crew. We'll be working mostly on weekends, since that's when people are available. Dinah and her mama are in charge of raising money for whatever building supplies we can't get donated."

"What do you expect me to do?" Maggie asked suspiciously.

"What you're told," Dinah said with a glint of amusement in her eyes. "Same as me. It'll be a refreshing change for us. At least that's what Cord says. We'll be hammering and painting right alongside everyone else."

Maggie turned her gaze on Warren. "And you?" she asked.

"That's up to you," he replied. "I said I'd help, but I'll stay away if you want me to, Maggie. I don't want to make you uncomfortable."

Maggie wasn't sure Warren had any essential skills

for building a house, so sending him away might not be much of a loss, but why bother? Maybe it was time to show all of Charleston that she was holding up just fine after her broken engagement. It was past time she held her head up high and behaved like the strong, independent woman she'd always considered herself to be.

"Do whatever you want to do," she told Warren with as much indifference as she could muster.

"Then you'll help?" Dinah asked.

"I'll help," Maggie agreed. "If I don't, who knows what sort of place you'll build? Everyone knows I'm the one with taste in this crowd."

"We're building a three-bedroom bungalow with the basic necessities for a single mom with three kids," Cord warned. "Not a mansion. Let's not lose sight of that."

"You're building a house," Maggie retorted emphatically. "I'll turn it into a home."

But just as she uttered the words, Maggie spotted the satisfied glint in Dinah's eyes and wondered if she wasn't making the second mistake she'd made that day. The first had been opening the door to these three.

2

The blessed ceiling fan was making so much noise Josh couldn't even hear himself think. Normally that would be downright terrific, but he was sitting on the edge of his motel-room bed, facing down his boss and his boss's drop-dead-gorgeous wife, who was trying valiantly to pretend that this sleazy dump was a palace. They all knew better.

Josh raked a hand through his hair and tried not to stare at Dinah Davis's elegant, long legs. Dinah Davis *Beaufort,* he reminded himself sternly. He had a hunch if his gaze lingered one second too long, Cord would punch him out and forget all about whatever scheme had brought the two of them over here at the crack of dawn on a Saturday morning.

Which might not be a bad thing, Josh realized. He didn't like that matching gleam in their eyes one damn bit.

"Why exactly are you here?" he asked, wishing like hell he hadn't had that fourth beer the night before. It had knocked him out so he could sleep, but it was muddying his thought processes now and something told him he was going to need all his wits about him before this conversation was over.

"I need you to do me a favor," Cord said.

"A huge favor," Dinah amended.

Josh regarded both of them suspiciously. He turned his gaze on Dinah, since he had this gut-sick feeling she was the one who'd come up with this *huge* favor. Cord was a businesslike sort who laid things on the line, said what he needed and then left his crew to get the work done. Dinah was sneaky…or clever, depending on your point of view. Her mere presence here was enough to fill Josh with dread.

"I am not going out with one of your friends," Josh announced, since that was always what women seemed to want from him. They assumed that if he was single, he was lonely. He wasn't, at least not in the way that made him accept blind dates intended to lead to something serious and permanent. In fact, he'd had enough experience with the female population to last him a lifetime. He was currently dedicating himself to a life of celibacy. Of course, he'd only been at it a week and it was already getting on his nerves, so the odds weren't great he'd stick with it. Still, permanency was absolutely, positively out of the question, and that was the only thing any friend of Dinah's was likely to be interested in.

"Of course not," Dinah said sweetly. "I would never dream of imposing on you like that, Josh. I don't know you well enough to presume to know your taste in women."

Even though he'd only encountered Dinah a few times in his life, Josh knew for a fact she only laid on that thick, syrupy accent when she was lying through her teeth. Her mama was the same way. He'd run into Dorothy Davis a few times when he'd helped out with the renovations Beaufort Construction was doing at Covington Plantation, her pet historic preservation project. She'd always poured on enough syrup to send a man into a diabetic coma just before she moved in for the kill. Watching her work on Cord had given Josh all the lessons he needed to know to watch his backside around the Davis women.

"What, then?" he inquired cautiously.

"Actually it's going to be a real challenge, something downright rewarding," Cord said in what sounded like an overly optimistic bit of spin. "We're going to be building a house for a particular family and I need you to oversee the project. I'll keep you on the company payroll, but everyone else will be volunteer labor."

"You don't build houses," Josh said, trying to get a grasp on what Cord was saying. "You do historic renovation. So do I."

Cord's lips twitched. "I'd say we both have enough skill to build a house from the ground up if we put our minds to it. Besides, this is a one-shot deal. I'm not asking you to take on an entire development in the suburbs."

Josh still couldn't hide his bemusement. "I don't get it. Why me? For that matter, how did you get sucked into this?"

Cord cast a glance at his wife, which answered one question, then he leveled a look straight into Josh's eyes. "I want you on this because the Atlanta renovations are finished and there's nothing going on over there till we get that new deal finalized. The Covington renovations are almost done. I need to finish up out there if we're going to keep my mother-in-law happy. She's got some big gala scheduled in a month to show it off, and if every little detail isn't just right, she'll have my hide. You've got the time for this right now. I don't."

"I do historic renovations," Josh reminded him again. "I don't build cute little houses with amateurs."

"You do if that's what I need you to do," Cord reminded him mildly, pulling rank.

"It's a bad idea," Josh argued. In fact, it was a lousy idea in ways too numerous to mention. He settled on one. "It's a waste of my skills. I should be helping you out at Covington. Then you'll be done that much sooner."

"Hey, come on, pal," Cord cajoled. "It's a few months out of your life for a good cause. What's the big deal?"

Josh shuddered. He knew more than most about good causes. For most of his life he'd been on the receiving end of other people's charity. He hadn't much liked it. It had reminded him that there was nothing normal about his family, that his dad had disappeared before Josh had needed his first diaper change and that his mom had tried to fill that void with one creep after another. They'd run from cheap motel to cheap motel in more cities than he could count, trying to get away from the worst of the creeps. It was the reason he picked rooms like this one. It reminded him of his so-called homes. That kind of history didn't exactly qualify him to build anybody's dream house.

"This is like one of those Habitat for Humanity things?" he asked.

"Exactly like that," Cord said. "But this is just a one-shot deal being put together by a church in Charleston. One of the parishioners has had a run of real bad luck and the church wants to help her out. They've got the land. They've got people beating the bushes to get building materials donated. I'm putting together the construction crew and I want you in charge."

"You say it's for someone who's had a run of bad luck. What kind of bad luck?" Josh inquired, despite his intention to nip this whole scheme in the bud.

"A woman with three kids," Cord said. "Her husband was killed in a car accident and left them with nothing but a mountain of debt. They had to sell their house and move into a cramped apartment. They were about to be evicted from that till the church stepped in and took care of the rent, but they need a bigger place, a home that really belongs to them. Building this will give them a new start in life." He gave Josh a pointed look. "I'm sure you can relate to that."

Josh cursed the day he'd spilled his guts to Cord about his lousy childhood. He should have known it would come back to bite him in the butt.

Before Josh could stop her, Dinah whipped out a picture of a pretty, but exhausted-looking woman with three solemn-looking kids. Every one of them appeared beaten down. Unfortunately, just as Cord had guessed, Josh could relate to that. His mother, Nadine, had looked exactly like that way too often. He felt his heart twist. How the hell was he supposed to say no now that he'd looked into those sad, vulnerable eyes that reminded him of her? His mother always bounced back quickly, but something told him this family might not have her resiliency.

"I suppose they're all going to be underfoot?" he asked, resigned. If there was one thing he was more skittish about than women, it was kids. He didn't know what to make of them. He sometimes wondered if that was what had sent his father fleeing, the jittery sense that he was in way over his head when he found out Josh was on the way.

"That's part of the deal," Cord said. "They have to help, right down to the littlest one."

"I'm not babysitting a bunch of kids," Josh declared fiercely. "It's way too dangerous for them to be anywhere near a construction site."

"You won't have to worry about them," Dinah assured him. "I'll make sure they're kept busy and out of your way."

"And the mother?"

"She'll do whatever you need her to do, the same as the rest of us," Dinah promised. "And we've already rounded up a lot more volunteers. You'll have plenty of help."

"I don't suppose any of these volunteers will actually know what they're doing," Josh said, resigned to his fate.

"We'll bring in professionals for the plumbing and electrical," Cord promised him.

Josh sighed. "Great. The house might fall down, but at least the toilets and lights will work."

"It's up to you to see that the house doesn't fall down," Cord chided. "So, is it a deal?"

"Do I have a choice?" Josh retorted wryly.

"You can always go off and look for another renovation project to fill the time till our deal comes through in Atlanta," Cord said.

Unfortunately, Josh knew that high-end historic renovation projects were few and far between. He also knew that Cord was better at them than anyone else he'd ever met. He didn't want to work on some half-baked job for an idiot who barely knew one end of a hammer from the other. He owed Cord for making him foreman of the Atlanta project when a lot of contractors would have turned their backs on a man who'd wandered from place to place as much as he had. Cord had trusted him to stick around and see the job through.

Josh had done that, and now would be the perfect opportunity for him to move on, the way he usually did. But he was damn tired of staking out new turf for a few months, then leaving it behind just when he started to feel comfortable. He'd worked in Atlanta and Charleston for Cord, so he knew his way around in both places. It wasn't as if he was going to be putting down any roots if he stuck around awhile longer. Nobody in his right mind would put down roots if this dump of a motel room was what he came home to at night.

As long as neither Dinah or Cord had any ulterior motives, Josh couldn't see much of a downside to staying. Maybe one good deed would make up for some of the miserable stunts he'd pulled in his life. Maybe he'd start to feel better about who he was if he gave something back, instead of living in the lonely isolation that had become a habit as far back as he could remember. People who were always on the run had few genuine friends. Maybe that was what had made Nadine latch on so desperately to anyone who showed her the least bit of kindness.

He gave Dinah a hard look, because she was the one he suspected of not being entirely truthful about her motivations. "This is just about the house, right?"

She beamed at him. "Of course. What else could it possibly be about?"

In Josh's humble opinion, she sounded just a bit too

cheerful. "You tell me," he pushed. "You don't have any ideas about me and this single mom, do you?"

"Absolutely not," she said. "I haven't even met Amanda yet. That's her name. Amanda O'Leary. We wanted to get everything in place before we told her what was going on. We didn't want to get her excited and then have to let her down if we couldn't make it happen. I'm sure she's still grieving the loss of her husband, so I seriously doubt she's looking for a new relationship."

Josh stared Dinah down, but she never so much as blinked. He turned his gaze on Cord. "Is she telling the truth?"

"Dinah's a journalist," Cord said. "She always tells the truth."

"We'll see about that," Josh said, still skeptical.

"You're saying yes?" Dinah asked eagerly.

"Sure," Josh said without enthusiasm. "Like Cord said, I've got time on my hands. I might as well do something productive with it."

"You're an angel," Dinah declared.

Josh chuckled. "Not even close, darlin'. Not even close."

Now that she was back in Charleston, Maggie knew she had no choice but to drop in to see her mother. If Juliette Forsythe heard from someone else that her daughter had returned, Maggie would never hear the end of it. It would be added to her already lengthy list of sins.

The Forsythe mansion faced Charleston Harbor, its stately elegance protected by a high wrought-iron fence. The front lawn was perfectly manicured, and in spring azaleas spilled a profusion of pink, white and gaudy magenta blossoms over the landscape. But in July, as it was now, everything was unrelentingly green. Juliette didn't believe in "tawdry" annuals along the walkways or hanging in pots from the porch ceiling. One brave gardener had edged the walkway with cheerful red geraniums and been fired on the spot for his audacity.

Maggie had timed her visit carefully. Juliette had a standing hair and manicure appointment at 10:30 a.m. Thursdays, so that she would be looking her absolute best when she met her friends for lunch and shopping in the historic district. By arriving at nine forty-five, Maggie knew she would only have to endure a twenty-minute grilling before being dismissed. No one kept Madame Monique waiting, not even Juliette. In fact, the hairdresser was the only person in all of Charleston that Maggie had ever seen intimidate her imperious mother.

"It's about time you came to see me," Juliette declared when Maggie walked into her upstairs sitting room, where she was drinking her morning coffee and finishing her raspberry croissant. She was already dressed in a stylish knit suit. A pair of one-carat diamond studs winked at her ears. Her makeup was flawless. Every highlighted blond hair on her head was in place, which seemed to mock the need for the impending salon appointment.

Juliette was fifty-seven, but looked ten years younger, the result of obsessive control of her diet and enough skin-care products to stock a spa gift shop. Her self-absorption might annoy Maggie, but it was simply the way Juliette had been raised. Her duty was to be an asset to her wealthy husband and a doting mother to her

children. Unfortunately, there had been only Maggie
upon whom to lavish all that attention. Maybe if there
had been sons or another daughter to distract Juliette,
Maggie wouldn't have been the focus of so many maternal rules and regulations and would never have felt
the need to rebel.

Now Juliette did a disapproving survey of Maggie's
simple red dress and sandals, then sighed before adding, "I thought you'd vanished."

"Obviously you weren't too concerned or you'd have
hired a search party," Maggie replied, bending down to
give her mother a dutiful peck on the cheek. "How are
you? You're looking well."

"I'm humiliated, that's how I am," Juliette declared.
"I can barely hold my head up as a result of that debacle
with your wedding."

"You should be in *my* shoes," Maggie retorted,
though it was clear the sarcasm went right over her
mother's head. Everything was always about Juliette,
how events affected *her.* By the time Maggie had hit her
teens, she'd given up expecting a sympathetic ear.

"You still haven't said why you haven't been by," Juliette complained.

"I've been away," Maggie said, regretting that she'd
bothered to rush right over, since it was evident her
mother hadn't been especially worried about her absence.

Juliette looked momentarily startled. "Away?
Where? You never said anything about going away."

"I rented a house on Sullivan's Island. I've been out
there for nearly a month now."

"My heavens, why would you do a thing like that?
What if your father and I had needed you in an emer-

gency? Do you ever think of anyone other than yourself, Magnolia?"

"If you'd needed me, I would have known about it," she said. "I checked my phone messages every day. Since there weren't any from you, obviously there were no emergencies, so don't make a big to-do about it now, Mother."

Juliette regarded her with a familiar expression of dismay. "Sometimes I just don't know what to make of you."

Maggie bit back a grin. "Now there's a news flash," she muttered under her breath.

Her mother frowned. "What did you say?"

"Nothing important," Maggie said. "I should run along now. I know you need to get to your appointment and I have to go to the gallery and check on things there. I just wanted you to know I was back."

Her mother glanced at her watch, obviously torn. "I do need to go, but we really must talk soon, Magnolia."

"About?"

"This fiasco with Warren."

"The fiasco with Warren is over. It's not open for discussion."

"But I'm sure you could mend fences if you put your mind to it," Juliette persisted. "He's a reasonable man. I'm sure he'll forgive you for whatever you did to upset him."

"He'll forgive me?" Maggie said incredulously. "Are you kidding, Mother? I didn't do anything. He's the one who called off the wedding. If there's any groveling to be done, let Warren do it."

"There it is again," her mother said accusingly. "That stubborn streak of yours. It's always been your downfall, Magnolia. If you don't reconcile with Warren, what will you do?"

"I'll survive, Mother. In fact, I've already gotten involved in an exciting new project that will take up a lot of my time for the rest of the summer. I'll tell you about it next time I see you. Now, we both really need to get moving." She leaned down for another quick kiss. "Love you."

Duty done, Maggie was out the door and down the stairs at a clip an Olympic runner would envy. With her visit to Juliette behind her, life already looked brighter.

Maggie's improved mood lasted only until she walked into Images and took a good look around at the displays that had been created in her absence. They were chaotic. Of course, she had no one to blame but herself. She was the one who'd gone off and left the decision making to her employees. She could hardly expect a twenty-one-year-old who dressed all in black and had pink streaks in her hair, or an art-school dropout whose mind tended to wander when she wasn't in front of a canvas, to arrange the gallery with the same expertise and attention to detail that Maggie would. She was probably fortunate that they'd even bothered to uncrate the new shipments and price them.

"You're back!" Victoria exclaimed when she stirred from reading her book. Judging from the cover, it was something dark and depressing, suitable for a woman in black.

"Indeed, I am," Maggie said. "I see the new shipments came in."

"Last week," Victoria acknowledged. "I didn't want to touch them, but Ellie said we probably should. The gallery was starting to look kinda empty, like we were going out of business or something."

"Ellie was exactly right," Maggie said. "Is there coffee made?"

Victoria stared at her blankly. "Coffee?"

"Yes, coffee. We make it every day in case a customer would like a cup."

"Oh, I thought it was just for you, and since I didn't know you were coming back today, I didn't make any."

"Never mind. I'll make it, and as soon as I have a cup you can tell me what business has been like while I've been gone."

"Actually, you'll need to ask Ellie. I have an appointment at eleven, so she's coming in early. Since you're here, I'll go now so I won't be late."

Maggie had always given her employees a lot of flexibility in scheduling, but usually she expected them to work longer than an hour before taking off. "When will you be back?"

Victoria shrugged as if the concept of time was of little importance. "How should I know? It depends on how long Drake can get away."

"Drake?"

"My boyfriend," Victoria explained impatiently as if Maggie should know that.

Maggie searched her memory. "I thought your boyfriend was named Lyle."

"He split, like, three weeks ago, so now I'm seeing Drake."

"In the middle of a workday?" Maggie said, subtly trying to suggest that there was something inappropriate about that. The notion apparently was utterly foreign to Victoria.

"It's when he's free," she said reasonably. "After work, he has to go home to his wife."

Maggie stared after Victoria as she fled to keep her "appointment" with her new, married boyfriend. And Juliette thought Maggie made bad choices. Her mother should spend an hour or two with Victoria. Maggie would begin to seem downright traditional after that.

A few minutes later, as Maggie was sipping gratefully on her first cup of very strong coffee, Ellie came in. In comparison to Victoria, she looked thoroughly professional in her tan slacks and white blouse. Her hair might be short and carelessly styled, but it was a perfectly normal shade of golden blond.

"Where's Victoria?" Ellie asked, obviously startled to find Maggie behind her desk. "You didn't fire her, did you?"

"No, though the thought has crossed my mind. She went to see Drake."

Ellie grimaced. "Can you believe it? She's dating a married man. And he must be having some kind of midlife crisis or something. Why else would he pick somebody as flighty as Victoria? He's old. He must be thirty-five, at least."

Maggie herself had issues with men that age. Warren was thirty-five. "Maybe you could sit here and tell me what's been going on. Has business been good?"

Ellie looked vaguely disconcerted by the question. "I guess," she said eventually. "The deposit slips are all in your desk."

Maggie sighed. She should have known better than to expect any kind of overview of the gallery's business the past month from either Victoria or Ellie. She was lucky they'd managed to keep the place from burning to the ground in her absence.

Ironically, the customers loved them. The two young women, with their off-beat quirkiness, seemed to fit the artistic stereotype people anticipated when shopping in a gallery. Her own contribution, she supposed, was class, necessary to assure the customers that the works and antiques on display were genuine and worth every penny of their exorbitant price tags.

"Thanks for looking after things," Maggie said, meaning it. "I really appreciate the way you pitched in."

"Sure. No problem. You know me. I can always use the extra cash." Ellie's expression brightened. "But I did sell two of my paintings while you were gone."

Maggie beamed at her. What Ellie lacked in business skills, she more than made up for as an artist. "Congratulations! I told you it was only a matter of time. I think we should talk about having a real show one of these days. You're ready for it, don't you think?"

Ellie's joy faltered. "Maybe you should come by the studio and take a look before you decide," she suggested worriedly. "Maybe there aren't enough good paintings yet. I don't want you to be embarrassed."

"You could never embarrass me. You're the most talented artist I've discovered yet," Maggie assured her with total sincerity. "I can't wait to really give your work a big splashy show. Why don't I come by one evening after we close and take a look. Then we can decide. I'd love to schedule something for this fall."

"Really?" Ellie said, her eyes shining.

"Sweetie, you're going to be showing in the Museum of Modern Art in New York before you know it, and I'm going to be bragging that I knew you when."

"Don't even tease about that," Ellie said, bright spots of color in her cheeks.

"Who's teasing? Don't you know how good you are?" She could see by Ellie's doubtful expression that she did not. "Don't worry. You'll see. I promise you."

In fact, seeing Ellie's career take off the way a few of Maggie's other discoveries had before her was exactly the kind of achievement that kept Maggie in business. It was reassuring to know that in one area of her life, her judgment was impeccable.

3

There were at least forty people milling around in the church parish hall when Josh arrived there on Saturday morning. A long folding table was loaded down with a coffee urn, pottery mugs and trays of doughnuts and pastries. He wasn't convinced there was enough caffeine or sugar in the world to get him through the weeks to come, but he filled a cup to the brim and grabbed a couple of glazed doughnuts before going in search of Cord.

He found him in an alcove, deep into what sounded like a very serious conversation with an unfamiliar man. Josh was about to back away when Cord spotted him.

"Hey, there you are," Cord called. "Josh, get over here and let me introduce you to Caleb Webb. He's the minister here and the driving force behind this project."

Surprised, Josh took another look at the man dressed in worn jeans and a polo shirt. He didn't look like any preacher Josh had ever known. For one thing, he was built as if he'd been working construction all his life. For another, he was young. Certainly no older than Josh's age, thirty-four.

The few preachers Josh had encountered in his brief

brushes with religion had all been old and mostly crotchety. They'd spent a lot of time talking about fire and brimstone, which had been pretty scary stuff to a kid. Caleb looked like someone you could enjoy a beer with at the end of the day. He also didn't seem like the kind of man who'd try to frighten a youngster into behaving.

"Sorry for interrupting," Josh told them. "I just wanted to let Cord know I was here."

"Not a problem," Cord assured him. "Caleb was just filling me in on a couple of problems that have cropped up."

Josh should have guessed this project wouldn't be the picnic Cord had promised him. "What kind of problems?"

"Nothing for you to worry about," Caleb assured him. "I just have a little rebellion in the ranks among my parishioners. Some of them don't approve of what we're doing. It's gotten a little ugly, but I'll get it straightened out."

"Ugly in what way?" Josh asked, trying to imagine why anyone would disapprove of building a home for someone in need.

Caleb gave him a wry grin. "There's a camp that thinks I ought to be run off for doing this for Amanda O'Leary. They're very vocal."

Josh didn't get it. He looked blankly from Caleb to Cord. "Okay, what am I missing here?"

It was Caleb who responded. "I assume Cord filled you in on Amanda's situation."

Cord nodded. "I know her husband was killed a while back."

"It was more than that," Caleb said. "He'd gotten himself into serious debt and she was forced to declare bankruptcy. She's been working two, sometimes three, jobs to try to pay off all the bills. She was about to be evicted from her apartment when we stepped in. At first we were just going to help out with the rent, which we did, but then someone had the idea to build her a house. Most of the congregation jumped on board, but a few people think we've picked the wrong person to help."

"Why?" Josh asked.

"Because Amanda's daddy is William Maxwell," Cord explained. When Josh shook his head, Cord added, "Big Max is one of the wealthiest men in Charleston. Some folks think Big Max is the one who ought to be helping Amanda, not the church."

There was obviously still some critical piece of information that Josh was missing. If getting this woman a place to live were that simple, it would have been done long ago.

"Why isn't he?" Josh asked. "I assume there's a reason."

"There's a lot of bad blood between the two of them," Cord said succinctly.

"That's an understatement and it's not without reason, at least on Amanda's part," Caleb said. "Since you're involved in this now, you should know what's going on. Here's the short version. Big Max disowned Amanda when she got married. He didn't approve of Bobby O'Leary. He dug in his heels. Amanda refused to cave in to his pressure, so he hasn't had a thing to do with her for almost ten years now. He's never even set eyes on his grandkids. I think he regrets all that now, but he's too stubborn to fix it, and Amanda's too hurt and has too much pride to turn to him now that she's in trouble because of Bobby's mistakes."

Josh got the picture. "But some folks think she should swallow her pride and go running to daddy now, instead of taking this opportunity away from some other family, one with no other resources."

"Exactly," Caleb said.

"I suppose I can see their point, but obviously she doesn't think she can turn to her father or doesn't want to after the way he treated her," Josh said. "I can't say I blame her." He could empathize. Even if he discovered tomorrow that his father was rolling in dough, it would be a cold day in hell before he ever turned to the man for help, no matter how dire his own circumstances.

"As far as Amanda's concerned, her father burned that bridge," Caleb said. "She won't ask him for a dime. So as far as I'm concerned, she's a struggling single mom who's as deserving as anyone else. And she's doing everything she can to get back on her feet. It's not like she came looking for a handout. People just saw a need and wanted to help. She's one of our own. We have an opportunity to help her and we'll all get something out of doing it."

"So you want to go ahead, even though it'll anger some members of your congregation?" Josh asked.

"Absolutely," Caleb responded without hesitation. "And it's really only one member who's dedicated himself to stirring the pot. He just happens to be wealthy and powerful in his own right. He could complicate things if he switches from talk to action."

"What sort of action?" Josh asked.

"Let's just say he's politically well connected and could hold things up," Caleb replied. "Especially if he thinks he's doing Big Max a favor in the process."

"Has he threatened to throw up real roadblocks?" Josh asked.

Caleb shook his head. "Not yet. Mainly he's been working to get the congregation on his side. He's succeeded with some. We expected a larger turnout than this initially."

"And as of this morning, Amanda's balking," Cord explained.

"Last night she got wind of the battle that was brewing, and she doesn't want the congregation divided over this," Caleb said. "I've tried every way I can think of, but I can't get through to her that it's only George Winslow flexing his muscles."

Silence fell as they all pondered how to break the impasse. It was several minutes before Josh realized that Cord was studying him speculatively.

"You know, Josh, you might have better luck than Caleb did," Cord suggested mildly.

"Hold it," Josh protested. "When did this become *my* problem? I'm here to build a house, not to provide counseling services. Besides, I don't even know this woman. Why would she listen to me?"

Cord didn't answer.

"There won't be any reason to build a house unless we get Amanda back on board," Caleb pointed out.

"Hey, that suits me," Josh said.

Cord regarded him with disappointment. "Josh, take a look out there," he said, gesturing toward the main room. "See those kids. Who do they remind you of?"

Reluctantly Josh turned to look at Amanda O'Leary's three children. They were sitting on metal chairs, their expressions glum. Two little boys, who should be out running and playing ball on a Saturday morning, and a pint-size girl with huge blue eyes who looked as if she might cry any minute. She was clutching a worn stuffed bear by one arm. Josh saw himself in each of those solemn faces. Once again he cursed the day he'd ever confided in Cord about his past.

"Well?" Cord prodded.

Josh wondered how different his life might have been if someone had ever sat his mother down and had a heart-to-heart with her about giving him a real home, instead of dragging him from city to city, from motel to motel. He heaved a resigned sigh.

"Okay, where is she?" he asked.

"Over in the corner trying to stay out of Dinah's path. Dinah's already tried and failed to persuade her," Cord said. "Knowing Dinah, she's just taking a breather, but maybe you can head her off."

"I think you're giving me way too much credit on all fronts," Josh said. "But I'll give it a shot for the sake of those kids."

Rueing the day he'd ever met Cord, much less agreed to take on the building of this house, Josh crossed the parish hall to where Amanda O'Leary was sitting all alone, her jaw set stubbornly and her chin lifted high.

"Mind if I sit down?" he asked, already sliding onto the chair next to her.

"There's nothing you can say to change my mind," she said before he could say another word.

He grinned at her defiance. She might be down, but she was definitely not out. He had to admire her for that. "What makes you think I'm here to change your mind?"

"Oh, please," she said disdainfully. "I saw you with Caleb and Cord. I'm sure they've given you an earful about how stubborn I'm being."

Josh grinned. "They did say something along those

lines. To tell you the truth, I get where you're coming from. I grew up with folks thinking I was the perfect target for their good deeds. It wasn't much fun."

Amanda regarded him skeptically. "Then why are you over here pressuring me?"

"Pressure?" Josh scoffed. "Sweetheart, this isn't pressure. This is just two people having a get-acquainted chat. Obviously I know who you are, but since we haven't been introduced, I'm Josh Parker."

Her gaze narrowed. "The builder Cord hired?"

"That's me."

"So you're out of work if I don't go along with this thing," she said with a biting edge of sarcasm. "Not my problem."

"It's not about me. I don't need the work." He studied her intently, then glanced toward her kids. "But those children over there look to me like they could use a nice home."

"And I'd love for them to have it, but not if it's going to split this congregation apart," Amanda said spiritedly. "That's too high a price. Things might be a little cramped where we're living, but we've been managing for the last year."

"With a little help, I understand… Anyway, Caleb seems willing to pay the price, however steep it is." He leaned toward her and confided, "Personally, I think he has visions of teaching some lessons about humanity and generosity."

Her lips twitched. "I imagine he does, but it's not up to him. I will not be responsible for him getting fired or friends taking sides against each other."

"Friends might disagree, but they'll patch things up. As for Caleb, who said anything about firing him?"

"Some anonymous caller left a message for me yesterday, and I heard a few people talking about it this morning. Word's getting around that George Winslow wants Caleb gone. He's not going to let this drop, not as long as he has my father whispering in his ear. He's determined to stir up trouble if we go forward. Caleb doesn't deserve the aggravation."

"People talk about a lot of things. It doesn't mean they'll act on it. I'm sure whoever left the message figured you'd cave in, because they knew instinctively that you'd back away from a fight."

Her eyes flashed. "I've never backed away from a fight in my life," she said indignantly. "But George is as rich as my daddy and just as powerful. He and Big Max are allies. When it comes to me and my father, there's little question about whose side he'd take. He'll happily bring down anyone who tries to help me, and he'll consider it a favor to my daddy."

"He doesn't seem to scare Caleb. Isn't that what counts?" Josh asked.

"I'm not willing to take that chance." Her gaze narrowed. "Besides, didn't you just say it wasn't much fun being the object of pity? Maybe I've thought it over and decided I don't want to be in that position, either. I'll be indebted to these people forever if I let them build the house."

"I could certainly understand it if you were to come to that conclusion," Josh agreed.

"Then we're agreed. I'm doing the right thing."

"No, we're not agreed," Josh said. "Because I don't think that's what happened. I think you got scared off, just the way this Winslow person—or your daddy— wanted you to."

Despite her earlier indignation, she didn't seem to have enough fight left to argue. "Does it really matter?"

"I think it does. There's a big difference between being proud and being scared," Josh told her. "And even if you think this is all about pride, I'm not sure you're in a position to let pride get in the way of doing what you need to do for those kids of yours."

She studied him intently. "Something tells me you would have thrown this offer right back in their faces, too, especially once it got complicated."

"Possibly," Josh agreed. "But I like to think that I'd have taken another look at it if someone had offered my mom the one thing that might have made a real difference to us."

"What was that?"

"A home," he said simply. "I'm not just talking about four walls and a roof over our heads, Amanda, but a real home with a community of people who cared enough to build it for us. That's what you've got happening here. I'm not sure you should be so quick to turn your back on it, especially not just to protect Caleb, a man who doesn't seem to think he needs your protection."

"But there are a lot of people, not just George Winslow, who think building this house for me is the wrong thing to do. Maybe they're right."

"Thumb your nose at them," he advised. "After all, what do they know? You have your reasons for not asking your daddy for help, and those reasons are none of their concern. If they knew, they might just admire your gumption. *I* do."

"I suppose," she said, though she still sounded doubtful.

"Sweetheart, there are always going to be people who find fault with everything. Are their opinions more important than your kids?"

"Of course not," she said.

"Well, then?"

"I can't stop thinking about the fallout for Caleb. He's been such a good friend. I don't want to repay him by causing him trouble."

"He strikes me as a man who stands on his principles. He wants to do this for you and your family. I think you should respect his wishes."

She sat silently, her expression thoughtful. Josh waited, knowing that he'd pushed as hard as he dared. The decision was hers to make. He suspected when it came right down to it, she would make the only choice a good and decent mother could make.

Finally she met his gaze. "Are you married, Josh?"

He shook his head. "No."

"You should be."

He shuddered at the certainty in her voice. "I don't think so." Curiosity got the better of him, so he asked, "Why would you say that?"

"Because it's a shame to let all that compassion and sensitivity go to waste," she said.

She grinned and Josh saw a glimpse of the beautiful woman she must have been before tragedy had weighed her down.

She studied him thoughtfully. "I think I'd better let you build this house for us."

He regarded her with suspicion, not feeling nearly as triumphant as he might have before she'd made that comment about him needing to be married. "Oh?"

"It'll give me more time to find just the right woman

for you." She winked at him, then added, "I'll go tell Caleb and the kids what I've decided."

Josh sat there feeling doomed. He'd seen firsthand just how stubborn and determined and principled Amanda O'Leary could be. Fortunately he'd had quite a few years to perfect his own stubbornness and determination. Amanda O'Leary wouldn't get to first base with her matchmaking scheme.

Besides, from what he could see in a glance around the parish hall, the few females there were already paired off and unavailable. He didn't have a reason in the world to worry.

So why the hell were his palms sweating as if he'd just made a pact with the devil?

Maggie slipped into a seat beside Dinah an hour after the organizational meeting had begun. "What did I miss?" she asked.

"The nail-biting when Amanda announced she didn't want the house, after all," Dinah said.

Maggie was shocked. "Why? What's wrong with her?"

"Don't blame her. She was trying to protect Caleb."

"And Caleb is?"

"The minister."

Maggie was confused. "Was he in some sort of danger?"

"A few people think he ought to be fired over this project. It's a long story. Bottom line, the deal is back on."

"And I thought this was going to be boring," Maggie said to herself, settling back in her chair as Cord began to speak. Of course, Dinah didn't hear her wry comment. All of Dinah's attention was focused on her husband. It was disgusting, actually. All that rapt attention from a woman who'd once been in the thick of some of the world's most important—and dangerous—stories. Now the most important thing in her life was a man. Of course, Dinah was barely back from her honeymoon, so Maggie supposed she ought to cut her some slack.

Cord didn't waste time getting to the point, which seemed to be introducing the man who would be in charge of building the house. "As long as you follow his directions, he's going to make you all look like master carpenters," Cord promised. "Josh Parker."

The man who walked to the podium looked embarrassed by the introduction. It must have been the combination of that hint of humility with the most gorgeous biceps and chest Maggie had ever seen that made her snap to attention. This was a man made for blue jeans and tight T-shirts.

"My, my," she whispered to Dinah. "Where has Cord been hiding *him?*"

Dinah chuckled. "In Atlanta mostly. I met him when I went looking for Bobby when you and Cord refused to tell me where he was."

"Ah, yes, your failed quest for your backup guy. Yet even after seeing Josh you still came back here and married Cord," Maggie said with exaggerated amazement.

"Fortunately for you I was interested in more than a great body. I love Cord for his mind," Dinah said piously.

"Yeah, right," Maggie retorted. "As I recall, Bobby Beaufort had a great mind. It wasn't enough."

"If you're interested in Josh, I could introduce you." Dinah offered, her tone casual.

"I'm a big girl. I can introduce myself," Maggie said. "If I decide I want to."

"If? You're practically salivating now," Dinah said.

"All the more reason to wait," Maggie said. "I don't want to appear too anxious. Besides, I've sworn off men, remember?"

"Maybe so, but can I assume that in the last five minutes you've experienced a miraculous recovery from your heartbreak over Warren?" Dinah inquired wryly. "It would be fitting if it took place here in a church."

Maggie frowned at her. "Warren didn't break my heart. He just put a dent in my ego and threw a monkey wrench into my self-confidence. None of that means I can't appreciate a fine male specimen when I see one."

"So you're simply admiring the view?"

"Exactly."

And to prove her point, Maggie waited to be the very last person in line to get her assignment for the start of construction next weekend. After all, nobody on earth recognized trouble as readily as she did. Why would she rush right into it?

And if waiting in line gave her a few more minutes to study Josh's fine body, so much the better.

Josh had done his share of hiring and firing on the various jobs he'd held through the years. He'd been on the receiving end of more interview questions than most people here today combined. He approached the task of assembling this roomful of volunteers into a construction crew with guarded optimism.

So far he had twenty-seven people who'd never done a home repair more taxing that plunging a stopped-up drain, five who'd painted the interior of their homes, three who owned decent tools and one who'd actually worked construction—thirty years ago as a summer job. It was discouraging.

"Next," he called out, already sliding a form across the table.

The well-manicured hand that reached for it immediately caught his attention. Long, slender fingers, silky-looking skin and nails painted fire-engine red. He sighed at the sight and snatched the form back almost before she'd put her fancy Mont Blanc pen to paper.

"You don't need to fill this out," he said, his dismay complete when he realized the owner of those hands was his last chance to complete a decent crew.

Dark eyes clashed with his. "Oh? And why is that?"

"Because…" He glanced at the form she'd begun to fill in. "Ms. Forsythe, I'm assigning you to the lunch team."

"Excuse me?" Her voice shook with indignation. "Did I hear you correctly? You want me to fix lunches?"

"And coffee," he said, meeting her gaze for the first time. The fire in those eyes could have seared the paint off old lumber. It certainly sent a jolt through his system.

"What sort of macho head trip are you on?" she demanded. "I'm female, therefore I cook?"

"Works for me," he said, gathering up the forms that had been filled out and trying not to meet that disconcerting gaze.

"Well, it doesn't work for me, Mr. Parker. Dinah and Cord talked me into volunteering because they thought

I could make a real contribution on this project, and I intend to do just that. I'll be here on Saturday with my tools. I plan to use them."

"You want to hammer a few nails after lunch, we'll talk about it," he countered. "Make sure there are plenty of sandwiches. Construction is hard work."

Ms. Maggie Forsythe whirled around and stalked away. Josh had a hunch it was the last he'd see of her. That suited him just fine. The woman spelled trouble. The last thing he needed on this job was some hoity-toity society woman going crazy because she'd broken a fingernail.

Then, again, if she ever wanted to rake those nails down his back, something told him he wouldn't say no.

"Do you realize that not one single person in that room has ever built anything bigger than a birdhouse?" Josh grumbled when he, Cord and Caleb went out for a beer after the meeting at the church. "How am I supposed to get this house built? I'll be spending all my time fixing what they screw up."

"Think of this as your chance to teach others the skills that have made you a great carpenter," Cord said. "You'll be sharing your knowledge. It's a noble endeavor."

Josh lifted his beer in a mocking toast. "Nice spin. You should go into PR."

"Thanks, but I'll stick to working with my hands," Cord responded. "My brother's the spin master."

"All in all, I think it went really well," Caleb said, appearing more relaxed now that the organizational session was over. "I think it will be exciting to build something substantial and enduring. In the end, despite whatever Winslow has up his sleeve, I think this project will be a unifying thing for the church. How long do you think the house will take to build?"

"With any luck, good weather and at least a few people on-site who are quick learners, Amanda and her kids should be in there by Thanksgiving," Josh said. "The plans aren't that elaborate or complicated."

Cord chuckled.

Josh regarded him with a narrowed gaze. "Okay, what was that for?"

"You're assuming that everything's going to go according to the blueprints."

"Of course I am," Josh said. "That's why we have them. What's your point?"

"Let me ask you this. Did you meet Maggie Forsythe?"

Josh didn't have to give the question that much thought. "Yeah, we met."

"I don't suppose you noticed that she's…opinionated," Cord said.

It had been a brief but definitely memorable encounter. "I noticed."

"She's bossy," Cord added meaningfully.

"Doesn't surprise me a bit," Josh replied.

"She thinks it's her duty to turn this from a bare-bones house into a home," Cord concluded.

Josh ground his teeth. "If it's not on the blueprint, it's not happening."

Cord and Caleb exchanged a look, then burst out laughing.

"Good luck with that," Caleb said. "I don't know her but I do know her reputation for getting her way."

Josh didn't like the implication that he didn't stand a chance against Maggie Forsythe and her whims.

"You hired me to get this house built, right?" he said, his gaze locked with Cord's.

"Absolutely."

"And I'm the expert."

"No question about it," Cord said.

"I'm in charge," Josh added for good measure.

"Certainly," Cord said cheerfully.

"Then my decisions are the ones that count," Josh said with finality.

"It ought to work that way," Cord agreed, his smirk still in place.

"That's the way it *will* work," Josh said.

"Unless Maggie has other ideas," Cord said mildly.

Josh was more relieved than ever that he'd assigned her to the lunch detail. Maybe that would keep her out of his path, maybe even off the site entirely if she considered the insult grave enough.

"I don't think it's going to be an issue. I assigned her to make lunch," he informed Cord.

Cord's mouth gaped, as Caleb murmured, "Oh, brother!"

"How did she take that?" Cord asked.

"Not well, if you must know, but I didn't back down."

"Really?" Cord said, his amusement growing. "And you think you won?"

"I know I won. She'll be fixing sandwiches, period."

"Let me give you a friendly little warning, Josh. I've known the woman most of my life," Cord said. "Trust me, her powers of persuasion were honed from birth. If Maggie wants things her way, you don't stand a chance. If she went along with this assignment you gave her, it's because she's lulling you into a false sense of complacency. You'll pay eventually."

Suddenly Josh recalled the first discussion with Cord and Dinah about this house-building thing. He realized now that he'd asked all the right questions that morning in his motel room, but they'd been about the wrong woman. It had never been about him and Amanda O'Leary. It had always been about him and this Maggie person.

"She's the reason you were so hell-bent on getting me to agree to build this house, isn't she?" he demanded, glaring at Cord. "You and Dinah figured you'd toss us together and watch the sparks fly, am I right?"

Cord looked only moderately guilty. "You'd have to ask Dinah about her motivation," he insisted. "Me, I just wanted to get the right man in charge of the job. I won't even be around to watch the fireworks, assuming there are any."

"There won't be," Josh said grimly. "I quit."

"You can't quit," Caleb protested, looking horrified.

"I just did."

"You'd run this whole project off into a ditch just because you're scared of a woman you've barely even met?" Cord asked.

"No, I'm walking off the job because you and Dinah lied to me. You told me it wasn't about hooking me up with some woman."

"It's not," Cord protested. "It's about getting a house built. Besides, you're a grown man. You don't have to hook up with any woman you're not interested in."

Josh regarded him with suspicion. "Then you and Dinah aren't going to be standing around cheering from the sidelines, matchmaking every chance you get?"

"Of course not."

"You swear it?"

"Cross my heart," Cord said, sketching a very large X across his chest.

He looked sincere. He even sounded sincere. "I don't believe you," Josh said.

Cord looked wounded. "Have I ever lied to you?"

"Not about anything work related," Josh admitted.

"About anything?" Cord persisted.

"I suppose not," Josh conceded reluctantly.

"Okay, then, you have no reason to distrust me now."

"You don't worry me half as much as your wife does."

"Understandable," Cord said. "But Dinah won't be around that much, either. She's usually working at the TV station on weekends."

Josh was only moderately placated by Cord's reassurances. "In that case, I won't quit." He shot a meaningful look at both men. "Yet."

"You're not going to regret this," Caleb said cheerfully. "It's going to be a rewarding experience for all of us."

Josh had his doubts. From the moment he'd met Maggie Forsythe, he'd known in his gut it was going to be a disaster.

4

There was something about a man in low-riding jeans and a tool belt, especially if he had rock-hard abs instead of a beer belly. Maggie sat on a stack of lumber in the shade of an old oak tree and admired the view as Josh stretched to hold a beam in place. Thanks to the typically humid weather, most of the men had stripped off their shirts hours ago. She hadn't seen so much pale flesh and so many flabby bellies in years. Josh's tanned, well-honed physique provided an absolutely fascinating contrast.

Then, of course, there was the remarkable fit of his well-worn jeans. Even her most recent bad experience with the male gender hadn't robbed her of her ability to appreciate the sex appeal of a very fine derriere, even if this one did happen to belong to the annoyingly arrogant Josh Parker.

She was still irritated by his assumption that she was incapable of making a contribution more demanding than brewing coffee and fixing sandwiches. When she'd arrived today, dressed to work, he hadn't budged from his original position.

"You're assigned to lunches," he said, his gaze unrelenting. Then, as if to deliberately taunt her, he added, "I like my coffee strong."

She'd almost asked if he also liked it dumped over his thick skull.

But because she was here to help, not stir up trouble, she'd made coffee by the gallon and enough sandwiches to feed a starving army. She'd also vowed to set Josh straight about her capabilities before the day was out.

She'd done all of the renovations on the gallery when she'd first bought it. It had given her a deep sense of satisfaction to look around those cozy rooms and know that she'd turned the space from a shabby, deserted storefront filled with cobwebs into an upscale gallery. She'd painted every nook and cranny and hung every track light herself. She'd even replaced the crown molding. In fact, she'd become something of a whiz with her saw and miter box. Wouldn't the superior Mr. Parker be stunned to know that?

She was debating just how to knock him off his high horse, when Dinah slipped into place beside her. Maggie frowned at her.

"I thought you were working at the TV station today," she said.

"I took a break to check on things here," Dinah said, then grinned. "Aren't you glad you said yes?" she inquired, following the direction of Maggie's gaze. "Working here sure beats moping around out on Sullivan's Island, don't you think?"

"There were plenty of gorgeous, bare-chested men out there," Maggie retorted. "It was a beach, for goodness' sakes."

"Then why are you staring at Josh with such fascination?"

Maggie turned her gaze toward Dinah, sacrificing the fantasies in which she'd been indulging. "Is that what you think I was doing?"

"Yes, I do."

"Maybe I was just plotting how to destroy the man's enormous ego."

Dinah grinned. "Because of the lunch thing? I heard about that. I don't suppose you added anything extra to his coffee, did you?"

"Not this time. I'm trying to decide if I want to kill him or make him suffer for a few hours. I'm leaning toward the latter."

Dinah studied her worriedly. "You're not really that furious with him, are you? He was just being a guy. You have this ultrafeminine look about you that makes men misjudge you. Show him what you're capable of doing and he'll put you to work. He needs all the qualified help he can get."

"I don't think he's all that interested in my construction skills," Maggie said.

"Few men think of drill bits and hammers when they first see you, Magnolia. Give the guy a break."

"Why would I want to do that?"

"Because he's sexy and available, for starters."

A warning bell sounded in Maggie's head. She knew all the signs of Dinah on a mission. "Don't get any ideas," she warned, once again dragging her gaze away from that delectable backside. "I'm here to work. Nothing more."

"Then you're insane," a lilting, unfamiliar voice chimed in. "I loved my husband and I'm not looking for a replacement, but that one could change my mind, at least for a night."

Maggie turned and saw that they'd been joined by a woman with dark circles of exhaustion under her eyes. She was so fragile-looking, Maggie was sure a strong wind could pick her up and carry her off. Yet there was something about her, an indefinable spark of amazing strength, as well as a glint of humor in her eyes. Maggie had no doubt that this was the woman for whom the house was intended. Dinah confirmed it.

"I'm with you," Dinah said, grinning at the newcomer. "Amanda O'Leary, this cynical woman is Maggie Forsythe. She owns Images."

Amanda's eyes lit up with unmistakable approval. "Oh, what a lovely shop. I was in there not long after you opened. Even before…" Her eyes welled with tears, and she brushed them away impatiently. "It was always out of my league, but I certainly admire your taste."

Maggie was pleased with the compliment. How could she help but like anyone who admired her taste? "You'll have to come by again and I'll help you choose something for your new home. It will be my housewarming gift to you."

"That's very sweet of you, but I couldn't possibly accept," Amanda protested. "You being here to help is more than enough. I knew people from church were going to be here, but I'm overwhelmed that so many other people are willing to pitch in and do something like this for a stranger. Having a home of our own again, well, it's practically a miracle to me and the kids. After my husband died, I thought we'd never get back on our feet, not with all those creditors hounding us."

"I thought declaring bankruptcy protects you from them," Maggie said.

"It does…it did," Amanda said. "But it took me a

long time to admit that I needed to take that step. I was determined to pay back every dime Bobby owed until I finally saw that I would never catch up and that I was hurting the kids with my stubborn pride."

"Speaking of the kids, where are they?" Dinah asked.

Maggie saw the question for what it was, a deliberate attempt to change the touchy subject. She understood Dinah's motive. Despite her brave front and evident resiliency, Amanda O'Leary was the kind of woman people instinctively wanted to protect. Men had probably been leaping to her defense ever since the tragedy that had taken her husband's life. Even as that thought crossed Maggie's mind, she realized how petty it sounded.

"Oh, good grief, the kids were right here a second ago," Amanda said, her expression alarmed. "I told them to stay put and not get in anyone's way. Unfortunately, Larry and Jimmy love anything to do with tools, and Susie tags along right after them. She's going to be quite the tomboy."

Maggie spotted them before Dinah or Amanda did. All three kids were lined up watching Josh Parker, their expressions unsmiling. He was staring back at them as if they were aliens. Given the way he'd treated her, Maggie caught her breath, anticipating some harsh remark that would send them fleeing in tears.

Instead, Josh hunkered down until he was at eye level with them. She couldn't hear what he said, but it was enough to earn him a shy grin from Susie, who looked to be about four. The boys were still stoic, as if they'd become used to being shunted aside by grownups and anticipated it happening yet again despite Josh's attention at the moment.

"I'd better go rescue Josh," Amanda said, worry knitting her brow as she hurried away.

An odd sensation settled in Maggie's chest when she saw a warm smile spread across Josh's face at Amanda's approach. When the woman placed a protective hand on each of her sons' shoulders, he said something that made her laugh, and Maggie's heart flipped right over. The jealousy-tinged reaction was disconcerting.

"Looks as if they're getting along just fine," she said to Dinah, unable to keep a certain edge out of her voice. "Did I get it wrong, after all? Was that what you had in mind? Not matchmaking for me, but giving Amanda a house and a man to go with it?"

Dinah gave her a knowing look that came from years of being able to read Maggie's innermost thoughts. "What exactly are you seeing when you look at those two, Maggie?"

"Two people who are flirting with each other," Maggie said, then couldn't resist adding, "it's a little unseemly, don't you think? Didn't Amanda just lose her husband?"

Dinah merely grinned. "The accident was almost a year ago and last I heard, flirting's not a crime. Maybe you should give it a try, Maggie. You used to excel at it. A flirtation might loosen you up."

"And who would you suggest I flirt with? I'm sure you have someone in mind. If not Josh, it must be someone around here. Caleb, maybe? Didn't you learn anything after hooking me up with Warren? Caleb seems sweet, but I'm not cut out for the steady, reliable type."

"I didn't have anyone in particular in mind, to be honest," Dinah said with just the right touch of sincerity. "And it doesn't matter who you flirt with. Just do it. You need to get your blood pumping again."

"My blood is pumping just fine," Maggie retorted irritably.

Dinah's grin spread as she glanced pointedly from Maggie to Josh and Amanda, then back again. "Why, yes, I believe it is. Jealousy sometimes has the same effect."

With that insightful barb, Dinah sashayed off, leaving Maggie wondering how fast her blood would race if she decided to strangle her best friend.

Josh spotted the purposeful glint in Maggie's eye from halfway across the yard. He'd actually been surprised when she'd shown up at the building site this morning. He'd been doubly surprised when she'd taken on the lunch assignment without a complaint and done a fine job of it. The coffee had been hot, strong and plentiful. The thick sandwiches had been served on paper plates decorated with little slices of fruit. There had even been homemade brownies for dessert, which suggested she'd been out to prove that she could handle any assignment, no matter how disagreeable, with grace and aplomb.

Now, however, with most people leaving for the day, she looked as if all those words she'd no doubt been biting back since their first meeting were right on the tip of her tongue. He braced himself to tune out the expected harangue.

"I'm surprised you're still here," he said when she planted herself in front of him. "I thought you'd take off the minute your assignment was done."

"We need to talk."

He wiped the sweat from his brow with a bandanna and resigned himself to letting her have her say. "What about?"

"My capabilities versus your insulting view of women."

Josh grinned despite himself. "In that case, I think I could use something cold to drink." Without waiting for her response, he headed for a cooler and pulled out an icy can of soda. "Want one?"

"No, thank you," she said primly.

He shrugged. "Suit yourself." He tilted the can and took a long, slow swallow. Drops of ice-cold water dripped from the can and fell on his overheated flesh, which had warmed a few more degrees since Miss Maggie had stepped into his line of vision. The effect she had on him was downright dangerous.

She was a picture of pure femininity, he thought, but he doubted she'd planned it that way. In fact, it was clear she'd set out to prove just the opposite in her blue chambray work shirt with the sleeves rolled up and the tails knotted at her tiny waist. Her jeans were well worn and her shoes were dotted with paint spatters. She'd pulled her long hair up into some sort of knot and secured it to the top of her head.

But none of that took away from her flushed cheeks, shiny lips or the very feminine curls that had escaped to brush the delicate nape of her neck. Some women were simply born sexy, and Maggie was one of them. She could have worn a burlap sack and she'd still have set his pulse racing.

Didn't matter, he told himself sternly. After what Cord and Caleb had told him about her determination, he knew he couldn't afford to lose focus around her, not for a second.

"I thought you wanted to talk," he said, aware that her gaze seemed to be locked on his chest. On another occasion he might have considered her expression flattering or interpreted it as an invitation to something more interesting than conversation.

Her head snapped up and the flush in her cheeks deepened.

"I don't like you, Mr. Parker."

Josh bit back a grin. "You're breaking my heart."

Undaunted, she went on. "But that's beside the point. I came here to help and you're wasting my skills."

"Really? I thought lunch was fairly good."

She immediately rose to the bait. "Fairly good? Have you ever had anything better on a construction site?"

He shrugged. "Maybe not. Those little fruit things were a nice touch. What do you call that?"

She rolled her eyes. "Garnish. Do you really care about that?"

"Not especially, but you seem to be fishing for compliments on your cooking."

"I was not fishing for compliments," she snapped. "Anybody can make sandwiches and slice up some fruit. I was trying to have a serious discussion about how you should be using me."

"Well, now that you mention it," he began, giving her a slow once-over, "a few ideas have crossed my mind on that score. But just so we don't get our wires crossed, what exactly are you offering, Miss Maggie?"

The fire in her eyes flared into a full-fledged inferno. "I'm offering to help you frame this house, you idiot, but you are sorely testing my patience."

Josh looked into all that heat in her eyes and absorbed the scathing note in her voice and concluded he might have made the tiniest miscalculation about Maggie. "You're serious? You actually want to get your hands dirty?"

"Yes, I'm serious."

"You've worked construction?"

"Not the way you mean," she admitted. "I've never built a house before, but I have renovated an entire building."

His gaze narrowed. "Meaning slapping a few coats of paint on the walls?"

She gave him a scathing look. "Meaning tearing out plaster and replacing it with drywall, reinstalling crown molding and matching up baseboards, installing track lighting, switching out electrical boxes and, yes, painting the whole damn thing when I was done."

He didn't even try to hide his skepticism. Maybe she'd supervised a professional crew but done the work herself? Not a chance. "Really?"

"Have you ever been in Images?"

Josh stared at her blankly.

"Of course not. It's an art and antiques gallery. What was I thinking?" she said sarcastically. "At any rate, it's mine. The building was a disaster when I bought it. I did all the renovations. Did a damn good job of them, too. Ask Cord, if you don't believe me."

He regarded her with disbelief. "You did the work yourself?"

"Yes."

"Why didn't you hire somebody?" Josh asked.

"Because that's what everybody expected me to do. I don't like doing what people expect. I never have. I wanted to prove I could build my business from the ground up, almost literally."

"How bad was this building?"

"Let's just say that a lot of people laughed themselves silly when I said I'd bought it. My father almost had a stroke when he saw it, and he's not prone to overreacting."

"How old was it?" he asked.

"It had been around since the mid-1800s. The outside was in good shape, but the inside had deteriorated."

A building that old would definitely have been a challenge, Josh thought. A lot of people would have leveled it and started over. He was impressed that Maggie hadn't done that. "Did you have Cord take a look at it?" Josh asked curiously.

"He was the first one I called before I signed the papers. He said the building had good bones."

Josh still wasn't entirely convinced that she hadn't exaggerated the transformation. "Mind if I come by to take a look?"

"Did you ask everyone else who volunteered to work on this house to prove their credentials?" she demanded.

Josh waved off the question. "It's not about that. I'm curious. I'd really like to see it. My expertise is in historic renovation, just like Cord. What can I say? I love old buildings." If he'd had to explain it, he'd have to say it had some deep-rooted connection to the lack of permanency in his own life, but he didn't know Maggie well enough to get into all that with her.

She studied him for a long time before nodding. "We can go by there now."

Josh glanced down at himself. "Like this? I'm a mess. So are you, if you don't mind me saying so."

"It's hot as blazes out here. Anyone who's been outside today is a mess. Besides, the gallery closes at six. We'll have the place to ourselves."

Once again, she'd caught him off guard. He'd figured her for a woman who'd want people to take off their dusty shoes on the front steps. Then, again, she could hardly ask such a thing of customers. Maybe running a retail business had forced her to lower her high standards.

"Then let's go have ourselves a tour," he suggested, eager to get a look at the place. "You tell me where and I'll meet you there."

Maggie gave him the address, which turned out to be not that far from his motel, though he suspected it was light-years away in terms of class.

"Does a half hour work for you or do you have things to finish up here?" she asked.

"A half-hour suits me fine if you're sure you don't mind me coming like this. Otherwise I can swing by my place and shower and be there in forty-five minutes."

She grinned at him. "As long as you don't sit on the antique furniture and keep your hands off the paintings, you'll be fine. And before you get all offended, I say the same thing to anyone who comes into the gallery. The ice-cream cones from the shop next door stay outside."

"I know how to mind my manners in a fancy place, Miss Maggie."

Maggie didn't look as if she believed him, but she merely nodded and headed for her car. Josh's gaze followed her as she settled behind the wheel of a snazzy little Saab convertible—which cost just about half of his annual salary. It suited her, though.

Maggie Forsythe might want him to believe she was as down-to-earth as anyone else, but he recognized privilege in every delectable, pampered inch of her. That meant they were about as suited as corn bread and champagne.

That didn't seem to stop him from wanting her, though. He wondered just how long it would be before he made the mother of all mistakes and did something about it.

Maggie liked showing off Images, but she hadn't been this jittery since the gallery's opening night, when the invitation-only crowd had dressed in black tie and included all her parents' high-society friends.

She'd driven crosstown as fast as she'd dared—she'd already received warnings from several easily charmed Charleston policemen. The extra speed had given her just enough time to wash her face, brush out her hair and add a touch of lipstick and gloss before she heard Josh coming in the front door.

He'd pulled on a navy blue T-shirt and tucked it into his jeans, but the additional clothing hadn't done a thing to take the edge off his sex appeal. Too bad. She'd been hoping her reaction, which had centered on his bare chest, would vanish once that chest was suitably attired.

She studied his face as he stood in the middle of the main room and surveyed it from top to bottom. She couldn't tell for sure if he was looking at the art and sculptures, the antiques or the renovations, but she was on edge as she tried to gauge his reaction to any of it. Why she wanted this man's approval was beyond her. She doubted he knew anything at all about art, possibly even less about antiques. He did, however, know renovations, so maybe that was why she was so edgy. Then again Cord had said she'd done an excellent job.

"Well?" she prodded when she couldn't stand it a moment longer.

"Do you have any *before* pictures?"

"A whole scrapbook full," she said, leading him over to the leather-bound volume she kept on a desk near the front door. Josh flipped the pages, glanced up several times as if to make comparisons, then slowly whistled.

"Is that approval?" she asked tentatively.

"Well, the place is definitely not what I expected," he said at last.

Maggie couldn't interpret the comment or his expression. "Meaning?"

"I'm not exactly an expert on galleries," he said, turning slowly to take in the rest of the room, "but the ones I've been in were a little cold, a little too, I don't know, impressed with themselves."

"Yes," Maggie said cautiously. That was exactly what she'd been trying to avoid.

"I feel at home here," Josh said. "I felt it the minute I came in the door. This place makes me want to buy something so my home will feel the same way. Those other places just make you want to possess something because someone else has judged it to be great art."

Maggie was so overwhelmed by his insight that she only barely resisted the urge to throw her arms around him. "That's exactly what I wanted people to feel when they walked in here," she said. Maybe she'd have to take back all the thickheaded, macho labels she'd been pinning on him.

He nodded distractedly and hunkered down on one knee beside the baseboards. "These are original?"

"Most of them. I had to replace some."

"Do you know which ones?"

She grinned. "Do you?"

"Looks like a perfect match to me," he admitted.

"Cord was able to find me some from the same time period at another site."

"Atlanta," Josh said at once, his expression oddly triumphant. "Damn, I knew this looked familiar. We had some old baseboards left over and they disappeared one day. No one would own up to taking them. I never thought to ask Cord."

Maggie winced. "Sorry. I hope you didn't need them."

"Cord wouldn't have taken them if we had, but it was a mystery that kept nagging at me." He stood up and met her gaze. "So, did you and Cord have a thing before he got together with Dinah? He said he's known you practically forever."

Maggie was thrown by the out-of-the-blue question. She debated how to answer it, then settled for the truth. "I was attracted to Cord for a while, but he never even gave me a second glance. Dinah's the only woman he ever had eyes for."

"You don't seem weighed down with regret," Josh noted.

"Not over Cord," she agreed.

He studied her intently. "Over someone else?"

Her pulse scrambled under that steady, speculative gaze. "Does it matter?"

"I'm not sure yet."

She liked his honesty. "Let me know when you decide."

"Until then, you don't want to share any deep dark secrets?"

Maggie chuckled. "There's nothing especially dark or secret about it. Half of Charleston knows the story of my pitiful love life."

"Then why keep it from me?"

"It would only bore you to tears, unless you decide you're fascinated by me." She recalled what Dinah had said to her about putting her flirting skills to better use. She tilted her head and looked deep into Josh's eyes. "Are you fascinated, Josh?"

To her chagrin, he laughed. "Miss Maggie, you could fascinate the pants off a saint, and I am only a humble, mortal man. I am most definitely intrigued."

She rested her hand lightly on his chest and kept her gaze locked with his. "In that case…"

A tiny little muscle in his jaw worked. "Yes?"

"Could I persuade you to let me help on the construction team next week? Don't you think I've proved myself?"

A startled grin spread across his face. "Sugar, just the thought of you with a hammer in your hands makes my heart palpitate."

She studied him warily. "Is that a yes or a no?"

"As much as I'm going to miss those little fruit garnishes, it's a yes. But I balk at letting you anywhere near a circular saw."

Maggie was about to tell him that she was quite an expert with a circular saw, but decided to leave that battle for another day. She might as well savor one victory at a time. She had a feeling they were all going to be hard won.

5

After she closed Images on Sunday afternoon, Maggie decided she had time to pay that impromptu visit to Ellie to try once again to persuade the talented young artist to schedule a showing at the gallery. Until now Ellie had been reluctant to do anything more than bring in an occasional painting. Maggie attributed her hesitance to insecurity. She was determined to put that to rest and build her employee's confidence once and for all.

She knew that Ellie lived in a loft apartment that had been created in an old warehouse along the waterfront. Since it wasn't that far from the shop and the humidity wasn't too oppressive, Maggie walked over, pausing along the way to chat with neighbors and customers who were taking advantage of the break in the weather to get some work done in their gardens.

It was nearly seven when she reached Ellie's, but there was plenty of summer daylight left.

As the creaky old elevator neared the top floor, Maggie could hear an unmistakably angry argument. It was loud enough and heated enough that she decided to go right back down and come another day when her visit wouldn't wind up embarrassing Ellie.

Before she could begin her descent, she heard a crash and the shattering of glass. That was enough to change her mind. Ellie's embarrassment was a small price to pay to be sure that the young woman was safe.

Locking the elevator so it would be available for a quick departure, Maggie stepped off, ran to Ellie's door and pounded on it. "Ellie, it's Maggie. Are you in there? Is everything okay?" When there was no reply, she pounded some more. "Ellie, open this door, dammit, or I'll call the police!"

The door swung open and a towering man stood there, his rugged face contorted with rage. "What the hell are you doing here?"

Though she was trembling inside, Maggie defiantly stood her ground and tried not to let him see even a flicker of emotion on her face. She took a slow survey of his features—the dark eyes, thick golden brown hair, thin slash of lips. She wanted to remember every detail in case she ever had to describe him to the police. He wore jeans and a grubby formfitting T-shirt.

"I stopped by to see Ellie," she said more calmly. "Is she home?"

"Now's not a good time," he said, and started to close the door.

Maggie stepped over the threshold before he could stop her. "I'm not leaving till I've spoken to her," she said, meeting the man's angry gaze with an unblinking stare, even though she felt sick.

He seemed thrown by her determination. "Look, lady, you can't just come barging into someone's home. It's called trespassing."

"You could always call the police," she suggested mildly. "In fact, I think that's a very good idea. Why don't we do that?" She extracted her cell phone from her purse and flipped it open.

For a minute she thought he might snatch the phone right out of her hand, but he didn't. Instead, he stormed past her and headed for the elevator.

Maggie waited until the elevator doors closed and it began its creaking descent before she breathed a sigh of relief. "Ellie?" she called softly. "It's okay. He's gone. Where are you?"

"Go away," Ellie pleaded from behind a closed door. "I know you were trying to help, but you've only made things worse."

Maggie's stomach churned at the quiet desperation she heard in her employee's voice. "Ellie, please, come out here. Let's talk about this. I want to help."

Slowly the door to what was apparently a bathroom opened.

Maggie wasn't sure what she expected, but it certainly wasn't Ellie looking shaken but otherwise unharmed.

"Are you okay?" she asked, surveying Ellie closely for signs of bruises.

"Brian would never hurt me," Ellie said. "Not physically, if that's what you're thinking."

"From the elevator it sounded like a pretty violent argument," Maggie said. "I was worried about you. I'm sorry if I embarrassed you by insisting on coming in."

Ellie sighed and sank down on a leather sofa. "It doesn't really matter. He'll calm down eventually. He always does."

"Then this has happened before?"

"A couple of times, but not like tonight. This was the worst he's ever been. I upset him when I told him you might do a showing of my art."

"I heard something break. Did he throw something at you?"

Ellie shook her head. "Not at me. At one of my paintings."

Maggie heard a defeated note in the girl's voice that spoke volumes. She finally understood that this was why Ellie was so reluctant to agree to a showing—she could never be certain if she would have anything to show. "He does that a lot, doesn't he? Destroys your work," she guessed.

Ellie nodded miserably. "He says I have no talent, that he doesn't want me to be humiliated."

Maggie felt her indignation rise, but she kept her voice under careful control. "Who is he? Your boyfriend?"

"He was," Ellie admitted, shamefaced. "He wasn't always like this. He's changed lately. I've been trying to break things off with him. I know Brian's no good for me, but he was my mentor, you see, so it's hard. There was a time when he encouraged me, when he taught me technique and composition, when he helped me settle on the right medium for my work."

"Then he's an artist, too? How did you meet?"

Ellie nodded. "He was my instructor. Everyone said Professor Brian Garrison was the most talented artist on staff. I was flattered when he took an interest in me."

"But eventually he realized that your talent was greater than his own," Maggie guessed.

Ellie seemed startled by her assessment. "I don't know. Maybe."

"Oh, Ellie, I'm so sorry," Maggie said, reaching for her hand. "Don't let Brian or anyone else ruin this gift of yours for you. Let's take a look at what you have here. You trust my judgment, don't you? You know I'd never lie to you about anything this important?"

"Of course I trust you, but I don't think I can look right now. You go ahead," Ellie said. "I don't know how much damage he did this time."

Maggie moved into the huge open space that comprised the studio portion of the apartment, then winced at the destruction. Brian had obviously been at it long before she arrived and heard that crash. What she'd heard had apparently been a jar of turpentine that had been thrown at a huge still life of sunflowers. The style was reminiscent of Van Gogh, but Ellie had a unique vision that brought a touch of lightness and whimsy to the work. Of course, now the paint ran in distorted streaks, so it was impossible to get the full effect.

Another canvas had been slashed, another splattered with paint. One had a giant X painted cross it in vivid red. Apparently he'd been indiscriminate in his rampage, choosing whichever works were most convenient, not those of any particular theme. Still lifes had been damaged, as well as street scenes.

Maggie's fury rose. Seeing such incredible paintings destroyed in a jealous rage made her almost physically ill. What a terrible waste!

"How bad is it?" Ellie called out in a voice that trembled.

"Half a dozen are destroyed," Maggie told her, struggling to keep the outrage out of her voice. "But there are quite a few he left untouched, more than enough for a show."

She went back to sit next to Ellie. "I think we need to get these paintings over to the gallery where they'll be safe," she told her. "And then you need to get your locks changed here. I'd do it myself, but I don't want to leave you alone while I pick up my tools and try to find a lock at this hour. Besides which, we need someone with a truck to take the paintings. I'll call some friends. We can take care of both of those things tonight. In the morning, if you'd like, we can go to the police and get a restraining order against him."

Ellie shook her head. "That will only infuriate him more. Besides, I told you he'd never hurt me."

Maggie squeezed her hand. "But he *has* hurt you," Maggie said gently. "This is meant to hurt your soul, Ellie. It's meant to destroy your self-confidence and rob you of something that's very important to you."

Ellie shook her head stubbornly. "I can't ask for a restraining order. Changing the locks will be enough. He'll get the message."

Maggie had seen the rage in the man's eyes. She doubted his mood would mellow significantly anytime soon. Nor did she think Ellie should ever risk trusting him not to explode when she least expected it, but she bit her tongue for now. She didn't want to add to Ellie's distress. "If you change your mind, I'll go with you, okay?"

"Thank you."

"Now, let me make that call and we'll secure your apartment and move the paintings."

She pulled her cell phone from her bag and punched in Dinah and Cord's number. Unfortunately no one answered. She debated the wisdom of calling Warren, who might also be able to counsel Ellie on dealing with Brian, but she doubted he had the tools to deal with changing a lock, and that was a top priority. Nor did he have a truck to help with moving the paintings.

But Josh could help on both fronts, she realized. And if he'd been convinced to assist with the building of Amanda's house, then he must have something of a knight-in-shining-armor complex. Fortunately he'd given all the volunteers a card with contact information on it, including his cell-phone number. Maggie found the card in her purse and dialed his number.

"Yes," he answered so irritably that Maggie almost hung up.

"Josh, it's Maggie."

"Well now, this *is* a surprise," he said, his tone immediately changing. There was a sexy vibe that hadn't been there ten seconds ago.

"I need some help," she said. "Are you busy?"

"Maybe you ought to tell me what sort of help you need before I say just how busy I am," he said, a sudden note of caution in his tone.

Walking away from Ellie, Maggie spoke in a low voice and gave him a condensed version of what she'd walked in on a half hour earlier.

"I'll pick up a new dead bolt and be there in twenty minutes," he said without hesitation. "You two going to be okay until then?"

"We'll be fine. Brain's gone. He took off when he realized I wasn't budging."

"If he turns up, though, call nine-one-one and then scream your head off till all the neighbors come running," Josh said. "Don't hesitate, okay?"

The genuine concern in his voice was comforting. It confirmed her gut instinct that he was the right man to call.

"You want me to stay on the line till I get there?" Josh added.

"I'd rather you concentrate on getting that lock and driving over here like a bat out of hell," she said honestly.

"I'm on my way," he said.

"Thanks."

She turned to smile at Ellie. "Help is on the way. Why don't I make us some coffee."

Ellie grinned. "I thought all Southerners lived on sweet tea this time of year. Lord knows, we did at my house. What is it with you and coffee?"

"A minor part of my rebellion," Maggie told her. "I've always hated going with the crowd on anything. That doesn't mean that drinking sweet tea isn't one of my guilty little secrets. I'll go pour us a couple of glasses, okay?"

"Sure."

En route to the kitchen, Maggie paused to give Ellie's shoulder a pat. "It's going to be okay, you know."

"I hope so."

"Come on. You know so. I keep telling you how talented you are. I'm an expert, remember? You need to start listening to me, rather than a man who's pea green with envy."

"It's not that," Ellie said. "I'm just worried if you store those paintings at the gallery, it'll make you a target. What if Brian comes after them there? I don't want to be responsible for him ruining your wonderful gallery."

"He won't," Maggie replied with a confidence she wasn't entirely sure was justified. "He knows he can intimidate you, but he won't try it with me. He's already seen that I don't back down. He knows I won't hesitate to put his sorry butt in jail."

But despite the forceful words, Maggie resolved to have the security system at the gallery checked and the locks there beefed up, as well.

It took Josh longer than he'd anticipated to find a halfway decent lock and then locate the warehouse. Every second of the delay was torture. Despite her brave front, he'd heard something in Maggie's voice he'd never expected to hear—fear. Despite her declaration that she and this other woman were fine, he'd been tempted to send the cops over there to keep an eye on things. Only her promise to call the police herself if this nutcase showed up again kept him from doing so.

When he finally found the darkened warehouse, he was appalled that anyone was living in such an area, especially a woman alone. It was clearly a place that someone had hoped to turn into a trendy section of funky studios and shops, but the transformation was far from complete. It was mostly dingy and run-down, with way too few streetlights for his comfort.

By the time he finally got to the right address and rode the groaning elevator to the top floor, he was cursing a blue streak. Not that anyone could have heard him over the music blaring from the apartment beneath. It sounded as if a garage band on speed was rehearsing inside. No one would ever hear screams over that racket.

He pounded on the apartment door for what seemed like an eternity before Maggie finally opened it.

"Why didn't you ask who it was?" he demanded.

"I did. Apparently you didn't hear me," she said, even now shouting to be heard over the din.

"How the hell does your friend stand that?"

"It just started," she told him. "Ellie says they only rehearse on Sunday nights."

"Lucky for her or she'd be deaf by now." He knelt down and studied the door and the current lock. The door was solid enough. In fact, it felt like steel. Nobody would get through that, he concluded. Add the new lock, and she should be safe.

"Do you want anything to drink?" Maggie asked.

Josh finally met her gaze, which he'd been avoiding up till now. Hearing her voice earlier had cut into one very hot fantasy he'd been having about her. He'd been afraid seeing her in person would kick those hormones right back into gear. It did.

"Nothing," he said gruffly. "Let me get to this."

"Sure. I can't tell you how much I appreciate you coming over here like this."

"Not a problem. I wasn't doing anything." Except thinking about her sexy body, but that definitely didn't bear mentioning.

She gave him an odd look, as if she was trying to figure out what to make of his suddenly irritable mood, then went back into the apartment, leaving a trail of some seductive perfume to torment him.

Installing the lock took less time than he'd hoped. He could have used an hour or two to get his equilibrium back. Instead, he was forced to go into the apartment.

"Okay, ladies, you're all set. The lock's in, and combined with that door, you should be safe enough," he said to the woman seated beside Maggie.

"Thank you," she replied softly. "It was really nice of you to come over and do that for me."

"Ellie, this is Josh Parker. He's in charge of building that house I told you about."

"Of course," Ellie said. "What a sweet thing to do!"

Josh shrugged. "I don't know about sweet. It's a job."

Maggie grinned at him. "Don't be modest. You know you did it to rack up points."

"Really? And just who do you think I was angling to rack up points with?"

"Cord," she suggested. "Maybe Amanda."

Josh laughed. "Miss Maggie, you have me all wrong. I don't need points with Cord and I'm not interested in Amanda."

She studied him curiously. "Then why did you agree to do it?"

"Just in case I'm a little short on recommendations when I arrive at the pearly gates," he claimed. He wondered if she'd buy that his admission wasn't all that far from the truth.

"I suppose your fate there all depends on who's checking in the newcomers," she retorted. "If it's a female, you won't have any problem at all sweet-talking your way inside."

"Well, just in case, I'm trying to accumulate a few good deeds. Speaking of which, where are these paintings you want me to move?"

"I'll show you," Ellie offered.

Maggie gave her a concerned look that Josh couldn't quite interpret.

"Are you sure?" she asked Ellie worriedly. "Want me to move the others out of the way first?"

"Which others?" Josh asked.

"The ones Brian destroyed," Maggie explained.

Josh got the message. What Ellie was facing was that first gut-wrenching sight of the destruction of something that was important to her. He'd known that feeling once when vandals had gotten into a historic house he was renovating and had themselves a field day with paint. The devastation had clawed at his gut for days.

"How about you just point me in the right direction and I'll take care of it?" he suggested.

Ellie shook her head. "I'll have to see them sooner or later. I'm ready now."

As soon as he followed her into the studio area and she switched on the bright overhead lights, Josh saw why Maggie had been so concerned. Ellie took a look around and swayed. He caught her and led her to a stool in front of an empty easel. He gently turned it away from the worst of the destruction.

"Why don't I bring over the rest of the paintings and you tell me which ones go and which ones stay?" he suggested.

She nodded, color finally coming back to her face. "Thanks."

Maggie came over and stood beside her, a hand resting on her shoulder.

Josh didn't know enough about art to make an educated judgment, nor did he want to waste much time examining each of the works, but something in his gut told him to treat the paintings with extra care. He supposed people tossed around the word *genius* a little too casually, but he had a hunch he'd just stumbled onto one.

In the end, there were a dozen paintings Maggie wanted to take to the gallery. She and Ellie stood guard at the truck, while he brought them downstairs one by one and loaded them carefully into the back of his pickup.

Then all three of them rode to the gallery, where Maggie supervised their storage in a secured vault in the back. Josh checked all the locks and nodded with approval.

"They'll be safe enough here. How's your security system?" he asked.

"Top-of-the-line," Maggie assured him. "But I'm going to have the security guys go over it just the same."

"Then let's lock this place up and I'll take you two out for something to eat. I'll bet neither one of you has had dinner."

Maggie regarded him with surprise. "To be honest, I'd forgotten all about food, and you're right. I'm starved. Ellie, what about you?"

"I think I'd rather go back home," she said. "I can walk."

"Not a chance," Josh said. "If you insist on going home, we'll take you. I want another look around before I leave you there alone."

"You don't need to do that," Ellie protested.

"Yes, I do," he said flatly.

"Let the man get his full quota of brownie points for this," Maggie advised. "He probably has to overcome a lot if he wants to get into heaven someday."

He winked at her. "You have no idea."

"Oh, I think I do," Maggie retorted.

But Josh thought he detected a glint in her eyes that suggested she found this reply intriguing. It seemed Miss Maggie might just have a thing for dangerous men.

Only after she and Josh were seated at an all-night diner in a part of town she rarely visited, did Maggie start to tremble. It could have been hunger, but she had a hunch it was a delayed reaction to her encounter with the out-of-control Brian Garrison.

Josh's hand immediately covered hers. "You okay? The worst is over. Don't fall apart now."

"It's probably low blood sugar. I'll be fine as soon as I've eaten something."

Magically, a waitress appeared at that instant, her artificially red hair sprayed into a dated beehive style and adorned with a frilly white cap held in place with bobby pins. A pin on her pocket said her name was Linda Sue.

"Hey, sugar, you're out late," she said to Josh. "You want your usual?"

Maggie regarded Josh curiously. "Come here often?"

"Most nights like clockwork, right at seven. I could set the clock by him," Linda Sue claimed. "Hasn't changed his order once in all these weeks, either."

Josh looked vaguely unsettled by the revelation. "Maybe I'll do something totally unpredictable tonight."

"Such as?" the woman asked skeptically.

"Yes, Josh," Maggie encouraged, eager to see what he would consider a daring break with tradition. "Do something wild."

"Okay, you two," he chided. "Stop trying to turn this into some sort of dare. I happen to like burgers and fries."

"But not tonight?" Linda Sue asked. "Is there something different about tonight, besides the fact that you finally have a good-looking woman with you?"

Maggie watched as Josh struggled to find a suitable comeback for the question. She grinned at his obvious dismay, then decided to give him a break.

"Well, while you're making this life-altering decision, Josh, I'm ordering the burger and fries. If you have it every night, it must be good."

"Best in town," the waitress assured her. She turned to Josh. "Made up your mind?"

He shrugged finally. "What can I say? I like the burger. But I will be daring. I'll have onion rings tonight."

Maggie chuckled. "That *is* daring. I'm impressed. And just so you know, if you try to sneak even one of my fries, I will hurt you."

Josh sighed dramatically. "Then you'd better bring me a side order of fries, too."

"Coming right up," Linda Sue promised.

The whole exchange had succeeded in calming Maggie's nerves, but as she met Josh's gaze, her pulse set off at a gallop all over again. However, he was the first to blink and look away.

"Why don't you tell me more about what happened earlier tonight?" he suggested. "What set the guy off?"

Maggie finally blinked and looked away. "I gather Brian was Ellie's mentor. When he heard I'd offered her a showing at the gallery, he freaked."

Josh frowned. "You think she'll stay the hell away from him after this?"

"She says she will. Problem is, he doesn't seem to want to stay away from *her*."

"Do you think he's dangerous? Does she need protection?"

"I wanted her to get a restraining order, but she refused. She says he would never hurt her." A look flashed across Josh's face that startled Maggie. "You think she's wrong, don't you?"

"Women make that sort of mistake a lot," he said tightly.

"And you know this because…?"

He shook his head. "It's not important."

"I think it is," Maggie contradicted, seeing the evidence in his stormy gaze.

But before she could press the point, Linda Sue came back with their food. The heavenly aroma and the gnawing sensation in her stomach forced her to push her questions aside for the moment. When she picked up her burger instead of prying into his life any further, there was no mistaking his relief.

Maggie met his gaze. "I won't forget what we were talking about," she told him, determined to put him on notice.

"Have a French fry, sugar. They're just about good enough to make you forget everything."

"Nothing's that good," Maggie countered, but she popped one into her mouth. It was excellent. Crisp on the outside, tender inside and sprinkled with just the right amount of salt.

"Well?"

"Not bad," she said, deliberately playing down the tastiness.

His eyes locked with hers. "Oh, really? That's the best you can come up with?" He picked up another fry, dipped it in ketchup and held it to her lips.

Maggie swallowed hard, then accepted the unspoken dare. She licked the ketchup off the fry, then slowly took it into her mouth. When she did, Josh's fingers brushed her lips.

And *that* had the effect he'd desired. She promptly forgot everything except the sensation of his work-roughened finger skimming across her lower lip. The jolt shot right through her. Something told her she'd be remembering that long after she was home—alone—in bed.

6

Maggie hated nothing more than having her curiosity aroused and then not satisfied. Once the impact of Josh's touch finally wore off sometime in the middle of the night, she recalled why he'd deliberately set out to distract her. He'd wanted her to forget all about his inadvertent mention of his past.

Unfortunately, there was nothing she could do this morning to track down any answers. She was scheduled to open the gallery at ten and was hoping to hear from Ellie that everything was quiet at her studio. With any luck at all, Brian had gotten the message that he wasn't to return.

When she arrived at the gallery, she found Dinah already waiting on the doorstep. Maggie regarded her suspiciously.

"What brings you by this early?" she inquired as she unlocked the door and turned off the security system.

"You called last night. I just came by to see what you'd wanted."

"How did you know I called? I didn't leave a message," Maggie said.

"That's the wonder of modern technology. Answering machines reveal all sorts of things. Cord insisted we have a top-of-the-line machine so we could screen calls."

"Were you home when I called?" Maggie demanded, suddenly irritated. What good were best friends if they didn't pick up the phone when you needed them most?

Dinah blushed. "We were, but we were otherwise engaged."

Maggie knew she should have seen that one coming. "Is this honeymoon of yours ever going to end?"

"Goodness, I surely do hope not," Dinah replied, a grin spreading across her face. "So, what did you want? I figured it couldn't be that important since you didn't leave a message."

"It was an emergency, as a matter of fact," Maggie retorted. "So I had to call someone who actually answers the phone when it rings."

"Warren?"

"No." Maggie hesitated, then reminded herself that she was dealing with Dinah, the intrepid reporter who'd made world leaders squirm. There would be no peace until Maggie revealed who she'd turned to. "Josh."

Dinah's eyes widened. "Really? How absolutely fascinating!"

"Is that all you can say?" Maggie asked in disgust. "Aren't you the least bit curious about the emergency?"

"Did Josh handle it?"

"Yes."

"Then that's all that matters. I'm more interested in why you chose him."

"He had technical expertise I required, along with a truck."

Suddenly Dinah looked worried. "You weren't disposing of a body, were you?"

"Good Lord, no. You really do need to rein in that imagination of yours." She frowned at Dinah. "And what on earth makes you think Josh would have the technical expertise needed for that? What kind of background does he have, anyway?"

Dinah shrugged. "He's an edgy kind of man. Something tells me he has all sorts of dark secrets."

"And yet you're encouraging Amanda O'Leary to get all cozy with him," Maggie said wryly.

"I am not encouraging anything between him and Amanda," Dinah said impatiently. "That's *your* imagination working overtime. The woman made an offhand comment about how hot Josh is, and you've pictured some sort of relationship blossoming ever since. Since you claim you're not interested, I have to wonder why it even matters to you."

"It doesn't matter," Maggie insisted irritably. "At least, not the way you mean."

"Is there some other way it could matter?" Dinah asked, amusement dancing in her eyes.

"Would you just drop it?"

Dinah chuckled. "Happy to, now that I've got the answer I was looking for."

"You don't know squat."

"That's what you think," Dinah replied mildly. "So what happened that had you calling for reinforcements?" she asked, pushing to get the topic back on her track.

Maggie described the scene she'd come upon when she'd gone to visit Ellie. "I wanted to get a new lock installed and those paintings of hers away from there before that Neanderthal came back and tried to destroy any more of them."

"They're here now?"

Maggie nodded. "Secured in the vault in back. I'm not taking any chances that he'll figure out they're here and decide to come by to ruin a few more." She shuddered at the memory of the fury in his eyes just before he'd stormed out of Ellie's studio. "The man's scary."

Dinah studied her with increased concern. "For you to say that, Maggie, he had to have been awful. Notify the police."

"I can't. I promised Ellie I wouldn't do that, at least for now."

"I think you're being foolish. At least tell them to keep a closer watch on the gallery," Dinah pleaded.

"The vault's secure enough," Maggie insisted.

"And the rest of this place? If he can't get to Ellie's work, he might take it out on the gallery."

"I don't think he's that stupid or that crazy," Maggie said, though her certainty was shaken by Dinah's concern. "This is personal between him and Ellie. He's jealous of her talent."

"Really? Her paintings are that good?"

Maggie's enthusiasm for the paintings overcame the last of her irritation at Dinah for shutting her out the night before. "They're fabulous," she confirmed.

Dinah's eyes gleamed the way they did when she was on the scent of a great story. "May I peek?"

Maggie grinned. "Are you asking as a reporter or as a friend who's capable of keeping a secret?"

"As long as you promise me an exclusive when the time comes, I'll keep your secret," Dinah bargained.

"Okay, then," Maggie said, knowing that she could

trust Dinah's promises. They'd both kept silent about an awful lot of youthful misadventures. "Come with me."

She opened the vault and switched on the overhead light, then gestured at the individual storage bins. "The paintings are in those." Then she waited, holding her breath for Dinah's reaction.

The hundred-watt bulb in the humidity-controlled vault was nothing compared to what the gallery lighting would be when it came time for the show, but Dinah gasped at the first painting she pulled out to view.

"Oh my, she really is talented, isn't she?" Dinah said in a hushed voice, stepping closer to the still life. "Not that I'm half the expert you are, but this is amazing."

Maggie beamed as relief flooded through her. "Don't sell yourself short, Dinah. The art collection your folks have is nothing to sneer at. You grew up being able to tell a masterpiece from junk the same way I did."

Dinah gently retrieved each painting from its protective bin. At last she turned back to Maggie. "When's the show?"

"I want to take my time planning it, so I'm thinking September at the earliest, maybe October," Maggie replied. "That will give me time to create a certain amount of buzz and maybe lure a few art critics down here from New York."

Dinah regarded Maggie with evident curiosity. "What did Josh think? I assume you paid close attention to his reaction."

"He seemed impressed," Maggie said carefully. "But he was more interested in getting these things out of Ellie's place and tucked away here than he was in examining them."

"So he's not an art lover." Dinah studied her. "Is that a problem?"

"I needed his muscle last night," Maggie said defensively. "I wasn't interested in his opinion of Ellie's work."

Dinah looked doubtful. "But you're attracted to him. Don't even try to deny it. Could you start seeing someone who doesn't have something this important in common with you?"

"I'm not seeing Josh or considering seeing Josh. He came to the rescue last night. Period," Maggie said flatly. "Don't try to make this into something it isn't."

"Maybe you're the one who should heed that advice," Dinah warned. "I know you, sweetie. You listen to your hormones before you pay the slightest bit of attention to your head. Your head's saying all the right things, but I'm willing to bet that your hormones are doing a fancy tango right about now."

"Oh, for pity's sake, you're making way too much out of this," Maggie repeated.

But even as she spoke, she wondered if Dinah wasn't right. Her reaction to Josh's touch the night before was enough to set off alarms all over Charleston. She couldn't deny it.

For once in her life, maybe she ought to do the smart thing and steer clear of a man so obviously unsuited for her. There were things in life she valued, and art was definitely one of them. If Josh didn't value it, how could there possibly be anything meaningful between them? Then again, her parents' world was filled with couples who went their separate ways when it came to cultural events.

She might have heeded Dinah's advice for once and

steered clear of Josh—if she hadn't recalled his reaction to the gallery. He'd said exactly the right things about the atmosphere she'd achieved. Maybe he didn't know a Monet from a Picasso, but he had good instincts. He might not have gushed over Ellie's paintings, but she'd seen the care he demonstrated when handling them. He'd known instinctively that they had worth. And he was a fine craftsman, which was a brand of art in itself.

"Don't you worry about me and Josh," she told Dinah staunchly. "We're not even friends, much less lovers. I'm not convinced yet that he doesn't have a thing for the lovely Amanda, so why would I risk anything under those circumstances?"

Dinah smiled. "Because there's nothing you like more than a risky challenge, Maggie, especially if you know it will set your mother's teeth on edge. I recognize all the signs. Josh Parker is a little rough around the edges and he has danger written all over him, therefore you're going to fall for him. Hard, more than likely."

"You don't know everything," Maggie said, scowling.

"When it comes to the way your heart works, I do," Dinah contradicted. "Just be careful, okay? Take your time for once. Get to know the man before you fall into bed with him."

Maggie studied her friend with a narrowed gaze. "I thought you liked Josh. What's with all the warnings?"

"He seems like a good guy, but like I said before, he's edgy. He doesn't say much. I doubt even Cord knows him really well, and they've worked together for a couple of years now." Her expression turned thoughtful. "Of course, I could dig around a little, see what I can find out."

"Don't you dare," Maggie said.

"Lots of women these days, especially wealthy ones, hire private investigators to be sure they're not dealing with some sort of scoundrel. You don't need to go that far," Dinah advised cheerfully. "You have me."

"Stay out of it," Maggie said again. "If I decide there are things I need to know about Josh, I'm perfectly capable of finding them out for myself."

"It could be too late. Let me at least do some sort of basic background check."

"Don't you think Cord probably did that before he put him in charge in Atlanta?"

"I doubt it," Dinah said. "Cord goes on gut instinct."

"Has it failed him yet?"

"I suppose not," Dinah conceded reluctantly.

"And Josh did excellent work for him in Atlanta, right? That *is* what you told me?"

"Yes. But trusting a man to renovate a building is hardly the same as trusting him with your best friend's heart."

"I'm not worried, so leave it be, Dinah. I'll be spending a few hours with the man on Saturdays, surrounded by lots of people. How much trouble can I possibly get into?"

"It's not Saturdays I'm worried about," Dinah argued. "You've already come up with one excuse to see him away from that project. I suspect that's just the beginning. You can be pretty creative when you want to spend more time with a man."

"I didn't manufacture an excuse to see Josh. This was an emergency," Maggie stressed. "Besides, I called you and Cord first." Tired of the whole debate, she gave Dinah a pointed look. "Don't you need to go to work or drive your husband crazy or something?"

Dinah sighed. "Okay, I'll go. But I'm keeping my eye on the two of you. If I don't like what I'm seeing, I won't keep my mouth shut."

Maggie laughed. "No surprise there."

Dinah grinned. "Yeah, I suppose not. Love you."

"You, too."

Maggie's smile faded as Dinah left the gallery. She was not going to fall for Josh in the same headlong, impulsive way that always got her into trouble. She wasn't.

She sighed when she recalled her response to his touch. Famous last words.

Josh was shaken by what he'd come close to revealing to Maggie the night before. He never talked about his mother and the steady parade of men through their lives. He'd only told Cord that he was from a single-parent home and they'd moved around a lot. He'd never explained why, never said that Nadine had a tendency to fall for the losers of the universe.

She'd always done it with such incredible optimism, too. Each man had been the love of her life, the one who was going to turn their lives into a bed of roses. When she discovered those roses were riddled with thorns, she'd packed Josh up and moved on, defeated for a time, but always bouncing back as soon as the next handsome scoundrel gave her a second glance.

At first Josh had hated her for getting sucked in again and again, but now that he was older he'd almost come to admire her determined ability to ignore history. He'd stuffed down his own considerable emotional baggage from losing a prospective dad again and again.

He'd come away from all those years of observing his mother's emotional ups and downs with a grim determination of his own to play fair with the women he met. He never made promises he had no intention of keeping. Hell, most of the time he never made promises at all. And he never, ever dated women with kids who could be hurt when he took off, as he inevitably would.

In recent months he'd pretty much lost touch with Nadine. She had his cell-phone number and over the years she'd checked in from time to time, usually when she needed money. But when things were going good for her—in other words when there was a new man in her life—he heard nothing. Last he'd heard a few months back, she was getting married in Vegas.

He wished her well. Maybe she'd finally get what she wanted. Maybe this one would last. He wasn't holding his breath, however. History told him that sooner or later she'd be on the phone, in tears, begging him for cash for a new start in some other city.

And he would send it to her. Anything to keep her out of his life, while keeping his conscience clear.

In the meantime, though, it was not a story he intended to share with anyone, especially Maggie. She was the kind, he was certain, who'd get all misty-eyed and sympathetic and the next thing he knew, she'd be bugging him to send Nadine a plane ticket to come for a visit.

Nope, better to let everyone believe he had no family. They might pity him, but they sure as hell couldn't start meddling and trying to bring about some cozy mother-son reconciliation. He supposed he loved Nadine, screwy as she was, but that didn't mean he wanted to be around for any more of those wild roller-coaster rides her life invariably became. Besides, he doubted she harbored any deep maternal feelings for him. When he was a kid, she'd pretty much viewed him as necessary baggage. Now he was fine for the occasional meal ticket.

Nope, the whole distance thing worked for them just fine. There was no way in hell he'd let some sentimental female get a notion to change that.

Nadine Parker Rollins Jensen had had another run of bad luck. It turned out that Nathaniel Jensen, husband number three, had just the teensiest little problem with the law. The cops had hauled him out of their Vegas hotel room on their wedding night, which even by her standards had seriously shortened the marriage.

It had taken a few weeks to use up their remaining cash, but now she was dead broke again. She'd spent a day or two wondering what to do next. She could have gone back to work as a waitress in Vegas, but she was afraid the cops would eventually start looking her way to see if she was involved in Nate's scheme.

Rather than take that risk, she decided to hop a bus and head for Charleston, where Josh was working some cushy job. Surely he'd have room in his life for his mama, or at least enough cash to stake her till she could get on her feet again.

It wasn't the first time she'd turned to her son. Josh had bailed her out of trouble more times than any kid should have to. She was embarrassed about that, but every single time she managed to pick herself up, dust herself off and get going again, something went wrong.

Like Nate. Who would have thought the man didn't have sense enough not to try to cheat a casino out of the take at the roulette wheel? Even she knew there were cameras watching.

When she got off the bus in Charleston, she looked at the address she'd scribbled on a piece of paper, asked directions, then walked the few blocks to a run-down motel that looked no better than the places she'd spent most of her life in. That was a disappointment, but she knocked on Josh's door, then plastered a big smile on her face.

When the door swung open, she brushed right past her incredulous, openmouthed son before he could block the way. "Hi, sweetie. Mama's come to visit."

The string of curses that crossed Josh's lips would have gotten his mouth washed out with soap twenty years ago, but he figured after all the stunts his mother had pulled, he'd earned the right to say what he damn well pleased.

Hurt welled up in her big brown eyes at the tirade, but he steeled himself against it. Hadn't he warned himself about a scene just like this barely a few hours ago? God must have been laughing his head off, knowing Nadine was already en route to Charleston.

"I thought you just got married," he said tightly.

"It didn't work out," she said cheerfully, plunking her suitcase on the bed, then sitting beside it.

The action hiked up a skirt that would have been too short for a twenty-year-old. On his mother, the look was ridiculous. Not that Nadine didn't have great legs for a woman who'd just turned fifty, but did she have to bare them for all the world to see?

Josh's bad mood intensified. "So you thought you'd drop by and make my life hell?"

"It's been ages since we spent any time together," she reminded him, unfazed by his lack of welcome. "I thought we could catch up."

"How much do you need, Mother?" Josh asked, cutting to the chase.

She looked as if she might deny that she'd come for money, but then she sighed. "A couple thousand? That ought to get me set up someplace new and hold me till I can get back on my feet."

Josh told himself to write the check and send her on her way, but something in her eyes this time got to him. She looked genuinely, deep-down defeated. Nadine never looked defeated for more than a minute, no matter how bad things got. For the first time ever, she looked as if she might not have the will to bounce back. Even her blond, highlighted hair looked a little limp, as if it had given up just as she had.

"I'll tell you what," he said, knowing he was going to regret this till his dying breath. "I'll get you a room here and put you to work on this job I'm doing right now. When it's finished, I'll give you some cash so you can move on."

"You want me to work construction?" she asked incredulously, looking pointedly at her bright red acrylic nails. "I don't think so."

"Sorry. That's the deal," Josh said, his manner unyielding.

"What does this job pay?" she asked suspiciously.

He grinned at her. "Nothing. That's the beauty of it,

Mother. You're going to be doing something nice for someone who deserves it. That ought to be a pleasant change for you."

"I've never built anything in my life," she argued. "Why not let me stick around for a week, then I'll move on. I was thinking I'd take a look around Savannah. I used to love it there."

"Until we left the motel in the middle of the night owing a month's back rent," Josh said wryly. "I don't think you ought to rush back to Savannah anytime soon."

"Atlanta, then. Atlanta was nice. Maybe that restaurant's still there. I always made great tips. The truckers loved me."

"The truckers loved you everywhere we went," Josh said, "and never brought you anything but heartache. Why not set your sights a little higher this time?"

She frowned at him. "When did you turn into such a snob, Joshua?"

He frowned at the accusation. "I don't have a thing in the world against truckers, just against the ones you chose. I've never in my life seen anybody who could zero in on the losers in the bunch like some sort of heat-seeking missile. It was the one thing you always had a real knack for."

Looking hurt, she rose to her feet and reached for her suitcase, then staggered just a little. Josh grabbed her and held on, barely containing another curse.

"When was the last time you had a decent meal?" he asked.

"Yesterday, I guess. I had a couple of doughnuts this morning, though. That should hold me for a few more hours."

"Yeah, I can see how steady you are on your feet," he said wryly. "Put the damn suitcase down and let's go have dinner. I'll get you a room when we come back. It's not as if this dump will fill up while we're gone."

She tilted her chin stubbornly. "I won't stay where I'm not wanted."

"Do you have someplace better to be?" Josh asked, then waved off his own question. "Doesn't matter. You're staying right here."

Her frown finally faded. "I won't get in your way, Josh. I promise. Your mama would never try to cramp your style."

He laughed at that. "It's not as if I have some hot-and-heavy romance going on."

"Why on earth not?" she asked indignantly. "What's wrong with the women in this town?"

Josh immediately thought of Maggie. "Not a thing. I just learned a long time ago to steer clear of trouble."

Worry, something he'd rarely seen on Nadine's face, puckered her brow.

"Did I make you that way?" she asked with a rare burst of insight. "Well, never mind. I'll have plenty of time to fix it while I'm here. We'll find you the perfect woman."

Josh shuddered at the thought of what Nadine would consider to be the perfect woman. "No meddling, Mother, or I promise you I will find the filthiest, most disgusting job on the construction site and assign you to it."

She regarded him with skepticism, but something in his eyes must have warned her that he meant every word, because she nodded. "No meddling. Got it. But if there are any more rules, sugar, you'd better write 'em down. Mama's memory isn't what it used to be."

Josh sighed and tucked her arm through his as they headed down the street toward his favorite diner. "Mother, your memory never was worth a damn. Have you forgotten the time you left me in the bus station?"

"You know perfectly well I thought you were already on the bus," she retorted at once, rising to the familiar bait. "You were when I went to the little girls' room. And I made that old bus driver turn right around and come back for you, didn't I?"

Josh could laugh about it now, but it had been the most terrifying thirty minutes of his life when he'd realized the bus and his mother had left without him. He'd been six. In that instant, he'd learned not to count on Nadine to remember anything.

Which meant, he concluded now, that he'd probably have to remind her a thousand times a day not to meddle in his life. He mentally counted the weeks till Thanksgiving, the date he'd promised to have Amanda's house finished. It hadn't seemed that far away just this morning, but with Nadine around and his impulsive, misguided insistence that she help, it was going to feel like an eternity.

7

Between her overreaction to Josh's simple touch and the warnings from Dinah, Maggie was not especially looking forward to working on the construction site on Saturday morning. But because she always faced her fears head-on, she was determined to be the first one there. If she was there even before Josh, so much the better. It would give her some sort of psychological edge.

Unfortunately, when she arrived just after dawn, dressed in work boots and the oldest, least attractive jeans and shirt she could find in her closet, Josh was already giving less-than-patient instructions to a woman who looked as if she wasn't one bit happy about being up at this ungodly hour. Dressed in brightly flowered capri pants and a masculine shirt big enough to belong to Josh, she was clinging to a giant-size cup of coffee like a lifeline. Maggie might have been able to relate to that if she hadn't been stunned by the streak of jealousy that slashed through her.

Reminding herself that she ought to be grateful for the presence of anyone who could serve as a buffer, Maggie crossed to them, snapped a jaunty salute and announced, "Reporting for duty, boss."

Josh barely spared her a glance. Keeping his gaze on the other woman's belligerent expression, he said, "It's not that complicated, Nadine. You take the lumber from that pile over there and stack it up over here next to the saw. Then I'll show you how to use the saw."

"You've got to be kidding," the woman said. "Josh, honey, how many times do I have to tell you that this isn't a good idea. I'm not cut out for manual labor."

Maggie bit back a grin. She had a hunch that was a massive understatement if the woman's perfect manicure and soft, pale skin were anything to judge by. Now that she was closer and could see the obvious age difference between the two her jealousy vanished. There might be some relationship between Josh and this woman, given the apparent tension, but it wasn't a romantic one.

"Maybe I could help her," Maggie volunteered, curiosity kicking in. She wanted to know just how Josh had persuaded a woman who obviously didn't want to be here to show up to work.

"That's okay," Josh said, still without looking at her. "She can do it."

"But if she's never done it before," Maggie began, only to have him skewer her with a look that told her to shut up and leave this battle to him.

"Okay, okay. I suppose I can give it a try," the woman said grudgingly.

Ignoring Josh's sour expression, Maggie gave her an encouraging smile. "You can do it. It really isn't that difficult. I'm Maggie, by the way."

"Nadine," the woman said, giving her a nervous smile. "I just got into town a few days ago from Las Vegas. Josh insisted on putting me right to work."

"Really? Well, it's very nice of you to pitch in around

here," Maggie said. "We can use all the help we can get."

"That remains to be seen," Josh muttered. "Maggie, you come with me."

He latched on to her hand and half dragged her along behind him.

"Well, that was rude," she said. "What is your problem?"

"The little unexpected twists and turns of life," he retorted.

She stared at him. "Am I supposed to understand what that means?"

"Not really."

"Who was that woman, and why does she seem to irritate you so much?"

"Because that's what she does. It's her God-given talent."

Maggie stopped in her tracks. "You know her, don't you? I mean, really know her. Who is she, Josh?"

His expression remained guarded. "She told you her name's Nadine."

"Nadine what?"

"Jensen, I believe, though I think that one's on its way out. She'll probably get rid of it when the divorce comes through."

Maggie's intuition kicked in. "Oh, my God, she's your mother," she said, "isn't she?"

Josh sighed, but didn't try to deny it. "She is."

Maggie was speechless as she tried to understand all the ramifications of Nadine's sudden and apparently unexpected appearance. Clearly Josh wasn't overwhelmed with joy to see her. He acted as if he could barely stand the sight of her.

"Why did you put her to work here if she gets on your nerves so badly?" she asked finally.

"She needs something productive to do besides fall into another disastrous relationship." He scowled at her. "And I really do not want to discuss Nadine."

Maggie smiled. "Yes, I can see that. Maybe you should explain why. She seems perfectly nice to me."

"Oh, she's a real peach."

"You sound bitter."

"Do I? Imagine that. The woman pops up whenever she needs some cash and I'm bitter."

Maggie was surprised he'd made no attempt to censor his remarks.

"I guess that makes me a terrible son," he added.

Maggie noted the turbulence in his eyes and knew there were things going on between Josh and his mother she couldn't begin to understand. She put a hand in the middle of his chest and shoved him toward a sawhorse. "Sit. Tell me what's got you so worked up."

"I don't want to talk about it."

"Well, you obviously need to. If you growl at all the volunteers who show up today, you'll wind up building this house by yourself."

"That might not be such a bad thing," he said stubbornly. "I spend Monday through Friday correcting mistakes as it is."

"I don't doubt it," she consoled. "But it will pretty much defeat Caleb's vision for this happy little project. He wants it to bring people together."

"Caleb's a cockeyed optimist."

Maggie bit back a smile. "He's a minister. I think it's in the job description."

"More than likely."

"I think in his case, it's called faith and hope."

"Whatever."

Maggie saw that she wasn't going to get anywhere with Josh in his present mood. All she could do was run interference between him and the source of his irritation. "Okay, in the interest of keeping the peace around here, how about this? You keep everyone else on track this morning. I'll work with Nadine."

He looked doubtful. "I don't know."

"Do you have a better idea?" At his lack of response, she nodded. "I didn't think so. That's what we'll do, then."

"She'll try to slack off," he warned. "Next thing you know she'll go into her helpless act and sucker you into doing everything for her."

Maggie gave him a disbelieving look. "Do I look like a sucker? Trust me, I won't let her get away with a thing."

Josh still looked as if he wanted to argue, but apparently he finally saw the wisdom in her suggestion. "Keep her the hell out of my way."

"Not a problem. If the woman has a lick of sense, she won't want to be anywhere near you."

"That's just it," he said grimly. "Nadine's not noted for her good sense."

"Well, fortunately for you, I am," Maggie said cheerfully. "We'll have that lumber cut to specifications in no time."

Thrilled that she'd found a way around his previous determination to keep her away from the saw, she was halfway across the site, when she heard his loud oath. Obviously, he'd remembered last week's edict.

"Maggie, you're not supposed to be anywhere near that saw," he shouted.

She merely waved.

"Don't you dare touch it till I've checked you out on it."

She frowned, but decided it was a reasonable request. "Hurry up, then. We're wasting time."

When she reached Nadine, she saw a speculative look in the older woman's eyes. Now that she knew the relationship, she could see that Nadine's and Josh's eyes were the same shade of dark brown. She judged the roots of Nadine's blond hair to be about the color of Josh's dark brown hair. But where Josh was about as down-to-earth and unpretentious as anyone Maggie had ever met, she had a feeling that Nadine, when she wasn't dressed for construction work, was all about flash and dazzle, the kind that would showcase well in Vegas.

"You handle him real good, sweetie," Nadine said approvingly. "How well do you know my son?"

"Not that well," Maggie said. "But I live by one rule when it comes to men."

"Oh?"

"Never let them get the upper hand."

Nadine chuckled. "You and me are going to get along just fine, sugar."

Maggie grinned, instinctively liking her. How could she help liking a woman who was as friendly and uncomplicated as a new puppy? "Yes, I believe we will."

And if that gave Josh fits, so much the better.

Josh's concentration was pretty much shot. Watching his mother and Maggie laughing and talking like a couple of old friends made his blood run cold. His mother's promise not to meddle in his love life was probably going right down the tubes as he watched. If Nadine got it into her head to start matchmaking, he and Maggie were doomed. He might as well go out and pay for the marriage license now. Weddings were one of Nadine's specialties. It was the marriages she couldn't seem to master.

"Interesting woman," Warren Blake commented, startling Josh so badly he dropped his hammer on his foot.

"Who?" he asked tightly.

"Nadine."

"You've met her?"

Warren grinned. "Nadine's made it a point to meet every man working here today. I'm pretty sure she has a mental dossier on those of us who are single. Where did you find her? She's definitely not from around here."

"Unfortunately, I didn't find her. She gave birth to me," Josh admitted reluctantly. "And the truth is, she was from around here years ago, but she's moved a lot. Most recently she was living in Vegas."

Warren studied her intently, then nodded. "Yes, I can definitely see her in Las Vegas. Was she a showgirl?"

"Waitress," Josh said automatically, then gave Warren a startled look. "Why on earth would you think she was a showgirl?"

"She has the legs for it, don't you think? And the flamboyance."

Josh heard something worrisome in Warren's voice and gave him a penetrating look. "You're a little young for her, don't you think?"

The psychologist looked startled by the question, then burst out laughing. "Don't panic. I'm not angling to become your daddy."

"I should hope to hell not," Josh muttered.

"I was just making an observation."

"I suppose you shrinks do that a lot," Josh said.

"Occupational hazard," Warren agreed. "I also sense that there's a lot of tension between the two of you."

Josh frowned. "You're not here to go skulking around in my psyche."

Warren didn't seem to take offense. "Consider it a perk of having a shrink underfoot."

"Did Maggie put you up to this?" Josh inquired suspiciously.

"Maggie? Hardly. We're barely speaking these days."

"Why is that?"

To Josh's surprise, Warren looked decidedly uncomfortable.

"You haven't heard?" Warren asked.

"Heard what?"

"About our engagement? I called it off just a couple of weeks before the wedding."

Josh stared at the man as if he'd grown two heads. "You and Maggie? Engaged?"

Warren chuckled at his stunned reaction. "If only we'd had the sense to see how ridiculous it was sooner, it would have saved us both a lot of embarrassment."

Josh wasn't sure why he was so shocked. Warren was a nice enough guy in a bland, steady way. He was probably rolling in dough, given the number of people in Charleston who had the kind of issues that sent them running to a shrink. Some women probably considered him good-looking, if the preppy, clean-cut type was their thing.

But Maggie? Josh would have expected her to be bored silly with him in a week.

"You said you broke the engagement?" he asked, to be sure he'd gotten it right.

"Came to my senses in the nick of time," Warren confirmed. "Maggie would have seen it sooner or later, too, but right now it suits her to blame me for humiliating her."

Josh nodded. "Some women are touchy that way. They want to call the shots if there's any dumping to be done. It's an ego thing."

"Unfortunately, I didn't think it was wise to wait around till she came to her senses. She was so hell-bent on keeping up with Dinah and Cord, she would have walked down the aisle with just about anyone."

Josh took another surreptitious look at Maggie, whose head was tilted back as she took a long, slow drink of Coke from a can. He tried to imagine a woman with that much sensuality with straight-arrow Warren. He failed.

"If she's still furious with you, maybe it's not about her ego at all," he suggested slowly, hating the idea even as he voiced it. "Maybe she really did have a thing for you."

Warren shook his head. "Maggie needs the kind of man who's a challenge. Someone a little mysterious and edgy." He gave Josh a speculative look. "Someone like you, as a matter of fact."

Josh stared at him. "I doubt she'd appreciate you trying to hook her up with me or anyone else."

Warren shrugged. "It was just another observation. I think I'll go have another chat with your mother. I've always wondered what Las Vegas is really like."

For a moment Josh was tempted to order the man to stay the hell away from Nadine. He had the perfect excuse. He needed another man to help with some of the framing work he was trying to get done today.

Instead, he decided to stay out of it. Hadn't he always believed that his mother was in serious need of a shrink? Maybe Warren Blake could fix whatever it was that drove her to make so many foolish mistakes when it came to men.

Maggie planted herself in front of Josh and waited until he met her gaze. "What are you up to?"

"I'm building a house. What about you?"

"You know that's not what I'm talking about," she said impatiently.

"Then you're going to have to spell it out for me. I don't have my decoder with me today."

"Warren and your mother, for heaven's sake! What are you thinking?"

"I didn't have anything to do with him deciding to spend time with her. He seems fascinated by the whole Vegas thing." He gave her a curious look. "Which seems odd since you couldn't be less flashy."

She frowned. "He told you about the engagement," she said flatly.

"He did. I'm still wrestling with that one. I have to say it doesn't make a lick of sense. What were you thinking?"

"I chalk it up to a momentary lapse in judgment," she admitted. "Not that there's anything wrong with Warren. He's a wonderful man."

"That's a given," Josh said, his amusement plain. "But isn't he just a little bit too tame for you?"

"Well, that was certainly his conclusion."

"And you? What did you think?"

Maggie considered the question for a long time before opting for the truth. "That he was perfect for my family."

Josh nodded sagely, though there was a definite glint of amusement in his eyes. "Ah, one last attempt for parental approval."

"Afraid so."

He glanced in his mother's direction. "At least that's one thing that will never trouble me. Nadine's standards aren't that high. Not that she has any right to pass judgment in the first place." He studied Maggie curiously. "Do you still figure your folks have that right?"

"It's not exactly a right," she said. "It's just what they do."

"And you care about their opinion?"

"To be honest, for years I did everything I could to show I didn't. My rebellion didn't turn out so well, so I changed course."

"Which explains Warren."

"Exactly."

"Now what?"

"I wish I knew. I think celibacy may be the answer."

Josh laughed. "I've come to that conclusion a time or two myself. Seems a shameful waste, though."

Maggie grinned. "I couldn't agree with you more."

She turned in Nadine's direction and saw that Warren was beginning to look just a little shell-shocked. "I think I'd better get over there and rescue Warren. Your mother can be a little overwhelming."

"Tell me about it," Josh said.

Maggie had taken only a few steps when he called her name. She glanced over her shoulder.

"Thanks for being nice to her. She drives me nuts, but I do care about her."

Maggie regarded him in bemusement. There was something in his tone she didn't quite get. "She's fun. Why wouldn't I be nice to her?"

Josh seemed startled by her response. "I just thought…" His voice trailed off and his cheeks flooded with color.

"You thought I might consider her beneath me?" Maggie suggested, her tone cold. "I'm not sure if that's more insulting to her or to me."

"I'm sorry. You're right."

"She may not be polished or wealthy, but she has a good heart, Josh. Maybe you're the one who should take the time to get to know her."

She could feel his gaze on her as she turned and walked away. Hopefully, his face was burning with shame.

With Maggie's disdain ringing in his ears, Josh felt about two inches tall. He was cursing himself every which way when he felt a tug on his pants at knee height. He looked down into Susie's upturned face. Amanda's four-year-old tended to pop up when he least expected her.

"Hi, Mr. Josh."

He grinned despite himself. "Hey, squirt. What've you been up to today?" he asked, hunkering down so he could look into her eyes.

"I helped with lunch," she said solemnly.

Ah, so that explained the mustard and ketchup streaks all over her bright pink T-shirt. Today's menu had been burgers and hot dogs cooked on a grill by one of the volunteers.

"Was there any ketchup and mustard left after you helped?" he teased.

"Sure. There was lots," she said, taking the question seriously. "And lots of chips, too."

"Where's your mom?"

"She's giving Jimmy and Larry a talkin'-to," she said with disingenuous honesty. "They're in trouble again."

"I see. What did your brothers do?"

Susie shrugged. "I dunno. Somebody told Mama something about a gun."

Josh felt as if the earth beneath him had opened up. "Do you know where they are?" he asked, trying to keep the panick out of his voice.

"Over by the cars, I guess."

"Let's see if we can find them," Josh said. "You want a piggyback ride?"

Susie nodded at once, then frowned. "I don't know what that is."

"You come around behind me and climb up my back, then hang on tight."

Her expression brightened. "Okay."

As soon as Susie's little hands were linked in a death grip around his neck, Josh went in search of Amanda and the boys. He couldn't imagine anyone being stupid or careless enough to bring a gun onto the work site, but he wasn't about to take any chances that Susie hadn't heard correctly.

He heard Amanda before he saw her.

"What were you two thinking?" she demanded, even as Caleb tried to calm her down with soothing words that Josh couldn't make out.

Larry and Jimmy, hanging their heads, didn't reply.

"I asked you a question," Amanda said, her voice escalating.

It was Jimmy who finally looked up, his chin quivering. "We just wanted to help."

"Did Josh show you what to do?" Amanda demanded. "Did he?"

"No, ma'am."

"And isn't that the rule? That you only do what Josh tells you to do."

She apparently caught sight of Josh then and turned an apologetic look on him. "I am so sorry. It won't happen again. I'll arrange for a baby-sitter next time."

"But we're supposed to help," Larry protested. "You can't leave us home."

"Please, Mom," Jimmy begged, his eyes filled with tears.

"Okay, guys, calm down," Josh said quietly, shooting a questioning look at Caleb, who merely shrugged. "Maybe you'd better start at the beginning and tell me what happened. Susie said something about a gun."

"Oh, my Lord," Amanda said, staring at her little girl. "Not a real gun, sweetie. A nail gun."

Josh breathed a sigh of relief, though a nail gun could be just as dangerous in the hands of a kid who didn't know how to handle it. Both boys turned to him.

"We thought we could figure it out and then we could be a real help," Larry explained. "I watched you and saw how to use it, so when you walked away, I got a board and we were practicing."

"Why didn't you ask me to show you?" Josh asked.

"Because then you would have thought we were babies," Jimmy said.

"Any man who's responsible takes the time to learn how to use his tools the right way," Josh scolded.

"I had Josh show me," Caleb added. "That's just being smart."

Josh met Amanda's still-worried gaze. "Was anyone hurt?"

"No, thank goodness. But I'd say they wasted a lot of nails."

"Nails can be replaced," Josh said.

"I can pay for more," Larry offered, sounding seriously grown-up for an eight-year-old. "Mom can give you my allowance for a whole month."

"Mine, too," Jimmy piped up eagerly. "We don't get much and we won't have anything for candy or ice cream, but that's okay."

"I don't think that'll be necessary," Josh said, holding back a grin. "But I do think maybe you boys should go home now and think about what I just told you."

Larry looked shattered. "You're sending us away?"

Josh had seen how much they loved being at the site. They were always underfoot. Still, he forced himself not to relent. "Just for today. Next week, I'll show you how to use the nail gun properly and then you can do it as long as Caleb or I are around to supervise. Not on your own ever again. Understood?"

They nodded.

"You're not really mad at us, are you, Mr. Josh?" six-year-old Jimmy asked plaintively.

"Not mad, just disappointed. I'm a lot like your mom, you know. It would make me feel awful if something happened to either one of you. You might want to tell her how sorry you are that you scared her."

"I'm sorry, Mom," they chorused dutifully.

Then Larry launched himself at Josh, causing him to stagger backward. "I'm sorry, Mr. Josh."

"Me, too," Jimmy said, his arms tight around Josh's leg.

"Okay, then," Josh said, stunned by the emotions that welled up in him. Thoroughly disconcerted, he lifted Susie over his head and handed her off to Caleb. "See you guys next week, then."

He walked away before any of them could see the unexpected tears that were stinging his eyes. Crazy kids. He'd known they were going to cause havoc. He just hadn't expected it to be with his heart.

He'd barely gone two feet, when Nadine appeared in his path.

"You have a thing with the single mom?" she asked, studying him curiously.

"Hell no," he said.

She nodded. "That's good."

He studied her curiously. "Why?"

"She's all wrong for you," Nadine pronounced with authority.

Josh glowered at her. "You figure she's better than me?"

Nadine's lips curved. "Would my opinion matter?"

"Of course not."

She grinned. "Didn't think so."

He studied her and tried to reconcile this conversation with his earlier fear that she was going to try to set him up with Maggie. Maybe he'd gotten that wrong. "Don't try any of this reverse-psychology crap with me, Mother. I am not interested in Amanda. Period."

"Whatever you say, Joshua," she said sweetly, then walked away.

Josh muttered yet another curse under his breath just as he was joined by Maggie.

"Nice talk," Maggie commented. "Especially when there are children nearby. What did Nadine do now?"

"Exactly what I warned her not to do. She's match-making."

Maggie glanced from him to Amanda and unexpected patches of color appeared in her cheeks. "I see," she said, her manner suddenly stiff. "Well, then, I just came over to tell you that I'm leaving. See you around."

She was gone before Josh could figure out what the hell had just happened. "Women!" he said in frustration. Not one of them made a damn bit of sense.

8

"Magnolia Forsythe, what is this I hear about you working on some construction site?" Juliette Forsythe demanded the instant she walked into Images on Monday morning. Her arrival not five minutes after the door had been unlocked was a very bad sign. Juliette rarely left the house before noon, unless it was to have her hair done.

Maggie regarded her mother with dismay. She'd hoped that this whole volunteer effort would escape her mother's notice. Juliette was all for charity and good deeds, as long as nothing more strenuous than writing a check or lending her name to a committee was involved.

"Good morning, Mother," she said, pressing a kiss to Juliette's cheek and hoping she could get this ordeal over with before either of her employees arrived. Both Victoria and Ellie respected her, but once they'd heard Juliette raking her over the coals as if she were ten, they might not. "How have you been?"

"Humiliated, that's how I've been," Juliette declared in a put-upon tone. "Wasn't it enough that you insisted on opening this little shop of yours and putting some of our priceless family heirlooms on display for anyone to see? Wasn't it enough that you let Warren embarrass us all by calling off the wedding? Now this! I can barely hold my head up."

Maggie turned away before she snapped out a retort she'd regret. She knew her mother wasn't nearly as mean-spirited as she sounded. Something or someone had stirred her up.

To buy herself the time she needed to get her own temper under control, Maggie said, "I was about to make some tea, Mother. Would you like a cup?"

"I didn't stop by here to drink tea. I came for answers."

Maggie ground her teeth. "Consider the tea a civilized bonus," she bit out, and went into the back to heat the water. The coffee was already brewing, thank heaven, because she needed a very strong shot of caffeine before she faced the rest of this inquisition.

She put two Royal Doulton chintz cups on a tray, added a plate of paper-thin lemon slices, a bowl of sugar cubes, cloth napkins and silver spoons, then poured coffee for herself and tea for her mother. She carried the elegant service into the shop and set it on the low coffee table in front of her grandmother's Queen Anne sofa.

When she finally faced her mother again, Juliette's pinched expression made her look as if she'd sucked on one of those lemon slices.

"Is this the way you treat all your customers?" her mother inquired stiffly.

"If they have time to sit and chat," Maggie said.

"It's a gracious touch," her mother admitted grudgingly.

"You were the one who taught me to be a good hostess, Mother. You should be proud that the lesson took. Please sit down and have some tea."

Her mother sighed heavily and lowered herself gingerly to the edge of the sofa, then accepted the cup of tea. "If only some of the others had," she said wistfully.

Maggie bit back a sigh of her own. "I wish I weren't such a disappointment to you."

To her amazement, her mother stared at her in shock. "A disappointment? How can you say such a thing? Your father and I may not understand some of the choices you've made, but you've never been a disappointment, Magnolia."

"I didn't marry Warren."

Her mother shrugged. "Yes, well, that was lamentable, but perhaps in time you can work that out."

"Not in a hundred years," Maggie said with certainty.

"Stubbornness has always been your downfall," Juliette scolded, the refrain more a habit than anything else. Surely she knew Maggie was unlikely to change at this late date.

Maggie grinned, her tension easing slightly. "Where do you think I got that particular trait?"

Juliette regarded her indignantly. "Not from me, I'm sure."

"We dislike most in others what we see in ourselves," Maggie said. "I think you told me that once."

Her mother looked genuinely flustered. "Well, that's neither here nor there. I want to talk about this construction business. Why on earth would you get involved in such a thing? It's beneath you."

Maggie had a hunch that whoever had told Juliette had deliberately put a negative spin on the project. No doubt it had been one of those from Caleb's congregation who opposed the construction of a house for Amanda. George Winslow came immediately to mind. He'd been lying low lately. Now it appeared he might be taking his case to people like her folks, hoping to get them to do his dirty work.

"Since when is it beneath me to help with a good cause?" Maggie asked, curious about her mother's logic.

"Well, when you put it that way, there's nothing wrong with doing a good deed, but this is something else. George Winslow spoke to your father. George is quite overwrought about the whole thing."

Maggie sighed. "I thought as much. Mr. Winslow should mind his own business. He's only trying to make trouble because he doesn't want to see this house built for Amanda O'Leary. If it were anyone else, he'd never have said a word."

Juliette frowned. "Well, you have to admit, he has a point. The woman does have resources of her own. Why should she get something for nothing when there are so many truly needy families out there?"

"I'm sure there are plenty of needy families, but if you're referring to Big Max as her resource, he hasn't spoken to Amanda in years. I'm sure you're well aware that he cut her off without a dime. Now there's a *real* example of stubbornness, if you ask me."

Juliette's gaze narrowed. "I knew there was bad blood between Max and his daughter, but he cut her off with nothing? I can't believe that. Are you sure?"

"I'm sure," Maggie said, her expression grim. "He did it simply because he didn't approve of her marriage. He's refused to even meet his grandchildren."

"I had no idea it had gone that far," her mother said, her expression thoughtful. "That's really quite shameful, especially now that things have gone so terribly wrong for her."

Maggie risked asking a question that had plagued her for years. "Would you and Father ever go that far?"

Juliette looked shocked for the second time that morning. "Absolutely not. You're our daughter and we love you."

"But I've seen how infuriated you get when I don't do things your way," Maggie said.

Juliette regarded her speculatively. "So you've been testing us to see if we'd disown you?"

"Maybe I have been," Maggie replied, suddenly viewing her years of rebellion in a new light. "Maybe I wanted to see how far I could push before you kicked me to the curb."

The teacup in Juliette's hand rattled against the saucer. She set it down and met Maggie's gaze. "Get that notion right out of your head, Magnolia. We would never disown you. Never!"

"Good to know," Maggie said, oddly relieved by her mother's adamant statement. Her parents' wealth had never mattered to her, but as she'd conceded to Josh over the weekend, their approval mattered in ways she'd never fully understood. She'd craved it, even as she'd done everything she could think of to guarantee that she wouldn't earn it.

"Well, believe it," Juliette said fiercely. "You're our daughter, our only child, and that's that."

"For better or worse," Maggie declared, amusement threading through her voice.

"Oh, darling, it's mostly for the better," Juliette said,

her expression softening. "I think I could even tolerate all these rebellions of yours if I saw they were making you happy, but inevitably they lead to heartache. That's what your father and I find so upsetting."

Maggie sighed. "I've noticed that myself. Then again, Warren was supposed to change all that, and look what happened."

"He's not the only appropriate man out there," Juliette consoled her. "If you can't work things out with him, you'll simply find another one."

Josh immediately came to mind. Maggie seriously doubted that her mother would see him as "appropriate." Was that the reason she seemed to find him so tantalizing? Was he just the latest in a long string of tiny rebellions?

More than likely, she conceded with a sigh. And maybe for once she could stop herself before she went down that path.

She dragged her attention back to her mother and noticed that Juliette was studying her worriedly. "I'm not heartbroken about Warren, Mother. You don't need to fret about me."

"I know you're resilient," Juliette said. "You did get that trait from me."

"Then why are you looking so worried?"

"Because I know how impulsive you can be. You have to admit that the combination of your impulsiveness and construction work is a recipe for disaster." She gave Maggie a stern look. "I do not want to get a call that you've fallen and broken your neck. Is that understood?"

Maggie grinned. "Understood. I'd say we're in total agreement on that one."

"Okay, then. I'll tell your father to tell George to mind his own damn business."

"You do that," Maggie said with enthusiasm. "Even better, perhaps you and father would like to stop by some Saturday and help."

Juliette looked completely thunderstruck by the notion, but then she seemed to perk up. "You're probably teasing, Magnolia, but who knows? One of these days your father and I might just turn the tables and surprise you. We've done an impulsive thing or two in our time."

Maggie laughed. "Well, then, I'll look forward to it."

Juliette's expression turned thoughtful. "I wonder if they make hard hats in pink?"

"Call Dinah's mother," Maggie advised. "If they do, I'm sure Mrs. Davis knows, after all those months she's spent on the Covington Plantation renovations."

"Excellent idea," Juliette said. "I'll speak to her this afternoon." She leaned down and kissed Maggie. "Bye, dear. Come see us. Your father misses you."

She was gone before Maggie could recover from the shocking image of her mother on the construction site in her own pink hard hat. For a woman who prized predictability and tradition, Juliette had been full of surprises this morning.

Nadine sighed at the destruction of her acrylic nails. Most of the polish had chipped off, and all but one of the nails was broken beyond repair. She had Josh to thank for this. Her son seemed to be taking some sort of pleasure in working her to death.

As if the demise of her manicure weren't bad enough, every muscle in her body ached. She longed for nothing more than a long soak in a hot bath—she was running the water now. Waiting tables for ten or twelve backbreaking hours a day had been easier than this job Josh had dreamed up for her.

Maybe she'd go out first thing tomorrow and find a job as a waitress. Even working in some dump would be better than this, and at least she'd have her own cash, instead of being dependent on whatever handout Josh deigned to give her.

Thoroughly disgruntled, she was about to climb into the tub, when someone knocked on the door. Since it could only be her son, she shouted at him from the doorway of the bathroom to go away.

"Nadine, it's me. Warren Blake."

She stood stock-still and stared at the door to her room. Now, *that* was a stunner. Warren didn't seem like the kind of guy who'd come chasing after her. The man was a real straight-arrow and a shrink, to boot. Definitely not her usual type, and that was even before she took into account the age difference. It was flattering to think a man like Warren was here because he was attracted to her, but more likely he wanted her to be some sort of weird case study.

She wrapped herself in her old silk robe, then cracked open the door to her room and regarded him with suspicion. "Why are you here?"

"Josh sent me."

"Why?"

"He figured you'd be starving and he couldn't get back to pick you up. He said if I'd come by to get you, he'd meet us at the restaurant."

Nadine noted that Warren kept his gaze carefully averted from her robe-clad body. The man was a real gentleman, no doubt about it. With any other guy, she probably would have been insulted that he didn't sneak a peek.

"I figured I'd just order a pizza," she told Warren. "You can stay if you want." She grinned at his dismayed reaction. "I'd get dressed, of course."

He laughed. "Well, since you're planning to get dressed, anyway, maybe we should just meet Josh. He's already suspicious of my motives where you're concerned."

Nadine studied him with interest. "And what *are* your motives? I can usually tell with a man, but you're harder to read than most."

Warren held up his hands. "No motives. You're relatively new in town and I figured you could use a friend. Besides, I hate eating alone."

"You do that a lot?"

"More than I'd like lately."

"Why is that? You're a good-looking guy and you must make good money." She frowned before he could respond. "You're not gay, are you?"

"Nope."

"Sorry," Nadine said, even though he hadn't seemed to take offense at the blunt question. "It was the only explanation I could come up with. You should have women beating a path to your door."

"I think a lot of them are put off by the kind of work I do," he admitted. "And I was engaged until recently."

"Anyone I know?"

"Maggie."

Nadine couldn't help it. Her mouth dropped open. "You and Maggie?"

Warren laughed. "Your reaction seems to be the consensus. Do you think we could continue this discussion after you get some clothes on?"

"Sure," she said. She was about to pick up her clothes

and head for the bathroom when she was struck by an idea. "You know, Josh has forbidden me to interfere in his love life, so I have some time on my hands."

Warren regarded her suspiciously. "What does that have to do with me?"

Nadine beamed at him. "I'll have plenty of time to find the perfect woman for you."

"I don't think so. Thanks all the same, but I've been finding my own dates for a long time now," he protested.

She pinned him with a gaze. "And how's that working for you, Doc?"

A sheepish grin spread across his face. "You have a point."

He was so doggone cute, she pinched his cheek before heading for the bathroom. "Leave it to me. I have real good instincts about this sort of thing."

"Haven't you been married several times?"

"Three," she conceded. "And in love more times than I can count. That's how my instincts were honed."

Warren chuckled. "Somehow I find that oddly reassuring."

"Damn straight," Nadine retorted. "I just don't see why Josh doesn't understand what a help I could be."

"Probably because you're his mother."

"I suppose," she said, disgruntled about the situation just the same. Just this afternoon she'd tried warning him away from Amanda O'Leary, and he'd gotten his back up over that. She'd simply been trying to save him a little heartache. Sweet as Amanda was, she'd bore Josh silly in no time.

Of course, why should he listen to her? The sad truth was she'd done little through the years to earn

Josh's respect. In fact, she was probably lucky that he hadn't written her off entirely. Suddenly she changed her mind about the construction gig. She was going to do her level best to stick around and keep it. After all these years, it was about time Josh found out he had a mother he could count on to follow through with something.

Maggie heard the front door at Images being rattled on its hinges and nearly jumped out of her skin. All she could imagine was Brian on the other side of that door intent on destroying the rest of Ellie's paintings. She picked up the portable phone in one hand and a letter opener in the other and peeked into the darkened front room of the gallery.

Since the security system alarm wasn't ringing like mad, obviously the locks had held. She took a few steps into the gallery for a better view outside. When she saw who was making all the commotion, she sighed, put down the phone and stalked over to snap open the door.

"You scared me half to death," she told Josh. "Did you ever think about calling to let me know you were coming by after hours?"

"I didn't have the number," he said simply. "It was an impulse thing. I was driving past, saw the light on in back and decided to check on you."

She stepped aside to let him in. "I was finishing up some paperwork."

"You shouldn't be here at night all alone. What if it had been that maniac Brian?"

She held up the letter opener. "I was prepared."

"You intended to hold him off with a plastic letter opener?" he asked incredulously.

"It's sharp," she retorted. "Don't you watch prison movies? Those guys make weapons out of plastic utensils all the time."

"And they're not afraid to use them," he said mildly. "Knives require you to be up close and personal with the intended victim."

Maggie shuddered. "I hope you didn't come by to cheer me up, because you're not doing a very good job of it."

"Actually I had no idea you needed cheering up. Do you?"

Maggie smiled. "No, not really. Was there something else on your mind?"

He shoved his hands in his pockets and avoided her gaze. "I have to have dinner with Nadine. I thought maybe you might join us. She seems to like you."

"As opposed to not liking you?"

He grinned. "No, she likes me well enough to pester me to death, so I'm looking for buffers."

Maggie thought she detected a guilty expression in his eyes. "Plural? Who else have you invited?"

"Warren," he admitted slowly. "Is that a problem?"

Maggie had no idea why she was even considering such a ludicrous invitation. Maybe it was simply because he was asking her and not Amanda. Still, she wasn't ready to jump at the offer too eagerly.

"You want my ex-fiancé and I to join you and your estranged mother for dinner?" She gave him a wry look. "How could I possibly say no to such an attractive invitation?"

He winced. "Lousy idea, huh?"

"Really lousy," Maggie concurred. "What made you think I'd accept?"

"Curiosity?" he suggested hopefully. "The chance to hold it over my head for all eternity?"

"Ah, now we're getting somewhere," she said. "I'll be ready in five minutes. Just let me turn off the lights in back."

"You'll actually come with me?" he said, sounding shocked.

"For the chance to have you owe me big time? You bet."

"I knew you had a perverse streak," he said triumphantly.

"Oh, sweetie, you have no idea."

Josh was pretty sure he'd died and gone straight to hell. If he hadn't, he should have, for ever having come up with this cockamamie dinner gathering. He'd been so absorbed with protecting himself from having to deal with Nadine, he hadn't really considered all the other dynamics likely to be at work.

Then, again, maybe on some level he had wanted to observe Maggie and Warren in a social setting to see if there were any sparks left between them. So far, though, they'd maintained a facade of such polite civility, such polite *cool* civility, that Josh was surprised icicles weren't forming over their table. If Nadine hadn't been chattering incessantly, the silence would have been deafening.

Suddenly, however, even his mother fell silent and gazed around the table. "Well, this is awkward as the dickens, isn't it?" she said eventually. "Clearly my son doesn't have much experience with planning a successful dinner party."

Josh frowned at her. "Thanks for pointing that out."

"Only stating the obvious, sweet pea." She turned her

gaze on Maggie. "Since it's the elephant in the room, let's just face it. Anything you've been dying to get off your chest to Warren here?"

Maggie looked startled by the question. "Such as?"

"What a pig he is for breaking the engagement," Nadine suggested.

Josh saw Maggie's lips twitch. "I believe I've already mentioned that a time or two since our breakup," she said.

"Or twelve," Warren said.

"Hush," Nadine scolded him. "You'll get your turn. Anything else, Maggie?"

Josh frowned. "Mother, why are you doing this? You're embarrassing them."

"Oh, I am not. We're all friends here. And if I'm going to find Warren a new lady friend, I want to be sure I'm not stepping on Maggie's toes."

Maggie gaped at her. "You're going to find Warren someone to date?"

"Only if you don't object," Nadine said.

"By all means, go for it," Maggie said. "I can hardly wait to see who you come up with."

"Me, too," Josh muttered. Nadine would probably try to hook him up with a stripper.

"Wipe that look off your face, Joshua," Nadine said. "I am capable of finding some classy women who'll be ideal for a sweet man like Warren. I'd do the same for you if you'd let me."

Josh recognized at once that he'd just dodged a bullet, thanks to Warren. Maybe she'd forget all about making any more of her misguided attempts to get him to notice Amanda. "Please, feel free to concentrate on Warren," he advised his mother.

"Yes," Maggie said. "He can use all the help he can get, now that most of Charleston knows what a pig he is. Oh, wait, I've mentioned that before, haven't I? Sorry." The apology was uttered with a total lack of sincerity.

Nadine ignored it and seized on Maggie's permission to move ahead with her plan. "Good, then that's settled. There will be no hard feelings if Warren moves on."

"None," Maggie agreed firmly.

Josh studied her face intently when she spoke and concluded she meant it. Why he found that to be such a relief didn't even bear thinking about.

9

When she arrived the next morning to open Images, Maggie was still reeling from Nadine's announcement that she intended to fix Warren up with a new woman. The fact that those two had struck up such an instantaneous bond was mind-boggling. Given Nadine's rather flamboyant personality, Maggie couldn't help wondering if there was something about Warren she'd missed, perhaps some element of excitement and danger she'd never tapped.

But as absorbed as she was in trying to make sense of that, the sight of Ellie sitting in her darkened office, her eyes red-rimmed and swollen, swept away everything else in her head.

Immediately alarmed, Maggie hunkered down beside Ellie and clasped her icy hand. "What's wrong?"

Ellie regarded her miserably. "I have to quit," she said sadly.

"What? You can't quit. You're my right hand around here."

"I have to," Ellie said with more determination.

Finally understanding, Maggie regarded her grimly. "This is Brian's doing, isn't it? He's told you to quit."

Ellie nodded, looking utterly defeated. "He says if I don't get away from this gallery, he'll…"

Maggie's temper flared. "He'll what? He'll hurt you? Destroy more paintings?"

"No, no," Ellie said urgently. "It's not me he'll go after. He's threatening to destroy your reputation."

"How on earth does he propose to do that?" Maggie inquired. She was from one of Charleston's finest families. If all of her own antics through the years hadn't destroyed her reputation, she doubted there was much Brian could do. "You can't let him get to you, Ellie," she stressed. "He obviously knows he can't frighten me, so he's counting on your loyalty to me, instead. It's a head game, an idle threat."

"No, it's not," Ellie argued. "He has a plan, Maggie. He told me."

"What plan?"

"He'll tell everyone that my paintings are fakes, that I stole his work and put my name on it and that you knew about it." She clasped Maggie's hands tightly, her expression intense. "I won't let him ruin you, Maggie. Even a shadow of suspicion could hurt you, at least in the short term. You don't deserve that just for trying to help me."

"He's not going to ruin me," Maggie said emphatically, though she could see how cleverly the man's mind worked. As Ellie said, such a charge could cast a shadow over the gallery's reputation till she straightened everything out. In the end, she'd stack her family's good name against Brian's reputation any day of the week.

"But he could make trouble," Ellie insisted.

"Hush a minute," Maggie chided. "Let me think about this."

She noticed that despite her distress, Ellie had automatically made coffee when she arrived for the day. Maggie poured them each a cup, then took a seat at her desk and pondered Brian's threat. Surely there had to be a way either to seize the initiative, now that she'd been forewarned, or to minimize the damage if he went ahead with his scheme.

Slowly an idea began to take shape. It was an ingenious one, if she did say so herself. She met Ellie's unhappy gaze. "I think I see a way around this, if you're game for it."

Brian's psychological torment had clearly taken a toll. Ellie still looked worried. "I don't know," she said hesitantly. "He's determined to stir up trouble for you, and I've seen him when he gets like this. He's a master manipulator. He doesn't let up till he gets what he wants."

"Then we simply have to turn the tables on him," Maggie said decisively.

"How?" Ellie's expression was filled with doubt.

"What does Brian want most in the world?" Maggie asked, hoping she'd pegged the man's real motivation.

"To be recognized as a talented artist," Ellie said, confirming Maggie's assessment.

Maggie smiled. "I thought so."

"Then what? You'll let him have a show here?"

"No, never," she said fiercely. "That would only be rewarding him for his emotional blackmail." She smiled. "But Images will sponsor an art contest for a poster for this year's Spoleto Festival. We'll have all the entries judged by the faculty at Brian's school and perhaps one or two independent experts. We'll see that he's pressured to enter. So will you."

Ellie regarded her blankly. "What will that accomplish?"

"When the judges have these originals in hand, we'll also have them compare them to your other paintings and determine which of you painted the works in my vault. I doubt there will be any serious question about it. My hunch is that your style and techniques have evolved quite differently from his. Am I right about that? Could you bring me something of his to look at?"

"I have a couple of his paintings in my studio," Ellie admitted, though she still didn't look convinced. "Won't this be hard to put together? You have so many other things on your plate."

"Nothing's more important than nipping this scheme of his in the bud. We can't let Brian win, Ellie. It sends entirely the wrong message," Maggie insisted. "And actually the festival committee has asked me before to get involved in a poster competition. They'll be thrilled that I've finally agreed, especially when they see the size of the donation I'll be making."

"What if Brian refuses to enter the contest because it's sponsored by Images? He might figure out it's a trap."

Maggie could see how that might be problematic. "I'll talk to the committee. Perhaps there's a way to keep the gallery's name out of it."

"Then you'll lose the PR value," Ellie said. "That's not right."

"Sweetie, that's nothing compared to the PR I'll get for this place once we get your works on display and critics all over the country start raving about what a talented find you are."

Tears spilled down Ellie's cheeks. "I don't deserve everything you're willing to do for me."

"You most certainly do," Maggie replied emphatically. "Now get out on the floor and get to work. Victoria's not coming in till later, so you're in charge. I have all those calls to make to get this ball rolling, and I have a ton of paperwork left from yesterday."

"I thought you stayed late last night to do that," Ellie said.

Maggie flushed. "I got sidetracked."

Ellie regarded her with evident curiosity. "Really? By what?"

"Never mind."

"A man?"

"Two men, if you must know."

Ellie's expression brightened for the first time since Maggie's arrival. "One of them was Josh, I'll bet. The man is seriously hot for you."

Maggie gave her a startled look. "You think so?"

Ellie made an exaggerated gesture of fanning herself. "No question about it. Who was the other man?"

"Warren."

Ellie immediately sat back down, fascination written all over her face. "I have to hear this."

"No, you don't," Maggie said. "Living through it was awkward enough. I don't want to relive it today. Besides, it was no big deal."

"Just tell me this," Ellie pleaded. "Who won?"

"Won what?"

"The contest," Ellie replied impatiently.

"There was no contest."

Ellie's grin spread. "Josh, obviously," she decided, drawing her own conclusion.

"No, I mean there was *no* contest," Maggie repeated emphatically.

"Oh, come on, when there are two guys and one girl, there is always a contest."

"There *was* another woman—Josh's mother."

"She hardly counts. Anyway, my money's on Josh."

"You favor him just because he came to your rescue," Maggie said.

"No, because when he's around or even gets mentioned, there's color in your cheeks," she said with a wink as she headed for the front room of the gallery. "Artists pay attention to that sort of thing."

Maggie snatched a compact out of her desk and glanced at herself in the mirror. Sure enough, her cheeks were bright pink. Too bad she wasn't old enough to blame it on a hot flash.

Josh had gotten in the habit of taking his lunch break with Amanda and the kids. No one was more surprised than he was that he found their company enjoyable. Besides, it kept him away from Maggie. His attraction to her was beginning to be worrisome.

He'd just set aside his bottle of Coke when Susie crawled onto his lap and brought herself eye-to-eye with him. She patted his cheek with one dainty but decidedly filthy little hand.

"Mr. Josh…" she began solemnly.

He had to fight to keep his lips from twitching into a smile at her serious tone. It was such a somber contradiction to her bright pink sneakers with the flowers on them and the ponytail that was slipping free of its rubber band.

"Yes?"

"Do you got a girlfriend?"

He stared back into those round blue eyes and knew

she had a very definite reason for asking. Lord help him, she was probably matchmaking for her mama. He'd had no idea that particular feminine gene kicked in this early.

"No," he said, then added cautiously, "Why?"

"'Cause I'm thinking you and me should get married someday," she announced.

Jimmy and Larry made dramatic gagging sounds. Amanda turned away, but not before Josh caught the amusement in her eyes.

"Now, darlin', I have to admit you've caught me by surprise," he said, trying hard not to laugh. "You really think marriage is a good idea?"

"Uh-huh."

"Don't you think maybe I'm too old for you?"

Susie studied him intently, then shook her head. "Nope. You're just right. And I'll be bigger someday."

"And when you are, dozens of guys your own age will be swarming all around trying to get you to marry *them*," Josh told her with conviction.

"But I love you," she insisted. "Mama says any girl would be lucky to have a man like you."

Josh turned a quizzical gaze on Amanda. "Is that so?"

Amanda shrugged. "It's true, but believe me I was not trying to fix you up with my four-year-old."

"No, I don't imagine you were." He studied Amanda for a moment to see if he could read anything more into what she'd said, but she was regarding him with the same friendly amusement with which she usually regarded him when they talked. Even so, he wondered if he shouldn't have a let's-get-this-straight chat with her.

"Kids, why don't you go back over to the food tent?"

he suggested. "I hear they brought some ice cream today for dessert."

"All right!" Jimmy shouted, pumping his fist in the air.

He and Larry were about to race off, when Josh called them back. "Hey, guys, don't leave Susie behind. Look out for her, okay?" He set her gently on her feet and watched as she scrambled to catch up with her big brothers.

When they'd gone, Amanda faced him. "That was very smooth, Josh. What's on your mind? You worried I'm filling Susie's head with ideas?"

"No, I just want to be sure you don't share any of those ideas."

To his chagrin, she laughed.

"Not even close," she said.

Perversely, her certainty sparked a streak of irritation. "Why not?" he demanded.

She laughed. "Not five seconds ago you were warning me off. What did I do? Hurt your tender male ego?"

Feeling foolish, Josh grimaced. "Something like that. Or maybe I'm questioning my own sanity. I'd like to know, why not me? We get along okay, don't we?"

"Of course we do. And to be honest, it would be easier for me if there *were* some spark between us," she added wistfully. "You're a great guy. You're wonderful with the kids."

"But?" he asked. "Maybe we should test things, Amanda." His life would probably be a whole lot saner if he did fall for a woman like her, instead of Maggie.

She stared at him with alarm. "Test things? How?"

He leaned forward and stole a kiss, letting his mouth linger on hers, waiting for the spark that could be fanned into something more.

There was no spark.

When he pulled back, she gave him an odd look. "What was that about, Josh? Are you running scared?"

"Running scared? I don't know what you're talking about."

"Maggie," she said succinctly.

"Not an issue," he said staunchly.

Amanda merely grinned. "Keep telling yourself that. Meantime, I think you and I are destined to be friends, nothing more. The kids and I have really come to count on you and Caleb."

Josh grinned, despite her obvious sincerity. "I suppose everyone can use a saint and a sinner around. Kind of evens things out, when it comes to setting an example for the kids."

She nudged him in the ribs. "I would trust you with their lives, Joshua Parker, so don't you go selling yourself short."

Startled, he met her gaze. "You really mean that, don't you?"

"Every word. You're one of the good guys."

She stood up and brushed the dust off the seat of her jeans. In any other woman it might have been a conscious gesture to draw attention, but with Amanda he knew it was completely innocent. Didn't keep him from looking, though. She was too thin for his taste. Unfortunately, he found Maggie's curves more appealing.

"Josh?"

He blinked and looked up into her face. Her mouth was curved into a knowing smile.

"I'm going to get those kids before they eat all the ice cream and make themselves sick, okay? Let me know what you need us to do this afternoon." She leaned down and brushed a kiss across his forehead. "I meant what I told Susie—any woman would be lucky to have you. Though it's beyond me why, I don't think you believe that. You should."

He stared after her, an odd sense of contentment settling in his chest. Praise like that had been in short supply in his life. He hadn't realized before now how much he craved it.

Then he glanced up and caught Maggie staring in his direction. Judging from the glint in her eye, she was not happy about something. He sighed and the contentment died. He had no idea what might be bothering her today, but he didn't have a doubt in his mind that sooner or later he'd be hearing about it. In detail.

Well, that had been a touching little scene, Maggie thought with annoyance. Amanda's kid crawling all over Josh, then the lip lock and finally Amanda planting one last kiss on him right here in front of God and everyone. Maggie wasn't sure why it grated on her nerves so badly, but it did.

In fact, a lot of things grated on her nerves, including Josh's stubborn refusal to accept that he was mostly wasting her skills. When she spotted Cord arriving at the site at the end of the day, she headed straight in his direction, determined to deal with at least one of her major annoyances.

"Hey, handsome, what brings you by?" she inquired, giving him a kiss on the cheek.

"Don't let my wife see you flirting with me, Magnolia," he taunted. "She's the jealous type." He studied her. "So, what are you after?"

"What makes you think I'm after anything?" she asked testily. "Can't I just greet an old friend?"

Cord laughed. "You can, but when you go all Southern and syrupy on me, it's usually because you want something. You and Dinah learned that technique at your mothers' knees."

"Does it work on you? Or have you gotten immune to it?" she asked, her curiosity piqued.

"It depends on how far she takes it," he admitted with a grin. "I think it might be better if you take a more direct approach and just tell me what's on your mind."

"I want to see the plans for the house," she said at once.

"Then why are you talking to me instead of Josh?"

"Because he guards them as if they're some sort of huge secret or maybe more like the rest of us are too incompetent to understand them."

"Have you actually asked him?"

"Of course I have," she said, not even trying to hide her disgust. "He told me to stick with the assignments I was given. The man is on a serious ego trip. I have no idea why you put him in charge of a job that requires cooperation."

"Maybe it's because he's the one on this site with actual construction experience," Cord suggested. "And he's never had any problem getting people to do their jobs before. Maybe you're the one who's crossing the line."

"I can read a damn blueprint," Maggie said, chafing at the implied criticism.

"But why, precisely, would you want to?"

"Because something tells me this place fits some sort of cookie-cutter plan that's all wrong for Amanda and the kids," she grumbled.

"It's what we can afford to build," Cord corrected.

"That doesn't mean it can't be improved on," Maggie argued.

"Then talk to Josh," Cord repeated. "I'm staying out of it. I just came by to take a look around and make sure things are on schedule."

"Okay, then. Why don't I give you the fifty-cent tour?" Maggie suggested, tucking her arm through his.

Cord regarded her with undisguised suspicion until he spotted Josh bending over the blueprints. "Oh, no, you don't, Magnolia!" he said, disentangling his arm from hers.

"What?" she asked innocently.

"You are not going to pit the two of us against each other by implying that I back your desire to see the plans. Work it out with Josh. He's a perfectly reasonable man."

"Oh, for goodness' sakes, it's not like they're secret blueprints of the White House."

Josh looked up, saw them and put down the plans. "What's going on, you two?"

"I'm just taking Cord on a tour, but he'd probably rather you took him around so you can discuss all the technical stuff," Maggie said, devising a whole new approach, since the last one had failed abysmally.

Cord's gaze narrowed. "No, I'm perfectly happy to let you take me around."

"Uh-uh, that's okay. You two go right ahead," she encouraged. "I'll be leaving in a few minutes, anyway." She gave Cord another peck on the cheek. "Tell your wife I said hey."

"Will do," he said, amusement lurking in his eyes when it finally dawned on him what she was up to. "Josh, shall we?"

Josh cast another suspicious look over his shoulder, but he walked away with Cord, leaving all those lovely blueprints behind.

Maggie spread them out and studied them. It was just as she'd feared. The house was going to be cut up into little boxes barely big enough to turn around in. She knew they couldn't change the overall size of the place, but surely there were ways to make it seem more spacious. She'd told Cord weeks ago that she was going to turn this house into a home, and she intended to do it. After that intimate little scene she'd witnessed between Josh and Amanda, it might turn out that she was doing it for the two of them. Well, so be it.

She pulled a pencil and pad from her pocket and began jotting down notes. First thing in the morning she and Mr. Control Freak were going to have a chat about this house.

Josh had never worked a job where so blasted many people had an opinion about what ought to be going on. Maggie was the worst of the lot, just as Cord and Caleb had predicted. She seemed to have some misguided notion that she knew as much about construction as he did. He'd done everything he could to keep the blueprints away from her to minimize her input.

Unfortunately he'd left them in plain sight yesterday when he'd gone off with Cord, and apparently she'd had herself a field day. He'd come by the site this morning to check on a couple of things, and Maggie had been right here waiting for him. He'd wasted an hour trying to explain why she couldn't have the wall between the living room and dining room taken out to "open things up," as she put it.

She'd finally given up on that idea, but she'd remained undaunted, Right this second she was hovering over the plans yet again, a pencil tucked behind her ear and a list as long as his arm in her hand. He did not want to know what was on that list, but judging from the determined glint in her eye as she turned in his direction, he was going to find out. He swore this was the last time he was ever coming by the site by himself to check on anything less urgent than a reported flood.

He eyed the paper warily as she got closer to him. "What's that?"

"Just a few tiny little changes," she said breezily. "They don't amount to much."

"Then why bother with them?" he asked.

"Because they'll make the house much more inviting and comfortable."

"Didn't we go down this road before?" he asked wearily. "I thought the purpose was to put a roof over their heads, not to build them Tara."

She frowned at the comment. "I'm not trying to make the house luxurious. I'm trying to make it more livable. Surely you can understand the difference. Then, again, I'm familiar with that dump of a motel where you live, so perhaps you don't."

Josh ignored the gibe about his living quarters. Better not to get drawn into that discussion. He had a hunch if he gave this woman any opening at all, she'd be all over his place like white on rice with her homey little touches. It was hard enough to keep Nadine from filling his room with her smelly candles.

"That last little change you came up with would have taken out a bearing wall," he reminded Maggie.

She scowled at him. "Which you explained to me ad

nauseam. I got it. I'm not recommending that you take out any walls."

"Putting any in?" he asked suspiciously.

"Not exactly, just some more closet space. There's not enough built-in storage in the plans."

"I don't think these folks have a lot of things to store," Josh said reasonably.

"That doesn't mean we shouldn't plan ahead. The kids will get older. Amanda might marry again."

She studied him intently as she said that, as if it should somehow matter to him what Amanda O'Leary did with her future. "What's your point?" he asked.

"That we shouldn't be shortsighted."

Josh barely stopped himself from rolling his eyes. "Who designated you to be in charge of these details?"

She smiled sweetly. "No one. I volunteered. Aren't you lucky?"

"That's a matter of opinion," he said. "You also volunteering to foot the bill for the extra materials?"

"If need be," she said without hesitation. She whipped out another paper. "I have the cost projections right here. If there's not enough in the budget, let me know."

Josh heaved a resigned sigh. "Okay, then, hand over today's list and I'll see what I can do."

"Thank you."

"I don't suppose you talked any of this over with Amanda?" he inquired.

She frowned just a little at the question. "No," she said, then gave him a pointed look. "But I'm sure you'll be happy enough to do that. The two of you seem so cozy these days."

She whirled around and left him staring after her,

wondering what in the hell that last little dig had been about. The kiss, he realized with a sudden burst of insight. She had witnessed his experimental kiss and wasn't one bit happy about it. Well, now, wasn't that interesting?

10

"Tell me again why you wanted to treat me to dinner," Josh said. "Not that I'd ever turn down a chance for free steak and some decent wine, but you and I are not in the habit of socializing."

"Since we're both so busy these days, I wanted to catch up with you on how the house for Amanda O'Leary is coming along," Cord said, his expression neutral. "And I've been wanting to try this place. Dinah refuses to come to a steak house."

"You toured the site less than twenty-four hours ago. Not much has changed," Josh retorted, amused. "Maybe you should have spent a little more time thinking about your excuse to pump me for information about whatever it is you really want to know. That one's pretty transparent."

Cord grimaced, then shrugged. "I told Dinah I was no good at this kind of thing."

The remark caught Josh off guard. "Your wife is behind this dinner?"

Cord nodded.

Josh sighed heavily. "Then I'm guessing it's about Maggie."

"What makes you say that?"

"Because it's always been about Maggie with her. I am building this house because your wife wanted to set me up with Maggie. I didn't get that at first, but we both know it now. You've all but admitted it, so there's no point in pretending otherwise."

"Maggie's pretty special. You could do worse," Cord said.

"I can and have," Josh conceded. "But nothing is happening between me and Maggie, aside from her determination to drive me nuts. She's in a frenzy over closet space at the moment."

Cord chuckled. "I warned you about that."

"You certainly did. If only I'd taken you more seriously, I never would have retracted my resignation or, at the least, I could have insisted on hazardous-duty pay. I may still ask for a big bonus."

"Don't ask me. There's no room in the budget for bonuses." Cord's gaze narrowed. "So, what do you think of Maggie?"

Josh didn't even hesitate. "She's intelligent, talented and annoying as hell."

Amusement filled Cord's eyes. "Yep, that's our Maggie, all right. It can make her quite a challenge. You up for it?"

"Are you pushing me to ask her out?"

"Maybe," Cord admitted. "She's Dinah's best friend. She wants to see Maggie settled."

"Therefore it's in your best interests to help the process along," Josh guessed.

"Something like that."

"I've been finding my own dates for a long time,"

Josh said, phrasing it as diplomatically as he could. "If I wanted to ask Maggie out, I would."

"Then the thought hasn't even crossed your mind?"

"Sure. I'd have to be dead not to consider the possibility that she and I could stir up some real heat, but she's a handful. I don't think I want the aggravation. Then there's the definite disadvantage of knowing that you and Dinah would be poking your noses into our business every time we turned around. This dinner is proof enough of that."

"The way I hear it, you've already seen Maggie a time or two away from the construction job," Cord said, ignoring the complaint, or perhaps just adding to the proof of it. "What was that about?"

"Those weren't dates," Josh replied. He frowned at his boss, hoping to forestall further questions. The whole discussion was getting damn uncomfortable. If his future with Beaufort Construction was tied somehow to his relationship with Maggie, it was going to make life awkward. He gave Cord a penetrating look. "Are we finished with this topic yet?"

"Not quite." Cord leveled his gaze with Josh's. "Don't mess with her head, okay? She's been through a lot."

Josh nodded, accepting that Cord was bound to have Maggie's best interests at heart, since the two of them went way back. "I know all about the Warren thing. I don't have a clue how they got together in the first place, but I do know his ending it took a toll on her. Since I don't do the whole engagement-commitment thing, it's never going to be an issue between us."

"Which is precisely my point. If you're just playing games, don't even start with her," Cord warned. "Maggie deserves happily-ever-after, not some summer fling because you've got the hots for her."

"Who says I have the hots for her?"

"I do," Cord said. "I recognize the look, since I wore it for years whenever I crossed paths with Dinah. It's on your face every time you spot Maggie. You've got it bad, pal. And, as the song goes, that ain't good."

No, Josh agreed silently. No, it wasn't, especially if a man like Cord could pick up on it after being around the two of them for no more than ten minutes.

"Let me get this straight. Are you seriously warning me away from her?"

Cord regarded him evenly. "You're both adults. Neither one of you has to listen to a thing I say. I'm just letting you know that Maggie has friends who worry about her and don't want to see her hurt."

Cord held his gaze until Josh finally broke eye contact. "Duly noted. For the record, though, I'm not in the habit of hurting women. I saw the misery my mother went through with men. I'm not about to inflict that kind of emotional pain on anyone. I always lay my cards on the table up front."

"One last piece of advice, then," Cord said. "You can say the words, Josh, but if your actions contradict them, women will buy the actions every time and resent it like hell if you throw those words back in their face when you're on the way out the door."

"Voice of experience?" Josh asked him.

Cord nodded. "Until Dinah and I got together, I was a whole lot like you. That's what makes me worry about Maggie. She had a little thing for me once and I hurt her without even meaning to."

Josh felt his gut clench. "You dated Maggie?"

"Only once, in what I thought was a lark. She won the bidding for a date with me at a bachelor auction for charity. We went out, had a nice evening and that was that. It was only later than I found out she'd hoped for something more. There was never any relationship, but that didn't mean her feelings weren't hurt. She's got a tough exterior, Josh, but her heart's been bruised, by me and Warren and who knows how many others. I'd like to see her find the real thing."

Josh got the picture. Cord didn't think he had what Maggie needed or deserved. Truthfully, neither did he. That didn't mean that somewhere deep inside he didn't wish it were otherwise.

Nadine was positively stir-crazy. Going from her motel room to the construction site and back again wasn't half enough excitement for a woman who liked being around people. She'd waited for Josh to come home, hoping they could go out for something besides burgers, but when he hadn't gotten back by six, she'd called Warren, then remembered he was out on a date, one he'd chosen for himself, more's the pity. He wouldn't even give her a name or tell her where they were going. Since the man had no imagination when it came to women, this one was probably dull as dishwater.

Unfortunately, she hadn't come up with a viable alternative for him yet. All the women working on Amanda O'Leary's house were married or such Goody Two-shoes, she wouldn't wish them on anyone. Only Maggie had some spunk, but she and Warren had already been there and done that. Besides, she'd seen something in Josh's eyes when Maggie was around. She'd promised not to interfere, but she sure as heck hoped those two woke up and smelled the coffee before it went cold.

Sitting around her cramped room with time on her hands was beginning to get to her. She checked her purse and found twenty bucks. It was hardly enough for a night on the town, but maybe she could buy a couple of drinks in a nice bar and parlay it into some conversation with an attractive man who'd be willing to buy dinner.

A half hour later, she'd put on her best blouse, some formfitting capris and high-heeled sandals, and spritzed herself with White Diamonds for luck. Hey, it'd worked for Liz Taylor...

When she walked into the dimly lit steak house, she paused long enough to survey the bar. There were a couple of men seated together at one end, already hitting on women young enough to be their daughters. A gray-haired man, wearing a perfectly tailored suit, was all by himself in the shadows at the far end of the bar. He was staring morosely into his glass of whiskey. If ever there was a man in need of company, he was it. Nadine had perfected the cheering-up routine years ago. It came naturally to her now.

"Hey, sugar, is this seat taken?" she asked, already sliding onto the bar stool next to him.

He shrugged, but never even glanced her way. Nadine didn't take offense. His lack of interest only made the encounter more challenging. She smiled at the bartender.

"I'll have a double scotch, neat," she told him, then pushed her lone twenty across the bar.

When the bartender returned with her drink, she took a sip, then turned to the man beside her. "You look as if you've got the weight of the world on your shoulders. Want to talk about it?"

He gave her a cursory glance, then turned back to his drink.

"I'm Nadine," she persisted. "I'm not coming on to you or anything. I'm just looking for a little conversation. I got tired of staring at the walls at my place. Does that ever happen to you? You start to feel like home is closing in on you?"

This time when he faced her, his expression was a little more open. "Where are you from, Nadine?"

"Right here in Charleston, originally, but I've been away a long time. I came back to see my son."

"Where is he?"

"Beats me. I suppose he got tied up with work or something."

"It's not very considerate of him not to let you know," he said disapprovingly. "Especially if you're just here for a visit."

"Well, it's more than a visit, I suppose. He put me to work on this job he's doing, so I'll be around until that's wrapped up at least."

"What sort of job?"

"Construction."

This time when he looked at her, she could see she finally had his full attention. His eyes glinted with disbelief. "You don't look like any construction worker I've ever seen."

"Believe me, it's new to me." She held up her hands and regarded them with dismay. "It's hell on a manicure, I can tell you that."

"What on earth was your son thinking?" he demanded indignantly. "What's the world coming to when a man treats a lady like that, especially his own mother? It wouldn't have happened with my generation."

She gave him a rueful look. "Actually I'm pretty sure he thought it might be nice for me to do a good deed for once in my life. We're building this house for a woman who lost her husband a while back."

To her surprise, instead of the approval or interest she'd expected, a frown crossed his face.

"This wouldn't be the house being built for Amanda O'Leary, would it?" he asked.

"It sure is," Nadine said, immediately perking up. "You know about it?"

"The whole thing's a bunch of damn nonsense," he said heatedly. "If Amanda O'Leary needs a house, her daddy ought to be building it for her. She shouldn't be taking the opportunity away from a family that really needs it. Somebody ought to go over there and bulldoze the whole thing."

Something in his forceful tone alarmed her, but Nadine decided she needed to keep her cool and find out if this man posed a real threat to Amanda or the house they were building. Maybe they needed to beef up security around the site.

"That's not a very charitable outlook," she chastised him. "Seems to me that a woman who's been forced to declare bankruptcy because her husband left her with a pile of debt could use a helping hand. Did you know she's been working two jobs to try to support her three kids and give something back to her creditors?"

"Bankruptcy!" he scoffed. "Now there's a scam for people who don't know how to manage their money. I still say she ought to go to her family for help, not rely on the kindness of strangers."

"From what I hear, her daddy cut her off without a dime. Why on earth would she want to go crawling back to a man like that?" Nadine asked, indignation overcoming her intention to remain calm. "So he can throw a bunch of I-told-you-so's back in her face? No woman with even an ounce of pride would do such a thing, and no decent man would expect her to."

Patches of red instantly colored his cheeks. "What are you saying? Are you impugning my sense of decency?"

Nadine refused to back down. She'd been around too many mean blowhards like this one and kept her mouth shut. Not this time. "I'm saying that any man worth his salt would be siding with Amanda and doing what he could to help her, instead of sitting here badmouthing the folks who care about her and her kids. That attitude of yours explains a lot about why you're sitting here all by yourself," she said, no longer finding him half as attractive as she had when she'd first noticed him. A bully was a bully, no matter how well dressed he was.

"How dare you!" he said, his tone suddenly filled with icy fury. He rose to tower over her. "Do you have any idea who you're talking to?"

"A self-important lowlife, from the sound of it," Nadine retorted loudly, not even flinching under his glare.

The bartender approached them then, looking worried. Nadine noticed that several people in the bar were studying the two of them curiously.

Before she could give the man an earful about what else she thought of anyone who'd display such a remarkable lack of charity, two men appeared behind her. She was about to elbow the closest one in the stomach when he spoke.

"Mother, why don't we get out of here?" Josh said, his tone pleasant but his gaze hard as he stared down the man who was unmistakably trying to intimidate her.

"Not until I speak my mind," she countered. "Do you have any idea what this old windbag said to me?"

"I think I can imagine," Cord chimed in. He offered the man a polite smile. "Good evening, George. I see you're out spreading good cheer this evening."

Nadine whirled on him. "You know this man?"

"George Winslow," Cord said. "Believe me, he's made his position about Amanda's house quite clear. He doesn't approve. He's even tried to stir up some folks to get Caleb fired." He faced the man. "What's the matter? Are you so furious at your lack of success in stalling this project that you have to take it out on the first person who dares to challenge you to your face?"

"I haven't done a blasted thing to this woman," George retorted. "She started the conversation."

Before Cord could say whatever else he intended to say, Nadine pushed between them. "Are you crazy?" she asked George. "You'd have a preacher fired for helping someone in need? Someone ought to teach you a thing or two about compassion. Apparently you missed that lesson in church, though I'm sure you take pride in sitting in the front row every Sunday. What were you doing? Counting your money?"

"I believe you've made your point, Mother," Josh said, his tone wry. "Let's go."

"But I'm not through with him," Nadine argued. "Besides, I paid for that drink and I intend to finish it."

Josh grabbed the drink from the bar. "You can finish it at our table," he said, tossing a tip on the bar. "Cord will deal with Mr. Winslow."

Nadine recognized her son's determination. It finally dawned on her that this man, whoever he was, was in a position to do some real harm to the construction project. She directed one last scowl his way, then let Josh lead her into the restaurant.

When she was seated, she said stubbornly, "I will not apologize for telling him what I thought of him."

To her surprise, Josh was regarding her with amusement. "I wouldn't ask you to. It's about time someone told that old windbag to shut his mouth. Everybody's been tap-dancing around him to try to pacify him because nobody wants to see him take out his anger on Caleb."

"Neither do I, but the only way to deal with a man like that is to lay it on the line," Nadine said. "He's not the kind who'll respect anyone who pussyfoots around."

"Well, judging from the little bit I heard, you definitely didn't do that," Josh said admiringly.

"You're not furious with me?"

"No, but I can't speak for Cord. He's the one who has to clean up this mess before it makes things worse."

Cord returned just then and slid into his chair. Nadine, who considered herself an expert at reading men, couldn't decipher his expression.

"Everything okay?" Josh asked.

"Actually, I think old George is a little shell-shocked. He hasn't had so many hard truths thrown at him in years, especially by an attractive woman."

"He deserved every word I said and then some," Nadine said, pleased by the compliment.

"He did, indeed," Cord agreed.

"He's not going to make trouble, is he?" she asked worriedly. "Did I make things worse for Caleb or Amanda? I know I have a tendency to act first and think later. If I need to, I can swallow my pride and apologize to the jerk."

"No, I think it's best if you steer clear of him for the

moment and let him stew," Cord said. "George doesn't like people thinking ill of him. Hearing you paint a pretty negative picture in public has put his actions in a whole new light for him. Maybe he'll come around, after all. It would make things a heck of a lot easier on Caleb if he did."

"Then maybe I did more good than harm?" Nadine asked hopefully.

"I'd say there's a very good chance of that," Cord said.

She looked at Josh and grinned. "Maybe for once you can be proud of your mama."

"Nadine, I was proud of you the minute I heard those words coming out of your mouth."

She felt something warm spread through her. "Really?"

"You scared the heck out of me when I saw you pushing the buttons of a man who towers over you," Josh admitted. "But when I realized what you were doing—standing up for Caleb and Amanda, two people you barely know—I realized just how big your heart is."

"Honey bun, it always has been," she told him. "I suppose you never noticed because I was usually wasting it on some useless man, instead of giving you the attention you deserved."

"Water under the bridge," he said, squirming uncomfortably.

Nadine would have reached across the table and given her boy a big ol' kiss, but she figured this was about as much of a Hallmark moment as he could handle, especially with Cord sitting there looking on.

"You know," she said, suddenly thoughtful. "There's

another aspect to this little incident we haven't even considered."

"What's that?" Josh asked.

"For the first time in my life, I actually recognized a jerk before I fell for him."

"Now that *is* cause for celebration," Josh said. "How about ordering a steak and joining us for dinner?"

"You mean it? I won't be interrupting your business?"

Josh gave Cord a look she couldn't quite interpret.

"Nope, I'd say our business is done, wouldn't you, Cord?"

"I've covered everything I set out to cover," Cord agreed. "Seems like a lot of people have been put on notice tonight."

Nadine wasn't sure she liked the sound of that, but since Josh didn't seem to be troubled by the remark, she let it slide. Battling with one man had already worked up a nice, healthy appetite.

11

The whole incident between Nadine and George Winslow had made Josh uneasy. He was proud of his mother for standing up to the man, but he also knew what a powerful man was capable of doing if his temper was riled. He wouldn't put it past Winslow to find some way to make trouble for Caleb or to bring the entire Charleston building and zoning staff down on their heads with a flurry of time-consuming inspections that could hold up construction for days.

His concerns turned to reality when he arrived at the site and found Winslow already there prowling around, his expression dour.

"Anything I can do to help you, Mr. Winslow?" Josh asked, determined to be as polite as possible.

"You're in charge here?"

Josh nodded. "I'm Josh Parker."

"Then that woman who ripped into me last night is your mother, is that right? That is what you called her when you rode in to save her from making a fool of herself."

Josh bristled at his derisive tone. "She is, though I'm not so sure she was the one who was making a fool of herself."

To his surprise, George ignored the remark.

"She has quite a mouth on her," George replied instead, a faint and surprising hint of admiration in his voice.

Since that was certainly accurate, Josh didn't take offense. "Nadine believes in being direct, that's true enough."

"Must have been hell on you growing up," he commented.

Josh didn't see any reason to discuss his issues with Nadine with this stranger. "Are you here for a reason, Mr. Winslow?"

"Just taking a look around."

"It's a hard-hat area. I'll get you one, if you'd like a tour."

His gaze narrowed. "You make all your crew wear hard hats?"

"Absolutely, especially since a lot of the folks helping out here aren't used to construction. They may not recognize the dangers."

"This place being built to code?"

"Of course."

Winslow looked skeptical. "You have a bunch of amateurs working and you're meeting all the city regulations?"

"I'm the expert, Mr. Winslow. Nothing gets by me if it's not top quality. And we'll have professionals in to do the electrical and plumbing to make sure they meet the highest standards."

"I see," he said, looking vaguely disappointed. "Then you won't mind if I have some of the city's experts take a look around."

Before Josh could utter the sharp retort that was on

the tip of his tongue, Maggie suddenly appeared at his side. She tucked a hand through his arm and gave it a gentle, warning squeeze.

"Good morning, Mr. Winslow," she said brightly. "What a pleasant surprise!"

Josh gave her a sharp look. Her tone suggested she was anything but pleased to find him here.

"Magnolia!" Winslow's gaze narrowed. "I'm surprised to see you here. I spoke to your father just last week. I thought we had an understanding."

"Yes, I'm well aware of your conversation with my father. My mother passed along your displeasure that we're building this house. I'm astonished that you honestly expected them to do your bidding or me to pay any attention to what you want."

"Is that why you're still here?" he said. "Another one of your infamous rebellions?"

"That's one reason," Maggie said sweetly. "Of course, I also stopped worrying about bullies when I was in grade school."

George Winslow's face turned so red, Josh feared for his health. "Maggie, perhaps we ought to go over those changes you wanted."

Under other circumstances, Josh might have laughed at her startled expression.

"You want to go over them again?" she asked.

"I most certainly do," he said, putting his hand over hers. "If you'll excuse us, Mr. Winslow, we have work to do. Feel free to pitch in and help, if you'd like. There's plenty left to do. We can always use another volunteer. As for those inspectors, bring them on, if that's what it will take to make you back off. You're not going to shut us down."

He steered Maggie away from the man before she could utter another word. Somewhere along the way she'd apparently forgotten all about her initial goal, which had been to rescue him before he said something to set Winslow off and make matters worse.

To his surprise, she went with him without complaint, but when they were a safe distance away, she planted her feet in the dirt and glared up at him.

"Why did you do that?" she demanded. "I was just getting warmed up."

"Yeah, I noticed," he said with a grin. "Between you and Nadine, the man's blood pressure is probably in the stratosphere. By comparison, I was downright diplomatic."

Maggie looked intrigued. "Nadine told him off?"

"Last night. They crossed paths in a restaurant. He said something about this project she didn't like, and that was that. She told him what she thought of him in front of a very captivated audience."

"Brava, Nadine!" Maggie said.

Josh grinned. "It was quite a show."

"Do you suppose that's what brought him out here first thing this morning?"

"Absolutely. I figure the housing inspectors won't be far behind," he said glumly.

"And that could hold things up, couldn't it?" Maggie asked, finally catching on to his real concern.

"More than I'd like," he agreed.

"Well, George Winslow isn't the only one in this town with contacts at City Hall," she said, yanking her cell phone out of her pocket.

"Hey, slow down," Josh said, amused by her readiness to take on the man. "Let's wait and see what he does, okay? Maybe we're getting worked up over nothing. Perhaps his conscience will kick in."

"Men like that don't have a conscience," she said derisively. "They have a checkbook and a big ego. George is even worse now that he stays at home all day long and studies his portfolio. Every little dip in the market turns his mood sour."

"All the more reason to try to stay on his good side."

"You'd pander to a man like that because he has money?"

"No. I'd pander to him to try to keep him from interfering in our work. Why waste the energy on unnecessary battles? Isn't the goal to get this house built?"

"I suppose you're right," she said grudgingly.

Josh held back a grin. "Why, Miss Magnolia, you sound disappointed. Were you hoping to start the day with a little rabble-rousing?"

She gave him a provocative look. "I can think of *much* better ways to start my day," she said in a voice laced with innuendo. "How about you?"

Josh stared into her eyes, trying to interpret the sudden shift in her mood. Was she actually flirting with him? It was one thing for him to have the hots for Maggie when it was a totally one-sided attraction, but if she was going to change the rules out of the blue, he was in serious trouble. Spontaneous combustion was just around the corner.

Even so, he couldn't seem to stop himself from playing the game she'd started. "Sweetheart, my blood always pumps a little faster at the sight of a woman in high dudgeon over something. Makes me want to see what other kind of heat she's capable of causing."

Maggie's gaze never wavered from his, but she swallowed hard. That was enough to tell Josh everything he needed to know. She'd changed the rules, all right, but she wasn't entirely comfortable with the outcome.

That little hint of vulnerability scared him worse than if she'd jumped up and locked her legs around his waist and her hands behind his neck. He could handle a woman with nothing but passion on her mind, but a vulnerable woman made his palms sweat.

"I need to get to work," he said gruffly. "Try to stay out of trouble the rest of the morning."

He heard her indignant little huff as he walked away, but he didn't turn back. He didn't dare. If he had, he might have hauled her into his arms and taken her up on that offer she was so plainly making. Something told him *that* experiment wouldn't end as tamely as his kissing Amanda had.

The man was a pig, no question about it. Maggie stared after Josh and cursed him every which way. That little game she'd played had certainly blown right up in her face. When had she gotten so lousy at flirting?

She'd shown up here this morning determined to prove to Dinah and herself that she was not the least bit jealous of Amanda. She'd also wanted to prove that she had no feelings whatsoever for Josh, that Dinah had misread the entire situation.

Then, seeing George Winslow wandering around trying to foment trouble had annoyed her, and the next thing she knew she was focusing all that pent-up irritation on Josh where it promptly turned into something else entirely. She was obviously in worse shape than she'd realized if her emotions could roller-coaster like this.

Getting herself a cup of coffee while she tried to get

her emotions back under control, she noticed that Josh and Amanda were together once again, their expressions intense. Josh looked as if he was hanging on Amanda's every word. Amanda seemed equally enraptured.

And there it was again, that little streak of pure, gut-deep jealousy. Maggie nearly groaned when she recognized it. What was wrong with her? Why couldn't she seem to spend ten minutes with Josh without making a fool of herself? She wasn't some inexperienced fifteen-year-old.

Hell, she'd grown up flirting with boys. It was second nature to every Southern woman, at least to every one who'd been raised by someone like Juliette Forsythe, who was not only Southern to the core, but had a few French genes romping through her DNA, as well.

Great-grandmother Juliette DuBois had come to Charleston from Paris at the turn of the century. She had brought with her a few prized antiques, which were now on display at Images, but barely a *sou* in her elegant silk purse. She had proceeded to enchant one of the wealthiest merchants in Charleston. With her flirtatious charm and excellent taste, they had made a fortune, which subsequent generations had tripled and quadrupled. Now none of the descendants worked in a trade, except for Maggie, much to her mother's dismay.

If Juliette ever actually saw Maggie working at the construction site, even though she'd offered tacit approval of the mission, she would probably take to her bed with heart palpitations. Forsythes did not get their respectable hands dirty, despite Juliette's hint that she might turn up here one day. Maggie figured that would be a cold day in hell, or in summertime Charleston, for that matter.

Juliette was outspoken in her opinion that Maggie would sooner or later bring disgrace down on all of them. Over the years, Maggie had done what she could to prove her mother right.

She and Dinah had made a mockery of their debutante ball. Maggie had come as close as anyone to flunking out of school without actually succeeding. She had a hunch money had changed hands to prevent that disgrace. She'd frittered away a few years taking advanced advanced classes in art appreciation, but had never bothered to aim for a college degree.

And then, of course, there were the men. The most unsuitable ones around, to hear her mother tell it. Maggie preferred to think of them as sexy and challenging, which, she couldn't help remembering, was precisely the label Dinah had pinned on Josh.

Until Warren. Juliette had adored Warren. She'd embraced the idea of the hasty wedding with a fervor that not even Maggie had expected. When Warren had bailed, Juliette had blamed Maggie for doing something to run him off and made her feel like a failure because of it.

"Your great-grandmama would be bitterly disappointed in you, *ma chérie,*" Juliette had said more than once. Unspoken was the fact that Juliette herself was just as bitterly disappointed, despite all her claims to the contrary.

Maggie was still pondering her track record with men when Josh propped a booted foot on a stack of two-by-fours beside her and inquired, "Aren't you supposed to be doing something besides staring off into space?"

"Am I?" she asked, surprised that he'd torn himself away from Amanda.

"You're usually busy finding some way to complicate my day," he said. "And not ten minutes ago, I sent you off to get to work."

"I got sidetracked. As for complicating your day, I'm fresh out of ideas."

He grinned. "I have to say that's a pleasant change. You want something to drink? I was about to get a Coke."

"Sure." It was too hot for the coffee she hadn't touched, anyway.

He started to head over to the cooler that was kept stocked with iced soft drinks, then hesitated, his eyes filled with real concern. "You okay, Maggie?"

She forced a smile. "Just peachy."

"Want to talk about it? You're not still worked up about Winslow, are you?"

"Hardly."

"Then what?"

"Do you really care?"

"Enough to listen," he said.

Now, *there* was an enthusiastic response. His eyes would probably glaze over if she started in on all the issues churning around in her head. "Thanks for the offer, but believe me, you really do not want to hear all about what a disappointment I am to my family."

He looked startled. "That's what you're thinking about?"

"Yep."

"Then basically you're feeling sorry for yourself?"

He sounded so incredulous she winced. "Ridiculous, isn't it?"

He nodded. "Pretty much. The way I see it you've got everything in the world going for you. You're gorgeous. You have friends. You have your own business.

You have the money to do anything you want. How many women would give anything for a life like that?"

"You mean women like Amanda?" She heard the testy note in her voice and cringed. She was pathetic.

"For one," he agreed. He sat down beside her and studied her curiously. "What is this thing between you and Amanda? Every time her name comes up, you act like you just got a taste of sour lemon."

Maggie wanted to deny it but couldn't. "Do you want the pitiful truth?"

"Sure."

"I'm jealous," she admitted, and despite what Dinah thought, it wasn't all about Josh, who was looking as stunned as if she'd announced a secret yearning to be locked in solitary confinement.

"You're jealous of a woman whose husband was killed a year ago, who doesn't have two nickels to rub together, and has three kids depending on her?" he asked incredulously. "Why?"

"Like I said, it's pitiful."

"No, it's crazy."

"Entirely possible," she agreed. It *was* just a little bit nuts to want what Amanda O'Leary had, but Maggie didn't see it quite the way Josh did. What she saw were three adorable kids, the strength to bounce back from tragedy and a man like Josh who treated Amanda like a valuable piece of crystal. No one had ever treated Maggie like that. No one had ever treasured what she had to offer, not even her own family.

Until recently she'd had enough self-confidence and pride in her accomplishments to weather whatever came her way, but lately she didn't seem to have the strength to fight back.

"I think you could use a reality check," Josh said. "Spend some time with Amanda. She's an amazing woman, but her life hasn't been a picnic."

"Don't you think I know that?" Maggie said impatiently. "I know all about her losing her mother when she was just a kid. I know what kind of man her father is and how badly her husband screwed up. Oh, forget it. I can't make you understand what I don't entirely understand myself."

He looked as if he wanted to argue, but he finally shrugged. "Still want that cold drink?"

She glanced at the cold coffee she was holding, then dumped it on the ground and tossed the cup in a nearby trash can. "Sure. Thanks."

Josh came back a few minutes later with the promised soda, handed it to Maggie in silence, studied her for an instant with a faintly troubled expression, then left her without another word.

"Oh, who needs you?" she muttered.

"I'd say you do," Cord said, settling down next to her. "Stop feeling sorry for yourself, Maggie. If you want him, go after him."

"Go to blazes, Cordell! This isn't about Josh."

"Isn't it? What happened with Warren has thrown you offstride, but if you want Josh, you can get him. No man can resist you."

She gave him a rueful smile. "You did."

"Barely."

She laughed. "You're revising history, Cordell. It was always Dinah for you. I never stood a chance."

"You stand a good chance with Josh, though."

"He has a thing for the single mom," she countered.

"Amanda?" Cord said, his surprise evident. "No way.

That's way too much hearth and home for Josh. He's an independent guy. You'd be good for each other. You both need space and you both could use the fireworks."

She grinned at that. "Have you and your wife consulted on this to make sure you're sending out a consistent message?"

He grinned. "We've talked. Or I should say, Dinah has expressed her views and convinced me she's gotten everything exactly right."

"Then what are you suggesting? Sex without commitment?"

"Sex, anyway," he responded. "Of course, that's just me talking. Dinah would add that you shouldn't go shutting any doors on commitment, either. She says you and Josh are the kind who'll fall hard once you realize you're worthy of being loved and let it happen."

"And you agree with that?" she asked curiously.

Cord nodded. "Josh may be the only person I know who puts up more barriers to being happy than you do. It'll be fun to see if you've got what it takes to tear them down."

"Is that a challenge?"

He winked at her. "You never could resist a challenge, Magnolia. Don't start now when it really matters."

That, of course, was the problem. She didn't want to believe that Josh could really matter, because if he did and she lost again, she wasn't sure she could survive it.

Better to build a house for a woman who needed it, better to fight to see that Ellie's artistic talent wasn't wasted, better to do just about anything than risk her heart and lose. That really would be flirting with disaster, because something told her if she failed again, she might not find the strength to bounce back.

12

Still in a major funk, Maggie left the construction site without another word to anyone. She headed straight to Images. This was her world, the one she understood, the one she was good at. She didn't need a lot of pitying looks from a man she barely knew and a lot of unsolicited advice from a man who'd once rejected her.

She also didn't need to have Josh's growing friendship with Amanda—*if* that's all it was—thrown in her face every ten seconds. She needed tranquility. She needed to be in charge of something, in control. She excelled at controlling things. Why waste time on anything or anyone that made her question herself?

Of course, her determined effort to regain her confidence wavered slightly when she walked into the gallery and saw Vicki's pierced eyebrow nearly hit her hairline.

"What happened to you?" Vicki asked. "You're all covered with sawdust. It's even in your hair. Were you in some kind of weird accident with a lumber truck or something?"

Maggie winced. She hadn't even considered what a sight she must be; she'd only wanted to get to someplace where she felt safe.

"Actually I was volunteering at a construction site," she said. "Don't panic. I won't scare the customers away. I have work to do in my office."

"Not now," Vicki said, blocking her way.

Maggie regarded her employee suspiciously. Vicki marched to her own drummer, but it wasn't like her to challenge Maggie so directly. She usually took a more passive-aggressive approach, simply doing as she wished and daring anyone to correct or stop her.

"Why not now?" Maggie asked, more out of curiosity than annoyance at the girl's insubordination.

"Because Ellie's in there with that guy," Vicki explained in a hushed undertone. "You know, the one who's scary as hell. He's got some burr up his butt about something. I don't know what."

Maggie's blood ran cold. "Brian's here? You left Ellie alone with him?"

Vicki shrugged. "What was I supposed to do? She didn't freak out at the sight of him, so I figured she had things under control."

Maggie supposed that was something. Hopefully Ellie was smart enough to stay in plain sight if she feared Brian was a danger to her or to the gallery.

Even so, she brushed past Vicki and headed straight for the back, anticipating some sort of commotion. She heard nothing more than the low murmur of conversation.

"You're sure she's okay?" Maggie asked, still not convinced she could trust Vicki's judgment.

"I pulled her aside and asked if she wanted me to call someone, but she said she'd be fine," Vicki told Maggie. "I wasn't convinced, so I've been listening at the door with my cell phone in my hand. After what happened at her studio a couple of weeks ago, I figured if I heard him so much as raise his voice, I'd call the cops."

It appeared the girl did have some solid street savvy, after all. "Good for you," Maggie praised.

"Why is Ellie with a loser like that anyway?" Vicki asked indignantly. "Anybody can see he's jealous of her talent. I may not be the brightest when it comes to men, but I do know jealousy is the kiss of death to a relationship. Like, I'm not jealous of Drake's wife. I know people think I'm nuts for going out with a married guy, but he's been straight with me from the beginning. That's more than some single guys have been."

How Vicki segued from Brian's jealousy of Ellie's talent to her own love life escaped Maggie, but she saw a not-to-be-missed opportunity to express her concern over Vicki's choices—even if it sidetracked them for a moment from the threat Brian presented. "We only worry, Vicki, because there's no future for you if he's married," she explained.

"I'm not even twenty-two yet. I'm not looking for forever. He treats me okay and that's what counts for now," Vicki insisted, dismissing Maggie's concern.

"What about his wife?" Maggie asked. "Do you think he's being straight with her?"

Vicki blinked.

"Well?" Maggie pressed, convinced that Vicki had never thought beyond her own infatuation.

"I guess not," Vicki admitted, seeming a bit shaken. "I never looked at it that way."

Maggie gave her hand a squeeze. "Maybe it's time you did. I'm not trying to tell you what to do. But just think about how you'd feel if you were in his wife's shoes."

In the meantime, Maggie suddenly realized, she needed to spend some time thinking about her own insecurities regarding Josh, and her jealousy of Amanda. If he and Amanda had something going, there was nothing she could do about it. If they didn't, then her ridiculous attitude only made her look petty.

Grateful that Vicki had inadvertently led her to a new perspective on her own situation, she reached out and gave the girl a hug. "By the way, thank you."

"Me?" Vicki said, looking startled by Maggie's impulsive action. "What did I do?"

"You've been looking out for Ellie, and I'm impressed with the way you handled things when Brian showed up. But mostly, thanks for what you said about jealousy and relationships. It was something I needed badly to hear." She nodded toward the closed door of her office. "Keep an ear out for those two, okay? Do not hesitate to call the police if you don't like what you're hearing."

Vicki still looked perplexed. "Sure, but where are you going?"

"I have to go home and formulate a battle plan."

Vicki's apparent confusion only deepened. "Am I supposed to get that?"

"Not really. I'll see you in the morning."

On her way out the door, she heard Vicki mutter, "And everyone thinks I'm the weird one around here."

Maggie chuckled. It appeared they all had a thing or two to learn about each other—and themselves.

Josh watched worriedly as George Winslow skulked around the construction site all morning. Obviously the man hadn't been put off by his earlier confrontations. He was here to cause trouble. It was only a matter of time.

Still, Josh couldn't find a reason to order him off the site. He wasn't interfering with their work. In fact, he rarely spoke to anyone until he encountered Caleb. Josh couldn't hear what those two said, but it didn't look like a very cordial exchange.

Five minutes later, a grim-looking Caleb came looking for Josh.

"God forgive me for saying it, but that man has the compassion of a gnat," Caleb said. "He told me he's calling the diocese this afternoon to see about having me removed, and meanwhile he's going to make sure the city inspectors are all over this site."

"What is his problem?" Josh asked irritably. "Doesn't he have enough to do? Why does he want to make everyone else's life miserable?"

"Because he can," Caleb said.

"Do you think he's acting at Big Max's behest?" Josh asked. "They're friends, right?"

"They are," Caleb said, looking vaguely uncomfortable.

"What?" Josh prodded.

"I can't get into it, but no, I don't think he's acting for Big Max. He might *think* he's doing it for his friend, but he's definitely doing it on his own initiative."

"And you know this because…?" Josh pressed.

"I can't tell you more than that," Caleb said. "It just infuriates me that he's so willing to condemn Amanda for not going to her father for help. It's bad enough that he's trying to get everyone else worked up. I just hope he keeps his opinions to himself around her. She doesn't need the aggravation."

"Surely he's enough of a gentleman that he wouldn't deliberately upset her," Josh said, just in time to see

Winslow heading straight in Amanda's direction. He shook his head in disgust. "Okay, maybe I was wrong about that."

"I'll deal with this," Caleb said, his face set.

Josh held him back. "Let me. You have more to lose than I do."

Caleb looked torn. "It's my duty to step in."

"And mine to see that nothing goes wrong on this site," Josh said. "Come on, Caleb, use your head. You'll do more good for this community from the pulpit than you will if he manages to get you tossed out on your behind. Don't give him any ammunition."

"I suppose," Caleb said, but he looked as if he'd relish going toe-to-toe with Winslow again.

Josh got to Amanda's side just as Winslow did. He saw her flinch when she looked up into the man's angry gaze, but then steady herself and face him calmly.

"Amanda Maxwell," Winslow began in a blustery tone that silenced everyone nearby, "you should be ashamed of yourself."

Before Josh could utter a word, she gave him a beseeching look and shook her head. Then she faced her father's ally, squared her shoulders and replied quietly, "It's Amanda O'Leary, Mr. Winslow, as you perfectly well know, since you walked out of my wedding when you saw that my daddy wasn't going to show up. I have no claim to the Maxwell name anymore, as I'm sure my father's told you."

Winslow's determination didn't wilt under her steady gaze. "He'd take you back in a minute, if you'd go to him. Then this house could be given to someone who really needs it."

Amanda's eyes flashed. "I'm a single mother with three kids who's working two jobs to pay off her late husband's debts. If I don't need it, I can't imagine who does. Even so, I didn't ask to have this house built. The kind people of my parish wanted to do it for my family."

"Your father—" Winslow began, only to have Amanda cut him off.

"As for my father, William Maxwell is a cold, heartless man who's made it plain he wants no part of me or my children," she said bluntly. "Did you know that I called him after Bobby died and he hung up on me? I was willing to grovel if it meant helping my kids, but he never even gave me a chance. After that, I saw no point in trying again."

Josh was startled but George looked completely taken aback.

"You called him?" George asked.

"Of course I did. It was my last resort. After that I knew that even if he subsequently agreed to take us in, I couldn't take my children into a home where they weren't even acknowledged, much less welcomed. How could I?"

"You should have tried again," George said stubbornly.

"If I inherited anything from my father, it's pride. I went to him once. Not again."

Winslow looked more uncertain than he had at the beginning of the encounter, but he still wouldn't let it go. "You have a strange way of showing gratitude for all the advantages your father gave you," he said eventually.

"I am exceedingly grateful for one thing he gave me," Amanda retorted. "He gave me the strength to weather adversity. When a man I'd loved and respected my whole life disowned me on my wedding day and I survived the blow, I learned I was strong enough to face anything. It prepared me for everything that's happened since, including dealing with the likes of you. You've lived the same sort of privileged life my father has, so you can't imagine what it's like to lose everything except the clothes on your back and your children. Until you've walked in my shoes, Mr. Winslow, you have no right to tell me what I should or shouldn't be doing. I've done whatever it was in my power to do to keep a roof over their heads and food in their bellies. I thank God for Josh and all these volunteers."

Giving Josh a tremulous smile, she whirled around to walk away, then turned back. "And don't even think about trying to take out your anger with me on Caleb. He's a fine man and the church is lucky to have him. If you disapprove so strongly of him and the rest of us, I'm sure you can find yourself another congregation that's more to your liking. If you decide to take on Caleb, we'll fight you."

Then she did leave, her back straight. Amid a smattering of enthusiastic applause from those close enough to have heard the exchange, she went directly to Caleb's side and left George Winslow sputtering with indignation.

"That girl is a disgrace to her daddy's good name!" he said.

Josh met his gaze evenly. "But I'd say she just did the O'Leary name proud."

"As if there were anything to be proud about," George scoffed. "The man left his family in hock up to their eyeballs."

Josh had no idea how that situation had come about, but he was determined to defend Amanda and her family any way he could.

"We all make mistakes from time to time. Some of us are fortunate enough to have the chance to rectify them," Josh said. "Bobby O'Leary never had that chance." He gave the older man a considered survey, then added, "You could rectify the mistake you made by coming here hoping to intimidate Amanda and everyone working to help her. You could put aside your judgmental attitude and help us build this house and show all of Charleston the kind of man you really are. Or are you too afraid of Big Max's opinion?"

"Oh, don't waste your breath on him, Josh honey," Nadine said, arriving just in time to add her two cents' to the discussion. "We can all see the kind of man he is. He's a pompous, self-righteous pig with nothing but time on his hands to meddle because he has no real friends. I suspect he leads a real lonely life what with spending all his time thinking up ways to make other folks miserable."

Josh winced inwardly. "Mama, I think he's probably heard enough of your low opinion of him."

"Then he can leave," she said, standing her ground.

The color climbed right back into George's cheeks, and his furious gaze clashed with Nadine's. "Fine," he said at last, then turned to Josh. "I'm going, but the next time I come back, you can be sure I'll have a housing inspector with me. You won't hammer a nail on this place without someone looking over your shoulder. By the time I've finished, you'll be lucky if this place is finished this time next year."

Josh groaned as he watched Winslow stride away without a backward glance.

Nadine gave Josh's arm a squeeze. "Don't mind him, honey. He's all hot air. He just had to get in the last word. I know his type. He won't set foot around here again."

"Did you have to rile him any worse than you did the other night?" Josh inquired, unable to keep the plaintive note out of his voice. "The last thing I need is building inspectors taking up all my time."

She smiled. "Some men just need to have the truth laid out for them again and again." She tapped a finger to her temple. "That man's head is hard as a rock. I doubt I even got through the first layer."

"That's true enough," Josh said, fighting a smile at her assessment. "But who appointed you to try to penetrate his thick skull?"

Nadine chuckled. "I volunteered. Weren't you hoping I'd get the hang of that, anyway?" she said as she, too, strode away.

Despite his desire to wring her neck for most likely making things worse, Josh couldn't help admiring her. In fact, Nadine, Amanda and Maggie had all showed some real grit today in the face of Winslow's bullying.

Josh suddenly realized that lumping his mother in with those two had to be some sort of turning point. Maybe he'd always been so caught up in how Nadine's actions affected him, he hadn't seen her for the scrapper she really was. Maybe she'd simply done the best she could under impossible circumstances. And maybe it was time he gave her credit for that and stopped blaming her for what she hadn't done.

Maggie knew exactly where Josh ate most of his dinners and where he'd shared a few meals with

Amanda and her kids. She suspected the outings were Josh's way of making sure the family had an occasional meal out. There wasn't a doubt in her mind that he was paying for them. Despite the disquieting feeling that gave her, she resolved to join them tonight and put the whole jealousy thing to rest once and for all. Just showing up would be a public proclamation of sorts. She was determined that after tonight no one would be able to accuse her of shunning Amanda out of jealousy.

When she walked into the diner, they were all there, the kids in one booth and Josh, Amanda and Nadine in another. The surprise was Warren, who'd pulled up a chair at the end of the table. His presence gave her pause, but before she could cut and run, Nadine caught sight of her.

"Maggie, I didn't know you were going to join us," she said brightly. "Come on over here right this second. There's plenty of room right beside Josh. Scoot over, honey, and let Maggie sit beside you."

Maggie still hesitated. "I just stopped by to…" She faltered, trying to come up with some lie that would allow her to bolt, after all.

"Yes?" Warren said, regarding her with amusement.

She didn't answer, just scowled at him and then sat down on the edge of the seat next to Josh. He looked almost as disconcerted by her unexpected arrival as she felt upon seeing them all here.

"Was there a reason you came by?" Josh asked, regarding her curiously. "Seems to me you were in a bit of a huff when you left the site this morning."

"I got over it," she said, regretting her change of heart now that she was here and squirming uncomfortably under so many fascinated gazes.

"The woman's hungry, same as everyone else here," Nadine said, coming to her rescue. "Stop trying to make such a big deal of it. The rest of us are having burgers, Maggie. What would you like? I'll go tell the waitress."

"A burger's fine," she said, then glanced across the table and caught Amanda looking at her. She forced a smile. "How did things go at the site after I left this morning?"

Amanda grimaced. "Fine, if you enjoy having a confrontation with a big blowhard."

"George Winslow, I assume," Maggie said sympathetically. "He didn't upset you too much, did he?"

"Oh, we exchanged a few words," Amanda said.

Josh chuckled. "That's like saying David just tickled Goliath with his slingshot. Amanda gave him hell."

His admiration for the woman grated on Maggie's nerves, but she couldn't help sharing it. She knew what it took to stand up to someone like Winslow, having done it herself, something Josh had obviously forgotten all about.

"Good for you," she told Amanda, then glanced at Nadine. "I don't suppose you jumped into the fray, as well."

"Does a chicken have feathers?" Nadine replied. "Of course I did. I couldn't let that old windbag have the final word, could I?"

Maggie laughed. "Sounds like things got interesting after I left."

"Where did you run off to?" Nadine asked. "You usually stay for the whole day."

"I had some things to take care of at my gallery," Maggie said. She glanced at Josh and added, "A good thing, too, since Brian had shown up."

Josh stiffened and his attention shifted fully to her. "He didn't get out of line, did he?" he asked, frowning.

"Hold it," Nadine interjected. "Who's Brian?"

Maggie gave them a brief description of the situation between Brian and Ellie. "But he was apparently on good behavior this morning. Vicki never heard him raise his voice, and she told me later that he left the gallery meek as a lamb, so obviously Ellie was able to placate him."

"I don't like the idea of him coming around there," Josh said. "I think I should have a talk with him."

"The situation is under control," Maggie insisted. "I think Vicki has more sense than I ever gave her credit for having. She won't let things get out of hand. And Ellie's on guard now."

"Even so, by the time either one of them had a chance to react, he could have destroyed some of the gallery's most expensive paintings," Josh countered. "You saw what he did to Ellie's work. I doubt it took him long."

"He was on a rampage and it was personal," Maggie said. "He doesn't care about the other works I have on display."

"You can't be sure of that," Josh protested. "Especially if he concludes you're interfering in his relationship with Ellie."

Maggie decided to downplay what Ellie had told her about Brian's threat to ruin her reputation. Better to let Josh think she and Ellie had everything completely in hand. "It's okay, Josh. Rest assured that Ellie and I have a plan to take care of Brian once and for all."

Rather than looking impressed, he scowled. "Why does that send a chill down my spine?"

Warren frowned, as well. "Maggie, are you sure this

plan of yours, whatever it is, won't just make things worse? You can't reason with a person who's out of control and capable of the kind of violence you described."

"We're not going to try to reason with Brian," she explained patiently. "We're going to counter his threats and humiliate him so badly he'll have to leave town."

Nadine whistled. "Honey, are you sure that's the smartest approach? Sounds to me a lot like waving a red flag at a bull."

"No, it's not smart," Josh said, his scowl deepening. "No way, Maggie. Whatever scheme you have in mind, forget it. You're playing with fire. Remember, I've seen what this man's capable of doing. So have you."

"I'm not afraid of him," she said stubbornly.

"Perhaps you should be," Warren said with evident concern. "I've seen cases like this before. Things can escalate more quickly than anyone anticipates."

"I think Maggie's doing exactly the right thing," Amanda said, startling them all.

Maggie was grateful for the support, but surprised it came from Amanda. "You do?"

"The only way to deal with a bully is head-on," Amanda said staunchly. "They count on people being afraid of them. That's how they win."

"Well, when you put it that way, I agree," Nadine said. She faced Maggie. "You need any help at all, sweetie, you can count on me."

Josh groaned. "Dear heaven, we've got a group of vigilantes on our hands," he said to Warren, who merely shrugged.

"No, son, what you have are three women who know

a thing or two about looking out for themselves," Nadine retorted.

Maggie nodded. "I'm sorry if that offends your deep-rooted macho need to come to the rescue."

Heat flared in Josh's eyes at her comment, and she knew at once that she'd pushed him just a little too hard.

He nudged her in the ribs with his elbow. "Out of the booth. We need to talk in private."

"Not till we've eaten," she said just as determinedly.

He leveled a look at her that would have intimidated her under any other circumstances, but with Amanda and Nadine in her corner, she felt braver.

"What?" she mocked. "Not soon enough?"

"Oh, I can wait, if you can. By the time we've finished dinner, I imagine I will have worked up a full head of steam over this."

Maggie's gaze never wavered. "Knock yourself out."

Nadine looked from Maggie to Josh, then slid out of the booth and beckoned to Warren. "Sweetie, why don't we get all those burgers to go and leave these two to finish their discussion in private? Amanda, you and the kids can come by the motel, too. It's a nice night. We'll have a picnic."

"Good idea," Amanda said cheerfully, regarding Josh with amusement. "Any objections?"

"Not a one," he said tersely, his gaze locked with Maggie's.

Amanda turned to Maggie. "You okay with this, or would you like backup?"

"I'll be fine," Maggie assured her. "I've dealt with one bully today. I'm sure I have strength left to battle one more."

"Don't you dare compare me with George Winslow,"

Josh said indignantly. "I'm only trying to look out for your best interests."

"I'm sure that's what Mr. Winslow was telling himself the whole time he was trying to push Amanda around," Maggie retorted.

"Let's go," Nadine urged the others.

"Something tells me they're not even going to notice we're gone," Amanda said.

Maggie acknowledged their departure with a wave, just to prove Amanda wrong, but Josh's eyes never left Maggie's face.

"Why are you being so damn stubborn about this?" he demanded.

"Because I know what I'm doing," Maggie replied evenly. "I've been taking care of myself for a long time now, Josh."

"And you've run across a lot of guys like Brian?" he asked skeptically.

She faltered at that. "Well, no, not exactly."

"I have," he said bluntly. "I admire your gumption and your independent streak, Maggie. I truly do. But use your head. The guy's already proved that he's out to make trouble for Ellie and you. Don't get in his face and encourage him to do it."

"Give me a little credit. We're not being that obvious. He won't even see this coming."

Josh groaned. "Why doesn't that reassure me? Tell me the plan, at least."

Maggie explained about the contest. "It's a countermove, something to take the wind out of his plan to discredit me and the gallery. That's all."

Josh appeared somewhat mollified by the explanation. "I suppose that could work."

She smiled at his grudging admission. "Thank you."

"Don't be smug. I still think you're taking a huge risk. If he figures out what's going on, he'll be out to do more than discredit you. Don't make the mistake of thinking that his temper can only be directed at Ellie's art."

She shuddered at his certainty. "He won't find out," she said bravely. "The people officially sponsoring the contest will never link it to me or the gallery."

"Just in case, I want you to make me a promise. Keep my number on speed dial on your cell phone, and if Brian so much as walks by the gallery and looks in the window, I want you to call me. There's no need to be taking chances."

"I suppose I can do that," she conceded. "I'm just not sure why you think protecting me or Ellie is up to you."

He grinned. "You don't see anyone else standing in line for the job, do you? Not counting Nadine and Amanda, of course."

"I imagine the three of us could make Brian regret ever stirring up trouble," Maggie said confidently.

"Lord knows you could probably talk him to death," Josh agreed. "But just in case brute strength is required, call me, okay?"

Maggie figured it was a small enough concession. "Okay," she said at last.

"Thank you," he said just as solemnly.

Maggie took a bite of her burger, then met Josh's gaze. "Do you think everyone expected us to resolve things so peacefully?"

"Oh, I imagine Nadine was hoping for fireworks," he said.

"Of the sexual kind?" she asked, prompted by a streak of pure devilment.

Josh choked on his sip of soda, but then a grin spread across his face. "Why, yes, darlin'! I'm sure that's exactly what my mother was hoping for. Were you interested in making her wish come true?"

She kept her eyes locked with his. "The thought has occurred to me from time to time in recent days," she answered honestly. "You?"

"To be honest, the thought's been on my mind since the day we met."

She regarded him curiously. "Why haven't you done anything about it?"

"Because I live my life according to one guiding principle, which is, avoid all emotional entanglements and complications." He gave her a look that could have singed steel. "You, my sweet Magnolia, have entanglement and complication written all over you."

"Really? I'll have to see if I can scrub it off when I shower tonight."

"I could help," he offered, his expression innocent. "Make sure you get it all."

Maggie swallowed hard. She didn't think the offer was being made entirely in jest. It was an important reminder that sometimes flirting led straight down the road to perdition.

"Slow down," she advised Josh. "We've never even had a date. I don't think showering together is the way to start."

"I don't know why not. It works for me," he said.

Truth be told, Maggie thought, it would work for her, too, which was why she forced herself to slide out of the booth and make a dash for safety. "Another time, then."

She was halfway to the door when Josh called her name. She paused and reluctantly turned back to face him.

"Next time you want to play dangerous games, Magnolia," he advised in a lazy drawl, "be real careful who you're playing with. Not every man understands the rules."

She winked at him. "You do the same, sugar. Most women get the rules, but some of us just plain enjoy breaking them."

The taunt hung in the air and had it crackling with electricity. Maggie decided this was one time when a hasty retreat, no matter how Josh interpreted it, was the wisest course of action.

The second she was out the door and out of view, she practically ran to her car and flipped on the air-conditioning. Something told her, though, that it was going to take a lot more than a blast of icy air to cool her down tonight.

13

Josh dreaded going back to the motel. Something told him the days were long past when Nadine would have been so caught up in her own drama that she wouldn't care about his. For all he knew he'd find Amanda, the kids and Warren sitting there, too, awaiting details about his time alone with Maggie. He wasn't sure whether he was up to facing all their fascinated inquiries about why he was coming home alone. He wasn't very clear about why that was himself. A few weeks ago, he might have chased after Maggie and done something about all that heat sizzling between them.

Despite his lack of enthusiasm for facing anyone, he dragged himself back to his place and was startled to find the courtyard empty and the lights out in Nadine's room. He was about to count his blessings when he opened the door to his own room and found Nadine stretched out on his bed watching a pay-per-view movie. The fact that it was a romantic comedy gave him hives. It meant she was all psyched up for a happy ending.

"Is there something wrong with the TV in your room?" he grumbled, cursing the fact that the motel owner had fallen under Nadine's spell and let her in whenever she came up with a plausible excuse.

"I was waiting up for you," she said, clearly not taking offense at his tone. Maybe she was oblivious to it. "I was afraid I wouldn't hear you come in if I waited next door."

"Yeah, that would have been a shame, all right."

Nadine frowned and switched off the TV. "How did things go with Maggie?"

"We talked. I think we're on the same page now."

Nadine regarded him with dismay. "You talked? That's it? What is wrong with you?"

"Did you expect me to throw her across the table and make love to her right there?" he asked, unable to keep the impatience out of his voice.

"Given the sparks flying when we left, it wasn't beyond the realm of possibility."

"She's a lady, Nadine," he explained with exaggerated patience. "And, believe it or not, I'm a gentleman. I do recognize some boundaries. Besides, Maggie and I do not have that kind of relationship. In fact, we don't have any relationship at all."

"Well, if you ask me, that's a crying shame. Both of you need to expand those boundaries to include a little more excitement."

"You turning up here was more excitement than I've had in a long time," Josh said wryly. "I'm still grappling with that one."

Nadine rolled her eyes. "Oh, please, it's hardly the same thing."

"Believe me, I'm aware of that. Now, could you skedaddle? It's been a long day and I'm beat."

She gave him a look filled with amusement. "Frustrated, too, I imagine."

He scowled at her. "I am not discussing this with you. You missed your chance to have the birds-and-bees talk with me twenty years ago."

"I could help," she persisted. "I know a lot about relationships."

"None of it good, from what I've observed."

"Yes, well, we learn more from the bad than we ever do from the good, which pretty much makes me an expert. You'd be wise to benefit from my mistakes," Nadine said.

"I'll consider that," he said, not intending to do any such thing.

She remained undaunted. "If you change your mind, I'm right next door."

"That's not something I'm likely to forget."

She actually looked a bit hurt, and Josh realized he'd been the cause, but before he could apologize, she pasted on a cheerful smile.

"I know you don't mean that the way it sounded," she said, giving him a peck on the cheek. "Good night, sweetie."

Josh sighed, swallowing his guilt. "Good night, Nadine."

He watched her leave with her spike-heeled sandals dangling from one finger. He noticed then that her nails were short and unpainted for the first time he could ever recall. It made her seem oddly vulnerable. After her initial protests, she hadn't complained once about losing her brightly painted acrylic nails, which confused him. It wasn't like her. In fact, she was complaining about very little these days. She was doing whatever he asked of her and then some.

Was Nadine less shallow than he'd given her credit for being? Or had she matured when he wasn't around?

Then, again, maybe he was the one who was finally growing up and learning to give his mother the benefit of the doubt.

There had been little question when her mother called at barely 9:00 a.m. inviting Maggie to lunch that it was a command performance.

"We'll have lunch at the club," Juliette said emphatically, not waiting for Maggie's reply. "I made a reservation for twelve sharp. Your father will be there, too, and you know how he hates to be kept waiting."

"What's this about?" Maggie asked, instantly suspicious. Her father never left downtown on a weekday. He had his routine down pat. He'd kept the same schedule for years. He and his cronies smoked cigars and discussed their investments. It wasn't something he'd give up lightly. If he'd canceled his usual lunch to drive all the way over to the country club, then there had to be some sort of catastrophe.

"We'll discuss it when we see you," her mother said, her tone giving away nothing.

"Is somebody dying?" Maggie asked, leaping to the only conclusion she could come up with for the unusual midday meeting. "Just tell me if you or Father are sick. Don't make me wait to hear it in a public place."

Juliette gasped at the suggestion. "Of course not. Your father and I are in perfectly good health. Why would you even mention such a thing?"

"Because Dad's a creature of habit. He doesn't go gallivanting off to lunch with the family on a Monday unless there's a real crisis."

Her mother sighed heavily. "Try not to let your imagination get the better of you, Magnolia. Your father can be flexible when it's required of him. We'll see you at twelve o'clock."

She hung up before Maggie could ask anything more. Maggie frowned at the receiver, then slowly placed it back in its cradle.

Not five minutes later, it rang again. This time Dinah was on the line.

"What is your mother up to?" she demanded before Maggie could do more than mutter a greeting.

"My mother? You've talked to her this morning?" The day was getting weirder by the minute.

"Not two minutes ago," Dinah confirmed. "She wants me to join you all for lunch today. Actually she didn't even wait for me to check my schedule. She just assumed I'd be there. Fortunately I don't have to go in to the station till three this afternoon."

"Oh, brother," Maggie said, beginning to get the picture. "Want to bet that Warren's invited, too?"

"Why on earth would your mother invite your ex-fiancé?"

"Because something tells me there's about to be another of those intervention things you're so fond of," Maggie said.

"Why would your mother stage an intervention now? Seems to me you're doing great."

Maggie laughed. "You must not know about me getting into a sparring match with George Winslow at the site day before yesterday. I'm sure he told my parents I was impertinent. In their world, that's worthy of immediate parental attention."

"Everybody's impertinent to George. It's the only way to deal with him," Dinah said. "I think I'll skip lunch, if you don't mind. It doesn't sound like much fun."

"Believe me, I'd skip it, too, if there wouldn't be hell to pay later," Maggie replied. "As for you, I need you there for moral support."

"I have a better idea," Dinah said.

"Oh?"

"Invite Josh. He ought to be quite a distraction. Something tells me he'll render your mother absolutely speechless."

Maggie smiled. He certainly had that effect on her from time to time. "That *is* a thought," she agreed. "Maybe I will."

Of course, her motives weren't entirely pure. If she did ask him to come along and he agreed, she'd be seriously indebted to the man. After that tantalizing little game they'd played the night before, finding out how he'd exact payment could be…interesting. Then again, maybe he'd just consider it payback for the night he'd dragged her to that first awkward dinner with Warren and Nadine and call it even. Whichever way things went, she might at least gain more insight into the way the man's mind worked.

Josh wasn't crazy about the gleam in Maggie's eye when she showed up on his doorstep just as he climbed out of the shower. Something told him she hadn't come to make good on her recent promise of sex sometime in the future.

"I need you," she said, trying to keep her gaze averted from his bare chest and the beads of water still trickling down his skin.

He brightened at her admission. Maybe he'd gotten it wrong after all. How convenient that he was wearing nothing more than the jeans he'd dragged on when he'd heard her knock. "Yes?" he said, determined to be sure. "For?"

"Oh, get that smirk off your face. I need you for lunch," she said.

"You have an odd way of inviting a man out," he said, trying to hide his disappointment. He reached for a T-shirt and dragged it over his head now that he knew sex wasn't on Maggie's agenda.

"Yes, well, I'm out of practice. Are you free or not?"

"When?"

"Now. I have my mother, my father and who knows who else waiting to ambush me at the country club."

"And I'm supposed to do what?"

"That whole macho protective thing you're so fond of," she said. "You should be in hog heaven."

"Why do you need protection from your folks?"

"To be honest, I'm not entirely sure, but I suspect it has something to do with my lack of manners when speaking to George Winslow. In my world, that's cause for alarm. Now, will you come or not? Do I need to remind you that you owe me one?"

He wasn't sure whether he was intrigued by the idea of meeting people who could intimidate Maggie or just plain hungry, but he nodded. "Oh, I'll come," he said. "It'll be fascinating to see how your world operates."

"That's what you think," she muttered darkly, then added more cheerfully, "don't let my mother scare you."

"Sweetheart, there's only one woman on the planet who scares me."

"Really? Who?"

"You."

Maggie grinned. "Then you'll love this," she assured

him. "Some say she and I have quite a lot in common, much as she dislikes admitting it."

"This I've got to see. Give me five minutes to change into something suitable for meeting and greeting the upper crust of Charleston society."

Maggie surveyed his jeans and T-shirt, then shook her head. "You'll do just fine like that."

Josh chuckled. "Going for the shock value, darlin'?"

"Exactly."

"If this weren't promising to be so much fun, I'd be insulted."

"Don't be. Out of all the men in Charleston, I chose you for this mission. That ought to tell you something."

"That you were desperate?"

"Nope. That you have certain essential qualities that are perfect for the occasion."

"Such as?"

"The only thing I've ever seen make my mother lose her train of thought," Maggie said, "is a gorgeous man. One look at you and she'll forget why she invited me for lunch. In fact, with luck, she may not even notice I'm there."

"What about your father? Didn't you say he'd be there, too?"

"He'll be so thrilled he can leave and go back to work that nothing else will matter."

Josh laughed. "Then this promises to be an all-around good time." He sobered and met her gaze. "Forget that prior debt. This is above and beyond. You're going to owe *me*."

"I suspected you'd see it that way. Can't say I blame you."

"Owing me doesn't scare you?"

"Not half as much as facing my mother does."

"Then I suppose I owe your mother. Kind of rounds things out, doesn't it?"

"You have no idea."

Josh thought maybe he did.

Even though Josh had backed every confrontation she and Amanda and Maggie had had with George Winslow, Nadine knew that Josh was genuinely worried that the man could stir up real trouble with the building inspector. She knew instinctively that delays would be costly and time-consuming and they all wanted Amanda to have her home by Thanksgiving. Maybe for once she could do something to make her son's life easier. Smoothing troubled waters when it came to men was one of her knacks. She picked up the phone and called Amanda at work.

"Honey, do you have any idea how I could track down George Winslow?" Nadine asked.

"Why would you want to talk to him?" Amanda asked.

"Somebody obviously needs to. This nonsense has gone on long enough."

"Oh, Nadine, stay away from him," Amanda pleaded. "You've seen what he's like. Nothing good will come of confronting him."

"I have to try. I know Josh thinks I made things worse when I told the man off the other day, so it's up to me to fix it."

"We all told George off and there's nothing you can say to fix the situation," Amanda insisted. "George will never listen to reason, not in a million years. We just have to let this play itself out and trust that things will turn out okay."

"That's not what you were saying to Maggie just last night. You were the very first one to say bullies needed to be taught a lesson."

"Some bullies, Nadine. Not necessarily George Winslow and definitely not by you."

"Are you going to tell me where I can find him or do I have to start poking around in all the restaurants and clubs in Charleston till I run across him? That could take days, and something tells me there's no time to waste. He's probably snooping around at the site again right now or down at City Hall raising a ruckus with the building inspectors."

"Then look for him there and leave me out of it," Amanda suggested.

"Are you going to tell me where the man goes for lunch or not?" Nadine persisted.

Amanda sighed. "I want to go on record telling you that I think this is a huge mistake."

"Okay, I get it. Now tell me where I'll find him."

"It's been a long time since I've run into him socially, you understand, but he used to play golf at the country club every morning, then have lunch there afterward."

"Perfect," Nadine said. "It's almost lunchtime now."

"But you can't go barging into the country club," Amanda protested. "It's members and guests only. They'll toss you right back out. You'll wind up in the middle of an embarrassing scene."

Nadine didn't mention that embarrassing scenes were nothing new for her. "Not when I tell them I'm there as Mr. Winslow's guest, I'm sure," she assured Amanda. "Trust me, sugar, I've crashed fancier places than this. I know just how to handle it."

As soon as she hung up, she sorted through the outfits in her closet and found the most discreet suit she owned. She added the one piece of tasteful jewelry she'd managed to keep after her last marriage had blown up around her, then put on the subtlest bit of makeup. She could look classy when she had to. Between the outfit and her charm, she figured no one would keep her out of that country-club dining room till she'd found old Mr. Winslow and had her say.

Too bad he had such a sour disposition. Otherwise she might almost enjoy the prospect of sitting down across from him for a little intelligent conversation over a fancy meal. She was sick to death of burgers, and much as she adored her son, he wasn't inclined toward chitchat, at least not with her.

Unfortunately, as it was, she had a hunch that even if she did manage to order and eat a few bites before Winslow had her tossed out she'd still wind up the day with nothing more than indigestion.

The country-club dining room preferred by Juliette was a place of damask napkins, fresh flowers and polished silver. Waiters moved silently among the antique tables, delivering food with impeccable timeliness. The stiff, formal setting had always made Maggie want to send china crashing to the floor just to set off some commotion in the room. Maybe her arrival with Josh on her arm would accomplish the same goal.

She stood in the doorway, letting her eyes grow accustomed to the darkened interior.

Beside her Josh muttered wryly, "Is anyone in here actually alive?"

"That's a matter of conjecture," Maggie responded. "I'm pretty sure that at least one of the men over in that corner had himself freeze-dried on his death and left there to read his newspaper in perpetuity."

Josh shuddered. "I don't suppose it's occurred to anyone to open the drapes?"

"Not when the candlelight is so flattering to aging complexions," Maggie said.

"No wonder you rebelled."

"Trust me, this place is only the tip of the iceberg that was my life. Now let's go meet Mother, who's the rest of it."

Maggie found Juliette at her usual table in the center of the room, from which she could observe and be observed by everyone else. Her mother's eyes widened, and not entirely in appreciation at the sight of Josh.

"Well, this is unexpected," Juliette said.

"Mother, meet Josh Parker. And don't worry, he won't throw your seating chart out of whack. He's taking Dinah's place."

"Mrs. Forsythe," Josh said. "I see now where your daughter got her beauty."

Juliette's gaze snapped from Maggie to Josh at that. "You flatter me," she said, but there was a hint of approval in her eyes.

"It's not flattery if it's true," Josh said, holding out a chair for Maggie, then seating himself between her and her mother. "Now, I expect you to tell me all about your daughter. She's an enigma to me."

Juliette studied him intently. "What is it you'd like to know?"

"Whether she's always as stubborn as a mule, for starters."

Maggie watched her mother's lips twitch at the question.

"She's always been a handful," Juliette confirmed, then leaned toward him. "But then, so was I."

Josh chuckled. "I imagine you were."

Mission accomplished, Maggie concluded, sitting back and starting to relax. This was going better than she could possibly have imagined.

At the stroke of twelve, as announced by the antique grandfather clock across the room, Frank Forsythe crossed the dining room and pulled out a chair. He scowled at Josh.

"Who're you?" her father demanded.

"Josh Parker, sir, a friend of Maggie's."

"Do I know you?"

"No, sir, I don't believe we've met."

"I know that name, though. Parker, Parker," he muttered. His expression brightened, then faded. "You're the one building the house that has George in such an uproar."

Josh nodded. "Indeed I am."

Juliette's eyes widened. "You are? Oh dear, this could prove awkward."

Maggie sat up straighter. "Why would it be awkward, Mother?"

"Because she invited me to join you," George said, pulling out a chair and sitting down next to Maggie. "Juliette, you've always arranged lively parties, but you may have outdone yourself today."

Maggie glanced at Josh to see how he was taking this turn of events, but she couldn't read anything from his expression. In fact, his gaze seemed to be directed toward the entrance to the dining room. When he muttered an oath, she whirled around to see what had caught his attention and spotted Nadine.

"What the hell is she doing here?" he said, getting to his feet just as Nadine saw him. "I'll get her out of here."

"Don't you dare," Maggie said, standing. "I'll ask her to join us."

"Magnolia, where are you going?" Juliette called after her.

"I'll be right back, Mother. I've just seen someone Josh and I know. I'm going to invite her over."

Josh was right on her heels. "Don't do this," he warned. "I'll take her home."

"You most certainly will not." She beamed at Nadine. "Come join us."

Nadine looked from Maggie's smiling face to Josh's scowling one and backed up a step. "I had no idea you two would be here."

"Then why are you here, Mother?" Josh demanded.

"Actually I wanted to talk to George Winslow. Amanda told me I might find him here."

Maggie beamed. "Then you're in luck. He's at our table. Isn't this the perfect coincidence?"

Nadine blinked at that. "He is? Whose idea was that?"

"Not mine," Maggie said. "My mother's the one with the strange taste in dining companions."

"Maybe I should go," Nadine said, looking more hesitant than ever.

"That was my suggestion," Josh said, then added grimly, "Maggie has other ideas."

"Absolutely. I say the more the merrier. Before you got here, the odds were definitely stacked against me and Josh. You'll even things up."

"Are you sure?" Nadine asked.

"Positive," Maggie assured her. "I can't tell you the last time I looked forward to a luncheon with more enthusiasm."

Beside her, Josh chuckled for the first time since Nadine's unexpected appearance. "Don't overdo it, darlin'."

Maggie patted his cheek. "You ain't seen nothin' yet, *darlin'*. It's going to be a genuine pleasure watching my mother's social graces be put to a real test."

14

From the moment he'd spotted Nadine in the doorway, Josh had been filled with a sense of dread. No good could come from her being here, not with George Winslow in the room, to say nothing of Maggie's folks.

He was especially worried about Juliette. She'd obviously had an agenda for this luncheon, and Maggie was turning it on its head. He didn't want Nadine caught in the crossfire, but he couldn't think of a single way to keep this disaster from playing out.

When they arrived back at the table, Maggie's father was deep in conversation with George. Still, at the arrival of the women, both men instantly stood, their manners instinctive. Then Winslow realized who was with Josh and Maggie.

"You!" he said, his voice filled with blustery disdain. He whirled on Juliette. "You invited this woman to join us? What on earth were you thinking?"

Juliette returned his indignant look with a considering expression. "I'm as surprised as you are, but I gather you've met?"

"More than once, unfortunately," George confirmed.

"Well, I haven't had the pleasure," Juliette said

smoothly. She held out her hand to Nadine. "I'm Maggie's mother and I'm delighted you could join us," she said graciously, though it was plain she had no idea on earth who Nadine was. It was apparently enough that Nadine's mere presence had riled George Winslow. To Josh she appeared surprisingly eager to fan those sparks.

No one looked more startled by Juliette's words than Maggie. Yet Nadine seemed to accept the greeting as her due. She gave Juliette one of her totally disingenuous smiles and said, "Thank you for allowing me to come at the last minute, Mrs. Forsythe. I didn't mean to interrupt your luncheon. I had no idea my son and Maggie would be here."

"Ah, you're Josh's mother," Juliette said, as if that explained everything. She waved to get the attention of a waiter. "Johnson, we need another place setting, if you please."

"Certainly, Mrs. Forsythe."

"You're allowing this woman to stay?" George demanded.

"Oh, sit down, George," Juliette said impatiently. "It's my luncheon. You don't get to approve the guest list."

"Perhaps not, but I also don't have to stay."

Nadine turned to him and inquired mildly, "You're not afraid of me, are you, Mr. Winslow?"

The florid color in his cheeks deepened. "Afraid?" he scoffed. "Hardly. But I've allowed you to offend me in public twice already. Why should I permit it again, especially here among friends and associates of mine?"

"And here I came all this way just to see you and apologize," Nadine said sweetly, leaning close and holding his gaze. "Won't you stay and allow me to do it properly?"

Winslow looked understandably confused by her cheerful demeanor. Even Josh was befuddled by this turn of events. What had possessed Nadine to decide to apologize to a man she clearly held in disdain, and justifiably so, in Josh's opinion? Not that his opinion seemed to count for much with this crowd.

"You really came here to see me and apologize?" Winslow asked skeptically.

"Indeed I did," Nadine assured him.

"Now will you sit down, George?" Juliette demanded. "You're drawing attention to us. If anyone's creating a spectacle, it's you."

Winslow finally sat, but Josh noticed he kept a careful distance between himself and Nadine. Josh leaned down and whispered in Maggie's ear, "What do you think she's up to?"

"I have no idea, but it's taken the heat off me, so I don't really care."

"I thought that's why I was here," he commented.

She grinned. "I think your work here is done. Nadine's stolen the spotlight."

Josh wasn't comforted. "Why does that scare the daylights out of me?" he muttered.

"I have no idea," Maggie said. "She's your mother."

"And I haven't known what to make of her since I was a toddler."

"Sit back and relax. Maybe you'll learn something," Maggie advised. "Nadine looks like she knows how to handle herself in any situation. She didn't bat an eye at this turn of events."

Josh didn't doubt for an instant that there would be a lesson learned from all this. He just hoped it didn't involve jail time.

Never in a million years would Maggie have dared to assemble this precise gathering of guests, but to her complete astonishment, it appeared to be working in some bizarre way. Nadine's appearance had caught George completely off guard, and he was slowly succumbing to her self-deprecating brand of humor. Even Juliette seemed to be watching their exchange with amazement.

"Mother, you've done it again," Maggie said with genuine appreciation when Josh excused himself to make a phone call, probably to report to Caleb the miracle that was taking place at their table—détente between George and Nadine.

Juliette regarded her with a puzzled expression. "Done what?"

"Pulled off the impossible. Your luncheon is a total success."

"Don't give me the credit for that. You can thank your young man and his mother for making things interesting. I'd been anticipating a dreary exchange between your father and George about how misguided you've been over this whole construction business. I assumed the most exciting moment would come when you got your back up and stormed out." She regarded Maggie with a knowing look. "I assume this has turned out precisely the way you'd hoped."

"I had nothing to do with Nadine's arrival," Maggie said.

"But you deliberately included Josh to distract me, did you not?"

Maggie grinned. "Perhaps."

"Well, the tactic certainly worked. He's quite distracting."

Maggie thought she heard a note of real approval in her mother's voice. It caught her by surprise. "Then you like Josh?"

"Does my opinion really matter?"

"Of course," Maggie said.

Juliette's lips curved slightly. "If I'm hesitant in expressing it, it's because my approval usually sends you running in another direction."

"I'm trying to get past that, but just so you know, Josh is not *my* young man. He's a friend."

Juliette studied her thoughtfully. "That's something new for you, isn't it?" she asked.

Leave it to her mother to understate the obvious. "I've been friends with other men," Maggie said testily.

"Very few, darling. You have passionate flings that you know will alarm your father and me, and then you move on. Warren was the one exception to that pattern."

"And just look how swimmingly that went," Maggie said. "I think it's probably best if we leave Warren out of this. He has nothing to do with anything anymore."

"And Josh? Would you prefer to leave him out of the conversation, as well?"

"That's probably a good idea." Though she'd said earlier she wanted to hear her mother's opinion, it was true that it did tend to affect her in a perverse way. If Juliette approved of Josh, it would send Maggie fleeing. If her mother had taken an instant dislike to him, Maggie would most likely fling herself into his bed later this afternoon. Maybe for once, she ought to base where things went on her *own* opinion of the man.

And that seemed to be changing hourly, given how he'd scored on every test she'd thrown at him.

Nadine knew there was a lot riding on her ability to get through to George Winslow. She'd grown quite fond of Amanda and her children since she'd gotten to know them. She wanted to see them settled in a home of their own. And, of course, she wanted to prove to Josh that she was determined to turn her life around and be the kind of mother he could be proud of. After all the mistakes she'd made, she knew it would take quite a lot to convince him she'd changed.

Every time she was tempted to tell George he was a pompous ass, she bit her tongue and smiled instead. It was taking a terrible toll on her, but it seemed to be having a mellowing effect on him. In fact, she was discovering he could be quite charming when they stayed away from the topic of building Amanda's house.

"You know, George, you should lighten up more often," she told him bluntly when everyone else at the table had their attention focused elsewhere. "You're a real handsome man when you're not scowling at everyone."

"And you're refreshingly honest," he admitted with evident surprise. "Of course, that's a less attractive trait when you're telling me off."

She laughed. "I'm afraid that's part of the package. I don't hold back."

"Sure you do," he corrected. "You think I don't know how hard it's been for you not to rip into me today? I can see it in your eyes, Nadine, but you're controlling your temper because you think it'll help your son."

She opted for honesty. "Okay, you caught me. This job's real important to Josh and I like Amanda. I don't want to see someone come along and mess things up for them. You have the power to do that."

"So you decided to make nice with me," he concluded.

She nodded.

"That took gumption, I'll give you that. So did getting up in my face when we ran into each other before. Not many people would risk that, knowing the influence I have in this town."

She shrugged. "I didn't have a lot to lose."

"But your son and Amanda did," he concluded. "Otherwise, you wouldn't have backed down, am I right?"

She smiled. "Afraid so."

He fell silent, his expression troubled. "I suppose you might as well know that I haven't let this drop. I spoke to someone in the diocese this morning about having Caleb replaced. They're going to look into it."

Nadine regarded him with shock. "You did what? What is wrong with you?"

His back stiffened. "I felt I had no choice."

"We always have a choice, George. I can't honestly say that I know Caleb all that well, but I know he's been a real rock for Amanda and the kids. Everyone else seems to like and respect him. That ought to count for something. You're just acting out of spite because he wouldn't do your bidding."

He studied her with a genuinely perplexed expression. "You really think I'm wrong?" he asked as if the idea had never before occurred to him.

Nadine realized he'd probably never considered the possibility that he could be misguided about anything.

He'd probably spent his entire adult life surrounded by yes-men who never questioned a word he uttered.

"I know you're wrong," Nadine replied flatly, trying to think what she could possibly say to get through to him and make him do the right thing. "Caleb surely doesn't deserve to be fired for doing something decent for a member of his congregation. And if you'd just stop throwing your weight around and take the time to get to know Amanda, you'd see how much she deserves this break the church is giving her."

"I've known that girl since she was in diapers," he countered with a dismissive wave of his hand.

"But that's just it," she said, regarding him intently. "You knew Big Max's girl. You don't know the woman. Not many people could have faced what Amanda has and come out of it strong, instead of beaten down. That's an admirable thing, George. I think even that stubborn daddy of hers would be proud of her if he'd give her half a chance."

He sighed heavily. "To be honest, I don't disagree with that. That's exactly why I stirred things up about this house. I thought if I stopped it, Amanda would have to go back home. In my own bumbling way, I've been trying to push those two back together. It's been hell seeing the toll their separation has taken on my friend, even if it was all his own stubborn, hotheaded doing."

"But you're going about it all wrong," Nadine protested. "It's up to her daddy to take the first step, not Amanda. The way I heard it—you heard it, too—she's tried before and he's turned her away. Not even a dog will keep coming back once it's been kicked enough times."

She turned to Maggie, whom she knew had been blatantly eavesdropping. "You agree with me, don't you? If Big Max wants his daughter back, it has to be on her terms."

"Absolutely," Maggie said.

Nadine turned to Mrs. Forsythe, who'd also been openly eavesdropping on their exchange. "What's your opinion?"

"I have to admit that I never understood how Big Max could turn his back on his child." She glanced pointedly at Maggie. "There's nothing my daughter could do that would make me disown her."

Nadine switched her attention to Mr. Forsythe. "You've been awfully quiet," she said. "Do you approve of the way Big Max handled things with Amanda?"

"All that's water under the bridge," he said. "Seems to me now that making amends is more important. Life's short enough and family's the only thing that matters."

Nadine's gaze caught Josh's as he slipped back into his seat beside Maggie. "The only thing," she agreed. "I wish I'd understood that sooner myself."

"Well, I think we've all gotten far too somber," Juliette said decisively. "I propose we ladies order dessert, something totally decadent, and let the men go smoke their cigars and talk about golf or whatever it is they talk about when we're not around."

Maggie chuckled. "Maybe the men would like dessert, too, Mother."

"Perhaps so, but I'm sure they'd be happier having it someplace where they don't have to listen to us talk about the latest fashions."

"Absolutely," Mr. Forsythe said at once, getting to his feet with an eagerness that was matched by George. Josh rose a little more slowly, but he dutifully followed the two older men from the room.

"I think you just threw Josh into the lions' den," Maggie observed when they'd gone.

"He'll hold his own," Nadine predicted.

Juliette nodded. "Yes, something tells me that young man can hold his own with just about anyone." She glanced at Maggie. "Even my daughter."

Nadine chuckled. "You know, Mrs. Forsythe, I've been thinking the very same thing."

Josh insisted on dropping his mother off at the motel after lunch, then riding with Maggie back to Images.

"But how will you get home?" she protested. "We're in my car."

"I've been known to walk from time to time," he said, regarding her with amusement. "Or I can hang around till you've done whatever you need to do and then you can drive me back. I'm in no rush. I have plenty of time on my hands this afternoon."

Maggie regarded him suspiciously. "Is this about Brian? Are you just coming by to make sure he hasn't been over there making trouble today?"

Josh returned her gaze with amusement. "Can't you imagine that I'd just like to spend a few more minutes with you?"

"I can imagine it," she said. "I just don't believe that's your motive."

"And here I've been on my best behavior all afternoon."

"Ha!"

"Did I get out of line one single time?" He grinned. "Or is that what you're miffed about, that I didn't run my fingers up your thigh under that fancy tablecloth and give folks something to gossip about?"

"Actually I am very grateful that you kept your hands to yourself," she replied, despite the very telling heat that shot through her at the wicked suggestion.

"Why? Because you know you wouldn't have been able to resist me?"

"I could have resisted you," she said. "No problem."

Josh laughed. "Not buying it, sugar."

"Well, that has more to do with the size of your ego than with any lack of conviction on my part," she declared.

"I could prove you wrong."

She frowned. "How?"

"I could pull this car over right here, do a little of that exploring I missed at lunch, and have you crying for mercy in sixty seconds flat."

Maggie wanted desperately to dare him to try, but she knew with every fiber of her being that it would be a huge mistake. It was what he wanted. Hell, it was what she wanted. And it would lead straight to disaster.

"No, thank you," she said primly.

"Chicken," he accused.

"More than likely."

"What are you afraid of, Maggie?"

She wished she could explain it. Maybe it was the past repeating itself. Maybe it was the present getting out of hand. Or maybe it was the inevitable heartache lying just down the road. Whatever it was, it was enough to keep her from giving in to temptation.

"I'm still trying to figure that out," she told him candidly.

"Want any help?"

"As if you could possibly understand what goes on in my head," she said scathingly.

"Oh, I think I could," he retorted. "You and I are a lot alike."

The claim astounded her. "We most certainly are not!"

He laughed. "You so sure of that, sugar?"

"Absolutely, positively."

"Have you ever in all your life dated someone with the expectation it would lead to marriage, aside from your ill-advised decision to get yourself engaged to Warren, of course?"

"Warren counts," she muttered, because he *was* the only one. She'd waltzed into every other romance knowing full well it would lead nowhere. "What's your point, anyway?"

"You and I don't do the whole serious, happily-ever-after thing. You have your reasons. I have mine. The fact is, though, that we make deliberate relationship choices that we know have a short-term life expectancy."

Maggie couldn't deny that he'd pegged her exactly right, after all. Most disconcerting. "So what if we do? What does that have to do with me being scared of you? I don't see that it proves anything at all."

He glanced sideways and held her gaze. "You know how they say opposites attract?"

"Sure."

"Well, we both can testify that they might attract, but they don't last. So, the way I figure it is, we're two peas in one very explosive pod. Once we start steaming up the sheets, there'll be no turning back. We might be risking that independence we're both so fond of."

"You're assuming that we're going to have sex," she said. "It's not going to happen."

"Because you're scared," he said, coming back to that again. He grinned. "You'll get over it, darlin'. So will I."

It took a minute for the full import of what he was saying to sink in. "You're scared, too?"

"Terrified. If I thought this was going to be nothing more than a fling, it would have happened by now."

"Your confidence is highly annoying," she said.

"But my assessment is accurate and we both know it."

"I don't know any such thing."

"Darlin', you can deny this from now till the cows come home, but I have chemistry on my side. Mix all these pheromones together and sooner or later there's bound to be something spectacular going on."

"Then why aren't you running for the hills?"

He grinned. "Maybe my track shoes are just worn out."

"Or maybe you can't resist trying to get one more notch on your bedpost," Maggie assessed.

Josh ran a finger along the curve of her jaw. The touch was enough to make her clamp her thighs together. Lordy, the man was dangerous.

Then he lowered his head and brushed his lips over hers. Maggie bit back a moan of pleasure. His mouth settled in place and he gave the kiss his all. Rockets went off in her belly as her body seemed to melt into his. She couldn't have gathered a coherent thought if her life depended on it.

When he pulled away at last, a soft little moan escaped.

He winked as if her reaction was totally predictable. "You could be right about the whole bedpost thing," he confirmed, acknowledging her less flattering assessment. "I guess we'll just have to wait and see how things turns out."

Maggie had a feeling it would be a whole lot smarter to start building an impenetrable fortress with a moat around it.

15

Josh couldn't imagine why he'd spent the afternoon tossing out dares designed to stir up the already simmering chemistry between him and Maggie. They both clearly understood that the attraction was hot enough to melt whatever resolve usually kept them safe without him pointing it out. Maybe he'd been taunting himself, as well as Maggie, which was a damn dangerous game.

He shrugged off the disconcerting subject as he trailed Maggie into Images, relieved to have something less provocative to focus on.

Once again, he was struck by the coziness of the gallery. It made him long for things he thought he'd gotten out of his system a long time ago. He'd never lived in the kind of place that had personal touches scattered around to turn it into a home. He and Nadine had been lucky if they stayed in a motel classy enough to have its own national brand name printed on the soap wrappers.

They'd traveled light, as well. He'd been fortunate if she'd let him bring along a favorite toy truck or a book, because too much baggage slowed down their often hasty retreats. The lack of possessions and the dingy surroundings of his childhood had pretty much kept his expectations low. Possessions simply weren't something that mattered to him. But he was beginning to think that hominess meant more than he'd ever imagined.

At the door to her office, Maggie turned to him. "I'm here all safe and sound. You can go now."

Her dismissal annoyed him. Mostly to exasperate her, he shoved his hands in his pockets and held her gaze. "I thought maybe I'd stick around for a bit."

She gave him a perplexed look. "Why?"

"Because it'll irritate you if I do," he admitted with complete candor.

To his amusement, she deliberately shrugged as if it made no difference to her at all. Only the telltale pink in her cheeks gave away her exasperation.

"Suit yourself," she said. "But I have work to do."

"No problem. I'll just keep Ellie company out front till you're done. There are a few things I'd like to talk over with her, anyway."

"What things?" she asked, instantly wary.

"I just want her take on how things are with Brian these days."

"I've told you we have that situation under control," she said impatiently.

He nodded. "That's your perspective. Now I'd like hers."

She regarded him incredulously. "You don't believe me?"

"I believe that you're convinced that what you're saying is true. You may not be the best judge of Brian's temperament."

"And Ellie is?"

"She's known him a long time, right? She dated him. And you, what? Met him for two minutes? Besides, she's seen him more recently than you have."

She frowned at his accurate summary. "Okay, fine. Talk to Ellie, and then what?"

"I'll take you home."

"I have my car," she reminded him yet again. "Besides, I only live a few blocks away."

His unyielding gaze locked with hers. "Then it shouldn't take long to get there, should it?"

She looked as if her patience was at an end. But instead of arguing, she heaved a resigned sigh, went into her office and shut the door very firmly in his face. Josh chuckled at the defiant gesture, then turned around and went in search of Ellie.

He found her using some orange-scented polish on an antique desk. She was concentrating so intently on the mindless task that she jumped when he spoke to her. The reaction told him a lot about the state of her nerves. He didn't have any trouble guessing the reason for it.

He studied her with a narrowed gaze. "Does Brian still have you that jumpy?"

She frowned at the question. "You're the one who scared me."

"You knew I was in the gallery, Ellie."

"I thought you were still in the back with Maggie," she said, apparently persisting with the denial that her ex-boyfriend had anything to do with her nerves being on edge.

Josh decided to let that particular subject drop and come back to it from another direction, when her guard wasn't up. "How's your work going these days?"

"Not as well as it would be if I could work in my own studio," she confessed, her expression resigned. "The light sucks in here, but Maggie's convinced it's better for me to work here than at my studio at home right now, even though you changed the locks. I don't know why she's so set on this. Brian's not going to do anything."

Apparently she shared Maggie's optimism. Josh wished he were half as certain as they seemed to be that all the danger with Brian had passed. He decided to test her candor. "Has Brian been bothering you at all?"

Ellie hesitated, then admitted, "He's dropped by here a couple of times, but he hasn't made any more threats, if that's what you mean." She spoke with a touch of defiance, then amended, "At least not to me."

Josh frowned at the admission, wondering if Brian's threat had been more serious than Maggie had led him to believe. "Who has he threatened?"

"Maggie, in a way. Not that he'd hurt her," she rushed to add. "He hates the idea that she's planning to show my works here at the gallery. He's trying to come up with some way to get even."

"And how do you think he intends to go about getting even?"

When Ellie remained silent, he stared her down. "Ellie, what does Brian have planned? He has something in mind, doesn't he?"

She regarded him with dismay. "He says he'll ruin her reputation."

"Which is why you two came up with this whole contest scheme," Josh concluded, putting it all together. Maggie had been so busy downplaying things, she hadn't given him the whole picture.

Ellie stared at him with evident surprise. "You know about the contest?"

"Maggie mentioned it. How do you think he's going to react when he finds out he was set up?"

"I…" Her voice faltered. "I'm not sure."

"Yes, you are," Josh said. "He's going to be furious, isn't he? I certainly would be. No man likes to be made a fool of, especially by a woman he cares about. And he will blame you, won't he?"

"I guess," she said shakily, then lifted her chin in a brave show of defiance. "But Maggie's sure the plan will work. She's usually right about stuff like this. Me, I just want to paint. She's the one with a head for business."

"But you're the one who knows Brian," Josh reminded her. "I think that's what counts in this instance."

"You're really worried, aren't you?" Ellie asked, suddenly looking as frightened and vulnerable as she had on the night Brian had gone on his rampage at her studio.

Josh didn't relent. "Aren't you?"

She nodded slowly. "I can't say anything to Maggie because she's trying so hard to help, but I'd feel better if we'd never put this whole plan into motion. Brian's all caught up in the contest. He's so sure he's going to win. He keeps talking about the fantastic trip we could take with the prize money, even though I've told him over and over that I won't go anywhere with him."

"What does he say to that?"

"That I'll change my mind once he's gotten the recognition he deserves by winning the contest."

"Maybe he will win," Josh said. "Is he any good at all?"

"I think he has talent," Ellie said loyally. "But I showed Maggie a painting of his the other day and she says his work is derivative and mechanical, that there's nothing original or passionate about it."

Josh almost felt sorry for the man. It must be hell to care so deeply about something and know that your work will never quite measure up. Renovating historic properties might not be art, but it was the one thing Josh had always cared about and he knew he was good at it. The craftsmanship required was its own art form, and not every carpenter had the patience and skill for it. He was fortunate that Cord Beaufort had recognized his talent and given him an outlet for it. Cord wasn't lavish with his praise, but the amount of work he'd given to Josh spoke volumes.

"Isn't art one of those subjective things?" he asked Ellie. "Maybe his work just doesn't appeal to Maggie."

"To be honest, I think he's heard the same thing before," Ellie confessed. "He just refuses to accept that he's a better teacher than he is an artist. It eats at him. It's no wonder he's bitter and angry."

"That still doesn't give him the right to destroy the work of other artists," Josh said.

"I know that," Ellie said at once. "I've done everything I can to cut him out of my life. He knows he can't get into the apartment anymore because I changed the locks, so he stops by here, because I can't very well throw him out of a business that's open to the public."

"You could get a restraining order," Josh suggested, knowing he was probably wasting his breath.

Ellie immediately shook her head. "It would only infuriate him more," she insisted. "And besides, I don't think he would ever hurt me physically."

Josh wished he were as certain of that as Ellie was. Maybe he could find out which cops worked this neighborhood of downtown and make sure they kept a close eye on the place. Ellie and Maggie wouldn't even have to know.

Since it appeared Maggie wasn't especially eager to spend any more time with him today, maybe he'd go take care of that right now. He'd let her think she'd won. With a woman like Maggie, keeping her off balance could only be a good thing.

"I'm gonna take off," he told Ellie.

"Without saying goodbye to Maggie?" she asked, clearly surprised.

"Trust me, I think she'll be relieved."

Ellie grinned. "Getting a little too close for comfort, Josh?"

He laughed. "So she says."

"Good for you. Don't let her scare you off. After that disastrous mistake she almost made with Warren, she needs to be shaken back out of her comfort zone."

"And you think I can do that?"

"*You* know you can. Otherwise you wouldn't be hanging around her as much as you are."

"Are you suggesting I wouldn't waste my time on a lost cause?"

"Something like that," she said.

"Sweetheart, you've got it all wrong. Lost causes are my specialty."

At least they had been till he'd run into one very complicated cause: Maggie Forsythe.

Maggie shuffled papers around on her desk and got precious little work done. The thought of Josh stubbornly waiting her out annoyed the daylights out of her. She'd been taking care of herself long before he'd come along and she'd be doing it long after he left. What gave him the right to take on bodyguard duty, especially when she and Ellie both were convinced that Brian posed no real physical threat?

Tired of being cooped up and accomplishing nothing, she eventually poked her head out of the office and took a surreptitious look around. It was surprisingly quiet in the gallery.

"Ellie? Josh?"

"Right here, Maggie," Ellie called out cheerfully. "At least I am. Josh left a while ago."

A startling sense of disappointment washed over her. "Oh? How come?"

Ellie's lips twitched. "He seemed to think you'd be relieved."

"Well, I am," she replied.

"Of course you are," Ellie said, her skepticism plain. "That's why you look as if somebody snatched the last cookie you'd been saving for a snack."

"You're imagining things," Maggie insisted.

"Oh, really? Then you came out here hoping to find me all alone?"

"Absolutely."

Ellie laughed. "It's a good thing you're basically an honest person, because you are such a lousy liar."

Maggie frowned at her and sat down on the stool behind the register. Ellie was the second person today who thought they understood her. How could so many people think they understood her when she didn't understand herself? She'd even lost track of why she was so mightily resisting Josh. Then she remembered. It was the old patterns-and-guaranteed-heartache thing. She needed to keep reminding herself of that.

"Could we not talk about Josh?" she pleaded.

"Suits me, but he's obviously on your mind," Ellie said.

"That doesn't mean I want to talk about him," Maggie said. "Anything happen around here today?"

Ellie looked as if she might persist despite Maggie's plea, but she gave her a resigned shrug and said, "Okay, then, I'll stick to business. I sold Cleo Anderson's sculpture and one of Mrs. Decatur's prints."

Maggie brightened. "That's wonderful. I didn't think we'd ever unload that sculpture. I can't imagine what I was thinking when I brought it in here. Who bought it?"

"Some tourist with a New York accent and more money than taste," Ellie said, grinning. "We're shipping it up to her co-op on Park Avenue."

"And Mrs. Decatur's print? Who bought that?"

"A very sweet older lady from Savannah. She said it reminded her of her grandmother's garden."

"Perfect," Maggie said, genuinely pleased.

Mrs. Decatur was already in her sixties when she'd taken up painting as a hobby. When Maggie met her, she'd had a garden room in her home filled with paintings stacked against a wall gathering dust. Her latest work had been on an easel and had immediately caught Maggie's eye. Her praise, though, had fallen on deaf ears. It had taken Maggie a full year to persuade the woman to let the gallery make prints of her lovely watercolors. The signed, limited editions were hot sellers long after the originals had been snapped up for top dollar. It had given Mrs. Decatur a nice nest egg for her retirement.

Satisfied with the report of the day's business, she turned her attention to Ellie's future. "Let's talk about your show. I'm still thinking September or October. You have plenty of paintings ready now, so there won't be any pressure on you to meet some sort of deadline, though we can always use more if you have them finished."

A frown immediately creased Ellie's brow. "Maybe we should wait."

"For what?"

"Until this whole mess with Brian is over."

"The contest will be over by then. Unless I've completely misjudged him, he'll be gone."

"Not if he's seen any publicity for a showing of my work," Ellie said with certainty. "You'd have to start publicizing it at least a month ahead, right? That's what you usually do."

"Yes," Maggie admitted.

"It'll be like rubbing salt in a wound. Who knows what kind of reaction it would trigger? Maybe we should wait till November or even December," she said. "Or next spring."

Maggie studied Ellie closely, trying to figure out why she was suddenly so jittery about setting a date. "Did Josh upset you earlier?"

"What do you mean?"

"You've suddenly turned skittish about this show again."

"No, I'm just trying to be smart. It makes sense to be considerate of Brian's feelings so he doesn't get all worked up and come after you the way he threatened to. Why ask for trouble if we don't have to? What's the rush?"

Maggie considered Ellie's view and reluctantly concluded she might be right. "Okay, you have a point," she conceded. "But we can't have a show in December. It'll get lost in all the holiday commotion. And I don't want to wait until after the first of the year. I'll look over the schedule and think about November, though."

"Thank you," Ellie said fervently. "I think that's best. Besides, you have a big show coming up in a couple of weeks. I predict it's going to be such a smash and you'll be so busy, you'll be glad you don't have anything scheduled for right afterward."

"I suppose," Maggie said. "I just wish I wasn't afraid that when I try to pin down a date for November, you'll find some excuse then as well."

"I won't, I promise." Ellie brightened. "Oh, wait. I almost forgot to give you a message from Mitzi Lewis over at the Spoleto Festival. She says the contest entries are pouring in. It's more than they've ever had before."

"Did you ask if Brian's entered?"

Ellie shook her head. "I didn't want it to look as if we were favoring any specific artist."

"Yes, I suppose that's wise, but he is going to enter, right?"

"He told me he was. I've been trying not to act too interested, so he won't get suspicious."

"Maybe I'll go over tomorrow to the festival offices and take a look at the entries that have come in so far," Maggie said. "I'll see if his is there."

Ellie suddenly looked worried. "What if he changes his mind and doesn't enter, after all? You will have made this big donation for nothing."

"Not for nothing," Maggie assured her. "Having a

poster contest for the Spoleto Festival is still a worthwhile cause." It just wouldn't accomplish the goal she'd set out to accomplish—protecting Ellie and taking away any leverage Brian might have had to destroy the gallery's reputation. She wasn't really worried, though. Brian's ego was too big for him to back out of the contest now.

Josh had his conversation with a sergeant at the police station and immediately got the man's promise to make sure the patrols in the area around Maggie's shop kept a close eye on the business and on the women working there.

"It might be best if they don't realize they're under surveillance," he told Sergeant Rick Danville.

The officer chuckled. "Believe me, I get that. I've known Maggie forever and I know how stubborn she is. The less she knows, the better. Otherwise she'll be down here in the chief's office raising a ruckus about us wasting resources on babysitting her when there are real criminals on the street."

Josh grinned. "You do know Maggie, no question about it."

"You know she's in the habit of walking home, don't you?" Danville asked Josh, his expression filled with concern. "Her hours aren't real regular, so it'll be tough to be sure we're around when she sets out."

"Do what you can," Josh said. "I'll try to discourage her from that particular habit for the time being."

Danville gave him a commiserating look. "Good luck with that one. The way I see it, you telling her to be careful will have her out taking walks at midnight."

"You're probably right," Josh conceded. "I might be

able to prevent that if I threaten to post myself on her doorstep around the clock."

"Let me know if it comes to that," the sergeant warned. "I'd hate to have one of our guys hauling you in by mistake."

"So would I," Josh said. "And I wouldn't put it past Maggie to call here to make sure that's exactly what happens."

The sergeant looked down at his notes again. "Josh Parker." He looked up at him again. "You're the one in charge of building that house for Amanda O'Leary, aren't you?"

Josh nodded.

"It's a good thing you're doing. She's had a tough time of it."

"Thanks. Everyone helping is happy to be doing whatever they can to make sure she gets back on her feet."

"You have any trouble over there with anyone who doesn't feel that way, let me know," the officer said.

Josh's gaze narrowed. Had Winslow already been here trying to make trouble? "You've heard about the problems with George Winslow?"

"The chief has. So have a couple of other folks. The news has filtered down. We're to do whatever we can to keep the peace over there and see that Amanda's house gets built without a hitch."

That was a twist Josh hadn't expected. "Any idea who spoke to the chief?"

"I have my suspicions, but I can't say for sure."

Josh nodded. "Thanks for the information. It's good to know we have backup."

"All you need and then some. Maybe I'll stop by next weekend and help out if you need another volunteer."

"We can always use another pair of hands," Josh assured him. "And thanks for your help with Maggie."

"No problem."

As he left the station, Josh wondered who'd gone to the chief of police to intercede on behalf of the construction project. Maggie's folks had the clout, but would they have used it? He decided to swing back by Images to see if Maggie had any idea. There was another possibility, but given what he knew about Amanda's relationship with her father, it was a real long shot.

When he got to Images, the door was locked, but it was evident that Maggie was still inside. He could see a light burning in her office. He knocked on the door, waited, then knocked again.

She finally came into the gallery, caught a glimpse of him and stopped in her tracks. Then, as if she realized that any delay made it seem as if his arrival had too much significance, she squared her shoulders and crossed the room.

"You again!" she said when she'd opened the door.

"Just like that bad penny," he taunted. "I'm going to keep turning up."

"Why?"

"I thought we'd established that I'm after the annoyance factor."

"Then it's definitely working. You are not endearing yourself to me."

He grinned. "Probably for the best, don't you think? Otherwise who knows what sort of mischief we could get into."

"We will not now or ever get into any mischief," she said emphatically. "But then, I'm wasting my breath telling you that, aren't I?"

"Pretty much. Can I come in? Or, if you're ready to leave, I'll walk you home or ride with you if you want to take your car. There's something I wanted to talk to you about."

"Not Brian again," she said. "I think you did quite enough talking about Brian when you were with Ellie earlier. She's all skittish now."

"I'm sorry if I rattled her, but you both need to be on your guard where he's concerned," Josh said. "That's not what I want to discuss, though."

"Then what?"

He regarded her patiently. "Are we going or staying?"

"I haven't decided. We may be staying right here," she said with a touch of defiance in her tone.

Josh shrugged. "Suits me."

She scowled at that. "Oh, for heaven's sake," she finally muttered. "I'll get my purse and lock up."

They set out for her place a few minutes later, strolling in silence for an entire block before she said, "I thought you had something to discuss."

"I was just enjoying the companionable silence," he said. "It's such a rarity with you."

"Well, we're almost to my place, so you'd better talk fast, because you are not coming inside."

"Whatever happened to Southern hospitality?" Josh inquired sorrowfully.

"Mine died when I met you," she retorted.

"You wound me, sugar."

"I doubt it. Now, talk."

"I heard something while I was out this afternoon and I was wondering if you knew anything about it. Apparently someone called the chief of police and suggested he keep an eye on our construction project."

Maggie's expression immediately turned indignant. "Is that George's doing? I thought the worst he'd done was to speak to someone in the diocese to try to get rid of Caleb."

"Actually I think whoever made this call is on our side. It appears someone is intent on seeing that George doesn't get away with stirring up trouble."

Maggie seemed as perplexed by that as he had been earlier. "Really?"

Josh nodded. "I know. I was surprised, too. Think it might have been one of your parents?"

Maggie shook her head. "Not that they're above calling in a favor or two, but I'm pretty sure it wasn't them. I don't think they perceive George as a real threat."

"Then who else might have called? It had to be someone powerful enough for the chief to sit up and take notice and pass along the word to his men to see that we don't have any problems over there."

Maggie stopped in her tracks, her expression thoughtful. "You don't suppose…?"

"I'm thinking Big Max himself," Josh said. "But I don't know the man. Could he have stepped in?"

"If he did, that's huge. It means George is really acting on his own, not for Big Max. That would certainly yank the rug out from under George." Her expression brightened. "Maybe Big Max and Amanda will finally reconcile, after all."

"Since we don't know if he was behind it, we can't say anything to her, though," Josh cautioned. "It would be a shame to get her hopes up, only to find out he had nothing to do with it."

Maggie gave him an odd look. "You really are very protective of her. Maybe you should think about why that is."

"I've already told you that Amanda is a friend," Josh said, tired of her insistence that there was anything more between him and Amanda.

"And I'm having a hard time believing that," Maggie replied. "I guess we'll see who turns out to be right."

Before he could reply, she opened a wrought-iron gate, stepped into a small yard filled with roses and closed the gate behind her. "Thanks for walking me home," she said stiffly.

"Get used to it, darlin'. Until Brian packs his bags and takes off, or proves he's turned into a pussycat, consider me your shadow."

His statement seemed to make her panic. "I don't want you underfoot every time I turn around," she declared. "I won't have it."

"You don't really get a say."

"I'll have you arrested."

"You could try," he said complacently.

Her eyes widened. "You talked to the police this afternoon, didn't you? That's how you heard about somebody talking to the chief about Amanda's house. You were down there telling them to keep an eye on me and Ellie and Images."

So much for his plan to keep her in the dark. Apparently he was his own worst enemy. "I was," he confirmed.

"You had no right to do that," she said furiously. "None."

"Maybe not a right, but an obligation," Josh told her. "Besides, I can't afford to lose one of my most skilled helpers, not if we expect to have Amanda's place done by Thanksgiving."

He watched as she struggled over whether to be furious at his presumption or flattered by his praise of her carpentry skills. Her fury lost.

"You have a point. You do need me."

"Then don't raise a ruckus about the patrols. It's just a smart precaution, okay?"

"Okay, fine. Whatever. Do you want coffee before you head home?" she inquired. "Or something to eat?"

Josh grinned at the grudging invitation. "No, thanks, sugar. I think I'll eat where the air's not quite so frosty. I'd hate to wind up a lovely day with indigestion."

"You are so not amusing," she shouted after him as he strolled away.

"But I'm growing on you," he called back.

And the hell of it was, she was growing on him, too. Which meant he needed to kick his usual defenses back into high gear before he did something completely nuts and fell just a little bit in love with her and all her fascinating contradictions.

16

"When are you going to break down and ask the woman out?" Amanda asked Josh during a break on the construction site.

Josh reminded himself of the decision he'd made a few nights ago to shore up his defenses around Maggie. He didn't need someone pushing him to do the exact opposite, least of all Amanda.

"When hell freezes over," he told her, his tone grim and, hopefully, forbidding.

"I could make it happen," she said, her expression thoughtful, clearly not scared in the least by his sour attitude.

"Don't you dare," he said. "I will not thank you for it. Neither will she. We've discussed it and concluded it's a bad idea."

"You've discussed it?" Amanda said, looking intrigued. "Really? When was that?"

"After we had lunch with her folks the other day," he admitted, realizing even as he said it that he was opening up a whole new can of worms.

Naturally Amanda seized on the opening immediately. "The two of you had lunch with her parents? Isn't that the sort of thing that usually happens after a relationship starts to get serious? Did her father ask you if your intentions were honorable?"

"Of course not," Josh said impatiently. "Where do you come up with this stuff? The Southern Girl's Rules of Courtship?"

Amanda laughed. "I'm not sure that precise book is on the market, but in certain circles those rules most definitely exist."

"Well, this lunch thing wasn't even about us. It was about you, as a matter of fact."

Now she was the one who looked disconcerted. "Me? If it had something to do with me, why wasn't I included?"

"I didn't set the guest list. Maggie's mama did. I was a surprise guest, along with Nadine."

Amanda was beginning to look more shell-shocked than fascinated. "Your mother was there, too?"

"She showed up uninvited in search of George Winslow. I gather you had something to do with that."

"Good God. Nadine never said she'd found him. He was there with Mrs. Forsthye?"

Josh grinned. "Yep. It was quite the little party. I suspect some people in that stuffy old dining room were taking bets on how long it would be before someone was stabbed with a sterling-silver butter knife."

"But no one was killed?" she asked as if she honestly thought it was a possibility.

"Not even bloodied," Josh assured her. "I'm surprised Nadine didn't mention it. She was rather proud of herself. She's convinced she almost has George won over to your side. Right now she's working on him to call the diocese and tell them he made a mistake about Caleb."

"That'll be the day," Amanda said, her expression grim. "Caleb's already gotten a couple of calls from his superiors asking what the heck is going on over here."

Josh hadn't heard about that, but then, Caleb wasn't the sort of man who said much about his own troubles. "I'll have to tell Nadine about that. Maybe she can try working a little more of her magic."

"It's going to take more than magic to make George back down," Amanda said unhappily. "You must not have noticed the building inspector poking around here earlier."

Josh stared at her. "What are you talking about? What building inspector?"

"He was on the roof counting the nails in the shingles," Amanda informed him. "He said it had something to do with hurricane standards."

Josh bit back a curse. He needed to save his anger for the inspector, assuming the man was still around. "Where is he?"

"He left, looking disappointed, I might add," Amanda said. She grinned. "Good thing you made us use even more than the code requires, huh?"

"I do know how to do my job, Amanda."

"Never questioned that for a second," she said sweetly. "However, we seem to have gotten offtrack. We were talking about you and Maggie."

"You were," Josh said. "I was finished with that topic."

She regarded him curiously. "Why are you being so stubborn?"

"Because avoiding trouble is what I do, and Maggie is trouble. I repeat, I will not thank you for sticking your nose into this."

"Maybe it's not thanks I'm after," she retorted, a glint of amusement in her eyes. "Maybe it's the entertainment value of watching you squirm on the end of her hook."

"What is it with women?" he inquired testily. "None of you are happy unless everyone's paired up."

"That's the way of the world," Amanda said. "Two by two ever since Adam and Eve and Noah's ark. I'm sure Caleb can fill you in, if you haven't read the Bible lately."

He regarded Amanda curiously. "Tell me, then. After what you've gone through, are you anxious to find someone new?"

"Sure," she said. "You seem to forget that I loved my husband. I'm a believer in marriage, despite how things turned out. I'd like to find someone I can feel that way about again, maybe not tomorrow, but someday."

"You're crazy."

"I prefer to think of myself as optimistic."

Josh shook his head. "I don't get it. You and Nadine should know better than anyone that there are no happy endings, yet you both get all starry-eyed over the love thing."

She gave him a look filled with unmistakable pity. "How can you say there are no happy endings? Just look at the way my life is turning around. Sure, I lost my husband way too soon. It wiped out every dime we had in savings and I've had to struggle some, but look around here, Josh. All these people are on the building site every weekend, working to give me a new home. I'm surrounded by people who care about me and my kids." She nudged an elbow into his ribs. "Even you, grouchy though you are. How can I not be optimistic?"

He regarded her with admiration. "You're remark-able."

"No. I just don't see what good it does anyone to focus on the negatives and expect the worst, in life or in love."

He got the message. "The way I do?"

She nodded. "Exactly the way you do. Ask Maggie out, Josh. You know you want to."

"Maggie and I see each other plenty," he reminded her.

"A date's different."

He grinned. "How? More kissing?"

"Stop making fun of me. I'm serious. Ask her out."

He gazed into Amanda's lovely upturned face and wondered once again why she wasn't the one he'd developed a thing for. Maybe it was because she was so darned cheerful. He didn't want to rain on her parade.

Maggie, however, was another story. Maybe they could commiserate over a few drinks without getting all sentimental or developing any unrealistic expectations. And, to be perfectly honest, battling wits with her had brightened his days considerably. He hadn't expected to have so much fun on this ho-hum job that Cord had roped him into. Nor had he expected to take on the role of protector despite her objections.

Of course, there was that danger he'd mentioned to her—that they were two peas in a very explosive pod. He wasn't sure he wanted to risk getting burned.

"Maybe I will," he told Amanda just to pacify her and get her off his back. "One of these days."

She grinned at him. "You're not getting any younger, Joshua. Do it today."

"Why are you pushing so hard for this?"

"Because I'm hoping that once you finally show the woman you're interested in her, she'll stop staring daggers at me every time you and I talk. I thought we'd gotten past it, but apparently not."

"What?" he asked, immediately scanning the site for some sign of Maggie. Sure enough, she was watching the two of them with a sour expression on her face. There was the jealousy thing, right there in plain view, no question about it. He'd half hoped she'd gotten past that craziness, too, especially since it had never made a lick of sense in the first place. It was even more distressing to know that Amanda was aware of Maggie's reaction and that it made her uncomfortable.

Since it kept popping up, sooner or later he supposed he would have to find some way to prove once and for all to Maggie that he wasn't interested in Amanda in that way. Words obviously hadn't gotten the message across. He just didn't know if he was ready for the consequences of the actions that would convince her she'd gotten it all wrong.

Caught now, Maggie immediately looked away and slammed a hammer in the general direction of a nail. She was probably imagining his head in its place. Josh winced, guessing from the string of curse words she uttered that she'd split the wood.

"Now!" Amanda said, giving him a push. "Before we have to go and beg for more supplies from the lumber company."

Reluctantly, Josh headed in Maggie's direction.

Maggie turned Josh down flat. She knew it was the smart thing to do. It also gave her a tiny shred of satisfaction to see the dull red color climb into his cheeks and the stunned expression spread across his face.

"You're saying no?" he asked, as if he couldn't quite believe his ears.

"It's not a difficult word to understand, though I'm not surprised you're having trouble with it. I doubt most women utter it in your presence," Maggie said tartly. "I'm sure Amanda hasn't."

"Dammit, Maggie, this is not about Amanda," he said, his voice rising. "It's about me asking you out for a drink. Why the hell would I do that if there was anything going on between me and Amanda? Don't you think she's been through enough?"

Maggie faltered a bit under the heat of his response. "I do, but I'm surprised you recognize that."

Josh shook his head. "What is wrong with you? If you don't want to have a drink with me, fine, but don't make it about anyone else, Maggie. At least have the guts to be honest and say it's because you're scared."

"Scared? Me?" She feigned indignation. "You don't scare me."

He took a step toward her. "Really? I thought we'd established this the other day, but perhaps you still need convincing."

Maggie's heart started to race harder and faster than it had in years. And not entirely in panic, either. After their earlier kiss there was a healthy dose of anticipation mixed in. She forced herself to stand her ground. She would not let Josh get the upper hand, not even for an instant.

"Really," she said firmly. "You don't scare me."

The corners of Josh's mouth tilted ever so slightly. "You should be terrified."

"Oh?" The breathless quality in her voice irked her, but she made up for it by meeting his gaze with an unwavering look.

He tucked a callused finger under her chin, then ran the pad of his thumb across her lower lip. Maggie was rooted to the spot, lost in the depths of his turbulent brown eyes. Her pulse scrambled wildly.

"Scared to death," he said quietly, then leaned forward and settled his mouth on hers.

Even though she'd been expecting just that, anticipating it and dreading it at the same time, Maggie wasn't prepared for the jolt the touch of his lips sent ricocheting through her. Even though he wasn't doing a thing to stop her from pulling away, she made absolutely no attempt to budge. She couldn't, in part because pride wouldn't let her, in part because she wanted the kiss to last forever, the same as she had last time. It was terrifying just how badly she wanted that, wanted him.

She was trembling like a leaf when he finally stepped back. She risked a glance into his eyes and saw that he was every bit as shaken as she was. Good, she thought. If the man was determined to rattle her, she liked knowing she could return the favor.

"Be ready at six," he said mildly.

"I haven't changed my mind," she said, though it was a halfhearted protest.

He grinned. "Then I'll pick someplace to take you that doesn't mind a little sawdust. Six o'clock, Maggie."

A part of her wished she were still five years old so she could stomp her foot and tell him he wasn't the boss of her. Another part of her—the grown-up woman part that had tromped right over too many men—admired the kind of gall it took not to take her at her word.

Round one had clearly gone to Josh, who was walking away whistling, happy as the dickens with himself.

Trying to see who could get the upper hand and hold on to it tonight was going to make for an interesting evening.

Nadine was sitting with Amanda watching Josh kiss the stuffing out of Maggie when a shadow fell across the two of them. She looked up into George Winslow's eyes, which were filled with surprising uncertainty.

"Now, you're the last person I expected to see around here," she said brightly, surveying his even more unexpected jeans and T-shirt. They looked well worn and were a far cry from the conservative suits he usually wore. "Did you come to help?"

"No, I'm sure he came to gloat," Amanda said.

Nadine studied him with a narrowed gaze. He suddenly looked awfully guilty. "Gloat?" she asked Amanda. "What would he have to gloat about?"

"He's got Caleb tap-dancing to calm down his bosses, and he's had a building inspector crawling all over the roof today trying to find some code infraction," Amanda said. "Isn't that right, Mr. Winslow? You're still determined to cause trouble for us, aren't you?"

"I—"

Nadine cut him off. "Don't even try to come up with some excuse," she said, latching on to his arm. "You and I obviously need to have another talk."

She dragged him halfway across the site until they had some privacy. "I think you'd better start talking, George. I thought we had an understanding."

He regarded her uneasily. "I'd already set some things in motion," he admitted. "It's not so easy to stop them."

"Sure it is," she said. "You pick up the phone and you explain you made a terrible mistake. If you have to, you grovel just the way you expected Amanda to." Her gaze clashed with his. "You have a cell phone with you?"

He nodded.

"Give it to me," she ordered.

"Now, Nadine," he protested.

"Do you want to fix this or not?"

He pulled his cell phone out of his pocket with unmistakable reluctance. "I'm not sure—"

"Well, I am." She faced him down, hands on hips. "You either make those calls or get off this site."

His lips twitched. "Damn, woman, nobody scares you, do they?"

"Certainly not you," she replied. "Do the right thing, George, then come see me when you've taken care of this."

She went back to Amanda.

"Well?" Amanda asked.

"I think he's calling off his dogs," Nadine told her. "At least he is if he knows what's good for him."

"Are you sure you can trust anything he says?" Amanda asked, regarding her curiously.

"Actually I am. I think I understand what he set out to do, even if he did go about it all wrong."

"Meaning?"

Nadine considered telling her that George had been trying to stop the construction so Amanda would be forced to reconcile with Big Max. But she didn't think that would be much consolation to Amanda. "Never mind," she said, then brightened when she spotted George coming their way. "Everything taken care of?" she called out.

"Would I risk coming over here if it wasn't?" he said, his mouth twisted wryly.

"Then you're ready to help us out?" Nadine asked.

George shifted his gaze to Amanda. "Would that be okay with you?"

Amanda regarded him warily. "Can you promise me you're not here spying for my father or trying to stir up any more trouble?"

George flinched at the direct question. For a minute he looked as though he was going to turn around and leave in a huff, but he finally swallowed hard. "I'm here to eat humble pie, if you must know. Someone showed me recently that it's not as distasteful as I'd once thought."

Caleb materialized just then and stood resolutely beside Amanda, his gaze forbidding. George faced him.

"Seems I owe you an apology, too," he told Caleb. "You've been doing what you knew was right all along, and I admire the courage you showed in standing up to me. I've spoken to your boss. I don't think there will be any more problems."

Caleb didn't look entirely convinced. "That's quite a mouthful, George. What changed your mind?"

"Nadine made me look at things in a different light."

Caleb looked at Nadine with surprise. "Then we owe you our thanks."

"I didn't do that much," Nadine demurred, uncomfortable being the focus of so much admiration for simply speaking her mind. For once it seemed to have done some good, instead of making matters worse.

"Of course you did," George said. "Getting a message through this thick skull of mine isn't easy, as I'm sure Caleb here would be happy to tell you."

"True enough," Caleb said, his expression finally relaxing into a grin.

"Then you don't object to my helping out?" George persisted.

"I don't," Caleb said, then turned to Amanda. "What about you?"

She studied George for a full minute before finally nodding. "We'll be glad to have you."

To Nadine's surprise, George seemed genuinely relieved. She realized then that it had taken a lot for him to openly admit to a mistake and risk rejection.

"Just tell me what to do, then," he said. "I've got some experience with building things, so put me wherever I'll be most useful."

Nadine tucked her hand through his elbow. "That'll be up to Josh. I'll go with you to find him."

As soon as they were out of Amanda and Caleb's hearing, she gave his arm a squeeze. "That wasn't so difficult, was it?"

"You have no idea," he muttered.

She laughed. "Not used to asking for forgiveness, huh? Trust me, it gets easier over time."

He gazed down at her, his expression curious. "How would you know a thing like that?"

"I've had to ask for my son's forgiveness more times than I care to remember."

He studied her intently. "Something tells me there's a story there."

"More than one, if you must know, but they'll have to wait. My break's almost over."

George looked surprised. "Your son runs a tight ship, then, even though he's relying on volunteers?"

"Josh is a hard worker. He only has the volunteers here on the weekends, so he likes to make sure we're not wasting precious time. He's determined that

Amanda and the kids will get to celebrate Thanksgiving in their new home." Just then she spotted Josh up on the roof, explaining to a couple of newcomers how to lay the remaining shingles. Given his precarious balance, she was not about to call his attention to George's arrival. He might nosedive off the other side.

Just as she was about to offer to get George something cold to drink while they waited to speak to Josh, she felt an urgent tug on her hand. She looked down and saw Susie's sweet little face.

"Hey there, cutie. What's up?" Nadine asked.

Susie cast a fearful look at George, then whispered, "It's Larry. He's climbing up the ladder so he can see what Josh is doing."

"Oh, Lord," Nadine said. "Show me where, sweetie."

George immediately caught her sense of panic. "Who's Larry?" he asked in a calm, level tone.

"One of Amanda's boys. He's only eight. He has no business going up on that roof. We have to hurry."

Without giving it another thought, George scooped Susie into his arms. "Where is he?" he asked her gently.

"Around the other side," she said, clinging to his neck. Tears were spilling down her cheeks. "Jimmy told him not to go, but Larry wouldn't listen."

"It's okay, sweet pea," Nadine reassured her. "We'll have him down in no time."

But when they turned the corner, they saw that Larry was already on the roof, trying to crawl up to the peak. Jimmy was on the bottom rung of the ladder, clearly intent on going after him. George shoved Susie into Nadine's arms and plucked Jimmy from the ladder.

"You stay right here, young man," he said in a commanding voice. Jimmy was too startled to argue. He stood silently beside Nadine. After a minute he tucked his hand into hers.

"What if he falls?" he asked in a quavering voice.

"George won't let him fall," Nadine said with conviction. "And Josh is up there, too."

"I told him not to go," Jimmy whispered. "Then he got to the top and told me I was a sissy if I didn't come, too."

"It's not being a sissy to stay off a roof," Nadine said, her gaze locked on George as he reached the top of the ladder and scrambled after Larry. "It's being smart."

Before George could reach him, Larry's feet slid out from under him and he began to slide down the roof just to the left of where George was. Nadine watched with her heart in her throat as George gingerly shifted position and grabbed the boy before he reached the edge and fell.

Holding Larry securely, George made his way back to the ladder and brought the boy down. By then a crowd had assembled on the ground and someone had alerted Amanda. She and Caleb rushed up just as the two of them reached the ground.

"Larry O'Leary, are you out of your mind?" she demanded, before hauling him into her arms, tears streaming down her face. She turned to George at last. "I will never be able to thank you enough for saving him."

George hunkered down beside them and put a hand on Larry's back. "You know what you did was very foolish, young man."

Larry nodded, apparently impressed by George's size and his somber tone.

"Next time you decide you want to go scampering

around on a roof, you make sure there's someone with you who knows what they're doing, okay?" George said.

"There won't be a next time," Amanda said direly.

George grinned at that. "Yes, there will. When a boy's as intrepid as this one, there will always be a next time. You just have to minimize the risks."

"If that's true, then God help me," Amanda said.

"He will," Caleb assured her.

George couldn't seem to tear his gaze away from Larry. When he finally looked directly at Amanda, he said, "You know, your boy is the spitting image of his granddaddy at this age, don't you?"

"I know," she whispered, her voice thick. "I have a few old pictures I took with me when I left home."

"He'd be proud of him," George told her.

Amanda sighed. "I wish that were true."

Josh came around the side of the house just then, and someone filled him in on what had happened. He walked over to Nadine and pulled her aside.

"They okay?" he asked, his face pale.

"They seem to be." Nadine assured him. "You don't need to worry. The whole thing's over now. They're safe, thanks to George."

He nodded toward George. "What's he doing here, anyway?"

"He came to work. We were on our way to ask you to give him an assignment, when this little crisis came up."

"You think he's serious about wanting to help? He was up to his neck causing trouble not an hour or two ago."

Nadine nodded slowly. "If I had any doubts about it

when he first showed up, I don't anymore. Look at him. You'd think Larry was *his* grandchild, not his best friend's. Big Max will hear about this, I'm sure. Maybe George will be the one who brings that family back together."

Josh looked skeptical. "There's that blind optimism of yours again."

"Josh, honey, when you stop being optimistic about people and about life, you might as well go off and live in a cave." She gave him a knowing look. "Which is pretty much what you've done, isn't it?"

"Maybe," he said, surprising her with the admission.

"It's no way to live," she scolded him.

"I think I'm beginning to get that," he said, looking around until his gaze finally settled on Maggie. His lips curved slightly.

Nadine suspected if she commented on his reaction, he'd swear up and down she'd misread him. Better to let him make the rest of this journey on his own.

But it sure was going to be fun to watch.

17

Josh had just showered and changed for his date with Maggie when someone tapped on the door of his hotel room. He opened it to find Susie, Larry and Jimmy staring up at him, which meant Amanda couldn't be far away. He found that more worrisome than the unexpected appearance of the kids. If she figured out where he was going tonight, she'd be gloating from now till doomsday. He'd never hear the end of it.

"What are you guys doing here?" Josh asked, hunkering down to put himself on eye level with them. "And where's your mom?"

"She's next door with Nadine and I came to 'pologize," Larry said.

Josh didn't think the boy looked very contrite. "Oh?"

"Climbing onto the roof was a dumb thing to do," Larry recited just as he'd most likely been coached to say.

"Yes, it was," Josh agreed. "I think maybe we should talk about the consequences of that."

For the first time Larry looked scared, probably more so than he had when he'd been scampering around on that roof and lost his footing.

"Consequences?" he said to Josh, his eyes wide. "You mean like getting punished?"

"That's exactly what I mean," Josh confirmed, determined to be stern enough to make his point even though a part of him admired the kid's daring nature. "What do you think would be an appropriate punishment to make sure you never do anything like that again?"

Larry lifted his chin defiantly. "Mr. Winslow said I probably will do it again 'cause I'm…I can't remember the word."

"Intrepid," Jimmy piped up. "I don't know what it means, though." He looked at Josh. "Is it a good thing? Mr. Winslow made it sound like it was."

Josh fought a grin. "It's sort of like bravery and it can be a very good thing, but not when it puts you in unnecessary danger." He paused solemnly to let that sink in, then added, "So, here's what I think. Next week, when your mom comes to help out at the site, I think you need to stay home and think about why being on that roof was a really, really bad idea."

"Me and Susie, too?" Jimmy asked.

Josh shook his head. "Just Larry."

Larry looked crestfallen. "But coming there is the best thing we get to do all week. And don't the rules say we gotta come?"

"I'm in charge of enforcing the rules. Just this once, I think this is more important," Josh told him. "And I'm hoping that since it is the best thing you get to do, you'll think twice next time before risking the chance to be there."

"But who'd stay with me?" Larry asked. "I can't stay by myself."

"Your mom and I will figure that out."

Larry's chin wobbled and tears filled his eyes. "Are you mad at me?"

Emotionally, Josh was usually out of his depth with these three, but he instinctively pulled the boy into his arms and gave him a hug. "Not mad, but you did scare an awful lot of people, Larry, me included. Worst of all, you scared your mom."

Amanda and Nadine exited the room next door in time to hear his last remark.

"You most certainly did," Amanda confirmed.

Nadine gave Josh a wry look. "And exactly how many times did I have to send somebody up onto a roof or into a tree to retrieve you when you were Larry's age?"

Josh frowned. Her sudden trip down memory lane was not helping. "Beside the point."

"Just a reminder not to be too hard on the boy," she scolded lightly.

"As I recall, you walloped my backside, so I think staying away from the site for one week is reasonable," Josh said, satisfied when he saw Larry's eyes widen at the punishment Josh had endured for a similar infraction. "Just enough to get the message across." He turned to Amanda. "We'll figure out the babysitting thing later."

She nodded. "I think that's definitely a fair punishment, don't you, Larry?"

Larry hung his head. "I guess," he said, scuffing the toe of his sneaker on the sidewalk. "How come it's not enough that I 'pologized?"

"Because Josh and I want to make very sure you remember this incident and don't repeat it," Amanda told him, then turned her attention back to Josh. "You look all scrubbed and gussied up just to go get burgers," she observed with amusement dancing in her eyes.

"Actually I have other plans," he admitted reluctantly. "They don't include burgers."

"Really? Care to tell us about them?" she inquired, her expression already too damn smug.

"No, I do not."

Nadine regarded the two of them with interest. "What's going on?"

"Unless I'm mistaken, Josh finally asked Maggie out on a real date and she agreed," Amanda said, not even trying to hide her personal sense of triumph over a successful matchmaking mission.

Josh grinned. "You only have that half right. I asked. She refused. I told her I'd be there at six, anyway." He glanced at his watch. "I'd better hit the road. I wouldn't want her to think she won, after all."

"It's a date, not a competition," Amanda reminded him.

"Not with Maggie, it isn't," he said. "See you."

"In the morning?" Nadine inquired innocently.

"Whenever I get back. Knowing Maggie, it could be thirty minutes from now."

But he was counting on his powers of persuasion to buy him a little more time than that.

"Do you know what that man had the audacity to do?" Maggie demanded indignantly when Dinah called her around five o'clock to see if Maggie was free to have dinner with her and Cord.

"That man? Can I assume we're talking about Josh?" Dinah asked, her voice threaded with amusement.

"Of course we're talking about Josh. Do you know any other man who's half as infuriating as he is?"

"Cord has his moments," Dinah replied. "They've made life interesting. I highly recommend a man with audacity."

"You are absolutely no help at all," Maggie accused in frustration. "Do you want to know what Josh did or not?"

"Please tell me," Dinah said.

"He asked me on a date," Maggie began.

"That is *awful*," Dinah commiserated, obviously choking back a laugh.

Maggie lost patience. "Will you just shut up and let me finish?"

"Yes, ma'am," Dinah replied dutifully.

"He asked me on a date. Being sensible for once, I said no. He accused me of being a coward. I denied it and then he kissed me in front of God and everyone right there on the construction site," she said, her voice filled with indignation.

"I'm shocked," Dinah said, though the opposite was plainly the case. She sounded even more entertained.

"Oh, for pity's sake, I'm not through yet," Maggie said. "That's not the worst of it. Then he said he was picking me up at six whether I was ready or not. Can you imagine? He actually thinks he can order me around. What's next? Tossing me over his shoulder and hauling me into his cave?"

Dinah chuckled openly. "I have to admire any man who thinks he can pull that off. In fact, I want to be the one who gets to sell tickets when he tries."

"You really aren't going to be any help at all, are you?" Maggie said in disgust. "I told you this so you could tell me what to do to show him that he is not in charge here."

"So this is a control issue with you?" Dinah asked. "It has nothing to do with you not really wanting to go out with him?"

"Yes," Maggie said at once, then backed off. "No. Hell, Dinah, I honestly don't know anymore. It started out as me trying to be smart for once in my life, but then things got a little murky."

"How does your mother feel about him? They met the other day, right?"

The out-of-the-blue question threw Maggie, even though she suspected exactly where Dinah was headed with it. "What does my mother have to do with anything?" she asked testily.

"Come on, Magnolia, don't play dense. If your mother adored Josh at first glimpse, then you're holding out just to be stubborn. Personally, I think that must be it, because if she expressed even a hint of distaste for Josh, you'd be all over the man."

"I'm way past choosing men just as a rebellion against my mother," Maggie claimed defensively, despite the fact that she'd made the very same assessment herself.

"Since when?"

"Remember Warren? He was the turning point."

"I think Warren was an experiment that didn't pan out," Dinah said. "I think you dipped your toe into safe, lukewarm waters to see how it felt and concluded that you preferred the excitement of a stormy sea, despite all the risks. I think you should be grateful."

"To Warren?" Maggie asked incredulously. "Why on earth would I be grateful to him?"

"Because he proved once and for all that you will only be happy with a certain type of man, and his type, sweet as he is, is definitely not it."

Unfortunately, Maggie couldn't entirely disagree. "Then why haven't I jumped into bed with Josh already? Goodness knows, he fits my old pattern perfectly."

"Because you see something in him you never saw in any of the others who came before Warren," Dinah suggested.

"Such as?"

"Staying power."

That was the most ridiculous thing Dinah had said yet. "You think Josh has staying power?" Maggie scoffed. "Who are you kidding? The man lives in a motel, probably with his bags packed."

"Only because that's all he's known. I don't think life with Nadine was all that stable. If someone gave him a reason to stay put, I think he'd settle down in a heartbeat."

Maggie paused and considered that possibility. "I know you're right about his childhood with Nadine," she said finally, "but what on earth makes you think he's ready to change his pattern? Look at his job history. He's always on the move."

"Until Cord hired him and gave him both the work he loved and the respect he deserved," Dinah reminded her. "He's not walking away from that. I don't think he'd walk away from a woman who gave him love and a sense of security, either. I just think he's afraid to want it too much."

"And based on my past history, you think I can be that woman?" Maggie asked skeptically. "I bolt at the first sign of commitment."

"No, you do not," Dinah contradicted. "You set it up so the man takes off and you can play the injured victim. I don't think Josh will be put off so easily, if you give him half a chance. And I think that's what terrifies you. Just look how he's shaken you up tonight."

"I am not shaken up. I'm annoyed. Besides, you hardly know the man," Maggie said, desperate to prove that Dinah's probably sage advice wasn't worth a nickel.

"Neither do you," Dinah reminded her. "If the attraction's there, and we both know it is, change that, Maggie. Get to know him. Let him into your life. Let him into your heart, not just into your bed."

Maggie sighed. Dinah knew her better than anyone on earth. Maybe, for once, she should listen to her, instead of dismissing what she had to say because she didn't want to hear it. "Okay, I'll think about it."

"Well, think fast, because according to my watch, he's due there in fifteen minutes."

Maggie glanced at her own watch and confirmed the time. "Oh, my God, I've got to go."

"Call me tomorrow," Dinah said. She paused, then added slyly, "Or the next day, if tomorrow's inconvenient."

"I thought you told me to keep him out of my bed."

"But I know you won't," Dinah said with conviction. "And what I actually said was to let him into your life and your heart, not *just* into your bed. Bye, sweetie. Have fun tonight."

Maggie slowly put the portable phone back into its charger and considered Dinah's advice. Her friend was right about her tendency to do most relationships totally backward. At thirty-two, it was probably time to consider changing that pattern.

Then, again, there was the whole upper-hand thing.

If Josh arrived tonight and she was dutifully waiting by the door to spend a nice sedate evening having a few drinks with him, just as he expected, he would win. It might be only a tiny victory, but it was unacceptable.

Which meant she had to come up with a fitting twist that would knock the man's socks off. If there was one thing at which she excelled, it was keeping wicked, dangerous men off kilter.

Maggie opened her front door wearing two skimpy scraps of silk and lace that left absolutely nothing to the imagination. Josh almost swallowed his tongue. He still hadn't recovered from the unexpected sight when she reached out, bunched a fistful of his shirt in her hand and dragged him across the threshold.

Okay, then, they apparently weren't going out for drinks, he concluded as she pretty much plastered herself to him and turned their earlier kiss into child's play by comparison.

He barely had time to glance around the living room, which had the same cozy ambience as Images, before she was shoving aside his shirt and reaching for his belt.

Josh put his hand over hers in an attempt to still her busy fingers. "Um, Maggie, not that I'm complaining, but what's going on here?"

"Isn't it obvious?"

"You're seducing me," he said, hoping he'd gotten it right and this wasn't some game she intended to halt any second now.

There was laughter in her eyes when she met his gaze. "Very astute. Any objections?"

He scrambled, trying to come up with one that made

a lick of sense under the circumstances, but the bene-
fits far outweighed any objection he could think of with
her hands all over him.

He grinned at last. "I guess not."

"Good answer. The bedroom's this way."

Rather than following, though, he backed her against
a wall and pinned her hands over her head. "We don't
have to get there in the next five minutes, do we?" he
asked, kissing his way along the side of her neck till he
reached the spot where her pulse was jumping. He ran
his tongue lightly over her burning skin.

"Two minutes," she said in a choked voice.

He glanced into her eyes. "What?"

"We have to be there in two minutes," she said.

"Oh? Why is that, sugar? You have a camera on a
timer?"

For an instant there was dead silence, but as his
words apparently sank in, she put a hand in the center
of his chest and shoved him back a step. "Are you
crazy?"

He laughed at her indignation. "Just checking, since
you seem to be on an urgent timetable. If you want
some kinky pictures to remember me by, it's okay with
me."

"You are so delusional," she snapped. "What made
me think for one single second that I wanted to sleep
with you?"

"Maybe this," Josh said, covering her mouth with his
and sliding his hand up her bare midriff till be could run
a finger over the hard bead of her nipple. Her hips instinctively swayed into his.

He pressed her back against the wall and continued
his assault on her mouth until she was whimpering with

pleasure. The movements of her hips became more and more restless. Josh was pretty sure they'd never make it to the bedroom if they kept up like this. Reluctantly, he backed up a step.

"No," she protested, trying to pull him back.

"Just taking a little break, sugar." To prove it, he scooped her into his arms and cradled her against his chest, then looked into her eyes. "You think you're gonna change your mind before we get to the good stuff?"

Her gaze remained perfectly level, as if she was responding to a dare. "Not a chance."

Josh grinned. "It's not supposed to be about pride, Maggie. You can back out if this is more than you wanted. Just because you started the game doesn't mean you have to finish it."

"It's not a game. This is exactly what I wanted," she said. "Didn't I make myself clear enough when I answered the door wearing this?"

Josh eyed the skimpy amount of lace still covering her. "It was an unexpectedly fascinating invitation, all right."

"Then you're accepting?"

"I may be a lot of things, but I'm no fool. When a woman like you says she wants me in no uncertain terms, I'm not likely to walk away. Only one thing I need to know."

"What?"

"Where's the bedroom?"

"Last door on the right," she said.

Josh carried her into the room, which was lit with candles. A bouquet of fresh roses scented the air. The luxurious flowered comforter on the bed was turned back, revealing sheets that looked smooth and soft and welcoming. A pile of pillows promised comfort.

The atmosphere was purely romantic, but it was the suggested permanence of it, the hundred and one little personal touches that screamed Maggie, that got to him. This was the bedroom of someone who understood what it took to make a home. Josh couldn't help wondering if he'd ever fit here, or anyplace like it.

Maggie touched his cheek. "What's wrong?"

"Just thinking how different your life is from mine," he admitted, settling her on the bed, then sitting on the edge beside her, not quite ready to join her.

"In what way?"

"I'll bet this big old bed has been in your family for generations," he said.

"It was my great-grandmother's," she confirmed.

He met her gaze. "Do you know I don't have one single thing from any ancestor of mine? Not even a snapshot."

"That's sad."

He shrugged. "It's just the way it is. Nadine never was one for sentiment. We didn't have room for it on the road."

"Sometimes family's not all it's cracked up to be," Maggie said as if that might console him.

"Your folks seem like good people. And you obviously like the links to the past. They're all around you, here and at Images."

"These are things, Josh. I appreciate them for their beauty and, yes, to a certain extent for the memories they carry with them. But sometimes the weight of responsibility that goes along with them can be a heavy burden."

"Which explains all those rebellions of yours," he guessed.

Maggie nodded.

"Am I another one?"

She looked away, then lifted her gaze to his. "I can't be sure."

He couldn't say that the truth didn't hurt, but he shrugged it off. "That's honest enough."

"Is it enough that I'm here with you now?" she asked.

He reached over and slid the strap of her bra off her shoulder. "I guess we'll just have to see whether it is or not."

Heat flared in her eyes. "Not to worry. This is the part I always get right," she assured him. "It's the rest I usually mess up."

"Then we're in the same boat, darlin'. Let's just see where it takes us."

The trip turned out to be spectacular, even if it was only the start of a journey. Josh had a hunch there might yet be rocky seas ahead. Surprisingly, that didn't make him want to bolt, as it had so many times in the past.

With Maggie still cradled against him, he sighed with contentment, then gazed down into her flushed face and commented, "You know, when we made this date, I promised you drinks. I don't want you to think I usually go back on my promises."

Maggie grinned and straddled him. "Things change. Besides, there's a bar downstairs if we get thirsty."

"And dinner," he said in a strangled voice when she took him in her hands, then shifted until he was deep inside her. "What about that?"

"There's plenty of food in the kitchen and I'm a great cook when I put my mind to it. I might have a little trouble focusing right this second," she said, beginning to move. "Are you hungry?"

She shifted provocatively and every thought of food vanished from his brain, along with all the blood.

"Only for you," he said, grasping her hips and settling her into place before giving in to sensations that made him wonder how he'd ever have the strength to crawl out of this bed again.

Maggie was right. She was a tantalizing expert at this. She knew just which of his buttons to push and when, but when he looked into her eyes, he had to wonder if there wasn't a part of herself she was holding back.

He deliberately slowed things down. "Maggie?"

She finally met his gaze. "What?"

"Keep looking at me, sugar."

"Why?" she asked, obviously confused.

"Just do it, okay?"

With their gazes locked, Josh began to move again. This time when the sensations ripped through him, when they shuddered through her, he knew with absolute certainty that she was with him.

His name was the cry on her lips when she came.

But as the tremors faded, she slowly slipped away, growing more and more distant without ever leaving his side.

For the first time in his life Josh got why it mattered whether someone made love or had sex. He'd just had the most incredible sex of his life, when what he'd wanted more than anything was to make love.

He tried to imagine what it would take for Maggie

to let that happen. Or would she always keep some sort of emotional wall between them?

And, he wondered, why did it seem to matter so damn much if she did?

18

"You must be pretty pleased with yourself," Josh said as he and Maggie ate cold roast-beef sandwiches in the kitchen at midnight.

She paused with her sandwich halfway to her mouth and regarded him suspiciously. She didn't like that glint of amusement in his eyes one bit. He looked as if he'd figured out the secret workings of her brain. Given how chaotic her thoughts were these days, especially when it came to him, that was troublesome.

"Oh?" she said carefully.

"You're back in control," he said succinctly, as if that explained everything.

She frowned at his knowing expression. "What is *that* supposed to mean?" she demanded, even though she knew exactly what he was saying. He'd seen straight through the whole seduction. He was aware that she'd set out to prove that he hadn't gotten the best of her with that unexpected kiss earlier in the day. She'd wanted him to know that she could be every bit as impetuous and daring as he could be.

"I kiss you. You seduce me." He grinned. "Do I get to choose what happens next? The escalation of this contest could get to be downright fascinating."

She frowned at his attempt at humor. It was the second time he'd acted as if taking her to bed were all some sort of game for grown-ups. "Not likely."

"I think I'll surprise you," he remarked thoughtfully as if she hadn't spoken at all. "Though tonight will be a tough act to follow."

"It's not a game, Josh." She spoke sternly, as if addressing a particularly mischievous child. Unfortunately, he didn't seem the least bit daunted.

"Isn't it?" He leveled a look into her eyes. "Isn't that what people like you and I do, Maggie? We play games. When things get too serious or when the challenge wears off, we cut and run."

"Maybe you do," she said to stress that they were entirely different. "I'm not the one who broke my engagement. I was ready to make a commitment."

"Oh, really?" he said with annoying skepticism. "To a man who would have bored you stiff in a month?"

"You don't know anything about my relationship with Warren."

"I know Warren and I know you. He's a nice guy. You're a woman who needs a challenge, someone who'll keep her on her toes. You don't want easy, Maggie. I think on some level you knew Warren would figure that out and call things off." He pinned her with another of those penetrating looks that made her shiver. "What about the men before Warren, Maggie? Weren't they a lot like me? Guys you knew would never call your bluff? Guys who were destined to walk away?"

She couldn't deny that, much as she wanted to. Dinah had called her on the same thing only a few hours earlier. Rather than replying, she tried to shift the attention back to Josh. "What about you? What do you expect when you start seeing someone?"

"Nothing," Josh said flatly. "I have no long-term expectations when it comes to relationships. I'm one of those guys who walks away, remember? At least I'm willing to own up to it."

The answer sounded rehearsed. Maggie was willing to bet he'd said it a thousand times before. Heck, he'd said it twice just now. But there was something in his expression, in the way he refused to meet her gaze when he said it, that made her question whether it was actually true this time. She couldn't help thinking about Dinah's claim that Josh had previously untapped staying power.

"Then all you care about is the sex?" she persisted, needing him to define things so there would be no misunderstandings down the road. It was another thing she did, getting all the cards on the table so there wouldn't be any unpleasant surprises when things blew up. Despite what Josh thought, Warren's action had been an unexpected and hurtful twist.

A faint flicker in Josh's eyes suggested she'd hit her mark with her assessment about his focus being all on the sex.

"Absolutely," he insisted. "Isn't that what matters to you? That's all tonight was about, right?"

Her pride kicked in, even though a part of her recognized that the moment called for honesty. One of them had to break old habits, but she wasn't ready to be the one. Why should she open herself up when he wouldn't? Why should she put all of her vulnerabilities on the line and let him get off scot-free?

"Of course," she said blithely. "How could it be about anything else? We don't know each other that well."

"And something tells me we never will," Josh said, his voice suddenly dulled by something that might have been disappointment.

Maggie was taken aback by the bleak assessment. "What do you mean?"

"You don't really let people in, Maggie," he accused. "Not even when you're sharing the most intimate moment two people can have. You look away as if to preserve some sort of anonymity."

She recalled his command earlier that she look into his eyes when they were making love and knew now why he'd been so insistent. His words resonated because the accusation was almost the same thing Dinah had accused her of earlier. It didn't sound any more complimentary coming from Josh. Her temper flared.

"As if you're any different," she said bitterly. "I thought you enjoyed yourself tonight. You certainly got what you came over here after. Now you're trying to make it seem as if I'm the one who shortchanged you."

"Didn't you?" he asked, his gaze unwavering. "Maybe you're not giving me enough credit, Maggie."

"I doubt it," she said, but with far less certainty than she might have a couple of hours ago. She began to gather up the dishes from their makeshift meal. "I guess that's that, then. Now that you've satisfied your curiosity or proved you've got what it takes to get into my bed, I'm sure you'll be moving on. I won't quit helping with Amanda's house, but I'll try not to make it awkward for you. I've never been the clingy type."

He frowned. "What the hell are you talking about?"

"Moving on, of course. Isn't that what usually happens next?" She almost choked on the words, but she managed to keep her tone even. She would not let him see that tears were stinging her eyes.

He reached out and snagged her hand as she tried to slip past him, then hauled her into his lap just as a tear spilled over and ran down her cheek. His expression surprisingly tender, he brushed away the trail of dampness with the pad of his thumb.

"Oh, darlin', you've got that all wrong," he said with quiet conviction.

"What did I get wrong?" she inquired stiffly.

"You and me," he said, his gaze locked with hers, "we're just getting started."

Her blood hummed at the promise in his words and in his eyes. A nagging little fear shuddered through her, as well. Maybe this time she'd met a man who wasn't going to make walking away quite so easy. Wouldn't it be ironic if the man who never settled anyplace for long turned out to be the one who took up permanent residence in her heart?

When the phone woke Maggie out of a sound sleep in the morning, she was still shaken by last night's realization that Josh could turn out to be important in her life if she allowed her defenses to slip and let him start to matter.

"Hello," she said groggily, aware that Josh was still in her bed. That was a surprise, too. She'd expected him to take off the minute she gave him a chance to do it, but he'd seemingly been determined to prove that she couldn't chase him off.

"Maggie, it's Ellie. I'm so sorry to wake you. I've been trying to call for a couple of hours now, but your line's been busy."

Maggie immediately snapped awake. She remembered deliberately leaving the phone off the hook so she and Josh wouldn't be interrupted when they came back to bed. She'd put it back in its cradle when she'd rolled over a half hour or so ago. She sat up now, filled with tension. "What's going on, Ellie?"

"There's a problem," Ellie began. "At the gallery."

"Tell me," she said.

She felt a shift in bed beside her and Josh settled a steadying hand on her shoulder, his expression quizzical. She gave him a slight shake of her head to indicate she didn't know anything yet.

"It's Images," Ellie explained again, her voice breaking. "The police couldn't reach you, so they called me."

Maggie's heart began to pound. She wanted to scream at Ellie to just get on with it, but she could tell that the young woman was deeply rattled and having difficulty finding the right words.

"Someone broke in last night, Maggie," Ellie finally blurted. "The police found the door open when they were patrolling the neighborhood."

"I'll be there in ten minutes," Maggie said at once, her stomach churning. "Are you at the gallery now?"

"I've been here for a while," Ellie said. "The police are still crawling all over the place. They have a lot of questions, Maggie."

For the first time, Maggie realized that there was more than urgency in Ellie's voice. There was real fear, suggesting that this wasn't some ordinary break-in by someone looking for cash or even valuable art.

"How bad is it?"

Ellie hesitated. "It's awful, Maggie," she whispered eventually, her voice thick with tears. "Hurry, okay?"

"Ten minutes," Maggie repeated, turning off the phone and tossing it aside as she haphazardly gathered up clothes and pulled them on.

"What happened?" Josh asked, already yanking on his own clothes.

"Someone broke into Images," she explained. Her hands were shaking so badly, she couldn't get her bra hooked. Josh shoved her hands aside and finished the job. For an instant she wished he would go right on touching her and make this whole incident disappear beneath a sea of sensation. Instead she just uttered a curt, "Thanks," and pulled a T-shirt over her head.

"So how bad *is* it?"

"I'm not sure. Ellie started crying before she could even describe what happened, so..." Because she couldn't bear to think about how bad, she put her own spin on it. "She's probably overreacting. After all, the police woke her up in the middle of the night to go over there. Anything would seem shocking under those circumstances, right?"

She regarded Josh hopefully, but judging from his tight-lipped expression, he wasn't buying it. "It was probably a burglary," she continued anyway, trying to put off jumping to a far more logical conclusion. "A lot of people know what we have in there is very valuable. Sooner or later, something like this was bound to happen."

"You know better than that," Josh retorted grimly. "This is Brian's doing. There's not a doubt in my mind."

She scowled at his assumption. It was one thing to imagine some anonymous burglar ransacking the place for cash and valuables and quite another to envision the kind of destruction of which Brian was capable. She couldn't bring herself to think that right now.

"Then it's a good thing you're not a policeman, isn't it?" she said testily. "They at least go through the motions of gathering facts before they make wild accusations."

Josh stilled her in midstep and forced her to face him. "Look, I understand why you don't want to believe it has anything to do with Brian, but face facts, Maggie. Have you ever had any problems with thieves before?"

"No," she admitted. "The alarm system seems to have been a good deterrent. Or maybe we've just been lucky. Even before you talked to the cops, my dad's probably had them patrolling around the building 24/7 since I opened the store years ago. What good is influence if you can't use it to protect your daughter's business, right? Somebody probably took a break at the wrong time last night."

"You know better," Josh pressed, his gaze steady. "Did Ellie even say anything had been stolen?"

"No." Before he could go on, she held up her hand. "Okay, let's just say the break-in was Brian's doing, is that really the point?"

"It sure as hell *is* the point," he said, raking a hand through his hair impatiently. "Can't you see that the man's getting more and more brazen? It's gone beyond threats now, Maggie. You and Ellie could be in real danger."

She simply couldn't face that possibility, not until she absolutely had to. Brian might be jealous of Ellie's talent and furious with Maggie for wanting to promote it, but that didn't make him some sort of psychopath. Or did it? She remembered the destroyed paintings. At least at Images, he probably hadn't been able to get to Ellie's paintings.

"Don't be crazy," she told Josh. "Even if he did this, he broke into the gallery. He didn't attack either one of us. He's basically a coward."

"And that's supposed to reassure me? Cowards like to pick on people they think are weaker, and in his case, I suspect, women fit the bill. Come on, Maggie, you saw him that night at Ellie's. You described him to me. Weren't you just a little bit afraid of how far he might go?"

She didn't like thinking about that night and the fury in Brian's eyes when she'd barged into Ellie's studio. "Can we stop arguing about this and just get over there?" she pleaded.

"I'll drive," Josh said.

"We can walk just as fast. It's only a few blocks."

"We might need the truck," he countered.

She stared at him blankly. "Why?"

"To haul away whatever he's destroyed, unless the police need it for evidence," Josh said. "Or to take what's left to someplace that's safe."

"The most valuable things are in the vault," Maggie reminded him—and herself. "Whoever did this can't have gotten in there, unless they're some sort of professional."

"Let's hope you're right," Josh said. "Is the alarm code kept anywhere around the gallery?"

"No."

"Does Ellie know it?"

She hesitated, then nodded.

"Think she's memorized it, or would she have written it down someplace?"

Maggie couldn't take another minute of uncertainty. "Dammit, let's stop speculating. We'll know what happened soon enough."

Josh drove the short distance to Images at a far calmer pace than suited Maggie. She would have broken speed limits. When he pulled to the curb, she was out of the truck before he'd even cut the engine. There were two police cars on the street and several officers standing on the sidewalk.

"Where's Ellie?" she demanded.

"If that's your employee, she's inside with the detective trying to make a list of what's missing and giving him some preliminary notes on the value of what's damaged," an officer told her.

Maggie rushed inside, relieved that Josh had stayed behind to talk to the police. As soon as she stepped across the threshold, though, she came to a screeching halt, her heart lodged in her throat.

"Oh, my God," she whispered and swayed. She wasn't sure how he'd gotten there so quickly, but she felt Josh's arm circle her waist to steady her, even as he uttered a heartfelt curse of his own.

"Hang in there, Maggie. Take a deep breath," he advised. "It's going to be okay."

"How can you say that?" There was red paint everywhere, on the oils and watercolors and sculptures, all over her great-grandmother's antiques. It was splattered on the walls and dripped over the glass-fronted counter where delicate blown-glass items had been displayed. The case's glass had been shattered and thousands of dollars' worth of art glass had been smashed on the floor. The colorful shards were everywhere.

Ellie spotted Maggie just then and ran across the gallery. "I'm so sorry," she said, folding Maggie into a fierce embrace, then bursting into tears. "It's my fault. It's all my fault."

"Shh! Stop it. It is not your fault," Maggie soothed. Ellie's distress, thankfully, gave her something to focus on besides the mess.

While she comforted Ellie, Josh went over to speak to the detective Ellie had been with. Now the two men turned and crossed the gallery to Maggie.

"Ms. Forsythe?" the man asked. "I'm Detective Dan Ryan. We've gotten a preliminary list of everything that's damaged and its approximate value from your employee, but I'd appreciate it if you could go over it with me, make sure we didn't miss anything."

"Of course," she said at once. She glanced at Ellie. "What about the vault? Did the vandals get in there?"

Ellie frowned at her. "It wasn't vandals, Maggie. You know it wasn't."

"We don't know that," Maggie said staunchly.

"Of course we do," Ellie retorted with absolute conviction. "I've already told the police about Brian."

"He threatened to ruin my reputation, not destroy this place," Maggie said, clinging to one last straw.

"Things changed," Ellie said wearily. "He and I had another fight last night. He came by here just as I was closing and realized I was painting here instead of at home. He added up two and two and concluded that you hadn't canceled the show, after all. He went on a rampage then about me not taking him seriously when he said he'd destroy you."

"Why didn't you call the police right then?" Josh asked.

"Because he left," Ellie said. "He just walked out and slammed the door behind him. I was too shaken to work, so I locked up and left right after that."

"Did you turn on the alarm?" Josh asked.

"I thought I had, but maybe I didn't," she admitted, looking miserable. "It would have alerted the police when he broke in, so I must not have."

Maggie felt sorry for her. She was beating herself up for the actions of that despicable man. "Ellie, you are not to blame for any of this. If it turns out to have been Brian who broke in here, and right now we don't have one shred of proof that it was," she said with a pointed look at Josh and the detective, "then Brian's the one to blame, not you."

"I should have stopped painting the minute he made the first threat," Ellie insisted. "I should have told you that I wouldn't do a show."

"And allowed a bully like that to win?" Maggie demanded indignantly. "You couldn't allow that jealous creep to rob you of something that matters to you, something for which you have such extraordinary talent."

"At least all these beautiful things wouldn't be ruined," Ellie argued.

"Speculating and casting blame isn't getting us anywhere. I need to start putting some solid evidence together. I need to know everything the two of you know about Brian Garrison," the detective said. "In the meantime, Ms. Forsythe, why don't you take a look in your vault and make sure everything there is okay."

Maggie nodded, relieved to be away from Ellie's self-recriminations for a moment. She was also grateful for Josh's steadying presence beside her as she went into the back. The vault was still securely locked, but she opened it and checked the contents just to be sure everything was in place and undamaged.

"No one got in here," she confirmed to Detective Ryan. "If you'll show me the list that Ellie's given you of everything damaged out front, I'll confirm the value for you. I have my inventories here in my office."

"Thanks, I'd appreciate it," he said, pulling a chair up beside her desk.

"Can I speak to you first?" Josh asked the detective, drawing him aside as Maggie sat down at her desk.

She began retrieving inventory file folders from a drawer while they talked, grateful to have a few minutes to gather her composure without having to look at all the destruction out front.

For the next hour Maggie went over the list with Detective Ryan, concentrating on the black-and-white figures of the loss, rather than the emotional impact of walking in to find the extent to which the gallery had been vandalized.

When they emerged eventually, she found Ellie seated behind the sales desk, tears still streaming down her face. There was no sign of Josh.

"Sweetie, why don't you go home and get some rest," she suggested. "This has been hard on you and you've been here for hours."

"I need to stay and help you clean up," Ellie insisted.

"It doesn't have to get done right this second. I probably need to get our insurance agent in here before we touch a thing," Maggie said.

"He's already here with an insurance adjuster." Ellie gestured across the room to where the Forsythe family's insurance agent, Dick Graves, was snapping pictures of the damage. "Josh asked me if I knew who to call. I guess it pays to be with an agent you've known forever. Mr. Graves said he'd make the arrangements for an adjuster and be here right away. They got here about ten minutes ago."

Maggie regarded them with relief. After all those years and exorbitant premiums, she supposed Graves didn't mind being rousted out of bed on a Sunday morning.

"That's wonderful," she told Ellie. "They can finish up today and we'll worry about cleanup tomorrow. Please go home. I'm worried about you. You look exhausted."

"I'm staying," Ellie said stubbornly. "And Vicki's coming in. She should be here in five or ten minutes."

"You called Vicki?"

"Of course I did. She might not act like it, but she cares about this place, too," Ellie said. "Besides, Josh said he'd be back soon with help, so Vicki and I need to be here."

Maggie stared at her. "Help?"

Before Ellie could explain, the front door opened and people began streaming in, led by Nadine.

"What are you doing here?" Maggie asked as Nadine enfolded her in a hug.

"We're here to help with the cleanup, of course," Amanda said.

"Josh called me and told me what had happened," Nadine explained. "I called Amanda and a couple of other folks. They called more people."

To Maggie's shock, George Winslow appeared, carrying a couple of ladders. "Your folks will be here soon," he announced.

Maggie stared at him, dumbfounded. "My folks?"

He grinned at her reaction. "I called them, since I figured you wouldn't have had time to do it. Won't kill 'em to miss church one Sunday. Caleb said he'd say a prayer for all us lost souls over here and then be here himself right after the service ends."

Maggie couldn't quite believe that all of these people had turned out here practically at the crack of dawn on a Sunday morning. The idea of her folks walking in here prepared to scrub walls and sweep up debris was even more astonishing. Her mother was going to be sick at heart when she saw the damage done to Great-Grandmother's furniture. Maggie could barely stomach it herself.

She looked around for Josh to thank him for setting all of this in motion, but there was no sign of him. "Where's Josh now?"

"Out picking up paint and cleaning supplies," Nadine said. "Cord and Dinah went with him. They should be here any minute."

Maggie turned to Detective Ryan. "Is this okay? Can we get to work already?"

"Your friend cleared it with me before he took off. Looks like you have yourself some pretty amazing friends, Ms. Forsythe. I'd be concentrating on that and let me worry about figuring out who's behind the vandalism. If it has anything to do with this Brian person, we'll nail him."

"You're welcome to track down the bad guy, Detective," Maggie assured him. "But when you have him in custody, I want to know so I can rip his heart out."

"Something tells me you actually mean that," he said, regarding her with a steady gaze. "So let me give you some advice. Maybe it would be best if you let the justice system deal with whoever's responsible."

Maggie had always been a great believer in the American justice system, but at the moment she was heartily in favor of getting some very personal revenge. She realized she'd better keep that to herself.

"We are going to need to take some of this stuff in for evidence," the detective told her. "I'll have my men take away what we need and make sure we have pictures of the rest. Then you all can get to work putting this place back in shape. With this many people helping, you should be ready to open for business in a few days."

"Thanks," Maggie said, then sank onto a chair, her legs once again unsteady as she surveyed the daunting task ahead. Then she looked around the room at all the willing workers who'd shown up thanks to Josh's distress call to Nadine and her immediate rush to help. Surrounded by friends like this, she couldn't help feeling she was more blessed than cursed this morning.

Josh wanted to track down Brian and strangle him with his bare hands. Only concentrating on the cleanup and Maggie's needs had kept him from doing just that.

"Leave it to the police," Cord said, apparently reading his grim expression correctly.

"Something tells me Maggie's heard the same thing this morning," Josh said, glancing across the gallery to where she was huddled with Dinah, her expression dark and forbidding. "You don't think she'll do anything crazy, do you?"

Cord grimaced. "Well, we *are* talking about Maggie…so I think we need to make sure she's otherwise occupied till she cools down."

"I think we can count on keeping her busy for the next couple of days getting this place back into shape. I thought we could whip through here in a day with all this help, but the destruction is worse than I realized," Josh said. "This might distract her till midweek, but what do we do after that?"

Cord looked at him. "I'm sure if you use your imagination, you can come up with something. Take her out of town. A few days over on Sullivan's Island or down in Savannah ought to distract her."

"And you think," Josh said dubiously, "she'd actually agree to go away with me when everything in her life is in turmoil?"

"She will if you make the offer interesting enough," Cord assured him. "Think you're up to it?"

Josh thought about how difficult it had been to get Maggie to accept a date with him for drinks. Getting her to agree to a trip seemed beyond his capabilities.

Then, again, he concluded thoughtfully, maybe he could make her think the getaway was her idea. That had worked out pretty well when it came to getting into her bed. She'd certainly snatched the initiative for that right out of his hands.

"I'll do what I can," he told Cord eventually.

It was a damn good thing he was so well acquainted with the way Maggie's mind worked. She might not even figure out what was going on till they were on their way to the beach.

Of course, the minute she did add up two and two, she'd probably make him pay, but that might just liven up the trip in some unexpected ways.

19

Nadine was steadying a ladder for George, but her gaze was on Josh and Maggie, who seemed to be having some sort of heated discussion across the gallery.

"Do you think those two have any idea what's going on between them?" she asked, not really expecting George to reply. How many men wanted to discuss other people's relationships?

To her surprise George descended the ladder and followed the direction of her gaze.

"You talking about your son and Maggie?"

She nodded.

"Seems to me there are enough sparks flying between those two to light a bonfire," George said. "What makes you think they don't see that themselves?"

"I know my son. He's a real smart guy and I love him to pieces, but I'm not sure Josh would recognize love if it came up and bit him in the butt. He has a pretty jaded view of it, thanks to me."

George's gaze narrowed. "You do that a lot, you know."

"What?"

"Blame yourself for the things Josh does or doesn't do."

"Well, who else should I blame?" Nadine asked. It was past time she accepted responsibility for the mistakes she'd made. "I was the one who raised him. At least, I tried. I have to say that there were plenty of times, though, when he was the adult. Josh had to grow up before his time, what with me making a mess of my life every few months, it seemed like."

"In what way?" George asked, studying her quizzically.

He had a habit of doing that, Nadine had noticed. He looked at her as if she were some strange species of butterfly he had pinned under a microscope. He always appeared bemused, but at least a little bit curious. She imagined that a recitation of her mistakes as a parent would soon erase that curiosity.

"You don't want to know all that ancient history," she said dismissively. "It's a boring story."

He gave her a chiding look. "I doubt there's anything about you that could possibly be boring, Nadine. And right this second the past is obviously on your mind, so let's get a cup of that potent coffee Maggie makes and sit a spell," he suggested, steering her toward Maggie's office where coffee, soda and sandwiches had been set up. "The world won't end if we take a break. Besides, I'm not as agile at the top of a ladder as I used to be. Let one of these young people climb up there and finish painting that molding."

In the deserted office, Nadine sat on a chair and accepted the cup of coffee George poured for her. "You're a real gentleman, you know that?"

"My mama would be real proud to hear you say that," he said with a grin that wiped years off his craggy, yet still-handsome face. "There were times she despaired of me ever learning to mind my manners. My wife, God rest her soul, had a similar opinion. Fortunately, she didn't much care about all the spit and polish that some Southern women insist on."

"I imagine there's a lot of scoundrel left in you," Nadine teased, enjoying the quick rise of color in his cheeks. Who'd have guessed that she could throw a powerful man like George Winslow off stride? A few weeks ago, who'd have even guessed she'd want to? "Tell me about your wife. You've never mentioned her before."

"Oh, no you don't. You're not getting away with changing the subject that easily," he said. He pulled a chair out from behind Maggie's desk and straddled it. "Now tell me why you think you're to blame for anything that your son decides to do or not do when it comes to Maggie?"

Nadine was tempted to push harder for information about his wife, but she could tell from his determined expression that she'd never get away with it.

"I'm not going to forget about your wife, you know," she warned him.

"Never thought you would," he said.

"Okay, then, do you want the condensed version or the whole ugly story of my life?"

"Whichever parts you think I need to hear to understand why you get so down on yourself," he said. "I imagine there's not a parent alive who doesn't feel he's failed his child from time to time, but you seem to carry that burden with you every second."

"For good reason," Nadine said candidly. "When I was young and impulsive, I met Josh's daddy. We had ourselves a wild fling when we were little more than teenagers. It's the oldest story in the book, but that doesn't make it any less sad when it happens to you. I got pregnant and we got married. I had my doubts, but Dwayne insisted it was the right thing to do, that no child of his would be born without his daddy's name."

George nodded sympathetically. "I can understand that. I'd feel the same way."

"Only trouble was, Dwayne didn't seem to care much whether Josh had an actual daddy around the house. We got a divorce and he took off, so it was Josh and me. It was a struggle, let me tell you. It's not easy raising a baby alone when all you can do are minimum-wage jobs and there's not one penny of child support coming in. More than once, I couldn't pay the rent, and we had to take off before the landlord evicted us. Most of the time, though, I kept a roof over our heads, and working as a waitress helped to feed us."

"In other words, you did the best you could," George said. "I don't see anything to be ashamed of in that. Josh ought to admire your strength."

"I think he does when it comes to that part," Nadine said honestly. "It was the men I chose that soured his view on me and on love. Every time I met someone new, I always convinced myself I'd finally found a real-life hero, someone who was going to treat me with respect, be a real daddy to Josh. I went into every relationship a believer and came out knowing that I'd just made another awful mistake. And each time, Josh just withdrew a little more into himself. No kid can go through that without wondering if he's to blame, if he's not worthy of being loved. He doesn't understand that it's not about him at all. I'm the one who kept screwing up."

"Or maybe you just managed to find yourself a string

of men who couldn't recognize gold when they had it in the palm of their hand," George said.

Nadine wanted to bask in the compliment, but she was realistic. "What does it say about me that I kept right on finding the same type of man?"

George shook his head. "I'll tell you something I heard on that Dr. Phil show one day. He said you teach folks how to treat you. I imagine after a time your expectations were pretty low, so these men of yours didn't feel they needed to do much. It surprises me that a woman with so much sass and vinegar could ever get to that point, but it's time to stop selling yourself short, don't you think?"

Nadine wasn't sure whether she was more stunned that George even knew who Dr. Phil was, much less was quoting him, or that he had the insight to understand what had gone wrong in her relationships. Over time her expectations had sunk lower than a pig's belly; it had only taken a winsome smile to charm her and a kind word to make her think she'd finally found the right man.

"You're probably onto something," she told George. "And you know what's really funny? It's Josh who's helped me to turn things around in terms of how I think about myself. When I came back here looking for a handout so I could get back on my feet, he insisted on me working on Amanda's house. I've made some real friends the last couple of months and discovered what I'm capable of."

She grinned at George. "I even stood up to someone who needed to be told a thing or two. When that house is finished and I move on, I don't think I'll ever sell myself short again."

George regarded her with unmistakable dismay. "What are you talking about, Nadine? You can't move on. You just said yourself that you've made real friends here. Why would you leave?"

"Because it's what I do," she said simply, accepting that some patterns were never likely to change. She didn't know anything about putting down roots. Neither, sadly, did Josh, which was why she despaired of him finding happiness with Maggie, who was all about roots and family history, even though she hadn't found the right man yet.

George grabbed her shoulders and looked into her eyes. "It's what you *used* to do," he said emphatically. "Now you stay and make things work right here."

"Josh isn't going to want me underfoot forever," she protested.

George shook his head. "You don't have to live with your son," he said impatiently. "We'll find you your own place."

"And how do you propose I pay for it?"

"If you need a job, we'll find one for you."

He said it with such confidence that Nadine almost believed it was a real possibility. Would she want to stay even if she could? She peered through the doorway into the main room of the gallery and spotted Amanda, Caleb, Josh and Maggie. Even Juliette Forsythe had been kind to her earlier today and thanked her for pulling together all these people to help Maggie. She and Juliette couldn't have had more dissimilar backgrounds, but this romance blossoming between their kids gave them something in common.

"Well?" George prodded. "Are you going to forget about this ridiculous idea of leaving town?"

She studied him curiously. "Why does it matter so much to you whether I go or stay? I thought I was nothing but a thorn in your side."

The question seemed to fluster him. "Isn't that obvious?"

"Not to me. I just told you, I'm the one whose instincts about men can't be trusted."

He leaned forward then and pressed a kiss to her lips, then sat back. "Does that tell you anything?"

She looked into his eyes and saw uncertainty and hope and determination. It was a heady combination, especially coming from a man whose respectability couldn't be questioned. "Why me, George?"

"Why not you?" he countered in a way that bolstered her self-respect by several notches.

Indeed, Nadine thought, why *not* her? There was promise in that kiss, but she'd learned not to trust promises.

"I don't suppose I have to make any decisions right away," she told him. "It'll be weeks before the house is finished."

"Then I'll just have to pull out all the stops and see what I can come up with to persuade you to stay," he said. "I used to be real good at closing business deals. I'm a little out of practice, but let's see what I can accomplish in the romance department. I imagine I can get the hang of it."

She touched his cheek. He hadn't shaved this morning and the slightly disreputable look suited him. He didn't seem nearly as intimidating as he usually did. "It'll certainly be flattering to have you try."

Maggie was arguing with Josh about his technique for removing the paint from Great-Grandmother Juliette's desk when she spotted Nadine and George emerging from her office looking flushed and awfully pleased with themselves. "Will you look at those two?" she murmured.

Josh turned to follow the direction of her gaze. "Dammit, not again!"

She frowned at his reaction. "You don't approve of your mother and George getting friendly?"

"I don't imagine it matters whether I approve or not. Nadine will do whatever the hell she wants to do and wind up getting hurt yet again. No man with a background like George Winslow's is going to be serious about Nadine."

"You're not giving her or George much credit," Maggie chided.

"Look, I can't blame George for latching on to whatever she's offering. Even *I* can see Nadine's appeal, though saying that about my own mother makes me cringe. It's Nadine. Why the hell hasn't she learned anything after all these years and all these mistakes? Why would she set herself up for heartache?"

"I think she's brave," Maggie said wistfully.

"Why? Because she repeatedly sets out to get her heart broken?"

"No, she repeatedly opens herself up to the possibility of love. You ought to admire that. Aren't you the one who accused me of being too closed off and not letting anybody in? Your mother's the exact opposite. Maybe she could teach me a thing or two."

"If you're looking for lessons, find somebody who's actually in a successful relationship," Josh advised. "Dinah, maybe. She and Cord seem ecstatic."

"They are disgustingly ecstatic," Maggie confirmed. "I'm not sure anybody can copy that."

His eyebrows rose. "Don't you even want to try?"

"Do you?"

"I don't know. Maybe. I think they've got a one-in-a-million thing, though." he said. "The rest of us are probably doomed to ordinary."

Maggie poked him in the ribs. "Are you saying sex with me is ordinary?"

"There you go mixing up sex and love again," he accused. "Two different things."

"Not always," Maggie said, again wistful. Sometimes lately, she had a feeling both were within her grasp if only she were brave enough to reach out and grab on tight. She couldn't help wondering if Josh ever felt the same way, but she was too scared to ask.

Instead, she forced her attention back to the desk. "I think we should send this down to Savannah to a professional furniture-restoration expert I know."

Josh sighed heavily. "What is it you think I do for a living?"

"Build things," she said, mostly because she knew it annoyed him to have his expertise diminished that way.

"I do historic renovation," he corrected patiently. "If you don't trust me, ask Cord. He seems to believe I'm reasonably skilled at what I do."

"You renovate buildings," she retorted. "We're talking about my great-grandmother's antique desk. I don't want to take any chances."

Josh rolled his eyes. "Okay, fine. We'll take it to Savannah."

She regarded him with surprise. The capitulation was almost too easy. "Just like that? You're caving in?"

He shrugged. "I know the desk has great sentimental value to you. If you'd feel better having it restored by someone you know and trust, it's okay with me," he said magnanimously. "We can drive it down tomorrow. I have some people I need to see down there anyway." He grinned at her. "Maybe this expert of yours can teach me some new techniques while we're at it. I'm always open to new ideas."

"He probably could," she said. "But you don't have to go. I can borrow a truck and take the desk down myself."

"Like I said, I have people I need to see in Savannah. Cord's been bugging me to get down there. Maybe you and I can stay over, have a great meal, walk along the river. I know a fantastic B&B on the waterfront— or there's one I've stayed at in town that has a room in the carriage house out back. You decide."

She regarded him suspiciously. "Since when have you spent a lot of time hanging out in fancy B&B's in Savannah?"

"Even a guy like me knows a little something about romancing a lady in style," he claimed.

"So you've stayed in these places with other women," Maggie said slowly, fighting the desire to slug him for past sins, as ridiculous as that would be. He might decide to start asking questions about her past and she definitely didn't want to go there.

"Does it matter whether I've stayed there before?" he asked.

"I think it does," she admitted. "I don't want to stay in some room where you've had a romantic tryst with another woman. I'll find us a place to stay."

"Fine. Suits me. You probably have better taste than I do. This way I won't have to listen to you complain about my choice."

Maggie wasn't sure she appreciated the suggestion that she might be too judgmental or picky, but she let the comment pass. "What time do you want to leave?"

"I'll pick you up early, say, around seven. We can stop for breakfast on the way down."

"If we're going that early, why not come back tomorrow night?" she asked.

"And miss the chance to romance you in some classy place? I don't think so."

Something didn't feel quite right about this whole excursion, but Maggie couldn't put her finger on it. Josh was saying all the right things, letting her have her own way. How could she argue with any of that?

"I'll be ready at seven," she said finally.

But between now and then, she was going to do her best to figure out just what Josh was up to.

Josh was pretty darn proud of himself. His little scheme had worked like a charm. He'd known from the outset of their conversation that Maggie would never in a million years let him lay a finger on her precious antique desk, no matter how qualified he might be to do the work. He'd seized the opportunity to get her out of town. Now all he had to do was entice her to stay there for more than one night—or at least until Detective Ryan had Brian safely in custody.

He'd had a couple of bad minutes when she'd questioned why they were staying at all. Once he had her in that room, though, he figured he could persuade her that there was no big hurry to get back. He'd stay in touch with Detective Ryan till Brian was behind bars before letting Maggie budge from Savannah.

Unfortunately, so far the police were having a hard time tracking the man down. If he was behind the destruction at the gallery, he'd wisely beat a hasty retreat out of Charleston once he'd accomplished his mission and wrecked the place. The cops had his apartment under surveillance 24/7. They'd assured Josh they would catch the man the minute he came back to town.

Meantime, Josh intended to keep Maggie otherwise occupied. She'd already started getting impatient that Brian wasn't locked up. Any second now Josh expected her to insist on looking for the man herself. The thought of Maggie and Ellie forming their own posse sent a shiver of alarm through him.

Relieved to be postponing such a potential calamity, he arrived at her place promptly at seven with the desk already in the back of the truck, wrapped in several blankets to keep it from sustaining any more damage on the trip to Savannah. He'd tossed his bag in the back of the truck, as well.

When Maggie opened the door, she gave him one of those long, lingering looks that might have raised the temperature of his blood ten degrees if there hadn't been so much suspicion behind it.

"What's wrong?" he asked.

"I'm not entirely sure."

"Did something happen?"

"No, not yet, anyway."

"Am I supposed to have the faintest idea what you're talking about?"

"You're up to something, Josh. I just can't figure out what it is."

"Me? I'm driving you to Savannah. What's so mysterious about that?"

Her expression remained puzzled. "I can't quite put my finger on it, but I will."

He shook his head. "Well, be sure to keep me posted."

"Oh, you can rest assured I will," she said.

"You know, Maggie, not everything in life is some big plot or conspiracy."

"No, not everything," she agreed. "But with you, I can't be sure."

He chuckled. "Maybe I just want to be alone with you someplace romantic. How dastardly is that?"

"I wish I believed that's all this trip is about," she said, crawling into the truck.

"If you're so suspicious of my motives, why are you going?"

"So I can have my way with you, of course," she said sweetly. "Why should I miss out on that just because I don't trust you entirely?"

"Why indeed?" Josh muttered. The workings of her mind would never cease to amaze him.

He stole a glance at her as he pulled onto the highway. "Tell me again how a woman from Charleston, which is loaded with people who are experts in restoring antiques, wound up using someone in Savannah?"

"Geoffrey Latham used to be in Charleston. Then he met someone and fell in love. Since his family disapproved, they set up shop in Savannah."

"Are we talking a gay couple here?" Josh asked.

She frowned at the question. "Does it matter?"

"To me? No. I was just wondering why his family objected. Sexual orientation seemed like the most logical reason."

"Well, you happen to be right, but there could have been dozens of other reasons."

"Such as?"

"Class is very important to some people in Charleston," she began.

"To your family?" he inquired, then held his breath. He'd been getting along with the Forsythes, but he doubted he was their idea of a good candidate for a son-in-law.

"To some degree, I suppose."

Josh felt a knot form in his gut. "So you figure you're slumming with me? Is this thing with us still about driving your mama crazy?"

"I don't go slumming," she said indignantly. "I choose my friends and my lovers because I enjoy their company, not because of who they are or how much money they have."

"But you can't deny that having your mama get all riled up is a nice bonus," Josh said.

"Okay, yes, sometimes that has been a factor," she admitted. "I'm not very proud of that."

"How about this time?" Josh pressed, unable to let the subject drop, even though he was hating every one of her answers.

"If that's what you and I were about, I'd be flaunting you under her nose, not running off to Savannah with you."

"Come on, sugar, you don't have to flaunt anything. You know she'll get wind of this. It's not like people don't know we're going."

"How could anyone possibly know? Have you been bragging?"

"No, I have not been bragging," he said with exasperation. "But there were a lot of people around when we made these plans. I had to tell Cord I was going to be away a couple of days. I'd be willing to bet you told Dinah, to say nothing of Ellie and Vicki, since they must be covering for you at the gallery."

"Okay, yes, but what does that have to do with my mother finding out?"

"Did you swear them all to secrecy?"

"No, of course not."

"Then odds are, your mother will find out. She'll call the store looking for you or she'll talk to Dinah. Whoever she speaks to will innocently mention that you and I are away together." He slanted a look at her. "Will she freak out?"

Maggie hesitated. "I honestly don't know."

"Maybe that's not even the important question," Josh said thoughtfully.

"What is, then?"

"Do you care if she flips out?"

"Truthfully, I don't care what she thinks."

Josh couldn't hide his skepticism. "Really?"

"Really," she said flatly. "This is not about my mother."

"Since when?"

"Since I realized a few days ago that there didn't seem to be anything I could do that scared you off," she said wryly. "Now it's all about me and whether or not understanding that will send me running for the hills."

That was an unexpected twist. Josh wasn't sure how he felt about it. He met her gaze briefly. "Come to any conclusions about that yet?"

"Nope. The jury's still out."

"You realize this is dangerous new turf for both of us," he teased.

"Tell me about it."

He liked the way her willingness to court danger made him feel. "I'll do what I can to make it worth your while."

"I'm counting on that," she said. "Which is why I made a reservation for an early check-in. I thought we might want to get started on that part right away."

Josh laughed. "Darlin' you surely are full of surprises."

"Something you should probably keep in mind."

"Oh, believe me, it's not something I'm likely to forget."

In fact, he had a hunch Maggie was capable of taking him on more nail-biting roller-coaster rides than any woman he'd ever met.

20

It was two days before they even considered emerging from the hotel room Maggie had reserved for them in Savannah. It was a good thing she'd instinctively chosen a place that had outstanding room service.

Wednesday morning they were lingering over fresh strawberries and Belgian waffles when she sat back with a contented sigh. "As amazing as this has been, we probably should deliver that desk to Geoffrey before he wonders what happened to me. He knows I'm in town and I'm beginning to run out of excuses for not getting it over to his shop."

"Maybe you should just tell him the truth," Josh suggested. "That you're having yourself a wild fling."

Judging from his expression, he spoke only partially in jest.

"As interesting as I'm sure he'd find that," Maggie said dryly, "I think maybe discretion would be better. He still knows a lot of people in Charleston."

"You ashamed of what we've been up to?" Josh inquired, his voice edged with tension.

"Don't be ridiculous," Maggie said emphatically. "Why would I be ashamed of this? It's been fabulous."

"Fabulous, huh?" He grinned, looking pleased with himself. "I certainly thought so. You do have a way about you, Magnolia."

"Very amusing," she replied, fighting a smile. "But it has to end sometime. We can't hide out down here forever, as attractive as that sounds to me right this second. Besides, you should see whoever it is you need to see and then we should get back home."

"What's the rush?"

"I hardly think we're rushing. We pretty much locked ourselves away in here for two days." She grinned seductively as she slid her bare foot up his calf. "I'd say we've taken our time getting to know each other a whole lot better, wouldn't you?"

"We've made some progress," he conceded with a renewed glint of desire in his eyes. "We can always do better."

"And I'm sure we will," she agreed crisply. "But now it's time to get back to the real world."

"I wasn't aware we were on a timetable."

"We're not," she said impatiently. "But we both have responsibilities." Until she'd gone into hiding after her aborted wedding, she'd never stayed away from work for more than a couple of days, and now, with so much going on, wasn't the time to start. With Brian still on the loose, it wasn't right to leave Ellie and Vicki on their own to deal with him if he went on another rampage.

"I suppose you're right," Josh agreed with unmistakable reluctance. He gave her a deliberately enticing grin. "But we could play hooky one more day without our respective worlds falling apart, couldn't we? I don't have any work to do on Amanda's house till Saturday, and I'm sure Ellie has your shop under control."

On the one hand, Maggie thought, his effort to keep her here away from their cares was flattering. On the other, something was screaming in her head that she shouldn't trust his motives one bit.

"I'm sure Ellie is doing just fine, but the gallery is my responsibility. Are you so anxious to stay because this has been so incredible?" she asked. "Or is there some specific reason you want to stay away from Charleston as long as possible?"

Before he could answer, the truth suddenly dawned on her. "That's it, isn't it? This has all been a ruse to keep me away from Charleston," she declared, not sure whether she was more furious with him for deceiving her, or herself for being stupid enough to fall for it. To think the trip had all been a calculated ploy was enough to ruin the fabulous time they'd had.

Her accusation didn't seem to faze Josh. His expression remained perfectly bland.

"A ruse? Where do you come up with this stuff? What makes you think I was trying to keep you away from Charleston?" he inquired without rancor. "Why would I do that?"

"Because you were convinced I'd go after Brian myself if the police didn't drag him into custody immediately," she charged, gathering steam as she mentally filled in the blanks for herself. "This whole trip has been about protecting me, about keeping me from doing something stupid. Well, what about Ellie? Did you ever consider the possibility that she might be the one who needs protecting?"

"Taken care of," he said calmly.

"How? What do you mean?"

"I mean there's someone looking out for her and the gallery every minute," he explained.

That was some comfort, she admitted, though only to herself. Still glowering at him, she said, "Which left you to guard me."

He still refused to confess. "And here I thought the past couple of days were all about you and me having some pretty amazing sex and a few gourmet meals."

"We could have had sex and great food in Charleston," she retorted.

"And I suspect we will," he said, amusement dancing in his eyes.

"Not if I find out you lied to get me down here," she said. "If you ever get lucky with me again, it'll only be because I decide not to kill you."

He held up a hand. "Hold on a second, Maggie. How do you propose to prove whether I lied? You're the one who wanted to bring that desk to Geoffrey. I agreed to bring you. For all I know, you're the one who had ulterior motives. Talk about a ruse! You could have lured me here just to get my pants off."

Her temper streaked into the stratosphere. "Don't you dare try to turn this around and question my motives," she said. "I could have had that desk down here and been back in Charleston by midafternoon. You were the one with all the big talk about romance."

"You weren't objecting that strenuously about an hour ago, or a few hours before that, or day before yesterday," he reminded her.

"A real gentleman wouldn't throw that back in a lady's face."

He laughed, then quickly swallowed it. "Sorry."

"If you say I haven't been behaving like a lady, I will

personally dump hot, scalding coffee over your head," she threatened and meant every word of it.

"Then I certainly won't say that," he said solemnly.

"Do you have any idea how much you're annoying me right now?"

He nodded. "Even I'm not dense enough to miss your point," he said.

She frowned at that. "Nobody ever said you were dense."

"Sorry. I must have misinterpreted. I was beginning to think I was nothing more than some sort of sex slave with devious motives."

She threw her napkin at him as she flounced into the bathroom and turned on the shower. The man was infuriating. Absolutely, positively infuriating! Sex slave, indeed.

It wasn't until she stepped under the shower that she permitted herself to grin. The whole sex-slave thing was an interesting concept. It was certainly a lot less threatening than what was really going on. The truth was that as infuriating as Josh might be with this whole protective mode he was in, she was beginning to fall just a little bit in love with him because of it.

Not one single man before him had ever thought she needed help or protection or even a shoulder to lean on. Heck, until Josh, *she* hadn't thought she needed any of that. She'd always prided herself on her competence and her ability to handle any crisis.

But she was discovering that sharing life with someone else—the good and the bad—made everything better.

"What's the word from Detective Ryan?" Josh asked Cord, keeping his voice low. He'd called as soon as he heard the shower running in the bathroom. Since things were rapidly spinning out of control here, he needed an update on what was going on back in Charleston. He wanted to know what sort of danger Maggie might be in when she got back, since it seemed inevitable that they were leaving here today.

"Brian's still among the missing," Cord said. "I don't like the fact that there's been no sign of him. Something weird's going on. I can feel it. Can you keep Maggie away for a few more days?"

"I'll be lucky to keep her away a few more hours," Josh confessed with disgust. "She's onto me. She figured out why we're here and she is not happy."

"Then you must not have been doing something right," Cord suggested.

"Oh, believe me, I got that part right. I just couldn't figure out any way to shut off her brain the rest of the time. Somewhere between the waffle and the strawberries and whipped cream, she got to thinking."

"I suppose that mind of hers would be a terrible thing to waste," Cord said, not even trying to contain his amusement. "So, you're coming back today?"

"Afraid so."

"Then we'll just have to make sure one of us is with her at all times to make sure she doesn't go off on her own in search of Brian. Or to make sure he doesn't get to her. Something tells me he's just biding his time."

"To be honest, I don't think she's going to let me anywhere near her for a while," Josh admitted. "She considers my motives suspect."

"Then we'll get a whole crowd of people together and tell them what's going on. We can see to it that she's never alone."

"We can't pull the people we've got keeping an eye on Ellie," Josh reminded him. "She's determined to make up for what happened at Images. She can be as impulsive as Maggie. She might get some crazy idea to go after Brian herself. Even with all he's done, I'm not sure she understands how dangerous he really is."

"I talked to Vicki," Cord said. "On the surface she seems like a bit of a flake, but I trust her to keep an eye on things. Ellie's not going anywhere alone if Vicki has anything to say about it. And the police have kept their promise to keep a close eye on the gallery in case Brian shows up there. There's been a cop nearby every time I've gone past the place. There's another one patrolling the area around Ellie's loft."

"Then I guess we've done what we can," Josh said, though it was small comfort. If only he were half as certain that Maggie wouldn't come up with some outlandish scheme that would put her in danger.

"Of course, there might be one more thing you could do," Cord said thoughtfully.

"What's that?" Josh asked at once. "I'll do whatever it takes to keep her safe."

"You could arrange for a flood at that motel of yours," Cord said. "I don't think it would take much to put your room underwater."

"Which would accomplish what?" Josh asked. "There are other rooms."

"Insist they're all booked," Cord said. "Maggie won't check."

"And my mother's room?"

"Too small for the two of you," Cord said.

Lord knows that was true enough, Josh thought with a shudder. "Okay, and then what?"

"You throw yourself on Maggie's mercy. She'll take you in. I can almost guarantee it."

"It's the *almost* that terrifies me," Josh said. "I could be sleeping on the street with a suitcase filled with soaking-wet clothes."

"It won't come to that," Cord said confidently.

"I don't know. Maggie's pretty furious with me right now."

"Then I suggest you mend fences on the way home so she'll be feeling all sympathetic when she hears about your sad plight later today."

Josh was filled with doubts. As desperate as he was to stick to her like glue, he didn't want to risk antagonizing her with yet another deception. When this mess was over, he wanted the two of them to have something left.

"You really think she'll fall for this?" he asked Cord.

"I think she'll ask to see the flooded-out room, but yes, I think she'll take you in," Cord said with certainty. "She has a big heart. Besides, you've been locked away with her in that hotel room for two days. Surely she must see some redeeming qualities in you."

Josh grinned, despite his skepticism over Cord's plot. "Not to brag on myself, but I think we get along just fine as long as we never leave the bed. It's when Maggie starts stirring around that things get a little dicey."

"Then I think your mission is obvious. Get her back up here and back into bed."

"You make it sound like a slam dunk. For a man who's known Maggie as long as you have, shouldn't you know better than that?"

"I have confidence in you," Cord said. "Keep me posted on how it's going. Meantime, I'll rally the troops."

"Does that include Dinah?" Josh inquired worriedly.

"Of course. Why?"

"Then you might want to keep a few of the details of your plan to yourself. In my experience, this is the kind of thing women can't wait to share with their best friends. They consider it their duty to stand together against a common enemy—us."

"You have a point," Cord conceded. "I'll just give Dinah the bare facts about the importance of keeping Maggie from doing anything foolish. I'll enlist her aid. She knows how Maggie's mind works. She could be a big help."

"Good idea," Josh said, relieved. He heard the water cut off in the bathroom. "I'd better go. We'll talk once I'm back in Charleston."

"Call me if you need any help in making sure those pipes in your motel room suffer a major leak."

"I don't think that's going to be a problem," Josh said wryly. "Nadine could make that happen with a couple of straight pins. The only thing left of those pipes is the rust."

He saw the handle on the bathroom door twist. "Gotta go," he said, then hung up the phone and feigned sleep.

"Who were you talking to?" Maggie asked as she walked into the bedroom.

"What?" he murmured groggily.

"Oh, stop it. I know you were on the phone. Who were you talking to?"

Josh sighed and sat up. "I was just checking in with Cord."

She didn't look as if she believed him. "And you didn't want me to know that because?"

"Because I knew you'd jump to the wrong conclusion and assume we were conspiring against you," he said.

"Weren't you?"

"No, we were going over the list of people he wanted me to see while I'm here," Josh claimed, amazed at how readily the lies tripped off his tongue. "I should be able to catch up with most of them while you're going over the desk restoration with Geoffrey."

Her face revealed undisguised skepticism, but she finally nodded. "I'll be ready in fifteen minutes. How about you?"

"I can be ready then," he agreed, pushing down the desire to try to tempt her back to bed. He might succeed, but she wouldn't thank him for it. "Just let me take a quick shower."

She nodded, her cheeks turning pink when he climbed out of bed buck naked and walked into the bathroom.

"Nothing you haven't seen before," he said as he passed her and shut the bathroom door.

"It's not going to work, you know," she called after him.

He opened the door and poked his head out. "What's not going to work?"

"You're not going to lure me into that shower with you."

"Did you hear me try?"

"No, but I know how your mind works," she claimed.

"Not half as well as I know yours," he retorted. "If I wanted you in this shower with me, I'd be more direct."

"Oh? How's that?"

He walked into the bedroom, scooped her into his arms and carried her into the bathroom and stepped straight into the tub, then turned on the shower. She was sputtering with indignation when he finally lowered her to her feet.

But then he lathered up his hands with soap and skimmed them across her breasts, and the protests died on her lips. The fifteen-minute timetable they'd been on pretty much went up in flames.

Maggie couldn't recall a time in her entire adult life when she'd been more sated…or more exasperated with the man responsible. Josh was sneaky and clever and seemed to know exactly how to make her body respond. He was thickheaded, however, about the way her mind worked. Unfortunately, in his arrogance, he didn't accept that.

She knew what he'd been up to in the shower. Okay, besides that! He'd been stalling. He and Cord had probably devised some new scheme to keep her from reneging on her promise to let the police track down Brian. Josh was no doubt buying time till they could put their plan into action.

She was more convinced of that than ever when he dropped her off at Geoffrey's, then disappeared with some halfhearted promise to be back as soon as he could. She'd been waiting for him for two solid hours and she was just about ready to rent a car and drive back to Charleston on her own. That would serve him right.

"Maggie darling, if you don't mind me saying so, you seem a little agitated," Geoffrey said, regarding her with amusement. "Did you and that gorgeous man have a little spat before you got here?"

"No, but we're going to have a humdinger of a spat when he finally gets back," she said grimly.

"Why is that?" Geoffrey asked.

"He's up to something."

Her old friend looked horrified. "You mean like sneaking off to be with another woman?"

"Good grief, no," she said.

"Then what else matters?"

"He's trying to keep me away from Charleston. He thinks it's for my own good."

Geoffrey shook his head in disbelief. "Speaking as someone who is quite happy to be away from Charleston," he said, "I'm not sure I see the problem, especially given the way you've always fought with your mother over your right to live life on your own terms."

"For once, this has nothing to do with my mother. It's about Josh trying to save me from myself. He's got this whole macho protective thing going on."

Geoffrey frowned. "Why would you need protecting?"

"It's a long story," Maggie said.

Geoffrey poured them both a cup of tea. "Do tell. It seems we have plenty of time."

Maggie summarized what she'd been through with Brian and his destruction of the gallery. "Josh doesn't want me back there till the guy's in custody."

"Because he's afraid that next time, this Brian will harm you," Geoffrey concluded.

"That, or that I'll take the law into my own hands and go after him. Believe me, if I knew where he was, I'd be tempted to do just that."

"Then I'm on Josh's side. Stay right here, darling. There's no need for you to risk your pretty little neck."

"The man destroyed things that mean something to me," Maggie said indignantly. "You saw that desk of Great-Grandmother's. That's just the tip of the iceberg. How can I allow him to get away with that?"

"You don't. You let the police handle it. He'll pay."

Maggie gave Geoffrey a rueful look. "I'm not sure I'll get the same satisfaction out of that."

"No, but in the civilized world, we have to make do," he said. "Now let's forget about that awful man for a minute, and tell me about you and Josh. Are you in love with him? He seems like the type you've always fallen hard for."

Maggie sighed. "You think so?"

"Well, of course. Sexy, handsome, dangerous. Does he have issues, too?"

"A million of them," she admitted.

Geoffrey's gaze narrowed. "But there's something different this time, isn't there? I can see it in your eyes."

She nodded, finally daring to admit aloud what she'd seen in Josh that scared her. "Dinah says he has staying power."

"She's good at reading people, no question about that," Geoffrey said. He paused to study her. "So, does that terrify you?"

"It should, shouldn't it?"

He chuckled. "That's not what I asked. Does it?"

"Not so much," she admitted, still amazed by the sense of peace that stole through her when she thought about the two of them and forever. "I just don't know whether I can trust any of it—what I'm feeling, what he's feeling, the little glimpses I keep getting of the future. I've never gotten that far before."

"Take it from a man who got hit by a bolt from the blue after about a thousand false starts, Maggie. If Josh is the one, grab on to him and don't let go. It's worth every roller-coaster up and down you'll go through."

She grinned at his blissful expression. "No regrets for you, then?"

"Not a one."

"Really?" She regarded him skeptically. "Have you had any contact at all with your family?"

"Martin is my family," he said determinedly, though there was no mistaking the sorrow shadowing his eyes when he spoke.

"Maybe your folks will come around," Maggie said. "They only wanted what was best for you."

"No, they wanted a heterosexual son who'd fill the house with grandchildren in the fine old Latham tradition. They'll never understand my choice, much less accept it."

"I'm sorry."

He smiled sadly. "So am I, some of the time. The rest of the time, I'm just grateful that I was brave enough to walk away and live the life I was meant to live."

The mention of bravery gave Maggie something more to think about. If Geoffrey was brave enough to risk everything for love, maybe she could be, as well. Not that she was in love with Josh just yet, but when the time came. *If* it came, she amended.

Needing a distraction from that line of thought, she asked, "Geoffrey, can I use your phone? My cell-phone battery died. I forgot to charge it."

"Other things on your mind, I'm sure," he said with undisguised amusement, then gestured toward his phone. "Help yourself."

She dialed the number for Images, growing more and more impatient when no one picked up. She disconnected, then dialed again. Same result. No answer. Panic threaded through her just as the bell over the front door rang and Josh called out.

"Back here," Maggie responded as she lifted the receiver and dialed one more time.

Josh walked into Geoffrey's office and automatically dropped a kiss on her forehead. "You two been catching up?"

She gave him a wry look. "You certainly gave us long enough to do it," she said as she listened to the phone continue to ring at the gallery.

Josh didn't rise to the bait. "One of the places I went had exactly the kind of crown molding Cord's been looking for. It took a while to make the deal and load up the truck."

She was taken aback that he'd actually been conducting the business he'd claimed to have. Until that moment, she realized she hadn't trusted that he wasn't sitting in his truck around the corner, on his cell phone with the Charleston police or with Cord.

Slowly she put Geoffrey's phone back in its cradle. "I think we need to go, Josh," she said, trying to keep the panic from her voice.

He picked up on it, anyway, and frowned. "What's going on?"

"I've been trying to reach Ellie at the gallery, and no one's answering."

"Maybe she's in the bathroom," he said, his voice calm as he took out his cell phone and punched in a number.

Maybe she was, Maggie conceded, but she couldn't seem to shake an image of Ellie being locked in there bound and gagged.

"Come on, dammit, pick up," Josh muttered, which told her he was as worried as she was.

"Are you calling the gallery?" she asked.

"No. I'm calling Cord."

"You'd probably have better luck with your detective friend," she said. "Cord and Dinah tend to be hard to reach these days."

He looked surprised. "Cord always answers his cell phone."

"Oh, really? Maybe that's the mistake I've been making. I've been trying their home phone."

Still frowning, Josh hung up and tried again. This time right after he hit the talk button, his expression brightened. "There you are. I was beginning to worry." He listened, then grinned. "Sorry to interrupt, but we have ourselves a situation."

He explained about Maggie's attempts to reach anyone at the gallery, then nodded. "We're about to hit the road. Call me back as soon as you know anything, okay?"

"What did he say?" Maggie asked.

"He's calling the police and heading over to the gallery himself. He'll call as soon as he gets there."

"I don't like this," Maggie said.

"I'm not crazy about it myself," Josh admitted. "Let's get going."

Maggie nodded, then bent down to give Geoffrey a kiss. "I know Great-Grandmother's desk is in good hands."

"It'll be good as new when I'm finished," Geoffrey promised. "You'll let me know what's going on up there?"

"As soon as we know," Maggie agreed.

Geoffrey turned to Josh. "Keep her safe, okay?"

Josh nodded. "That's the plan."

"No matter how she balks," Geoffrey added with a pointed look in her direction.

Josh chuckled. "Ah, I see you know her well."

"Most of her life," Geoffrey said. "Which means I know she won't make anything easy for you. Don't give up."

Josh looked vaguely perplexed. "Are we still talking about keeping her safe?"

"Not entirely," Geoffrey admitted. "Just keep that advice in mind whatever happens to come up between the two of you."

Maggie gave her old friend a frustrated look. "Stop going over to the enemy. You're supposed to be on my side."

"I am on your side, darling. Always." Geoffrey gave her a stern look. "But you don't always know what's best for you. It's up to those of us who love you to stick together to overcome that stubborn streak."

"Amen to that," Josh said, shaking Geoffrey's hand. "If I need any pointers, I'll be sure to give you a call."

"Always happy to oblige," Geoffrey said.

Exasperated with the pair of them, Maggie headed for the door. "I'm leaving. You all can continue this lovefest if you want to."

"Right behind you," Josh said, amusement threading through his voice.

She scowled at him when they were in the truck. "You enjoyed that, didn't you?"

Josh switched on the ignition. "What?"

"Winning over my friend."

"It's not about taking sides, sugar," he said as he pulled away from the curb. "You heard the man. It's about making sure you're safe. When it comes to that, I'll hook up with anyone who can help me get the job done."

"You're a little obsessed. You know that, don't you?"

"Would you like it better if I just sat back and let you get yourself killed?"

"I am not going to get myself killed," she said. "That's absurd."

"A few days ago you told me Brian was all talk," Josh reminded her. "Can you say the same thing after seeing the damage he caused at Images? Isn't that why you were in such a panic when Ellie didn't answer the phone? You know there could be a dozen different explanations, but the first thing that came to mind was Brian."

Maggie sat back. "Okay, yes," she admitted wearily as a vision of the mess and the viciousness behind it reeled through her mind.

"Then let me help," Josh said. "I know you're strong. I know you're capable. I know you've been fighting your own battles for a long time now. I just want to be around in case you need backup, okay?"

The request was so reasonable when he put it that way, she could hardly deny it. "Okay."

He seemed stunned by her easy acquiescence. "Will you let me stay at your place for a while?"

She regarded him with a narrowed gaze. This was a twist she hadn't seen coming. "You want to move in?"

He nodded.

"Maybe we should wait till we see what's happened today before making that kind of decision," she said, feeling even more uneasy now than she had when her calls to the gallery hadn't been answered.

"Come on, Maggie. Until this whole thing is over, I'm not going to feel good about you being alone. I'll sleep on the sofa, if that'll make you happier."

She frowned. "Why would that make me happier?"

He glanced at her. "I don't want you getting the idea that this is just about me getting into your bed."

"Since we've pretty much established that I *like* having you in my bed, I don't think that'll be an issue," she said candidly. She thought about his proposal for some time, then said, "Okay, you can move in."

"Thank goodness," he said.

"You sound awfully relieved," she noted.

He grinned. "I had a plan B. It was a little over the top."

"Which was?"

"You don't want to know."

"Oh, I want to know," she assured him. "You don't want me to know in case you have to use it later."

"That, too," he conceded. He reached for her hand and wove his fingers through hers, then lifted their hands and brushed a kiss across her knuckles. "Thank you for being reasonable."

"I'm always reasonable," she said stoutly.

When his laughter filled the cab of the truck, she was tempted to take back her offer, but then she chuckled, too. Who was she kidding? She was *never* reasonable.

And the fact that it hadn't scared Josh away was absolutely mind-boggling.

21

As satisfied as he was with Maggie's agreement to let him move in, Josh began to seriously worry when they'd driven for miles without getting a call from Cord. Something was obviously up at the gallery, and he didn't like his gut-deep sense that it wasn't good.

"Why do you think Cord hasn't called back?" Maggie asked eventually, her tone echoing his worry. "Something's really wrong. I can feel it."

"Let's try not to imagine the worst," Josh told her, even though his mind had traveled down that same path.

Just then his cell phone rang. At last! He had to gently bat Maggie's hand away to keep her from grabbing it from him. Whatever the news was, he wanted to be the one to hear it first.

"Cord?"

"Yeah. Sorry to take so long to get back to you, but I wanted to gather all the facts before I called."

"What the hell is going on? Is Ellie okay?"

"Ellie's fine. So is the gallery, but not for lack of trying on someone's part," Cord said, his voice tight with tension.

"Tell me."

"Someone started a fire out back in one of the trash bins. They set it so it blocked the back exit. It was also close enough for the door to catch fire, which I'm sure was just what they had in mind. By the time Ellie smelled the smoke at the same time the alarm went off, there was a pretty good blaze going back there. The fire department got here before there was any damage inside, but the whole place reeks of smoke. We've got fans going now."

"Water damage?"

"None. The worst of the fire was contained outside in that trash bin. I've arranged for the waste management company to haul away the trash bin as soon as the police and fire department give the okay. And I've already gone to get a replacement for the back door. I got a metal one this time."

"Thanks, pal. We'll be there in another forty-five minutes or so. Stick around, okay?"

"I'm not going anywhere," Cord assured him. "I can't help thinking how much worse this could have been if the fire had been set at night or at either Maggie's home or Ellie's."

"Believe me, the same thought has already crossed my mind," Josh said.

"You having any luck on that plan we discussed earlier?"

"Taken care of," Josh replied.

"Well, that's something at least."

"Yeah, but is it enough?" Josh said, his gaze shifting briefly to Maggie, who was looking way too pale. "See you soon and thanks, Cord. I appreciate it."

He hung up slowly, expecting Maggie to deluge him with questions. Instead, she was strangely silent.

"How much of that did you get?" he asked.

"Enough to know that I'm not going to like the rest," she said. "What happened?"

"Someone set a fire out back."

What little color there was in her face drained out. "Ellie?" she asked.

"She's okay. The smoke detector went off and she smelled the smoke and got help before there was any damage inside the gallery."

"God," Maggie said. "You were right. Brian really *is* messed up, isn't he?"

"I'd say so. The cops will get him, though, Maggie. And in the meantime, we'll make sure you and Ellie are safe. Do you trust me to see to that?"

"I know you'll try," she said wearily, then lay her head against the back of the seat and closed her eyes.

It wasn't the ringing endorsement Josh might have preferred, but it was something, at least from a woman who had plenty of well-honed trust issues.

Maggie didn't want to get out of the truck when they finally arrived at Images. Despite Josh's reassurances that there'd been no serious damage, she didn't want to see one more shred of evidence of just how dangerous and out of control Brian was. The sight of the fire truck that remained at the scene was proof enough of that. It shook her in ways that the vicious vandalism had not.

Before she could tell Josh she wanted to go home, though, Dinah was opening the passenger door of the truck. Ellie was with her, and Warren was lurking behind them, his expression filled with concern.

"Are things so bad you thought it smart to have a

shrink here in case I flip out or something?" Maggie asked the two women.

"Everything is just fine inside," Ellie said, "I promise. Warren stopped by just after I called the fire department. He stuck around to help."

"And you?" Maggie asked. "How are you?"

"A little shaky, but mostly from the adrenaline rush wearing off."

"You should be home resting," Maggie told her.

"I agree," Warren said, putting an arm around Ellie's shoulders protectively.

What was that about? Maggie wondered. Interesting.

Then Dinah said, "Ellie refused to leave till you got here. Vicki's inside, too. I think she has designs on one of the firefighters."

The comment actually succeeded in making Maggie smile. Things were getting back to normal if Vicki was using the fire as an opportunity to go on the hunt for a new man.

Inside, there was a faint whiff of smoke in the air, but the huge fans that had been brought in had dispersed most of it. In the back with the new door already in place, it didn't look as if anything had happened. She couldn't bring herself to open the door and look outside, though. She was relieved that Warren and Ellie hadn't come into the back with her. Dinah, however, hadn't left her side.

"Sit," Dinah ordered. "You look a little shaky."

"I'm okay," Maggie said, but she sat just the same.

"I think you should come and stay with Cord and me," Dinah said decisively. "I won't take no for an answer."

"And interrupt the eternal honeymoon? I don't think so," Maggie retorted. "Besides, I got a better deal."

"Oh?"

"Josh is moving in," she said, then quickly added, "temporarily."

Dinah's mouth gaped. "You agreed to that?"

"It seemed like the sensible thing to do."

Dinah's lips curved. "Sensible, huh? Did you agree to this before or after you heard about the fire?"

"Before, as a matter of fact."

"Even more telling."

"Oh, go stuff a sock in it."

"The response of a woman who knows I'm right. Josh is moving in because you like the idea, not because you're scared. If it were just a matter of being scared, you'd be moving in with us or your folks."

"You don't know what you're talking about," Maggie said.

"Tell me that when he's still underfoot months from now," Dinah responded cheerfully.

"That is *not* going to happen," Maggie replied.

But somewhere deep down inside, she was very much afraid that it might. Now, *that* was something that should really terrify her. Strangely, it did not.

Josh swung by the motel to pick up his things before taking Maggie home. He didn't want to risk letting her out of his sight, mostly because he feared she'd change her mind if she had time to think about letting him move in with her and all the possible motives he might have for requesting it, motives that went beyond her safety. He was a little muddy on that himself.

When he pulled into a parking space outside his room, Nadine immediately appeared next door. "You're home," she said, her face alight with curiosity. "Did you and Maggie have yourselves a real good time?"

Maggie emerged from the truck and Nadine flushed. "Sorry. I didn't see you in there," Nadine apologized, though she didn't look especially contrite.

To Josh's relief, Maggie merely looked amused.

"That's okay," she assured Nadine. "You're a mother. You have a right to ask your son if I've kept him adequately entertained."

"That is not what I was asking him," Nadine protested weakly. "Not exactly, anyway." She shrugged off her obvious embarrassment and, hands on her hips, demanded, "Okay, are you two ready to admit you're an item or what? I'm getting tired of pretending I don't see what's going on right under my nose."

Josh scowled at her. He figured the only way to shut her up about his personal life was to put her on the defensive. "What is it you think you see, Mother, or do I even have to ask? You always did start hearing the wedding march sometime after the first kiss. Are you hearing it when you're with George Winslow?"

Nadine scowled at him. "Don't drag George into this conversation. It's about you and Maggie."

"Maggie and I are just fine," Josh claimed. At least he thought they were. They might not have defined where they were or where they were going, but the current setup seemed to suit them. He'd see how it wore on them after he'd moved into her place for a few days. "I'm going inside to pack a few things."

Nadine's eyes widened. "Pack? You just got back."

"And now I'm leaving again," he said tersely, then went inside and shut the door behind him. He didn't want Maggie seeing the inside of this dump.

He could hear the murmur of voices outside the door, so he threw his stuff into a suitcase as quickly as he could to get back to the two of them before Nadine pried too much information out of Maggie. He had a hunch she might not be as reticent as he'd prefer.

When he stepped out into the bright sunlight, Nadine was alone and Maggie was back in the truck. His mother regarded him speculatively.

"What did you say to her?" he demanded. "If you did anything to upset her, I will never forgive you."

"Oh, for goodness' sake, calm down. Maggie's not upset. I just gave her a few things to think about."

"Such as?"

"That's between Maggie and me. Now I have a couple of things to say to you."

"I don't want to hear them," Josh said adamantly.

"Do you actually think that's going to stop me?" she asked, regarding him with amusement.

"Okay, fine," he muttered, resigned. "Get it over with."

Her gaze was steady. "You've never done anything like this before," she said quietly.

"Like what?" he asked, immediately defensive.

"Moved in with a woman."

"How the hell would you know that? You haven't been around in years."

"Okay, then, I'll ask. Have you ever lived with a woman?"

He felt as uncomfortable as he had at seventeen when Nadine had handed him a condom and told him to remember what it was for. "No, but I don't see what that's got to do with anything. Nor do I see how it's any of your business. Besides, Maggie and I are not living together the way you mean. We're sharing her house for the time being so I can keep an eye on her. Did she tell you about the fire?"

Nadine's eyes widened. "What fire?"

He gave her the condensed version. "And that's why I'm moving in," he concluded, ignoring the fact that the timing of the decision had been slightly different. This scenario would make sense to Nadine and get her off his case.

"Then you'll be sleeping in a guest room or on a sofa or something?" his mother asked, still skeptical.

"It is definitely none of your business where I sleep. I'm drawing the line right there, Mother." He tossed his bag in the back of the truck and started to step inside. "This discussion is over."

Nadine latched on to his arm. "Hold on just a minute and look at me, Josh Parker. I may not have earned the right to tell you what to do, but I am your mother, so I'm entitled to worry about you. No matter what you say to me or what you tell yourself, this is a big step. Don't do it if you're not making a statement to Maggie about your intentions."

"My intention is to protect her from that psychopath."

Nadine gave him a knowing look. "I know that's probably what you're telling yourself."

"It's the truth, dammit!"

She regarded him sympathetically. "Oh, sweetie, I think you want much more than that. I think you're going to walk into that house of hers and find everything that's always been missing in your life and it's going to kill you when the crisis is over and you have to leave."

Josh was startled by her insight. He wanted to deny

that there was any truth at all to her claim, but he couldn't. "Maybe so," he admitted. "But that's a small price to pay to make sure Maggie's safe, don't you agree?"

"Be honest with her, Josh," Nadine said urgently. "Tell her now that it's about more than that. Tell her you're in love with her and you want it all."

He closed his eyes, still trying to block out the truth in his mother's words. If he admitted that he loved Maggie, then he had to face the fact that the rest was true, as well, that it would kill him to walk away when Brian was behind bars.

"You know," Nadine said quietly, "Maggie might surprise you. She might be just as much in love with you as you are with her."

For the first time in years, Josh looked into his mother's eyes and saw the real concern there. When had their relationship changed? When had she once again assumed the role of parent? Didn't she know it was too late now? He'd needed her years ago and she hadn't been there, not the way he'd wanted her to be. Unfortunately, he couldn't waste time exploring all that ancient history now.

Instead, he said, "I can't take that chance. Because if you're wrong, she'll keep me out and I have to be there now."

She gave him a sad smile. "I knew you'd say that."

"How?"

"Because you've always put everyone's needs before your own, even mine at a time when I didn't deserve it."

"I'll be okay, Mother. I've always been okay."

"Yes, I imagine so. You're a lot stronger than I ever was. But something tells me you'll pay a terrible price just the same."

"You know, I used to think I was the strong one and you were weak," he said with rare candor. "But I've developed a whole new appreciation for you since you've been here. I think you're the strongest person I've ever met. Now, let me get out of here before Maggie changes her mind. I'll see you on Saturday."

"Or before," she said. "I think I'll check in from time to time to make sure Maggie's treating you right."

Josh shook his head at this belated display of maternal concern. He was way past the age when he needed anyone looking out for him, but, belated or not, he had to admit it felt good knowing that Nadine genuinely cared. It had been a long time since he'd believed anyone gave two hoots what happened to him.

"Nadine doesn't approve of this," Maggie said when Josh was in the truck and they were headed for her place. She looked oddly shaken by that.

He shrugged. "Doesn't matter."

"I thought she liked me."

"She does. It's the situation that has her acting a little crazy," he explained. "I never thought I'd live to see the day when she'd worry about my sleeping arrangements."

"What exactly is she worried about?" Maggie pressed.

Josh glanced at her. "I've already told you that it's not important."

"I could just ask her."

"I'm surprised you didn't."

"Well, she wasn't as straightforward with me as she appeared to be with you. I just picked up on this weird vibe that she wasn't entirely happy with the situation."

His lips twitched. "Since your curiosity was obviously all stirred up, why didn't you roll down your window and eavesdrop?"

"That would be impolite," she said primly, then added with a note of disgust, "besides, you have power windows and I couldn't get the damn things down."

Josh laughed. "Then you did consider the idea?"

"Of course."

"Maggie, you don't need to worry about my mother. Maybe the mother we ought to be worrying about is yours. How is she going to take this new development?"

"She'll deal with it," Maggie said. "She won't have any choice."

"You know, it's ironic how much those two women have in common," Josh said. "You sure as hell wouldn't guess it to look at them. Something tells me when news of our living arrangements gets out, they're going to be thick as thieves trying to decide what to do about it."

"They don't scare me," Maggie said.

Josh studied her unconcerned expression and shook his head. "They probably should, darlin'. These two are not lightweights when it comes to causing a ruckus."

"And we're not two teenagers sneaking off to some lovers' lane," Maggie countered. "We're both adults. I know exactly what the score is and so do you."

Josh thought about Nadine's belief that Maggie didn't have a clue what this move meant to him. Now was not the time to fill her in.

Besides, after he'd spent a couple of days dodging hose and lacy bras hanging from the shower rod or tripping on a pair of high-heeled sandals she'd tossed carelessly aside, he'd probably tire of the whole domestic-bliss thing. In fact, he was counting on it.

* * *

Her carriage house felt smaller with Josh underfoot every time she turned around, Maggie thought with annoyance. It had been different in that hotel room in Savannah. They'd been there for one reason and they'd spent most of their time in bed.

Now, with all the careful rules spelled out about their living arrangements and the fact it was just about protecting her from Brian, they spent way too much time avoiding the bed. Josh was taking the whole bodyguard thing to an extreme. She couldn't figure out when on earth he was sleeping, since he was wide awake on the sofa when she went to bed and wide awake at the kitchen table drinking coffee when she got up.

She took two days of this before she finally lost her temper. Climbing out of her cold and lonely bed at three in the morning, she went downstairs and spotted him sitting outside on the patio. She couldn't help the sudden rush of sympathy at the loneliness radiating from him. She had to find a way around or over or through that wall he'd built since moving in here. She knew it had something to do with whatever Nadine had said to him.

Pouring herself a cup of coffee, she took a seat beside him.

"This isn't working for me," she said bluntly.

He turned to stare at her. "What?"

"You living here."

He regarded her with a stunned expression. "I've been doing my best to stay out of your way."

"That's just it. It's weird. You're acting as if we hardly know each other. I thought—" She cut herself off before she could say that she'd thought it would be different, that they'd grow closer with him living under her roof.

"You thought what?"

"That we were past this awkwardness," she said finally, then decided to be perfectly honest. "I thought you'd be sleeping upstairs with me."

Josh met her gaze, then sighed. "To tell you the truth, that's what I thought, too."

"Then why are you downstairs while I'm in my bed all alone?"

"It seemed like a good idea to put a little distance between us."

"Why?"

"I can't protect you if I'm distracted," he said.

"Baloney!" she said at once.

A smile tugged at the corners of his mouth. "Not buying that one?"

"Not even close."

"I thought it was pretty good."

"For a professional bodyguard," she agreed. "Not for a man who's been my lover. Dammit, Josh, if your feelings have changed, I have a right to know about it."

"My feelings haven't changed," he told her. "That's the point, I guess."

"I'm sure that makes perfect sense to you, but not to me."

"It was something Nadine said," he admitted, confirming Maggie's suspicion. "She told me I was going to move in here and find all the things that had been missing in my life."

"Such as?"

"Little things, I guess," he began as if he was struggling to put it into words. He regarded her earnestly. "It's a home, Maggie. I never had that. This place is filled with heirlooms. It's filled with memories. I told you before that there was never anything like that in my life. Walking through these rooms, seeing the old family pictures, being surrounded by all these things that mean something to you, it makes me want something I can't have."

Maggie thought she was finally beginning to get it. "You can have anything if you want it badly enough."

"I wish I could believe that."

"What is it you want that you think you can't have?"

"Roots, I suppose."

Her heart turned over at the wistfulness in his voice. "You know, Josh, seeds don't have any roots when you first put them in the ground. They have to be nurtured. Next thing you know they're deep in the earth and a plant is flourishing."

He regarded her bleakly. "You can say that because it's something you've had all your life. It's harder to believe when you've lived the way I have."

"Maybe that's where faith comes in. You have to start somewhere, Josh."

He lifted his gaze to hers. "You know when it really hit me? I was in the bathroom, putting my toothbrush in the holder next to yours. Seems like a silly thing, doesn't it? But it hit me right in the chest that this was what it was like for two people to be together. It's a million tiny, intimate things that add up to a relationship."

"But it always starts with just one thing," Maggie said. "Like a toothbrush."

"And then what? Our underwear's all mingled together in the laundry? You steal the toast off my plate?"

She tried to fight a smile and failed. "If I promise never to steal your toast or turn your underwear pink by washing it with my red bra, will you come to bed with me? Please?"

He stared at her with undisguised longing. "I want to."

"Then do it, Josh. Don't try to analyze it or predict where we're heading. Just come to bed tonight. Tomorrow will take care of itself."

"Not fifteen minutes ago, you wanted me to move out," he said wryly.

"No, what I said was that it wasn't working for me the way it's been the last couple of days," she corrected. "I've been feeling isolated and alone. I like what we have together. I don't want to lose it, certainly not because either one of us is scared about what the future might hold."

He looked deep into her eyes and he must have found whatever he was looking for, because he finally nodded. "You're right. It would be foolish to walk away from something we both want."

Maggie stood and held out her hand. "Just so you know, it's not just about the sex."

He grinned at last, ignoring her outstretched hand and looping an arm around her shoulders. "Never thought it was."

"Yes, you did. You're a man, aren't you? Men always think it's just about the sex."

"I'll prove it," he retorted. "There will be no sex."

Maggie nudged him in the ribs. "Bet I can make you change your mind."

He gave her a bland look. "You can try."

She slipped her arm companionably around his waist and snuggled against his side as they walked toward her room. "I've missed this."

"What? Arguing with me?"

"Feeling close to you."

He sighed then. "Me, too, darlin'."

Once he'd made the move from the sofa into Maggie's bed, Josh kept waiting for panic to start clawing its way up the back of his throat, but a week later, it hadn't happened. Instead, it felt right, just the way the sight of those two toothbrushes side by side had felt right.

Even so, he kept reminding himself he was staying at Maggie's because Brian was on the loose. He told himself that would make it easier for him to go when the time came. Since the lie was beginning to wear thin, he was relieved when Saturday rolled around and he knew they'd be surrounded by other people all day long. Maybe that would help him keep things in perspective.

Instead, he arrived at the site and Nadine was immediately in his face.

"You look like hell," she declared. "Aren't you getting any sleep?"

"I'm getting plenty of sleep," he assured her. It was just coming in fits and starts since he and Maggie couldn't seem to keep their hands off each other for more than an hour at a time.

"Where's Maggie? Does she look as worn-out as you do?"

"Even if she does, I would advise you against commenting on it," he said.

Nadine rolled her eyes. "Give me some credit. I'm a woman. I'd never tell another woman she's a mess, unless, of course, it's someone I'm not overly fond of. So, where is Maggie?"

"I dropped her off at the gallery, as a matter of fact. She has a lot of work to catch up on. She's going to spend the morning over there, then come by here later."

"I thought you were supposed to be watching her every second," Nadine said.

"I had a chat with Detective Ryan. He's got someone stationed right outside the gallery. Maggie will be fine there for a few hours. She needs a break from me, anyway."

Nadine grinned. "Oh, really? Having trouble keeping your hands to yourself?"

"Mother!"

"Oh, for goodness' sake, I know how these things work."

"Yes, I imagine you do," he said. "How are things with you and George?"

"I wish you'd stop trying to make something of that," she said. "George and I are just friends."

"When have I heard that before?"

"Coming out of your mouth with regard to Maggie," she retorted. "Though in your case it was a blatant lie."

"And it's not in your case?"

"No. George is going to help me find a job, so I can stay here and find a decent place of my own."

"I thought by now you'd have found some way to suggest moving in with him."

Nadine looked about to utter a quick denial, but then she shrugged. "In the past, I might have."

Josh heard something in her voice he'd never heard before—caution. He studied her curiously. "What's different this time?"

"I'm just starting to figure out who I am."

Josh regarded her with surprise. "You've never known that before?"

Nadine shook her head. "I always let myself be defined by the men I was with." She smiled at him. "I owe it to you, you know. Making me work here has turned things around for me. I've realized that I have a lot to offer besides my body. I might even take some college classes one of these days."

He stared at her in shock. "You're kidding!"

"Why shouldn't I?" she asked defensively.

"There's no reason at all why you shouldn't. I'm just surprised you want to."

"To be honest, so am I, but George says I don't have to study for a degree. I can just take classes that interest me. He's taking art appreciation right now, something he never had time for years ago when he was getting his business degree. I thought I might sign up for music appreciation with him next semester."

"Good for you," Josh said, his admiration deepening.

"We're going to take tango lessons, too."

"George is going to take tango lessons?" The image boggled Josh's mind.

Nadine grinned. "I've told him it's a very sensual dance. I think that convinced him."

"Then there *is* a relationship here."

"There's a friendship," she corrected again, then winked and added, "with sexual overtones. Maybe it's something you and Maggie should try to get the hang of."

"Maggie and I are doing just fine," Josh said.

At least he thought they were, as long as he didn't think too far into the future. Maybe that was how relationships worked, like a twelve-step program—one tentative, hopeful day at a time.

22

It was still a shock to Maggie to walk into her house and find telltale evidence that a man was living there. Not just any man, she amended. Josh.

He'd kicked off his filthy work boots in the front hall, which might have made her cringe a few weeks ago. Now it merely made her smile. There were sports magazines mixed in with her interior-design and regional-lifestyle magazines. She found two coffee cups left in the kitchen sink and two juice glasses, one of them extra large. The laundry basket was overflowing with his jeans and work shirts.

It was the latter that actually shook her. She picked up one of his *work* shirts and breathed in the masculine scent that was all Josh. In one way it was still an alien, unfamiliar scent. In another it had become an aphrodisiac.

Panic began to twist in her gut. She had never gotten this far in a relationship before, had never allowed anyone to get this close. She'd been intimate, but there was a huge difference between allowing a man into your bed and permitting him to share your life. She'd always been about doing the unconventional. This seemed a whole lot like conventional. What was she thinking?

"Hi, honey, I'm home!" Josh called out just then, his tone filled with amusement at the trite phrase.

"How can he joke about this?" Maggie muttered, tossing aside his shirt and retreating to the kitchen, where she could pour herself a much-needed glass of wine. Out of habit, she pulled a beer from the fridge for Josh, then cursed yet another sign of this recent domesticity.

He walked into the kitchen and, as it had for more than a week, her heart did a little stutter-step at the sight of him. He leaned down, kissed the stuffing out of her, then reached for the beer she'd set on the counter. When he glanced back at her, he frowned.

"What's wrong?"

"Nothing," she said.

His gaze narrowed. "Not buying it. Try again."

"Okay, it's this," she said, gesturing around vaguely.

He merely looked confused. "The kitchen?"

She scowled at him.

"Okay, not the kitchen. You're going to have to clarify, sugar."

"You, me, all this domestic bliss," she said. "Doesn't it scare you?"

A grin began to spread across his face. "Bliss, huh? Yeah, I guess it should."

"But it doesn't?"

"A little, but not nearly as much as I thought it might," he admitted.

Maggie was unreasonably irritated by his reaction. "I'm doing your laundry, dammit. You're fixing my breakfast. Doesn't that bother you?"

"You want me to do the laundry, too?"

She studied his expression to see if he was making fun of her, but he looked totally sincere. "It's not about who does the laundry," she said impatiently.

He pulled out a chair and gestured toward it. "Sit down and tell me what's really going on here."

Maggie sat, but she couldn't find the words to express what was bothering her. "I don't know exactly," she said finally. "I got home just now and I looked around and you're everywhere."

He feigned indignation. "Are you suggesting I'm a slob, Magnolia?"

Her lips twitched despite her sour mood. "No, of course not. You're actually amazingly neat. It's the implication, I think. You're really living here."

"That's what we agreed to," he said.

"I know."

"Then what's the problem?"

"I like it," she said at last. "I didn't expect to, but I do."

"And that's what scares you?"

She nodded.

He hunkered down in front of her and gazed into her eyes. "Me, too. Sometimes, anyway," he admitted. "But there's nowhere I'd rather be."

"And that's not just because of Brian?" she asked.

He shook his head, his eyes still locked with hers. "Not anymore."

Maggie sighed. "Same with me."

He studied her intently. "Feeling better now?"

"I guess."

"You feel like having dinner now? I'll cook."

She laughed at the offer. "Not in my kitchen you

won't," she said. "Last time you cooked dinner, it took me two days to clean up the mess."

"But, admit it, the food was excellent," he said.

She stood up and he pulled her into his arms. Maggie lifted her mouth to his. "Dessert was better."

He chuckled. "Want to have dessert first tonight?"

"You read my mind."

Maggie couldn't imagine who was working on Amanda's house this morning, since half the people she knew kept popping into Images. Dinah was just the latest.

"Why are you here?" she asked wearily when Dinah settled into the chair beside her desk and took a sip of the latte she'd brought with her. She seemed prepared for a long visit.

"I thought we could catch up."

"It hasn't been that long since the last time we saw each other," Maggie reminded her.

"A lot can happen in a couple of weeks. How's it working out with you and Josh under the same roof? Are you getting any ideas?"

"Such as?"

"Making it permanent, of course."

"Josh had a minor freak-out when he saw our toothbrushes lined up," Maggie told her. "I freaked when I saw our laundry sitting beside the washer. Does that sound like two people who might walk down the aisle anytime soon?"

"He might have freaked, but he didn't bolt," Dinah pointed out. "And you didn't kick him out. I'd say that's significant."

"I suppose."

"Let's cut to the chase, Maggie. How do you feel about him?"

Maggie couldn't seem to stop the dreamy expression that she knew was washing over her face. "He's sexy and exasperating, gorgeous and annoying, protective and irritating."

Dinah's grin spread. "Admit it, Magnolia. You're in love with him. What did it? The whole protective thing?"

Maggie thought about it, then nodded. There was little point in trying to keep it from her best friend. Besides, maybe she needed to test saying the words aloud, see how the notion of love felt.

"That was a big part of it, I think. No man has ever thought I needed protecting before. Maybe Josh has gone a little over the top in that department, but it's so sweet. When it's not exasperating me, his attitude makes me feel cherished."

"Is he in love with you?"

Maggie's shoulders sagged at the question. "I don't think he has the first clue that love doesn't have to be this huge, sweep-you-off-your-feet craziness. Sure, there's passion, and goodness knows we have that, but it's about the million and one little things that make a relationship work. Nadine never set that example for him. I think all of her relationships involved high drama."

Dinah's grin spread. "And yours didn't?"

Maggie winced. "You have a point, but with Josh it's different."

"Then it's up to you to show him how to make this work."

"That could take forever," Maggie said with a trace of her usual impatience.

"There you go," Dinah scolded. "You always want what you want when you want it. Some of life's most valuable things are worth working for and waiting for. Cord could probably explain that one to you better than I can. It's still astonishing to me that he waited patiently for so many years for me to wake up and realize what a remarkable man he is."

"What if I work and wait and Josh still doesn't get it? He's happy enough with the way things are now. I don't see him taking any big leaps toward making anything permanent."

"At least you'll know you gave it your best shot," Dinah said. "But when have you ever not gotten what you went after?"

"There was Cord," she reminded Dinah, half in jest.

"You bought a date with him at a charity bachelor auction," Dinah scoffed. "That hardly constitutes one of your trademark campaigns to get your own way. Besides," she added with a grin, "you were competing with me. You didn't stand a chance."

Maggie laughed. "True enough."

"With Josh, you have a clear field. No competition at all."

"I thought there might be with Amanda for a time," Maggie admitted. "She's beautiful and sweet and has those three darling kids. I thought Josh's protective instincts would go into overdrive." She shrugged. "Turned out I was wrong. I really do think they're just friends."

"If you ask me, Amanda has other fish to fry," Dinah said.

Maggie's mouth dropped open. "You're kidding! Who?"

"Caleb," Dinah said with the confidence of a trained observer.

"What? Caleb's got a thing for Amanda? Are you serious? How did I miss that?" Maggie asked, bemused by the notion.

"Haven't you ever noticed the way he's always right by her side when he senses anything might be upsetting her? She turns to him instinctively. I'm not sure she even realizes what's going on, but he's been a real rock for her. She counts on him. I predict one of these days those two will wake up and see what's right under their noses, and when they do, watch out."

"Dinah, Caleb's a minister!" Maggie protested, then chuckled. "'Course he's also a man."

"And quite a hunky one, for that matter," Dinah added. "Have you seen that man with his shirt off?" She fanned herself dramatically.

Maggie covered her ears. "Stop saying things like that. I'm pretty sure there's a place in hell for people who ogle ministers."

"Okay, okay. I'm just saying I don't think you need to give another thought to Amanda and Josh."

Maggie nodded. "Actually I think the biggest problem I'm likely to face with Josh is all in his head. He's not going to fall into my arms, at least not on a permanent basis, without a fight."

"Just be sure before you go down that road that you are absolutely certain about what you want," Dinah warned. "I'd hate to see his heart broken because you were just playing some game to prove you could get him."

"I would never do that," Maggie retorted indignantly.

"You would and you have," Dinah said. "Mostly to annoy your mother."

"My mother does not have anything at all to do with my relationship with Josh," Maggie asserted.

"She did at the beginning. You can't deny that."

Maggie would have denied it, but she gave the idea a moment's thought and realized Dinah was probably right. Old habits died hard. Josh's initial appeal probably had had a lot to do with the likelihood her mother would have a cow when she found out Maggie was seeing him.

But she was long since over that. She really was.

Wasn't she? The question lingered in her head long after Dinah had gone.

When her mother called to insist she come to Sunday dinner, Maggie realized she had a chance to find out how much influence Juliette still had over her decisions. It was something she needed to know before things between her and Josh went any further.

"What do you really know about this man?" Maggie's mother demanded before they'd taken their first sip of the cold-soup course at Sunday dinner.

They were dining alone. Maggie's father was playing golf. That alone was enough to make Maggie suspicious about her mother's motives for inviting her over. Her father played golf on Sunday only when his wife had an agenda he might not approve of.

"I know enough," she said calmly, hoping they could get through this inquisition without a major blowup. She'd been through enough of them over the years, and they'd all ended badly.

"Really? Have you met his family? Aside from that common mother of his, that is."

Maggie saw red. "Nadine is not common," she said

furiously. "She's a perfectly nice woman who hasn't had the same kind of opportunities you've had."

"She is most definitely not like us," Juliette said with a little huff.

"You mean rich and stuffy?"

"No, I mean she lacks breeding. It's not her fault, of course."

Maggie was stunned by her mother's words. Juliette had her standards, but she'd never behaved so snobbishly.

"Where is all this coming from?" she asked. "I thought you liked her. You seemed to think she was a breath of fresh air that day at lunch."

"I was rather fascinated at first, mainly because she rattled George. And I appreciated the fact that she stepped in to help you clean up the gallery," she said grudgingly. "That doesn't mean I approve of her as your mother-in-law."

Maggie bit back a groan. "Who said anything about Josh and me getting married?"

"Then you're not serious about him?"

"I don't know where our relationship is headed," Maggie admitted.

"Then why on earth is he living under your roof?"

"To protect me from Brian."

"The man who destroyed Images?"

"Yes. He's still on the loose."

For a moment, Juliette looked so shaken that Maggie regretted saying anything. As usual, though, her mother promptly rallied.

"I wonder if your father knows that," she mused. "He would put some additional pressure on the police chief, I'm sure. He certainly doesn't hesitate to call him about everything else."

Maggie remembered the call that had been made to the chief to make sure George couldn't succeed in making trouble at the site. "Did Dad happen to talk to him about making sure that nothing held up the work on Amanda's house?"

Juliette shook her head. "The way I hear it, that was Big Max's doing."

"You're sure?"

"Of course, I'm sure. Your father spoke to Max and told him what George had been up to. He asked if it was what Max wanted. Max picked up the phone right then and there and made the call."

"Well, I'll be," Maggie said. "That's encouraging, don't you think so? Maybe his attitude toward Amanda is softening."

"I hope so," Juliette said. "But we're getting offtrack, Magnolia. I'm interested in where you see this situation with Josh heading. He's sleeping in your bed, I imagine."

"That is none of your business," Maggie said emphatically.

"It's a reasonable question," Juliette insisted. "You're a Forsythe, Magnolia. You're also thirty-two years old. It's time for you to stop behaving impulsively and settle down with someone suitable."

"Give it up, Mother. I'm not marrying Warren or anyone like him, for that matter. And, if you recall, I didn't know his family either, not at the beginning. And meeting them didn't do a thing to assure that we'd take a respectable walk down the aisle."

"Water under the bridge," her mother said with a dismissive gesture. "I'm talking about this current fling of yours. People are talking."

"Let them."

"You're embarrassing your father."

The litany was all too familiar. Juliette had a checklist she went through each time Maggie tried her patience. She lived with the hope that something on it would set Maggie off down a path of which she approved.

"No," Maggie corrected. "I'm embarrassing *you,* Mother. And disappointing *you.* Again. That's what this is really about. I'm sorry I can't live up to your high expectations. I've stopped trying. I'll never be quite good enough. And as far as I know, I have impeccable breeding, so that must not matter half as much as you claim it does."

Her mother looked genuinely shocked by the accusation. "Is that what you think?"

"Of course it's what I think," Maggie snapped. "You've as much as said it. More than once, as a matter of fact. I'm getting tired of having this conversation over and over again."

Her mother sat back with a sigh. "Oh, dear, I've gotten this all wrong again. Maggie, the only thing I want is your happiness. I don't think you'll find it if you insist on making choices just to spite me."

"That's not what I'm doing," Maggie said. "Believe it or not, Mother, Josh really is a good guy. He's decent and hardworking and kind."

"If he's such a paragon, then why haven't your father and I seen more of him?"

"Because I don't want to listen to you pass judgment on everything that's wrong with him. I like him and that's what matters."

An unreadable expression passed over Juliette's face

then. It almost looked like satisfaction, but Maggie couldn't be sure.

"Bring him around," Juliette encouraged.

"So you can cross-examine him? I don't think so."

"If he's half the man you think he is, I won't scare him off. He certainly didn't seem easily intimidated when you brought him to lunch at the club."

Maggie regarded her mother thoughtfully. "Maybe I should bring him by some evening. You might be pleasantly surprised."

And way back in the dim recesses of her mind, Maggie had to wonder what would happen if just this once she could win her mother's approval for a man she was already in love with. Would it send her fleeing for the hills? Would the thrill of being slightly outrageous be gone and ruin everything?

Or would she finally be able to claim the happiness that had been eluding her all these years?

Maggie had promised to call Josh when she was ready to leave her mother's, but she needed some time alone to think about why she'd gotten involved with him in the first place.

She walked back to Images, shut off the alarm and went inside. Even after working for a few hours Saturday morning, there was still a mountain of paperwork she needed to get to, but she couldn't seem to make herself focus on any of that.

She'd been there half an hour, staring blankly into space, when her cell phone rang—at the same moment the bell over the front door of the shop chimed to indicate that someone had come inside.

Her heart instantly climbed into her throat. Hadn't

she locked the door behind her? Surely she had. In that case, it had to be Ellie or Vicki coming back to check on something.

"Ellie?" she called out, scrambling to find her ringing cell phone at the bottom of her purse.

"Sorry, lady. Ellie's unavailable."

The sound of Brian's cold voice made her skin crawl. She lifted her gaze to meet his, and what she saw filled her with fear. He looked half-crazed, as if he hadn't slept or shaved or even bathed in days. Had he lived on the streets, knowing the police were looking for him for the break-in and the fire?

"Toss that cell phone over here," he commanded. "I can't have you answering it. That would ruin everything."

"If I don't, Josh will be here in two minutes," she lied. "He'll have the police with him."

"I can do a lot of damage in two minutes," Brian claimed, his face twisted into an ugly smirk. "You saw what I did to the gallery on my last visit. I did all that in sixty seconds flat. The fire didn't turn out quite the way I'd intended, but it did shake up Ellie."

"And you're proud of that?" she demanded furiously. "You terrified a woman you'd once claimed to have feelings for! And you destroyed work that talented artists had labored over. You claim to be an artist yourself. How can you do that to someone else's work?"

"That was just a warning, sweetheart. Today we're getting to the real thing."

"Which is?"

"Making you pay for interfering in my life, for demeaning my talent, for messing things up between me and Ellie and for trying to trap me with that whole poster contest scam."

Maggie was stunned.

"Didn't think I'd find out, did you? I have a few contacts in this town myself," Brian gloated.

Maggie knew she should let him rant and try to placate him, but she couldn't seem to hold her tongue. Besides, now that she'd had time to take a closer look, she saw him for what he was—a weak-minded bully who thrived on intimidation. As long as she gave as good as she got, she could keep him off balance, just as she had on the night they'd met.

"You and Ellie were doomed from the moment you figured out she had more talent than you do," she said bluntly.

"Ellie and I would have been just fine if you'd stayed out of it. Offering to give her a show here got her all worked up. She started thinking she must really be something."

"She *is* something," Maggie said. "She's an incredible artist. You see that, Brian, I know you do. Why can't you be happy for her? Why can't you be proud of the role you played in nurturing that talent?"

For an instant he looked flustered, as if he didn't know what to make of her unexpected praise for his teaching abilities. Maggie decided to capitalize on that. Maybe she could still get through to him.

"It takes a very special kind of teacher to recognize when a student has artistic talent," she told him. "There's such a fine line between letting that talent flourish and find its own way and molding it to fit into some preconceived idea. You gave Ellie room to grow. What she found in herself, what she's able to put on canvas is remarkable. You did that, Brian."

"I could have been a great artist," he said with more wistfulness than conviction.

"Perhaps, but then a lot of students would have lost an outstanding teacher," she said.

She knew she had to make a decision soon about what happened next, because once Josh and the police got here—and if that had been him on the phone, they would show up—things would spin out of control quickly. And if they weren't on the way, she needed to save herself from whatever mayhem Brian had in mind.

"Would you like to see what Ellie's done?" she asked, already out of the chair and moving toward the vault. "I think you'll be even prouder of how far she's come."

She didn't wait for his response, but quickly spun the combination and opened the vault. An idea was taking shape in her mind, but it was going to be tricky to pull off without risking everything she'd been trying so hard to protect.

"Let me show you," she called from inside the vault. She began pulling Ellie's artwork into the office and stacking it against the wall. At the sight of the brightly painted canvasses Brian seemed to freeze in place. "Aren't they spectacular?" she enthused, removing them as quickly as she could.

When the last one was stacked against the wall, she met his gaze. "There's one more, but it's too large for me to handle. You probably remember it from her studio. It's amazing, a real masterpiece. Help me bring it out, then you can take a leisurely look through all of them and tell me what you think."

Brian shook himself as if coming out of a trance. "What?"

"Help me bring out Ellie's last painting. It's the best of all, I think." When he didn't move, she grabbed at one last straw. "I predict it will hang at the Museum of Modern Art one day."

"You've got to be kidding me," he sneered.

"See for yourself." She stepped into the vault and waited.

It seemed like an eternity before he moved. She heard his approach and waited until he was just inside the vault.

"Where is this masterpiece?" he demanded.

"Against the back wall," she lied, allowing him to move past her.

Then she shot through the door and slammed the vault door closed. She was already dialing 911 when he realized what she'd done and let out a bellow that could be heard a block away.

At practically the same instant the front door of the gallery burst open and Detective Ryan and half a dozen policemen stormed in.

At her first glimpse of them, Maggie's knees gave way and she sank onto the chair behind her desk. "In there," she whispered, pointing to the vault.

"Give 'em the combination, sugar," Josh said, appearing out of nowhere and putting a steadying hand on her shoulder.

She looked up into his eyes. "I can't remember it," she whispered, starting to shake.

Josh knelt down in front of her and clung to her hands. "No rush," he told her. "Brian can wait. Is there anything in there he can destroy?"

She shook her head. "I got it all out," she said, nodding toward the paintings leaning against the wall. "Every last one of them."

"Good work," Josh said, grinning.

She kept her gaze on him, trying to steady herself.

"How did you figure out what was going on? You were here before I even finished calling the police. That was you calling a little while ago, wasn't it?"

"It was," he confirmed. "And when you didn't answer your cell phone, I called your mother. She said you'd left thirty minutes ago. I guessed you were here and that you might be in trouble, so I called Detective Ryan."

"You must be furious that I slipped out of your protective custody," she said.

"Yeah, well, it wasn't a huge surprise. You've been champing at the bit for days now. All that matters is that you're fine and that, thanks to your quick thinking, Brian's in custody." He glanced toward the locked vault. "Or will be if you can ever remember that combination."

"I wonder how much air there is in there," she said thoughtfully.

"Maggie!" Josh said.

"Okay, okay, I know I can't leave him in there to die, though it is a temptation."

"Did he hurt you?"

"Do I look hurt? He never laid a hand on me."

"And thanks to whatever scheme you devised, he didn't touch those paintings, either. I'd say you did a good afternoon's work."

Maggie thought about what might have happened, and a wave of dizziness washed over her. "I think I want to go home."

Detective Ryan ambled over. "You can go as soon as you tell us how to get into that vault. I assume you'd prefer we didn't blow it up."

Her eyes widened. "You would do that?"

"If we had to," he confirmed.

Maggie weighed the threat against whatever satisfaction she might get from Brian's continued screams. She rattled off the combination, then turned to Josh.

"Get me out of here. I don't want to see him when he comes out."

Josh glanced at the detective. "Okay with you?"

Dan Ryan nodded. "I know where to find you. I'll be by later to take a statement."

"Lock up when you leave," Maggie ordered.

"Yes, ma'am," Detective Ryan replied with a grin.

Josh gazed down into her eyes. "You're feeling more like your old self again already, aren't you?"

"A little controlling, you mean?"

He nodded.

"I'll work on that." She met his gaze. "In the meantime, we have a lot to talk about."

"Oh?"

"I think that's sufficient warning."

His eyebrows rose. "Warning?"

"I had Sunday dinner with my mother, remember."

"I'm drawing a blank here, sugar. What does that have to do with anything?"

"You'll see," she told him. It might be better if she didn't say another word till she had him right where she wanted him—in bed. It was the one place she could count on him being totally focused and attentive.

23

George had just arrived to take Nadine to the movies when Josh called to tell her what had happened at the gallery. Stunned, Nadine sank onto the edge of the bed.

"Maggie's okay? You're sure?" she asked. She was shocked by how much Maggie had come to mean to her, as well as to her son. "And you? Are you okay?"

"I'm fine. It was all over by the time I got inside. Maggie's remarkable. She had Brian locked in the vault. Now that it's over, she's a little shaken up," Josh said. "But we're at her place now. She'll be fine once she's had some time to settle down."

"I'm coming over," Nadine said at once.

"No, don't," Josh told her. "She needs to rest for a while. She doesn't need to be reliving what happened."

"Has she spoken to her mother?"

"No. I guess she'll call her as soon as I get off the phone," he said with a man's typical nonchalance.

"Mrs. Forsythe shouldn't hear something like this over the phone. I'll go by there and tell her in person," Nadine volunteered.

"Are you sure?" Josh asked doubtfully. "You hardly know her."

Actually she and Juliette knew each other better than their children could possibly imagine. "I'm still sure she'd prefer to hear something like this from me rather than from a TV newscast or over the phone," Nadine said confidently. "Besides, George is with me. He's known the Forsythes forever. He'll help me break the news."

"Fine. I'll let Maggie know you're taking care of it," Josh said. "Thanks, Mother."

Relieved that he hadn't asked a million questions about what George was doing in her room or why she was so determined to speak to Juliette, Nadine hung up. "You heard?" she asked George.

"Enough to figure out what happened. You can fill me in on the rest on the way over to Juliette's."

"You don't mind missing the movie?" she asked. A lot of people would rather eat dirt than break bad news. Of course, since Maggie was fine, the news wasn't that bad. In fact, Brian's being in custody was the best possible news.

"Of course not," George said readily. "I think it's very thoughtful of you to want to make sure Juliette isn't upset unnecessarily."

She gave him a chagrined look. "Actually I have an ulterior motive," she confessed.

"Oh?"

"Maybe it's best if you don't find out till we're over there," she told him. "Think you can contain your curiosity that long?"

"I suppose I'll have to," he grumbled. "You do love your little mysteries, don't you, Nadine?"

"A few harmless little secrets and mysteries keep life interesting," she informed him. "If we're going to spend much time together, you'll need to adapt to that."

He grinned. "I'll work on it. I imagine I'll get the hang of it eventually."

Nadine smiled contentedly at the implication that they would be together for a while. Not that she was counting on too much yet, but the promise was there. For once she was going to demonstrate a little patience and let the relationship progress at its own pace. It was her rush to seal the deal that usually landed her in trouble. Who would have thought that she'd wait till her fifties to finally grow up and mature?

When George pulled up in front of the Forsythes' home, she sucked in her breath. She'd passed a dozen houses like this over the years back when she'd lived in Charleston, but she'd never been inside one. The size of it daunted her. Thank goodness most of her conversations with Juliette had been over the phone or in little out-of-the-way restaurants where they were unlikely to be spotted by anyone they knew. If she'd known just what kind of wealth Maggie came from, she might have had second thoughts about trying to give Josh and Maggie a push down the aisle.

"How do you suppose they manage it without the slaves?" she muttered.

George laughed. "I heard that."

"Well, do you have an answer?"

"One good housekeeper can work miracles," he said. "I should know. My place is just up the road."

"You're kidding!" She'd known he was well-to-do and powerful, but if his home was anything like this antebellum mansion, he was way beyond rich. "Why didn't you say something?"

He regarded her with amusement. "Such as?"

"Oh, I don't know," she said wryly. "Maybe, 'Hey,

Nadine, I'm way out of your league, but I feel like slumming for a while.'"

George's jaw tightened. He cut the engine of his car without looking at her. When he finally faced her, his eyes were dark with barely suppressed anger. "Do you think so little of me?" he asked.

To Nadine's astonishment, he was genuinely upset by her comment. "No, of course not," she said, shaken that he'd taken her so seriously. "I guess what I said was more about me than you. You have to know this isn't my world."

"Nadine, you could fit in at a presidential ball. Not having money is no disgrace."

"It's not just the money," she said, helpless to explain why she suddenly felt so far out of her depth when only a few moments ago she'd been perfectly comfortable with this man. Suddenly she understood another reason that Josh was so terrified to acknowledge his feelings for Maggie. She came from a similar world, a world of privilege and roots. Because George deserved an explanation, she tried to find the right words.

"You have a history," she said, knowing that was only part of it.

He smiled faintly. "So do you."

"You can hardly compare the two," she said.

"One of these days I'll tell you all about my great-granddaddy the bootlegger," he promised. "But right now we'd better table this discussion and go inside. Juliette's peeking through the curtains to see what we're up to out here."

For a few minutes Nadine had actually forgotten where they were. "Of course. How could I forget the reason we came?"

Juliette had the front door open before they climbed the steps onto the veranda. She smiled at them. "This is an unexpected pleasure," she said with apparent sincerity. "What brings you by?"

"We have some distressing news, I'm afraid," George began.

Nadine shot a daunting look at him before he could blurt out the rest. "Everyone's fine," she said hurriedly as Juliette turned pale. "We should go inside and sit down."

Inside, Juliette's manners kicked in and overcame her distress. Apparently Nadine's assurances that no one was hurt had calmed her fears. Only after she'd insisted on ringing for tea and taken a few sips, did Nadine explain what had happened at the gallery. "Josh has taken Maggie home and he's there with her. She wasn't harmed at all, just shaken up a bit."

Juliette stood up at once, her dismay evident. "I have to call Frank. We need to see her."

Nadine understood Juliette's need to go despite assurances that Maggie was unharmed. She wasn't about to tell Juliette she shouldn't, either, even though Josh had told *her* to stay away. "Of course. You shouldn't be driving, though. We'll take you, won't we, George?"

"Absolutely."

"Of course, those two might prefer to be alone," Nadine said casually. "You saw Maggie earlier, didn't you? What was your sense of how things are going?"

Juliette gave her a sly look and sat back down. "You're very clever, Nadine. I haven't given you half enough credit. I'll settle for making a quick phone call to speak to Maggie, and then I'll tell you everything."

"Everything about what?" George asked, obviously

confused by the rapid change in plans. "Are we going over there or not?"

"Not," Nadine and Juliette confirmed together.

He sat back with a heavy sigh. "I will never in a million years understand women."

"Probably not," Juliette said.

"It's probably best if you don't even try," Nadine added, then sat back herself while Juliette called and had a brief conversation with Maggie. She looked relieved when she hung up.

"I think things are progressing quite nicely over there," she told Nadine.

Nadine grinned. "That's been my perception. So, what did Maggie say earlier?"

"The minute I raised a single doubt about her relationship with Josh, she leaped to his defense. By the time she left here, I think she was half convinced to propose to him herself."

George leaned forward, his gaze utterly fascinated. "The two of you have been conspiring?"

"We've been talking," Nadine corrected.

"It's our duty as mothers to look out for the best interests of our children," Juliette added in a prim, self-righteous tone. She ruined it by winking at Nadine.

"Lord help those two," George said fervently.

"His help is certainly appreciated, but they have us," Juliette said. "I doubt they'd get the ball rolling without a little push."

"I know Josh wouldn't," Nadine agreed.

"And Maggie's happiest when she's defying me," Juliette said. "I must say it's been more difficult than usual for me, because I genuinely like Josh. Keeping that from her hasn't been easy. I had to do something, though. Watching her try to twist herself into knots to make things work with Warren was painful, and she did all that because she thought I approved of him. I realized then she was trying to be someone she's not to please me, and I swore I'd never let her do something so ridiculous again."

George frowned. "Then you approve of Josh?" he asked. "But you don't want Maggie to know you approve? Have I got it right?"

"Exactly," Juliette said.

"Whatever happened to just keeping your opinion to yourself and staying out of the way?" he asked.

Nadine and Juliette exchanged a commiserating look.

"If you were a mother, you'd understand," Nadine told him.

"Not in a million years," he said with certainty. "And as a lowly man, I'm not even going to try."

"Just keep everything you've heard here today to yourself," Nadine told him. "You're privy to a huge secret. If those two find out what we've been up to, who knows what might happen. They might break up just to spite us."

George shook his head. "I don't think things were this Machiavellian when I was young."

"And just look how your marriage turned out. Even you have to admit you were unhappy long before Virginia Sue died," Juliette said. "Perhaps if your parents had done a little more meddling, things would have turned out differently."

"Perhaps so," he conceded. "But then I might not have been free when a woman like Nadine came along."

Nadine felt her cheeks turn pink. Sometimes the man said the sweetest things. "If you go on saying things like that, George, you're going to turn my head."

Juliette laughed. "Give it up, Nadine. I saw the way things were between you two that day you barged into my luncheon."

Nadine stared at her in confusion. "We didn't even like each other then."

"Of course you did," Juliette said impatiently. "What is it they talk about these days? Pheromones? They were flying all around. In my day, it was just plain old chemistry."

"Could we talk about something else?" Nadine pleaded.

"I'm sure I can't think of a better topic," George said, looking smug. "Seems to me that love is in the air all around these days. Why deny it?"

Nadine met his gaze and felt her heart take a familiar little lurch. Why indeed? The least an optimistic woman could do was open herself up to the possibility that this time she'd finally gotten it right.

Josh had done everything he could think of to try to get Maggie to lie down and rest after she'd spoken to her mother, but she was on a mission. She had things she wanted to discuss and she wasn't going to be happy until she'd gotten them off her chest. She'd even staged some sort of halfhearted seduction in what she claimed was an attempt to get him completely focused and attentive.

After he'd accepted that the seduction was going nowhere beyond the preliminaries, Josh had resigned himself to the fact that they were going to have this conversation, no matter what. Having it in bed with no clothes on was going to provide a real test of his powers of restraint.

"This has something to do with whatever you and your mother talked about today?" he concluded.

Maggie nodded.

"Okay, then, spill it. What did she want?"

"She was all over the fact that we're living together."

"But you told her why I'm here, right?"

"She saw right through that. She assumed you weren't sleeping downstairs, so she wasn't impressed by the whole bodyguard thing."

First Nadine, now Juliette Forsythe. When had mothers become so damn nosy, especially when it came to their adult offspring? "And this is her business because?" he asked.

"It's not, of course, and that's what I told her, but naturally that didn't shut her up. She thinks I'm only seeing you to exasperate her."

"I thought we'd established that you aren't."

"We did," Maggie said hurriedly. "But I can't be entirely sure. I have this pattern, you see. In the past, annoying my mother would definitely have had a lot to do with my motivation in going out with you. How am I supposed to know if it's really different this time?"

Josh didn't like the direction this conversation was taking. "So what? You want to clarify things for her? Prove something to her? What?"

"I want to figure things out for myself," she said. "It's only fair to you. You need to know what my real feelings are as much as I do."

"I always thought that was something you needed to figure out for yourself over time."

"It is, of course. I just want to speed up the process," she said, as if it were a simple matter.

The twists and turns of her mind were beginning to make his head spin. "How do you propose getting at this truth?"

"I've thought a lot about this and here's what I've come up with. We need to spend some time with my mother," she said. "A lot of time."

Josh wasn't sure he was following her logic. Or maybe he understood it too well. Maybe that was why he found it so damn depressing. "You want to trot me out for your mother's inspection?" he asked, his heart thudding dully.

"It won't be that bad," Maggie said, more cheerful now that her cards were apparently on the table. "She's not an ogre. She was totally charming the last two times you crossed paths, remember? I predict she'll probably be so polite, it'll give you hives."

"An attractive prospect," he muttered. "Okay, one more time now. Tell me exactly why you want to do this. What are you hoping will happen?"

Maggie, the most confident woman Josh had ever met, looked decidedly uncomfortable. "It's sort of a test."

"I think you'd better explain that one to me," he said irritably. "If I pass, what do I get? The Forsythe seal of approval stamped on my butt?"

She grinned weakly. "As intriguing as I find that notion, no. The test is more about me. I've already told you that Mother thinks I choose unsuitable men just to spite her. I think that's possible." She met his gaze. "So, I want you to win her over."

Josh stared at her. "That's a little convoluted for my

simple brain, but I think I should probably be insulted. What happens if I charm the socks off your mother?"

"That's what I want to find out."

"You've lost me."

"If my entire life has been one big attempt to rebel against my mother, I think it's time I figured that out. If she adores you, then based on past experience, I'll probably find some way to mess things up between us."

"Now, *there's* something for me to look forward to," Josh said, an odd feeling in the pit of his stomach. "Tell me again why I should participate in something that could ruin what we've got going?"

"What we've got going is great sex," she said blithely. "That's what we agreed. It won't be a huge loss."

"Speak for yourself," Josh retorted. Somewhere along the way it had gotten to be about more than sex for him. He didn't know where things were going, but he was in no rush to see everything flushed down the toilet as part of some stupid test Maggie had devised for herself. She might not know her own heart, but he knew his and he thought he had pretty good insight into hers. Unfortunately, she probably wouldn't take his word for anything. He sighed as he contemplated a future without her in it because he or she—he wasn't exactly clear on this—failed her test.

"You won't do it?" Maggie asked, regarding him with undisguised disappointment.

"No," he said flatly, coming to a decision. "I won't go along with your crazy scheme. What I will do is this…" His voice trailed off as he tried to formulate a plan more to his liking. Only one thing occurred to him, but the words stuck in his throat. Once he spoke, it would change things forever. They weren't the sort of words that could be unsaid.

"What?" Maggie prodded.

He took a deep breath and looked into her eyes. What he saw convinced him this was the only choice he had. "I'll marry you," he blurted before he could think better of it. "In Las Vegas. Next weekend."

As soon as he'd uttered the words, they sounded absolutely right to him. If Vegas was good enough for Nadine, it was just perfect for him.

"Are you out of your mind?" Maggie demanded, her expression stunned.

Josh remained undaunted by her lack of enthusiasm. "That's my final offer," he said. "Take it or leave it. We get married. Then I start spending all the time with your mother you want me to."

"But why?" she asked.

That was the mother of all questions, but for once Josh didn't even hesitate to say what was in his heart. "Because I love you and I am not letting someone else decide our fate for us."

"But that's so…"

"Unpredictable? Impulsive? Irresponsible?" he supplied when she couldn't seem to complete the sentence. "I thought that might suit you, that it might say a lot about us, in fact."

Just when he thought his outrageous idea was too over the top even for Maggie, her eyes began to sparkle.

"Perfect," she whispered. "It's perfect, Josh. I didn't know how desperately I wanted you to propose to me until you did. I guess I'm more conventional than I ever realized."

"Is that a yes?"

She flung herself into his arms. "Of course it's a yes!"

Holding her, Josh was suddenly filled with the sense that his world was exactly right. He'd learned a lot about the true meaning of home and family these past couple of months. And for him, Maggie would always be at the center of his world. Still, it wouldn't do for either of them to get too set in their ways.

"Promise me we'll never let convention get the better of us, okay?" he said, gazing into her eyes. "We'll always do the unexpected."

"Of course we will," she said, grinning. "Remind me to tell you about Great-Grandmother Juliette sometime. Unpredictability is in my genes."

Funny thing about that, Josh thought. He'd always thought he'd had his fill of that with his mother, but maybe Nadine had just been preparing him for the greatest love of his life. He'd have to thank her for that—next time he and Maggie got out of this bed.

24

"I will not have an Elvis impersonator singing 'Love Me Tender' at my daughter's wedding," Juliette declared when Maggie and Josh went by her house to tell her their plans to go to Las Vegas to get married. "If you insist on getting married on short notice…" She hesitated. "You do insist on that, right?"

"We do," Maggie said firmly.

"Are you pregnant?" Juliette asked, not looking especially appalled by the idea.

Maggie sighed. "No, Mother. We're in a rush because we want to get married and squeeze in a honeymoon before I have to focus all my attention on organizing Ellie's show at the gallery. And there's still a lot of work to be done on Amanda's house if she's going to move in by Thanksgiving. Josh can't be gone for long, and neither of us has any extra time to plan a big hoopla."

"You could wait until Christmas," Juliette suggested. "I've always thought holiday-season weddings were lovely."

Maggie frowned. "Two weeks, Mother. That's it."

"Okay, okay. I can live with that," her mother conceded. "We can do the ceremony right here in Charleston. Caleb can officiate. Nadine and I will make all the arrangements. You won't have to do a thing."

Maggie could barely bring herself to look at Josh. She had a feeling he'd been counting on the unpredictability of his plan. "We really want to go to Las Vegas, Mother. We only told you so you could decide whether you wanted to fly out to be there."

Juliette drew herself up. "Magnolia Forsythe, you are my only daughter and I will not allow this!" She gave Josh a look that would have sent most men fleeing to Alaska. "Little girls start dreaming of their wedding when they're flower girls in other people's weddings. You cannot take that away from my daughter."

Josh's gaze settled on Maggie. "You had this dream?"

"It doesn't matter," she said staunchly. "A Las Vegas wedding suits me now."

He sighed and shook his head. "No, it doesn't. If we're going to do this, we might as well do it right." He turned to her mother. "If you can manage all the arrangements in two weeks, we'll get married here."

Juliette beamed at him. "I always knew you were a reasonable man."

"You didn't know any such thing, Mother," Maggie declared in disgust. "You're just thrilled that he's going along with your wishes."

"No, I'm thrilled that he's willing to compromise to make you happy," Juliette corrected. "Now, unless you want to be a part of this, get out of here. I need to call Nadine and get busy. We don't have a lot of time. What about bridesmaids? Dinah, I assume."

"Of course." She glanced at Josh. "Maybe I should

ask Ellie and Vicki and Amanda. We might as well go whole hog. What do you think?"

"Whatever you want is okay with me. Do you think Vicki's hair will still have pink streaks? You might want to coordinate their dresses with that."

Maggie frowned at his idea of humor. "Vicki's hair is a perfectly lovely shade of brown now that she's dating that firefighter. Apparently he was a little put off by the pink."

"You don't say," Josh said wryly.

Maggie ignored him and faced her mother. "I'll let you know about the bridesmaids."

"And the best man? Josh, who do you plan on asking?"

"Maybe I should ask Warren," he said. "If he hadn't dumped her, Maggie and I might never have met."

"You are so not amusing," Maggie commented. "Be serious."

"I'll ask Cord."

Maggie nodded. "Perfect. Satisfied, Mother?"

"For now."

"Then we're out of here," Maggie said. "Tell me what time to show up for the wedding."

"Very amusing," Juliette said. "I'll need you for a gown fitting before that. And you might want to give us your input on the flowers, the music and the menu."

"You said you and Nadine were taking care of all that," Maggie reminded her. "I'm a perfect size eight. Don't choose anything too fussy."

"Then you trust our taste?"

Maggie thought about that. She figured her mother's preference for simplicity and elegance and Nadine's for outrageousness would land the wedding safely somewhere in the middle. And however it turned out, since she was marrying Josh, it would be perfect.

Though she was seriously tempted to stick around to watch the entertaining spectacle of her mother and Nadine attempting to compromise, she said without a qualm, "Yes, I trust you completely. Come on, Josh. Let's get out of here before she thinks of something we ought to be doing or deciding."

"Suits me," he said eagerly.

In the front hallway, he backed her against a wall and kissed her for what seemed like an eternity. She was weak-kneed when he finished.

"What was that for?" she asked breathlessly.

"I thought you might need reminding why we're doing this."

"Believe me, that is never far from my mind," she assured him.

And it was going to make the inevitable chaos of the next two weeks bearable.

Later that night, Josh gazed down at Maggie beside him. She looked more serene than he'd ever seen her before. Maybe that had something to do with making love for the past couple of hours, but he thought it was more than that.

"You're happy?" he asked.

"Deliriously, especially now that we know Brian's locked up until his trial. And Ellie has agreed to let me schedule her show in October."

"And you don't mind relinquishing control of your wedding to our mothers?"

"Not a bit."

"Really? I was convinced to skip Vegas so that you

could have the wedding of your dreams. Control freak that you are, I assumed you'd want to put your stamp of approval on every detail."

"I don't need to. What my mother didn't mention was that she has notebooks filled with everything we've ever discussed. If I passed a dress I liked in a bridal boutique, she wrote down the designer. If I mentioned an appetizer they had at a friend's wedding, the recipe is in the appropriate notebook, along with every caterer who's ever impressed either of us. She'll pull this off and it will make her happy."

"Then this is as much about making her happy as it is about you?"

"Of course. She was right. I'm her only daughter. She deserves this wedding even more than I do. How could I rob her of that, especially now that I'm actually marrying someone it turns out she approves of?" She grinned, then added without any hint of rancor, "Guess I'm still an approval junkie, after all."

"How do you know she approves?"

"Of you? Come on. Did you see the look on her face when we told her the news? The woman was triumphant. I realized in that instant that the whole disapproval thing was a ploy to push me into making the right decision. I imagine Nadine had a similar expression when you told her."

"Come to think of it, she did look awfully smug," Josh said. "You don't suppose those two were conspiring?"

"I wouldn't put it past them."

"Does that bother you?"

"Not much. You?"

He grinned. "I'm marrying you, aren't I? How could I complain?"

* * *

Nadine couldn't seem to stop the tears from spilling down her cheeks as she watched her son stand at the front of the church in his tux, his gaze riveted on Maggie as she walked down the aisle. His heart was in his eyes. She wondered if he had any idea how much joy she was taking in this moment, knowing that he was finally going to have the home and family she'd never been able to give him.

Beside her George took a second clean handkerchief from his pocket and silently handed it to her.

"I'm sorry I'm such a mess," she whispered.

"I think it comes with the territory," he said. "Mothers of the bride and groom are supposed to be a little weepy."

"I absolutely love weddings," Nadine said with a sigh. "But this is the best one yet. It's certainly better than any of mine."

"Maybe you just haven't walked down the aisle with the right man yet," he said, tucking her hand in his.

"Maybe not," she said, feeling more hopeful than she had in a very long time.

She turned her attention back to Josh and saw a smile spread across his face as Maggie reached his side. He clasped her hand as if he'd never let go, then turned toward Caleb, clearly ready to say the vows that would join him and Maggie forever. Unfortunately, Caleb seemed to be momentarily distracted by the sight of Amanda in her elegant bridesmaid dress.

"Um, Caleb, do you think we could get this show on the road?" Josh murmured.

Caleb's attention snapped back to the couple in front of him. "Dearly beloved," he began.

Nadine sighed. "Something tells me those two are going to make a grandmama of me before another year is out," she whispered.

A few months ago the idea would have appalled her. Now she could hardly wait. It wasn't a matter of making her feel old as much as it was of enriching her life. She realized then that she was gaining a family the same way Josh was. Fresh tears spilled down her cheeks.

"This is the last one I have," George said, handing her another folded handkerchief.

"I'm almost done crying," she told him. "From the minute those two say I do, it's going to be all about fresh starts and optimism."

George looked doubtful and she could hardly blame him, since she'd already turned it into a three-hankie occasion. She noticed that across the aisle, Juliette was just as teary-eyed. Nadine gave her a quick thumbs-up that had her smiling.

Yes, indeed. Fresh starts and optimism from here on out, she concluded.

She stole a glance at George.

And maybe, if her luck held out this time, just a touch of romance.

Church was over and most of the congregation had gone home for Sunday dinner, but Caleb was still in his office trying to feel his way through an unexpected and troubling counseling session. He studied the couple sitting across from him and wondered if he dared tell them what he really thought, that they were way too young to even be thinking about marriage. Mary Louise Carter was just a few months out of high school. Danny Marshall was barely into his sophomore year at Clemson.

They'd known each other since grade school, been sweethearts since Danny's freshman year in high school. They both thought their marriage was inevitable. So what if having a baby on the way had kicked up the timetable by several years?

"It's not the end of the world," Mary Louise said, her adoring gaze on Danny.

Though she rarely looked away from her fiancé, she evidently didn't see the barely concealed panic that Caleb spotted. He'd counseled enough couples during his years as a minister to recognize the signs of a man being pushed toward a commitment he wasn't ready to make.

"Danny, is this wedding really what you want?" Caleb asked carefully, aware that Mary Louise's eyes had widened with dismay. "I know you love Mary Louise and I think it's wonderful that you want to take responsibility for the baby and do the right thing for Mary Louise, but there are other options."

Danny squirmed uncomfortably and avoided Mary Louise's hurt expression. "What kind of options?"

"You could acknowledge paternity and pay child support. Or you both could agree to give the baby up for adoption to a family more prepared to give a child the life he or she deserves," Caleb suggested.

"No way," Mary Louise said, on her feet and quivering with outrage. She scowled at Caleb, then whirled on Danny. "This is *our* baby. How could you even think about giving away *our* baby, Danny Marshall?"

Danny gave her a sullen look. "I didn't say I'd do it. I asked Reverend Webb what the options are. Jeez, Mary Louise, settle down. What harm does it do to ask?"

"I'm keeping the baby and that's that," she said fiercely. "If you don't want to marry me, then don't. I don't want you, if you can't love both of us. And you can keep your stupid money too!"

"I never said I didn't want to marry you," Danny placated. "You know I love you, baby. It's just…"

"Just what?" she asked.

"How are we going to make it?" Danny asked reasonably. "I can't quit school. I worked too hard to get accepted and get a scholarship to throw it all away now. I don't want to wind up in some dead-end job for the rest of my life, like my dad."

"You won't have to. I can stay with my folks for now and keep working. It's only minimum wage, but I'll get another job," Mary Louise promised staunchly. "We can put all that money into savings so we'll have it when I have to go on leave to have the baby. I won't have to take off long. Once the baby comes, I'll move to be with you. We can figure out a schedule so you can take classes when I'm home. Then you can watch the baby while I work."

It was evident she'd already given this a lot of thought. Caleb admired her earnest conviction that she could handle a pregnancy and two jobs and that Danny could keep up with his classes and take care of the baby. Unfortunately Caleb was more realistic. He knew the toll that arrangement would eventually take on the marriage and on Mary Louise and Danny individually, for that matter. He also knew she'd never listen to him if he tried to tell her any of that.

However, he did know someone who might be able to get through to her in a way he couldn't.

"Okay, you two. I think that's enough for today," Caleb said, concluding they needed a cooling-down period. "I think you both need to spend some time thinking about all this. Danny, can you get home from college again next weekend, so we can talk some more?"

"I guess," Danny said, his reluctance plain, but the stoic lift of his chin telling Caleb he would do it. He'd always been a good kid, who took his responsibilities seriously. He'd worked hard to get a college scholarship, even harder to earn money to help with bills for meals and books.

"Great. Then we'll talk again next week right after church," Caleb told them. "In the meantime, Mary Louise, there's someone I'd like you to meet."

She regarded him with evident suspicion, clearly not

happy about the monkey wrench he'd thrown into her plans for a hasty wedding. "Who?"

"Let me speak to her first and get back to you," he said.

"I don't know why you're so opposed to this wedding," Mary Louise said to him plaintively. "You've known us forever. You know we're in love."

"I do," Caleb agreed. "But I want you to have the best possible chance to succeed, and the way to accomplish that is to make sure you've given this serious consideration from every angle before you rush into something. I've seen too many kids who start out crazy about each other wind up bitter and divorced because they did the right thing and then resented each other afterward. I really don't want that to happen to you."

Danny gave him a grateful look. "Thanks, Reverend Webb. I'll see you after church next week. Mary Louise, you ready to go?"

For a minute, based on her pouting expression, Caleb thought she might insist on having this out right here and now, but apparently she caught something in Danny's steady, unrelenting gaze that told her to wait till next time.

"Remember, I want both of you to do some soul-searching this week. See if there are some other solutions that might make sense. If marriage is what you both want, then think about the best way to make sure you have plenty of support around," Caleb suggested. "And I'll be in touch with you, Mary Louise, probably tomorrow."

"Okay," she said, and followed Danny from the room.

Just outside the door, Caleb saw Danny reach for her hand and whisper something in her ear that finally put a smile back on her face. Caleb sighed and reached for his phone to follow up on his brainstorm.

Okay, he'd been looking for an excuse to call Amanda all day long. Ever since he and the other church volunteers had finished building her house two weeks ago and had held a housewarming party just yesterday, he'd been suffering from some sort of weird withdrawal symptoms. He liked spending time with her and her kids, but he was all too aware that she needed time to adjust to being in the new house and finally getting her life back under control.

Though Bobby O'Leary had been gone for more than a year now, Caleb had a feeling Amanda's life had been so rocky that she was only now beginning to find her equilibrium. He didn't want to add any pressure that might throw her off course.

And yet, his feelings for her were there and getting stronger every time he saw her. He'd fought with them, struggled to pretend that she was just another member of his congregation in need of help, but the time he'd spent with her and with the kids had fulfilled him in unexpected ways. He'd come to admire her strength, to enjoy her sense of humor. Keeping their relationship in perspective hadn't been easy. Giving it up might be impossible.

Thus, he thought wryly, the need to find excuses to see her that she might not recognize for what they were...pitiful attempts to keep the connection between them going for just a little longer.

Before he actually dialed her number, he gave himself a stern lecture on remembering that he was her pastor, not a would-be lover, much as he might wish otherwise. It wasn't the first time he'd struggled to place duty above his needs and desires as a man, but it was the first time he was right on the edge of losing the battle.

In fact, the lecture didn't seem to stop the jolt to his heart when she answered the phone, her voice soft and just a little breathless.

"Amanda, you weren't taking a nap, were you?"

"In the middle of the afternoon, with three kids loose in the house?" she replied, laughter threading through her voice. "You must be kidding. No. If I sound out of breath, it's because Susie, Larry and Jimmy insisted I play tag with them in the backyard. They can't get over having so much room to run around. I can't get over it myself. Thank you again, Caleb."

"Would you stop thanking me?" he pleaded. "Getting that house built for you was something the whole congregation wanted to do." Well, except for a couple of obstinate holdouts, and eventually even they had come around.

"I just want you to know how much I appreciate it," she said. "If there's ever anything I can do to pay you back, let me know."

It was exactly the opening Caleb needed. "Actually, there is something you could do." He explained about Mary Louise and Danny. "I think Mary Louise needs to understand the realities of trying to work two jobs and care for a baby. Would you consider talking to her?"

"Of course I will," Amanda said at once. "But maybe I should clarify something. Are you asking me to help you talk her out of getting married?"

He considered the question, then answered honestly. "I just want her to know what's ahead. Right now she's all caught up in this romantic notion of living with

Danny and having his baby and being happy forever. She needs to know how exhausting it can be and what a toll it might take on their marriage. These two kids have been in love practically as long as I've known them. I don't want them to lose that because they've been backed into a corner by this pregnancy."

"Will their parents help them?" she asked, an unmistakably wistful note in her voice.

Caleb knew what it would have meant to Amanda if her father had stepped up when her life fell apart, but the divide between them had been too huge. Amanda had made a tentative overture, but as usual, Big Max had blown the opportunity. Sometimes Caleb wanted to shake the stubborn old man, but instead he'd settled for trying to gently nudge them back together. So far, he'd made precious little progress. And if Amanda ever found out what he'd been up to, she might very well hate him for his interference.

"Actually, even though I haven't spoken to them yet, I think their parents would help as much as they can. They're all good, decent people who want what's best for their kids," he admitted. "Even so, it's still going to be tough. Danny would probably have to give up his scholarship, quit college and come home."

"He could go to college here," Amanda reminded him. "It might take him longer, but he could do it."

"I suppose," he conceded, though he knew how much going to Clemson had meant to Danny. Caleb had made quite a few calls himself to assure Danny's acceptance there. He'd even spoken to the scholarship committee on Danny's behalf.

"And both sets of grandparents could help out with baby-sitting if they're here," Amanda continued.

"Maybe Mary Louise and Danny could even live with his folks or hers for a while. It wouldn't be ideal, but it might work. Have any of you considered that?"

"What are you saying?" Caleb asked, startled by the turn the conversation had taken. "Do you think I'm wrong for urging caution?"

"No, I think you're being a responsible, compassionate minister who's trying to make sure two kids get off to a good start. But sometimes things happen even when the timing sucks. Not every marriage is ideal at the beginning, but if the love is strong you can weather almost anything."

"The way you and Bobby did," Caleb concluded.

"The way I *thought* we had," Amanda corrected. "I lived the illusion right up until the day he died. Then reality set in."

"I'm sorry."

"Hey, I'll make you a deal," she said, a teasing note in her voice. "I'll stop saying thank you, if you'll stop saying you're sorry."

Caleb chuckled. "I can do that."

"So, knowing where I'm coming from, do you still want me to speak to Mary Louise?"

"Absolutely," he said at once. "I think you'd be an incredible role model for any young woman. Will tomorrow afternoon work for you?"

"I'll need to come straight home from work because of the kids," she said. "Can you bring her by here?"

"Will do," he said at once, trying to keep the pathetically eager note out of his voice. "Goodbye, Amanda."

"Bye, Caleb. See you tomorrow."

He hung up, a smile on his lips, then realized he was running late for his standing Sunday-afternoon get-together with Amanda's father. Big Max hated to be kept waiting. On the rare occasions it happened, he blustered and carried on about Caleb's impertinence and lack of respect.

Caleb had come to realize, though, that Big Max's temper didn't have anything to do with feeling disrespected at all. Big Max was simply impatient for every little tidbit of information he could get about the daughter he'd cut out of his life and was too proud to let back in. Caleb was simply the chosen messenger.

One Hollywood producer.
Five ex-wives.
Endless possibilities for murder.

LINDA L.
RICHARDS

After former stockbroker Madeline Carter reluctantly agrees
to tutor the current wife of A-list film producer Maxi Livingston,
she unwittingly becomes part of a murder investigation.
When Maxi's ex-wives are killed off one by one, Madeline finds
herself in the middle of a scenario worthy of the most imaginative
screenwriter—where she is the prime suspect.

"Smart and sophisticated...a bracingly intelligent whodunit."
—Laura Lippman, author of *To the Power of Three*

SHERRYL WOODS

32149 THE BACKUP PLAN	___ $6.99 U.S.	___ $8.50 CAN.
32048 DESTINY UNLEASHED	___ $6.50 U.S.	___ $7.99 CAN.
66815 ABOUT THAT MAN	___ $6.50 U.S.	___ $7.99 CAN.

(limited quantities available)

TOTAL AMOUNT	$ _____
POSTAGE & HANDLING	$ _____
($1.00 FOR 1 BOOK, 50¢ for each additional)	
APPLICABLE TAXES*	$ _____
TOTAL PAYABLE	$ _____

(check or money order—please do not send cash)

To order, complete this form and send it, along with a check or money order for the total above, payable to MIRA Books, to: **In the U.S.:** 3010 Walden Avenue, P.O. Box 9077, Buffalo, NY 14269-9077; **In Canada:** P.O. Box 636, Fort Erie, Ontario, L2A 5X3.

Name: _____
Address: _____ City: _____
State/Prov.: _____ Zip/Postal Code: _____
Account Number (if applicable): _____

075 CSAS

*New York residents remit applicable sales taxes.
*Canadian residents remit applicable GST and provincial taxes.

MIRA®

www.MIRABooks.com

MSW1205BL